Suzy Cox is deputy editor of *Cosmopolitan* magazine and has been working as a journalist since the age of sixteen, when she founded a monthly music page for teenagers in the *Oxford Times*. Suzy lives in London, but loves New York.

Also by Suzy Cox

The Dead Girls Detective Agency

DEAD GIRLS WALKING

Suzy Cox

Much-in-Little

Constable & Robinson Ltd.
55–56 Russell Square
London WC1B 4HP
www.constablerobinson.com

First published in the UK by Much-in-Little,
an imprint of Constable & Robinson Ltd., 2014

A copy of the British Library Cataloguing in
Publication Data is available from the British Library

ISBN: 978-1-4721-0660-5 (paperback)
ISBN: 978-1-47210-663-6 (ebook)

Printed and bound in the UK

13 5 7 9 10 8 6 4 2

CHAPTER 1

I hadn't lived until I died.

That's what I thought in the first days after my murder anyway. The days when my heart stopped beating, but was big enough to let new friends in. When I could no longer feel the heat of the sun, but I still felt hope. When my body became a lifeless corpse, but I learned to port and fly. When my pulse disappeared, but my determination grew and grew.

But newly deads are idiots. I know I was. Because when the acting stopped and the secrets came out, my world unravelled – again and again.

Yeah, whatever, I know. This isn't a super-happy intro-duction – not what you were expecting on page one. I mean, who wants to think their afterlife could unreservedly suck? That when you shuffle off your mortal coil, it's not all hot boy angels, fluffy clouds and sunny days without double Chem to mess them up, as far as the eye can see?

Because if your afterlife does blow, what was the point? Of every math test you sweated, every friend's mom you toler-ated, every subway seat you gave up, and every pimple you didn't squeeze.

What was the point of any of it, if all you had to look forward to was this?

A world where your boyfriend turns out to be a cheater, new friends can't be trusted and old ones aren't much better. And someone whose name you never even had the time to learn, hated you so much she pushed you under a speeding subway train.

A world where you realize every breath you'd hungrily taken in life had been a deep drawn lie.

No, living is easy. Pity I had to die to figure that out.

And know the true meaning of forever.

CHAPTER 2

'Charlotte, will you come on already? What's taking you so long? You're being such a scaredy hat.'

'Cat, Lorna, it's scaredy *cat*.'

'Don't be ridiculous. It's "hat". *Cats* are not scary. But *hats* can be horrible. Did you never catch a Lady Gaga video? Let me tell you, it's the hats you have to watch out for not the cats. Plus, like, also . . .'

I closed my eyes, pressing my head against the white plaster wall, and thought about how – before – this would have been the moment when I'd have taken a deep breath.

If only . . .

Click, click. Click, click.

I turned my head and uncrinkled one eye.

Click, click. Click, click.

Lorna clicked her French manicured fingers impatiently in my ear. 'Charlotte Louise Feldman, if you do not come with me right now, we're going to miss the entire show.' Even at a time like this I couldn't help but notice that her hand looked like something from a nail polish commercial. Maybe my mom was right to haul me out for biting mine. 'They don't wait for the Living, so they totally won't wait for us.'

Click, click. Click, click.

Groaning internally, I straightened up and turned to face my friend. 'Sorry. I'm ready. Really I am. I was just . . .'

Moping, hiding, turning sulking into a golden statue-worthy event?

'I was just thinking that if Nancy finds out about this she's going to go coastal. You know her feelings about us getting too near to the Living – especially members of our families. She's all, "If they sense you, there'll be epic trouble." It stresses her out more than untidy murder case files.'

Lorna swooshed her hand through the air and delicately placed it on one popped hip. Someone had been watching too much *America's Next Top Model*. Lorna totally made 'to Tyra' a verb.

'Look Miss Morals, will you stop with the Girl Scout act already? You weren't worrying about this kinda thing when you were hanging out with Edison, learning all those bad girl ghost tricks in the back of who-knows-where.'

A dull pain spread through my stomach and I felt my shoulders slouch. Edison. After what he'd done, could we please not bring up Edison?

Lorna's denim-blue eyes softened and she took a different tack. 'Come on, it'll be more fun than a sample sale in the Hamptons. You love watching bands live, right? This will be sooo much better. For starters, everyone in the theatre will have washed within, like, the last twelve hours. At least. There'll be none of those roadie guys hanging around and walking through us by mistake. No beer bottle throwing. No one sweating.' She grimaced. 'Plus, I'll be in a super-good mood if you come with.' Beam.

I looked out of the window where the late afternoon sun was tickling Washington Square arch with its final rays. In the other direction, up Fifth Avenue, the Empire State Building stood tall, majestic, proud. No matter how long I stayed in the Hotel Attesa – where all murdered teenage ghosts came to live in New York City – and no matter how bummed I felt, I always got a little rush when I saw that view. I imagined the Empire State was almost waving hello.

'Plus my old high school is way near the Guggenheim,' Lorna said casually twisting a long, glossy blonde lock around her finger. 'Maybe we could stop by afterwards and have a look at one of those exhibition things you love? I'll even look at the art and swerve the gift shop – this one time.'

Man, she knew how to press my buttons.

'Okay, okay, I'm coming,' I said. 'But if Nancy finds out and gives us of one her lectures, I am laying the blame for this little excursion squarely at your door.'

Lorna smiled, flipping her hair over her shoulder. Her neat bangs fell back into place. 'Like I'm scared of *that* dead girl.' Her eyes twinkled mischievously. If Abercrombie & Fitch scouted models from the afterlife, Lorna would have been on every billboard in Limbo. 'Just think: Upper East Side. East 88th. Palmer Peabody Academy for Girls. And away we . . .'

Pop!

Lorna ported out of my room. I enviously watched dust dance in the shaft of light where she'd been standing. No matter how much intense teleporting practice I got in – and I'd had plenty, thanks to the Attesa's resident dead boy next door, Edison Idiot Hayes – it was still my weakest spook skill. Which was a major bummer seeing as it was the way we ghosts got around the city. Sure, I didn't want to re-examine my breakfast every single time I ported any more – I had been dead for almost two Living months now after all – but I still felt as weak as a second grader on Space Mountain after most trips.

Then again, porting was a much better way to get around the city than the alternatives. Like, say, the subway. It's kinda tough to feel the love for the Manhattan Transport Authority when you met a sticky end by falling under 85,000 pounds of subway train. Well, when you were murdered getting pushed under one by a psycho sophomore who was desperate to get you out of the way so she could date your douchebag boyfriend.

Even if I lived in the Attesa until I was 903 years old, I would not be making peace with that.

Stop stalling, Charlotte, I told myself. It's nearly Christmas. An afternoon at Lorna's old high school watching her little sister perform in the end of semester play may not be my – or any sane person's – idea of fun! fun! fun!, but it would be way better than sitting around the hotel. Waiting. Watching the seconds tick by and night's shadows grow long. Wondering if this was all there would ever be to death.

I scrunched up my eyes, resolutely. Upper East Side. East 88th St. Palmer Peabody Academy for Girls. Easy. I could do this. Really I could. East 88th. East 88th. Concentrate, Charlotte, come on.

The familiar spinning began. Crazy-fast at first, a merry-go-round at top speed, then after less than two excruciating seconds, it began to slow.

Urgh. Barf city. Every. Single. Time. How lame was I?

I cautiously opened my eyes, to see Lorna beaming at me, an imposing red-brick building lightly smattered with snow behind her. Above the marble arched entrance, an American flag waved in the winter breeze. So this was Parker Peabody.

'We're here!' She bounced, her blonde hair flying and landing in perfect waves on the shoulders of her baby blue dress. 'Welcome to my old high school! The play's taking place inside! Let's go!'

Much as I loved her, I was so not in an exclamation mark mood.

Lorna grabbed my arm and we fell in step behind two immaculately dressed girls, all with the same glossy blown-out hair and box-fresh green-piped navy uniforms. There wasn't a pore out of place between them, let alone a follicle. Sixteen years of living and two months of dying in New York City had done very little to disprove every cliché TV teaches you about Upper East Side girls. I'd yet to meet one who wasn't groomed to *kill-me-now* perfection.

'You know there are totally days when I wish I'd been murdered in my school uniform like you were.' Lorna gave my arm a thoughtful squeeze. 'As Coco Chanel said, a well-fitting blazer *never* goes out of fashion. Though I suppose if I'm dead for another few seasons my Marc by Marc Jacobs shift will be so out, it'll come back in again. Jacobs is a master like that.'

I looked down at the wrinkled dull-as white shirt, blue and yellow plaid skirt and navy blazer I was destined to wear for eternity – ghosts being stuck in whatever outfit they died in and all – and for the one-millionth time, wished I'd changed into my J Brands and a cute top before I headed down to the subway tracks to, like, meet my maker. People prepare for death by making a will or checking their taxes are paid, but no one mentions the paranormal fashion dilemmas. Sure, the Living joke you should always wear a matching bra and panties in case you're hit by a bus, but people don't warn you to think about what you're wearing on top of them too.

I looked around, trying to take in Lorna's old high school. Jeez, even the snow up here looked more expensive than it did downtown near the Attesa. Pristine white flakes covered the emerald grass and ivy leading up to Palmer Peabody's entrance door like something from a Christmas card. Martha Stewart couldn't have sprinkled them more expertly if she'd tried. These people probably had stylists to cut their shrubs. I'd never even had one for my actual curly brunette hair.

'Hey guys, wait up!' a voice shouted behind us. I turned just in time to see a cute blonde girl with dark blue eyes running right at us. I tried to step out of her way, but was too slow. She crashed straight through me.

Wah! I felt a tickle – the motion of her Living spirit passing through my dead one. If it hadn't been two below, she'd have shivered as the Living always do when they accidentally walk through a ghost.

I was righting myself and wondering where I'd seen the blonde before, when a tall redhead strode right through me too. What was this, National Walk Through Charlotte Day? Major tickle. The blow-out sisters stopped and kissed the other girls hello.

'Nervous?' one asked red.

She snorted – somehow managing to make it look sophisticated not gross. Skills.

'Hardly,' she said. 'We did *Hamlet* for the first time in – what? – eighth grade. I could do Claudius's entire soliloquy in the middle of Bergdorf's and it still wouldn't use up enough brain cells to make me miss one piece from the new Thakoon line. I've got this one covered.' Her tone shifted from whatever to bitchy. 'Plus no one's going to be looking at me now, are they?'

'Why not? I saw you in rehearsal yesterday and you were amazing, Anastasia.' First blow-dry girl must have an Indian mom or dad. Along with her salon-styled walnut hair, she had the biggest brown eyes. 'You acted everyone else off the stage.'

'Maybe. But I suspect even Meryl Streep couldn't hold her own next to Mercy Grant and her – what does she call it? – *craft*.' Anastasia rolled her amber eyes. The others giggled. 'I'm not in the business of wasting my energy trying to upstage the likes of her. This is one play I'm going to downplay. Maybe then Miss Ballard will finally realize Mercy's the hammiest actress this side of Miss Piggy – and give me the lead I deserve next time around.'

9

'Ana, don't be so mean.' The blonde's hair was pulled into a high ponytail of perfect waves, which stopped just above her shoulders. 'You know Mercy's worked hard for this – we all have. Playing Hamlet? You have to give her some respect for that. It's one of the most famous parts ever, and it was written for a guy. She's just a bit . . . *intense* is all. Cut her some slack.'

'The only thing I'm cutting is the next drama class I have with Mercy Grant,' Anastasia shot back.

The blonde made a *please-don't-be-this-way* face, then slung her arm around Anastasia's shoulders. 'Come on, Moody, the sooner we get this show on the road, the sooner we can celebrate this semester being over – and the start of winter recess with drinks at Plunge.'

They walked up the steps and through Peabody's wood-panelled door.

'Wow,' I said to Lorna. 'Much as I'm enjoying our little excursion uptown, your classmates are doing about as much as Edith Wharton to break down the rich kid stereotypes.'

I turned to the spot to my left where Lorna had been standing. But she'd vanished. Awesome. She'd brought me the whole way up here, basically against my will, on a black-ops mission which was totally against the Rules – the laws all good teen ghosts were meant to abide by – and now she'd ported off already? Probably to, I don't know, look in some designer boutiques or check out cute guys skating in Central Park.

That was it. I was totally leaving. Right now. Well, maybe after a little trip to the Guggenheim. But after that, me and the snooty Upper East Side were so done.

'Pssst!'

I looked around. What was with the 'pssst'?

'Over here! Charlotte! Psst!'

The expertly coiffured bush to my left seemed to be talking.

'Has she gone?' it whispered in Lorna's voice.

'If by "she" you mean one of the girls who so rudely just walked right through me, then yeah, like the wind,' I said. 'They seemed to be in a rush to get inside. You know, for the *play*. That thing you were in a rush to get to too?'

Lorna clumsily stood up from behind the snow-covered shrubbery. It was such a non-Lorna moment that, for once, even I couldn't find anything smart to say.

'I hope she didn't see me,' she said smoothing down the skirt of her designer baby blue dress.

'Lorna, even if you weren't shielded by the fact you're a) a ghost and therefore b) invisible to the Living, you c) got your pretty ass in that bush in less time than it takes a Kardashian to launch a new fragrance. I think you're safe. And btw, who's "she"? You've been dead for four years – all your old classmates will have graduated by now. Except . . . Oh.'

There was my light bulb. 'Oh no, was that . . .?'

'Emma,' Lorna said, like I was a bigger dummy than George Clooney's latest girlfriend. 'That was my kid sister Emma. The super-pretty blonde one with the cute blue eyes. Did you get a good look at her? Isn't she the most gorgeous little girl ever?'

Of course. The blonde was Lorna's younger sister. *That* was what was so familiar about Emma's just-strutted-down-a-catwalk deal. While my parents had passed bulky ankles and hair that frizzed at the sight of a grey cloud down to me, poise and perfect follicles were what ran in the Altman family genes. Figured.

'The only thing is, she didn't look that "little" to me,' I said, taking a run at the door and passing through it into a dark hall. Lorna joined me, calmly stepping through the heavy wood like it was no thicker than air. See? Poise.

'Emma was only twelve when I . . . *you know.*' Lorna whispered the words, like she was discussing a scandalous uncle who'd had an affair with the help and run off to Acapulco. 'And she took it way badly, poor thing.' She sighed, twisting a lock of hair around her finger. 'Our parents, well, they're both very business-minded and they were – *are* – away a whole lot. On the upside, it meant Emma and I were really close. But on the down one, she found it hella hard when I was gone.'

Lorna leaned in. 'I'm not talking myself up here, but Emm kind of hero-worshipped me. She was always in my closet trying on new clothes I'd not even had a chance to wear yet, using my Mac make-up palettes, or borrowing my cell to text my friends . . .'

I really should have thanked my parents more for only having one child. Back in the days when me popping up wouldn't have resulted in, ohhh, let's see now . . . shock-induced heart attacks, fears they'd gone cray-cray, or calls to the nearest exorcist.

We stepped into a large hall – the kind of oak-panelled place you could imagine debating societies holing up or future world leaders playing the kind of drinking games they'd pay criminally large sums of money to buy any photographic evidence of when they got into power.

'So Emma's sixteen now? The same age we both were when we died?' I asked.

Lorna nodded. 'Yeah, though it's a head-wreck to think of it like that. Emma had always been such a shy kid, but after my funeral she shut everyone out. She hid in her room, skipped class, stopped talking to our parents. And then she—' Lorna stopped with a jolt so sudden three giggling seniors walked right through her.

In unison, they shivered, one stopping to stare at the ceiling, wondering what idiot janitor had put the air-con on in the middle of a big freeze.

Lorna didn't move. She didn't even shudder.

'Hey, Lorna! Limbo to Lorna. Come in Lorna!' I said, taking a step to the left just in time to avoid an especially large, beardy dad ploughing through me. He was twice my size. He would have tickled worse than a hay-fever nose in July. 'Lorna!'

Now it was my turn to snap my – epically bitten – fingers in her face.

'Hey,' I said, touching my friend's shoulder. 'What's up? You look like you've seen a ghost. Except if you had, it would most likely be Nancy – and she'd be giving us hell for coming up here. Or Edison – then I'd be giving him hell for being the jerkiest jerk in Jerkland. Or—'

'This is it,' Lorna said quietly, taking in every fibre of the room. 'I can't believe I didn't think we'd have to walk right through it.'

'It? What's it? Where are we?' I asked.

She turned and looked at me with big sad eyes. 'The Great Hall,' she said. 'My murder scene.'

CHAPTER 3

'The front? Are you joking? This isn't Fashion Week, Charlotte. And FYI, even if it was, I always thought the front row looked kinda sucky anyway. Like, whenever you see a picture of celebrities at the shows on The Cut or Grazia Daily, they're always craning to see the models from down there. Looking at a stage from that angle has totally got to give you neck ache.'

Lorna rubbed the back of hers like she'd been sat in fashion Hades for the last three hours. 'No, I think the best place for us to sit is definitely in the wings. It'll be like we're almost *on* the stage. Plus, we'll get to hear all the super-cute things the girls say before they go on. It'll be like when the contestants perform on those real-ity talent shows and the TV presenters, like, ask them how they're feeling beforehand and if they're okay. But, you know, more cultured. Because this is Shakespeare after all.'

I looked at my friend carefully, scanning for concrete signs she was about to flip. The freak-out-o-meter had totally moved to 'uh oh'.

Ever since we'd walked slap bang into her murder scene – where someone had hit her over the head with the prom queen's crown so hard she'd wound up dead – Lorna had been acting a little . . . well, like Lorna on the fullest tank of gas.

And honestly? It was a ride I was ready to get off.

'So let's go up there – the left side of the stage would be best, don't you think? Actors always "exit stage left", right? I heard that somewhere, for sure. Can you make it up the stairs in your heels without porting? I can. But then I am wearing ballet flats. I know you're not so good in them. We don't need to port, like, thirty feet, do we? It's kinda lazy and—'

Lorna was talking at a speed that would make a Bugatti eat her dust. Was it time to get worried yet? I mean, how much damage could she actually do? She'd been murdered already, so she couldn't talk herself to death. Or me for that matter. This was totally why super-sensible Nancy said interacting with our Living families was A Very Bad Idea. Maybe I should get her out of here? Then she'd resume her normal Lorna shopping-and-shoe-obsessed service. I hoped.

Back in the hall, Lorna had proudly shown me the last thing she remembered seeing before she woke up dead in Hotel Attesa: an ancient oil painting of old lady Palmer Peabody herself ('She opened the first kindergarten in America back in the whatever ages. That portrait always freaked me out because of her beady weirdy black eyes. I'd much rather have died looking at someone cute. But what school puts up portraits of hot people? Except if Ryan founded a school and you went to, like, Gosling High. That would be super-cool').

She'd pulled me down the corridor past her old home-room ('Boy, am I glad I died when I did. We had a math test on Monday and I'd not cracked one book'). And now we were here, in the school auditorium, picking our seats like everything was normal – and Lorna hadn't just had to face up to the memory of her gruesome murder.

'Oh! There's Dylan West!' Lorna squealed, pointing at a short boy with a mop of messy jet-black hair, a Roman nose and a pointy chin. 'I used to babysit for him when I was alive. I cannot believe how grown up he's got! Aww, and there's Anastasia De Witt!'

The rude redhead from the school steps stormed by, trussed up in a vintage red military jacket, leather mini-skirt and undone black Doc Martin boots, her neon laces trailing behind her. The look was more barfly than Bard. 'Ana's been Emma's best friend since, like, forever. She's a majorly sweet girl.'

Sweet? From the little I'd seen, Anastasia was only 'sweet' if you thought lemons tasted like M&M's.

'Shouldn't she be getting into her costume? This thing's got to be starting soon.' I really wasn't super-keen on Lorna sticking around here any longer than she had to. The sooner I could convince her to port back to the Attesa, the sooner I could 'fess all to Nancy – and get her to make with the head girl calming influence routine on Lorna until she forgot all about the Great Hall again. Sure, Nancy would be pissed I'd gone to such a stupid place with Lorna – even I could see this was up there with wax wings near the sun on the 'good idea' list – but once she'd got over that, Nancy would totally make everything right. She always did.

'I think she *is* in costume.' Lorna pointed to a graffiti-style poster at the side of the stage. 'This is *"Hipster Hamlet"*, so it's, like, a more contempoberry version of the play.'

Actually it was a good thing Nancy wasn't here. This was not the time to be correcting Lorna's misuse of vocabulary. And Nancy couldn't help herself from doing that.

'All the kids are speaking Shakespeare's script, but their outfits are modern,' Lorna continued. 'I guess they've adapted it a little. All the parts are played by girls, even though Hamlet was, like, a boy. And that Claudius guy too. And Polonius . . .'

I narrowed my bluey-grey eyes. 'You *guess*?'

Much as I adored Lorna and wanted to believe she was an English Lit genius of Harvard-proportions, there was no way she'd know that much about the production. Unless . . .

I turned to face her. 'This isn't the first time you've seen Emma act in this play, is it? Admit it, you've been porting to rehearsals to watch her, haven't you?'

Lorna flushed. 'Maybeee.'

'Lorna Altman!' I said, 'I'm not going all Nancy Bossy Boots on your ass, but you know that's totally against the Rules. *"#12: Ghosts can spy on their Living relatives only in the line of their personal murder inquiries, and not if it could interfere with the Living's wellbeing or course of their everyday lives."'* I parroted. 'What if Emma is spirit sensitive? If you're around her a lot, she could feel you.

You said before she took your death badly – imagine if she sensed your presence? Or you were so emotional at seeing her up there doing her thespy thing you accidentally appeared as an apparition?'

Not that I hadn't done that before myself. At the top of the Empire State. Inside my scumbag ex-boyfriend David's bedroom. On a football field . . . 'Emma would freak the hell out and—'

Boom! Boom! Pow! Pow! Boom! Boom! Pow! Pow!

A heavy bass line blasted out of the speakers next to us so loudly I nearly fell through them. Man, today was not about to be put in the file marked 'awesome'.

'Sorry, Charlotte, I can't hear you over this track,' Lorna said, as if she was Jay-Z's newest protégé and used words like 'track' on a daily basis. 'The curtain's coming up. The show's about to begin. I think we should find our places.'

Lorna pulled me up the stairs and positioned us by some set scaffolding, stage left.

Boom! Boom! Pow! Pow! Boom! Boom! Pow!

I jammed my hands over my ears. Yep, this was going to be a loooong night.

Three girls in fluorescent onesies, trucker hats and high-top sneakers body-popped onto the stage. Yellow dry ice snaked across the floor and epilepsy-inducing lights flashed as they rapped the opening lines.

'Who's there?'

'Answer me! Bernardo?'

'Yes, he!'

I thought back to my high school's last slightly pitiful performance of *Romeo and Juliet* (balcony painted by my mom, death scenes with flimsy cardboard swords) and tried not to roll my eyes. Here, graffitied battlements had been erected, probably by some professional stage crew on a Broadway break. The grey backdrop of – what I guessed – these kids thought a Williamsburg street looked like was painted on wooden slats.

'See, I told you it was the hipster version,' Lorna whispered, as the bass line died and Fleet Foxes careered out of the speakers. 'This is what happens when amazing kids like Emma are allowed to be totally creative.'

I sighed. 'No, this is what happens when "amazing kids" have too much time, trust fund access and ill-advised aspirations that joining the cast of *Glee* is a viable career option. If Shakespeare didn't go through whatever the British equivalent of the Big Red Door was 400 years ago, and he's still got a grave to turn in, believe me, he'll be doing back-flips right now.'

One girl dived into the splits, while another jumped over her head. How Julliard.

'And they will be way more graceful than *those* moves.'

Lorna gave me a playful shove. 'Stop being such a Grouchy McGrouch,' she said. 'The really good part's coming up – you'll totally get a kick out of this. It's where the ghost of Hamlet's dad shows up! He's, like, stuck in Limbo – just like us! How – what's that word Miss Ballard, my old drama teacher, used to use? – ironic.'

Splits Girl seemed stuck on the floor. Her friend pulled her up with the fakest to-audience smile. At least this gnarlfest of a show seemed to be taking Lorna's mind off the bad stuff.

'Oh! Here's Emma's big moment!' Lorna said.

Two more girls half danced onto the stage, wearing bowler hats, denim cut-offs and T-shirts with 'Wittenberg University' scrawled across the front.

This whole thing was basically an excuse to dress for Coachella in December.

The Foxes turned into Phoenix, then Vampire Weekend. One of the girls – the one wearing enormous ironic black-framed glasses – bounced way less enthusiastically in her slouchy boots than the other. As she pulled off her hat, she smoothed down her shiny blonde bangs. Emma.

'Say, what, is Horatio there?' Splits Girl asked Emma, jerking at her like a fish in a net.

Emma didn't dance back. Splits Girl twirled her trucker hat, throwing it up in the air and catching it back on her head. Eugh. This would never go down in Bushwick.

'A piece of him,' Emma said in a neutralist of neutral voices, making the others look super try-hard.

Someone in the audience sniggered.

'Isn't she brilliant?' Lorna beamed.

'Stand-out,' I said. Though possibly not for the reasons Lorna imagined.

'She doesn't need those glasses, btw,' she whispered. 'They're just for show.'

'I think the same could be said for half of Brooklyn.' I smiled.

Oh boy, now Splits Girl was spitting, spinning around Emma like a vinyl record. 'If again this apparition come . . .' She tediously over-pronounced every syllable before landing theatrically in a heap, centre stage, and looking out into the pretend night. 'The bell then beating one . . .'

An – it has to be said – eerie church bell chimed one o'clock. Splits Girl stared earnestly out into the audience, doing her best to appear spooked. Presumably waiting for the 'apparition' of Hamlet's dad. This better be good.

The auditorium fell silent. Waiting.

For a moment, nothing happened. Either someone had forgot their line, or decided to go *big* on the suspense. Then the edge of the giant *Hamlet* poster began to wave.

'This is *so* unrealistic,' I said. 'That never happens when we enter a room.' Woah, Lorna was all about the shoves today.

The pages of parents' programmes on the front row fluttered, then the second and third rows felt it too. A slow wind was whipping through the theatre, threatening to mess up mothers' salon-styled hair and make fathers' Armani ties fly.

Wooo! Wooo! A disembodied wail broke out, quietly echoing off chair after chair.

With a low boom, the lights cut, plunging the hall into inky darkness. Somewhere in the audience a little kid started to cry.

'Um, did this happen in rehearsal?' I asked Lorna.

'No.' I could just make out the movement of her shaking her head in the darkness. 'The dad ghost popped up in some ill-advised white skinny jeans and a lace crop top. *Lace.* They really should have got a better costume director. But it certainly wasn't this scare—'

Two hundred heads turned with an almighty jolt as the door at the back of the theatre blew open. A green light flashed onstage – and someone grabbed my shoulder.

21

In unison, Lorna and I screamed.

'Guys, it's only me. Calm down! I'm assuming you didn't want me to know about this off-curriculum excursion, but that's a tad of an overreaction.'

Only one person used that many three-syllable words in sentences on a daily basis. Nancy.

I turned to see her bespectacled face and white and blue striped top in the darkness. She dropped her hand.

Onstage the ghost appeared from behind the headache of green light, causing parents to shriek. I sat on the floor and put my sorry head in my hands.

'Wow, I guess they were saving the really sick FX until opening night.' Lorna looked down at me, her mouth forming a perfect O.

'Sorry, I didn't mean to scare you.' Nancy – the third member of the Dead Girls Detective Agency – eyed the 'ghost' suspiciously as it strode menacingly around the graffitied battlements. It seemed to be a projection of a small-ish Peabody girl with caramel hair and pillow lips. Which were more menacing than they sound when she was see-through and wailing manically. 'I just . . .'

'Just what? Thought you'd scare the death out of us?' I asked from the floor. To my left, the ghost wooed.

Nancy smiled weakly and tucked a strand of her squirrel-red hair behind her ear, making her black glasses wiggle. Unlike Emma, she *did* need those.

'No, I just wanted to find out where you were. I know you think I'm all Rules, Rules, Rules, but you can tell me if you're going to do this kind of stuff.' She looked at Lorna, kindly. 'I know I was an only child, but I do get why you wanted to be here, Lorna. I'm your friend, not your boss. It's not my job to get mad at you. I get why you took a risk to see Emma tonight.'

The ghost made a pathetic groaning noise at Splits Girl. She shook her shoulders at it and it disappeared off stage in a cloud of dry ice. I wondered if shoulder-shaking worked on us too?

Nancy sat next to me on the wooden floor. 'The thing is . . . Well, lately, I've been feeling kind of left out.' She hugged her knees into her chest. 'We've all been so disparate.'

I didn't entirely understand what that word meant. But I sorta knew what she was getting at. Maybe.

'Charlotte, you've – understandably – been needing some privacy and alone time to come to terms with what happened with your Key . . .' Nancy said.

The dull pain slooshed back, weighing low in my stomach. I didn't want to get into this right now. It wasn't the time. It would *never* be the time. We'd solved my murder. I'd found my Key – my passport through the Big Red Door to the Other Side – and Tess, the Attesa's fourth dead girl, had stolen it. She'd done with my Key what I'd never now do. Escape this world to whatever came next.

'. . . and I respect that, but I feel like we haven't talked in weeks. All the hiding in your room by day, and porting wherever every night . . . I can't fully imagine what you're going through at the moment, Charlotte, but wouldn't it be easier to go through it with Lorna and I there?'

Nancy tried to get me to face her, but I couldn't stand to see the look in her green eyes – the *Poor You* one which

23

confirmed that my future was every bit as dead end and ruined as I knew it to be. I was the ghost equivalent of those kids who fail high school over and over and have to keep repeating senior year. I'd be here forever, while everyone else graduated and got to be a grown-up. And in Limbo, you didn't even get to go to Prom.

Not that I was a fan of Prom. But . . .

Nancy removed an invisible speck of dirt from her Breton top. 'And you, Lorna – well, you've not been around so much either. I guess you've been avoiding me to keep Emma's play secret and sneaking off?'

'I didn't mean to. I just . . . I'm sorry, Nance.' Lorna pouted at Nancy sadly as the ghost disappeared.

'Anyway, it didn't take very impressive levels of detection to figure out where you'd been going every day. The fact you actually said you thought Tess was no better than Claudius yesterday was a dead giveaway.' Nancy shot Lorna a small smile. 'You're not usually into improving your knowledge of dead English playwrights when there are boutiques on the block. I know there haven't been any new arrivals at the hotel these past couple of weeks, but does that mean we can't hang out all together again like we used to? I . . . I really miss you guys.'

Poor Nancy. With all my mopey me-me-me-ing, I'd forgotten that I wasn't the only one who could get hurt. Boy, did I need to stop being such a brat.

'Group hug?' I asked.

Nancy grabbed me round the waist and lynched Lorna's leg before I had a chance to add that I'd been joking. I guess we'd upset Nance even more than she wanted us to know. Both Nancy and Lorna said they stayed in this world out of choice – Nancy to help other dead girls find their Key and Lorna because she wasn't ready to move on – but that didn't mean it wasn't a day at the beach all the time.

'You know what we need? A ghouls' night out,' I joked.

Lorna groaned, extracting her leg from Nancy's viper grasp. 'Sssh! with the truly terrible puns already, Charlotte' she said. 'This is it, Hamlet's big scene! We can't miss this.'

A tall, pale girl strode onto the stage. Her severe black bob was partly hidden under a sky-blue beanie hat. The reflective strips on her fluorescent blue and yellow sneakers caught the lights as she confidently walked to the middle of the stage, her navy leather-look leggings tight on her long, slim legs.

'O, that this too too solid flesh would melt, thaw and resolve itself into a dew!'

The instant the girl opened her mouth, everyone in the audience stopped shuffling. Even the little kids. She was like a bag of magnets. With this girl onstage, there was nowhere else to look.

'How weary, stale, flat and unprofitable seem to me all the uses of this world.' Her voice was deep – my mom would have called it 'commanding'. She didn't need to dance around the stage to make her point. It was in her every cell. She made Splits Girl look like an auditionee who'd brought their dancing dog on a TV talent show.

'I take it that's Mercy Grant?' I asked.

'Uh huh,' Lorna said. 'The queen bee of the drama

club. She always gets the lead role in every play. She's crazy-good, but her acting style's a little showy. In my opinion, Emma has way more chance of going on to awesome things.'

But of course.

'O, God! A beast, that wants discourse of reason, would have mourn'd longer – married with my uncle,' Mercy spat, the hood of her aqua sports jersey spinning out behind her. Her eyes were rimmed with so much black kohl it was impossible to tell if they were brown or green.

'I know one thing,' Nancy said quietly, 'I wouldn't want to have bad discourse of reason with Mercy Grant. She looks like she'd eat anyone who got in her way for dinner, then ask for a shake and a side of home fries.'

Mercy glided to the front of the stage, pausing to eyeball the front row. If they weren't watching, she wasn't speaking. 'But break, my heart; for I must hold my tongue.'

She rose onto the balls of her feet and looked mournfully up into the spotlight. *Her* spotlight. Mercy's hand was on her brow.

In the wings on the opposite side of the stage, Anastasia and the dancers waited for their cue. Mercy held her epically angsty position.

Nothing.

The silence lasted a beat too long. Kids began to shuffle; dads to adjust their ties. Something was wrong.

'Don't tell me she's corpsing?' I turned to Lorna. 'She can't have forgotten her next line – she doesn't seem the

26

type. I bet Mercy had the whole of *Hamlet* down while the rest of us were still watching *SpongeBob*.'

Mercy's leg wobbled as she struggled to hold her pose. She began to look a little uncomfortable. It so wasn't an emotion she was on board with.

'No, I don't think so,' Lorna said. 'If I remember what happens next right, she's just waiting for Emma – this is where she's supposed to come in again and say a line.'

A mother in the second row ruffled her programme loudly. The dancers exchanged lost looks.

Mercy cleared her throat. 'But break, my heart; for I must hold my TONGUE.' She said the line even louder this time, pronouncing 'tongue' as if she was talking to someone who'd only heard English on the radio in songs.

'Ohforgodssake,' Ana muttered from the wings. 'Emma, if you don't get your cute little butt out here right now . . .'

The front row giggled as Anastasia strode backstage into the blackness to find her best friend. Mercy sighed – disgusted at the amateur hour she was being forced to take part in – and took a step forward to speak. 'Oh that—'

Whoosh!

There was an almighty crack as a rope on the other side of the stage shot into the air with a violent force, lashing the scaffolding across the top of the stage.

'What the . . .?' Nancy jumped up. Head detectress on duty instantly. Without thinking, I jumped up by her side.

The sandbag that should have been holding the rope

down landed with a thud by Splits Girl's feet. She let out a petrified scream. Above the stage, the colossal lighting rig began to wobble.

'Ohmigod . . .' Lorna took a slow step onto the stage as her feet tried to catch up with her brain. 'Mercy.'

At the speed of a herd of snails, Mercy raised her head. Above her, the rig creaked, with an eerie low screech . . . then began to fall – right towards where she was standing.

'Mercy!' I shouted. 'Mercy! Move! NOW!'

But it was no use. I was dead. She couldn't hear my voice. No Living person could.

The lights toppled down, bringing the entire metal rig with them, like explosives in a disused building. An avalanche of metal raced towards Mercy Grant; I buried my face in Nancy's soft sweater.

With a sickening thud, the rig hit the stage.

There was silence. And then people began to scream.

CHAPTER 4

'Emma! Did anyone see Emma?' The wild was back in Lorna's eyes.

All around us, the teachers were moving with lightning speed: pulling down the curtain, moving sobbing students backstage, ushering parents into the Great Hall.

'No, but I'm a hundred per cent sure she's fine.' Nancy squeezed Lorna's shoulder. 'She was nowhere near the stage – we saw the lights fall and they only hit Mercy.' She grimaced. 'What a terrible, terrible accident. In all my years of detecting, I've investigated murder after murder, but I've never actually seen someone *die* before. That was . . .' She shuddered.

Someone had pulled a black sheet over the place where Mercy fell. I could make out the tips of two small sneaker-clad feet poking out from under it.

'Lorna,' Nancy said gently, 'we need to get out of here. Emma might have been lucky and not actually seen the accident happen, but Mercy was still her classmate. She'll be feeling all kinds of horrible right now and I don't think it's safe for you to be so close to her. For *either* of you. I know you wanted to watch Emma perform tonight, but the show's over. Plus, you know the Rules, we can only affect the Living's lives if it's in the interest of solving a case. And all three of us saw what happened here – it was a terrible mishap, pure and simple.'

The small black-haired boy, Dylan, was still standing at the side of the stage. It was as if his scruffy sneakers were attached to the spot with Krazy Glue. Poor kid. He looked totally traumatized.

'Do you think he's in shock?' Lorna asked. 'Maybe I should go help. I used to babysit him when he was a kid, remember?'

Nancy placed a hand on one hip. She'd been upset earlier for sure, but now her inbuilt leader gene had kicked in. She needed to get us out of here before Lorna did something to cause even more of a scene – more than, you know, the whole teenage death one.

'If Dylan is in shock, do you really think an appearance from the ghost of his dead *babysitter* is going to make the poor boy get over this horror show any quicker?' Nancy asked.

'Good point,' Lorna admitted, quietly staring down at her Pretty Ballerinas. 'My bad. You're right, as always. Maybe we should go. I can check in on Emma later.'

Uh oh, there was the world famous Harsh Nancy look. You didn't want to be on the receiving end of that.

'. . .That is, check in on her later from about a block away. When it's less dangerous,' Lorna quickly added.

'I don't get what happened,' I said. 'Why did the rope suddenly fly up like that?'

I touched the stage scaffolding next to me. A metal tower reached up, almost to the theatre's roof. It must have been used for putting up the backdrops and lights. I climbed up a step, then another, trying to get a better look at all the wires and ropes up there. Messy.

'Surely the lights would have been attached to the rig really, really securely. Like, getting whacked by a rope – even if it was a gigantic, speed-of-scary, out-of-control one like that – shouldn't have been enough to make the entire thing crash down, should it?' I asked.

Pop!

I clumsily swivelled to locate the source of the sound – and found myself staring into a pair of intense green eyes; ones that were punctuated by tiniest flecks of grey.

A disloyal tickle – totally the opposite of the one I'd felt in the Great Hall – fluttered from my fingers and all the way down to my toes. It momentarily made me forget I was dead, and that I could no longer feel heat or cold.

The owner of the eyes looked at me for a second too long, then brushed his midnight-black fringe to one side, never once losing hold of my stare.

'Hey,' I said.

'Hey yourself,' Edison answered.

Even three steps up, I was only on eye level with him. It had been so long since I'd stood this close to him, I'd forgotten he was so tall.

So tall and *so* trouble.

'Edison Hayes, what in the name of bad pennies, are

you doing turning up here?' Nancy asked, breaking the moment. Thank God. 'A girl's just died in an unfortunate accident. We don't need every teenage spook in the city showing up to take a look.'

She sighed, then eyed him sharply as a thought hit. 'Wait, how did you know where we were?' Nancy asked Edison.

'Maybe he's been following me around like a sneaky sneak too,' Lorna said, rocking on her heels.

He so had previous in that department.

Edison gave a little shrug – which I in no way found cute – and pulled a crumpled old letter from the back pocket of his very skinny black jeans.

'I was in the Attesa lobby, minding my Bs, when the place started sounding like something off a Kraftwerk album,' he said.

Nancy pulled a face which said she certainly didn't have time for his obscure musical references. Even if they weren't obscure to anyone who had, I don't know, used Spotify since they started puberty.

'He means the hotel siren started blaring,' I translated, refusing to meet Edison's eyes.

I didn't like him. I couldn't. Not when he'd known about Tess's plan to steal my Key and, for some inexcusable reason, not warned me about it like any sane person should. That day – just before she'd stolen my future – I'd heard Edison and Tess fighting, and from what he said to Tess, it was super-clear he'd known what she was up to all along. How could I ever trust him again after that?

'Look, while I've not been the Dead Girls Detective

Agency's best performing Girl Scout cookie seller, I do know what sirens going off and letters falling out of the sky from whatever freaksville outfit that sends them means – a new dead kid's on their way,' Edison said. 'And probably because they died in Snow White with an apple circumstances. Here.' He handed the letter to Nancy who unrolled it as carefully as she would an unread report card.

'"Mercy Grant, sixteen, died at Palmer Peabody Academy for Girls this afternoon",' she read aloud. '"She was murdered when a lighting rig crushed her body. Please expect her arrival within the next thirty minutes. As usual, until Mercy's Key is found, she must stay in the Hotel Attesa.'

Woah. So the flying rope and the falling lights weren't down to someone's shoddy stage-making after all. But how—

'The supportive tone of those things never fails to amaze me,' Edison said.

Much as I majorly hated him, the boy had a point. It was like the letters were written by some ghost who'd seen so many murders they didn't find them tragic any more. Which, to be fair, was probably the case.

Lorna tugged on Nancy's stripy sleeve. 'But you said Mercy's death was an accident "pure and simple"! The letter proves it's not.'

'Um, I . . . I guess I was wrong.' Nancy silently reread the faded page in disbelief.

'Wow,' Lorna said. 'So we just witnessed our first murder? That's creepier than a box of caterpillars.'

'Imagine someone wanting Mercy Grant dead.' I was

finding it majorly hard to take everything in. I needed a minute. Or maybe 400 of them. 'I mean, from the very little we've seen and heard of Mercy, she did seem sort of overconfident and annoying. But there's "annoying" and there's "making two hundred pounds of metal fall down on a person's head". They're kinda poles apart.'

'I'll say,' Edison agreed. Really? Did he have to be so agreey?

'I've never been at a murder scene this early before.' Nancy's confusion was clearing; her detective brain kicking into gear. She'd switched from mine and Lorna's hurt best friend to head of the Agency the second Edison gave her the note.

'Disturbing doesn't cover it. The body's over there under that blanket, like, five steps away.' Lorna unnecessarily pointed at the only dead-girl-shaped object within a trillion block radius. 'Like, she's still hot.'

Edison's attention shifted from me as he raised his eyebrows with a mischievous grin. 'Hot? Not *another* cheerleader? I know those girls are about as annoying as a room temperature IQ, but surely someone could give the pompom and peroxide posse a break from homicide for one week?'

Urgh. Honestly?

'Edison, look—' Nancy ignored his lame-as attempt at a not-even-joke '—what Lorna's trying to communicate is that we're incredibly lucky to be on a case this early – we actually *saw* the murder for the first time ever!'

Wow, was she enthusiastic now we knew this wasn't just some 'tragic accident', but a case to be solved. I thought back to my first day in the Attesa when Nancy had patiently explained that yes, I was dead, but hey, she'd help me get through this – like losing your life was no worse than losing a button off your favourite shirt.

'So these seconds now,' Nancy said, 'the ones I am currently wasting talking to *you*, Mr Hayes, are vital. The police aren't here yet. No one even knows it's a murder but us. We need to secure the crime scene so it doesn't get contaminated. Or try to possess some of these kids so we can interview everyone who wasn't onstage. Or – seeing as we can't photograph the scene – write down everything so we can remember it later.' She pulled her trusty spiral notebook out of the pocket of her A-line denim skirt.

'Been ODing on late-night cop shows again, have we?' Edison gently leaned on the tower. *My* tower. His arm brushed against mine as if it was the most natural thing in the world. 'Or you could just wait until the professionals arrive and copy their homework.'

Nancy scowled. Ever since the Tess Incident, she'd gone from ignoring Edison when he acted more Hyde than Jekyll, to actively looking like she might slug him. Which made me love her even more. Her Geekiness was way too professional to ever admit she was sore at Edison for the part he played in what happened to my Key, but the fact she so obviously was, was one of the gazillion reasons she ruled.

'When did this arrive?' Nancy coldly waved the letter at Edison.

He shrugged again. He was an evil Key-stealer's enabler. His shrugs were definitely *not* cute. 'One port and half a smoke ago.'

Nancy pushed a strand of auburn hair behind her ear. 'Then we've probably got one port and twenty minutes here to look for clues before we have to be back to the hotel to greet our newest member.'

She clapped her hands. 'Let's get going. Charlotte, it sounds as if all the students from the show have been kept backstage until the police arrive, so if you and Edison . . .'

I stared her down. Hard.

'. . . okay, if *you*, could go check out what's being said in the dressing rooms, Lorna and I can inspect the scene, see if there are any clues around the body.'

Edison reached into his other back pocket and pulled out a beaten-up packet of cigarettes. He absent-mindedly tapped the bottom of the box until a white stick jumped out and into his other hand, before bouncing it into his mouth. No matter how often he smoked – and it was *way* too much – Edison never seemed to run out. I'd been too out-of-my-mind mad at him for the last few weeks to ask how his little party trick worked. Maybe dying with an object on your person meant you had a supply of it forever. Was that why the ancient Egyptians buried their dead with gold and wine and all that jazz? Lorna must be majorly pissed she'd not been holding a suitcase of Chanel when that crown came down on her lovely head.

'Please don't smoke in here, Edison.' Nancy scowled again. 'It's not allowed and you know it. This is a place of learning, not a dive bar.'

'C'mon, Nancy, what's it going to do to the students – kill them?' Edison gently bit down on the cigarette as he lit it. 'Because the last time I looked, there seemed to be much bigger dangers than passive smoking. Like, I dunno, psychotic murderer dropping half of Broadway on their heads?'

'*Edison!*' Woah, from Nancy that was basically a bark. 'Please.'

He took a long lazy drag and leaned on the rig behind him. I practically heard Nancy count to ten in her head.

'So you – one, two? I do not care – go backstage and Lorna and I will . . .' She swivelled, her thick ponytail spinning. 'Where *is* Lorna?'

'If you'd been doing more detectressing and less judging, you'd have noticed that her little blonde doppelganger appeared, then Lorna followed her through there.' Edison pointed to a small door behind the stage's mean streets backdrop. 'I'm guessing the Lorna mini-me is her sister?' he asked me.

I nodded neutrally because – tight jeans and nice green eyes or not – if Nancy was still mad at Edison, I was still very mad at him too. He'd stood back and let Tess take my future without so much as a 'Hey Charlotte, heads up, this girl's a crazy.' And that was not easy to forgive.

Sadly I blew my ice maiden act by tripping down the steps and narrowly avoiding my face saying a big hello to the stage. Smooth. I'd died wearing my mom's super-high DvF heels – I barely make it to the subway in them, let alone through eternity. Turns out they weren't appropriate for the theatre either. Great.

Ed grabbed my arm, steadying me just in time. My traitor of a belly did its tingle thing. Why had my terrible taste in men not died with the rest of my body? My last boyfriend and supposed soulmate David had turned out to cheerleader-addicted manwhore who was cheating on me before I was even buried. Now I was feeling this total confusedness about a dead boy who was soo not worth my breath.

Not that I had any.

I stepped off the bottom rung with all the grace I could muster. Ed squeezed my hand before letting go. Must remember I'm mad at him. Must remember I'm mad at him. I pulled away fast.

'Lorna! Lorna! Ah, she's over here! Quickly, Charlotte, we've not got long before Mercy arrives.' Nancy motioned for me to follow her. 'Edison, do you think you can handle the preliminary inspection of the crime scene?'

His expression practically screamed, *Really*?, but he said, 'If I have to.'

'Charlotte, come on!' Nancy waved.

Backstage, the Peabody girls were sitting in small crumpled clumps of fours and fives on the wooden floor. There was a low rumble of talk; it hummed like the refrigerator in the corner of my mom's kitchen. An occasional muffled sob broke out across the room. In the middle of the horror and the shock, Nancy was weaving her way between the groups, bending down to forensically stare at the girls as if one of them might have accidentally written the word 'murderer' on her face in pen.

Lorna stood stone-still by the door, her back to the magnolia wall, her hands pushed hard against it.

'Do you think this is far enough away from Emma to be safe?' she asked. 'Don't tell Nancy, but I am feeling emotional. I don't want to accidentally appirate and scare Emm even more.'

I scanned the room. Emma was sitting with her 'sweet' best friend Anastasia, Miss Onesie, and the big-eyed girl from outside on the steps. Dylan had joined another group a way off, but he kept looking over. Not that any of the girls noticed. Even though he was the only guy in the room, Dylan was the kinda boy girls didn't notice.

'Is he friends with them?' I asked.

Dylan touched his nose, realized he had a booger on it and quickly whipped a dishevelled Kleenex out of his pocket.

'Dylan and Emma? When they were little, yes, but not now. Emma and Ana had always been in the cool crowd – just as you'd expect.' Lorna smiled in her sister's direction. I almost expected to see a halo shining over Emma's head. 'Dylan's a sweetie, but I think they started to run in different crowds when the girls joined PP.'

I bet they did. Very diplomatically put.

'To be honest, I don't know why he's here,' Lorna said. 'I think he goes to a boys' school a few blocks down.' She stared at Emma sadly.

'You've never appirated, appeared as a ghost to the Living, when you've been all angsty and emotional before, have you?' I asked.

'No, but—'

'Y'know, that might just be *my* thing.' I looked sideways at Lorna. 'Technically you *could* get closer to Emma now if you wanted. This is a murder inquiry and all. It's basically called doing your job.'

Three, two . . .

'Oh!' Lorna let her hands drop from the wall and shuffled forward as she got my full meaning. 'You're so

39

right. Any contact I have with Emma now *would* be in the line of detectressing, right? And we both know how seriously Nancy takes that.'

We looked up to see Nancy putting her head inside one girl's canvas tote. Because whoever did this was bound to have a saw, knife and copy of *The Murderer's Handbook* on their person.

'In fact if she wasn't so busy, I bet she'd be super-annoyed at us now, just standing here by this wall instead of gathering evidence.' Lorna smiled slyly. 'We should probably go over there and listen to what they're saying. It's what Nancy would want us to do.'

'And if Nancy would want it . . .'

We picked our way across the room, careful not to walk through any more girls and over to Emma's group.

'I'm not being a bitch, I'm just saying that sometimes karma is.' Anastasia had taken off the heinous baseball hat. Her long red hair was two shades lighter than her soldier coat. She looked like a dancer from a Beyoncé video.

Emma lightly slapped her friend's knee. 'Ana, will you stop with that already? You didn't see that thing crash down. Poor, poor Mercy.'

'Hello, you didn't see the accident either because you were as off-stage as me, so don't make with the whole I'm-so-traumatized act,' Ana shot back. 'Where were you anyway? I know you weren't exactly volunteering to paint props when you could be painting your nails, but it's not like you to miss a cue.'

Emma picked at the frayed edge of her cut-offs. 'I told you – I went to the bathroom and the lock jammed,' she said. 'By the time I got the hell out, I heard the crash, then everyone was running and screaming.' She held up her right hand to show she'd broken a couple of nails wrestling with the busted door lock. 'Someone should talk to the janitor about it before another girl gets trapped in there. It smelled really bad.'

'Emm, I think the janitor is going to have enough on his hands cleaning up the mess Mercy made on that stage without worrying about faulty locks.' Anastasia wrinkled her freckle-covered nose.

'Please tell me she regularly uses humour to deflect her true feelings and pain,' Nancy said, coming to join us and pulling a face.

'She's totally, definitely joking.' Lorna sounded as convincing as a real estate agent. 'Emma wouldn't be besties with someone who was out and out mean. I think I know my sister.'

Or you did when she was twelve.

'Find any leads?' I asked Nancy, trying to switch up the subject.

'No, but it's incredibly early to put any pieces of this puzzle together. More than half of murders get solved in the first forty-eight hours, so I'm not putting pressure on myself just because the first sweep of the suspects hasn't come up golden.'

'I suppose as Student Body President I'll be expected to say a few words.' Ana rolled her amber eyes. 'It's going to take me forever to write something that doesn't make Mercy sound like the biggest waste of space the Upper East Side's seen since the Citi Bike rack was installed. Way to ruin a weekend, Mercy.'

The door flew open and a woman exploded into the room. Anastasia stopped bitching long enough to look up. The woman was probably in her late twenties and definitely into floral prints. Her floaty chiffon sundress was completely wrong for this time of year, so she'd thrown a mismatching knitted red cardigan on top. The bulky ensemble hid her curves, a purple velvet headband held her Rapunzel-long mouse hair back from her make-up-free face. Even if she weren't a teacher, she'd never be given membership to Palmer Peabody's glossy posse.

'Great, and now Miss Ballard's here.' Ana threw her baseball hat at Emma. 'Can we go yet already? We had a reservation at Plunge Bar for six. Our table's totally going to go to some idiot tourists at this rate.'

'Miss Ballard?' Nancy asked.

'Peabody's drama teacher,' Lorna explained. As if she'd be anything but. 'I had her when I was at school too. She's kinda—' Lorna bit her lip, searching for the word '—kooky.'

'Students, this is Detective Jefferson Lee,' Miss Ballard announced, ushering someone else into the room. 'He's going to be handling the inquiry into Mercy's . . . Mercy's . . .' She dissolved into tears unable to finish her sentence.

'Wow, I'd forgotten that these drama types, can be so, like, dramatic,' Lorna said.

I looked at Nancy, expecting her to tell Lorna to ssshhh! and listen for any clues, but Nancy's face was as still as the Jackie O Reservoir. She looked like a girl who'd been zapped by a freeze-ray in some loser sci-fi

42

film my dad would have made me watch on a Saturday afternoon.

'Nancy! Woo hoo! You okay in there, Radley?' I waved my hand in front of her face. Nancy blinked. Then blushed. 'Yes, sorry, I was . . .'

Then I saw him – all six foot four, two-day stubble, slightly baggy nonchalant suit of him – and *totally* realized why murder had slipped even Nancy's mind.

'Hey everyone, I'm Detective Jefferson Lee,' Mr Dark Stubble said, scanning the room. 'And, as Miss Ballard explained, I'll be the head detective on this case.'

'He's not old enough to be a head anything – unless it's head *boy*.' Edison smirked. 'No one grows stubble like that unless they want to make the point that they can.'

I channelled Nancy and did my level best to ignore him.

'I know this afternoon has been . . . well, I can't imagine how you're all feeling right now, to have lost such a dear friend.' Detective Lee had a trace of a Southern accent. It made everything he said sound super-proper and polite. Moms must love him. 'Some of you witnessed a horrific accident today, and I am so sorry you had to see what you did. But I need you ladies to be strong for Mercy for a little longer. It's police procedure that we get some information from you before we can let you all go – we need to figure out what happened today, so it never happens again. Quite rightly, I imagine Mercy's family will have some questions about how an accident like this could have occurred. I need to get them the answers they deserve.'

Someone in the room sighed.

'Right now, some of my team are out there securing and photographing the scene. The rest of them would like to start interviewing you so we can work out what went wrong out there,' he said, pushing his blue-black hair out of his grey eyes.

Securing, photographing and interviewing . . . Nancy flashed me a triumphant smile. Boy, did she love it when she was right.

'This is going to take some time—' Detective Lee smiled weakly at Miss Ballard as she delicately blew her nose '—but we owe it to Mercy to do things properly and find out how this could have happened.'

'But time's the one thing we don't have, right, Nancy?' I said.

She was staring at Detective Lee the way Lorna stared at a Marc Jacobs bag.

'Nancy?'

'Uh? Oh, yes. *Time*. No, time is one thing we do not have a lot of.' She checked the clock on the school wall. 'You're completely right, Charlotte. The police still think this was an accident – I guess that's why they're being so calm. But Mercy's going to arrive at the Attesa any minute. Some of us need to go back there right now and do the new-ghost induction.'

'Some of us? I thought new-ghost inductions were a "three deads are better than one" thing?' Actually only one girl had died since me, but I wasn't sure I was settled in enough to be handling anything right now. 'Me, you and Lorna always do it together – one for all and all for that nonsense?' I asked.

'Charlotte, Charlotte, I think we can both agree this is a very strange case,' Nancy said. 'The fact we were all here right from the get-go . . .'

Get-go? Yep, Mercy was going to love hearing her sudden, violent death described like that.

'. . . means we've got a jump start *and* a good in with the police—' she smiled in Detective Lee's direction '—so I think I, as the most senior detective—'

'Um, Nancy, I was here before you!' Lorna interrupted.

Nancy ignored her. 'As the founder of the Dead Girls Detective Agency, I should stay here, shadow the police through these first interviews, get all the information I can, then report back.' She turned to a clean page in her little spiral notepad to show she was poised for detection.

'You can handle an induction, Lorna,' she said without looking up. 'You've seen me do them enough times. It's easy: reassure the newbie, tell them they're dead, give them the Rules, then show them to a room. Simple.'

Simple. That was exactly how I'd found the news I was spread all over the F Train tracks. Simple. Hadn't flipped out. Not at all.

'By the time Mercy understands what's happened to her and you all come back, the police should have figured out they're actually dealing with a murder case, and we'll all be working from the same page.' Nancy practically ran over to Detective Lee's side.

'You know what?' Lorna said as we prepared to port back to the hotel. 'I don't think it was just Mercy who lost her life today, I think Nancy may have lost her mind too.'

'Happens to the best of us,' Edison said quietly, slowly turning to follow Nancy. 'When we meet the right person.'

Once again, I tried to pretend I hadn't heard him. Or let my mind get hung up on exactly what he might mean.

CHAPTER 5

Lying on the Attesa's black leather couch, Mercy Grant was a lot smaller than she'd seemed onstage. Her neat black bob was still partly covered by the sky blue beanie she'd been wearing. Her long legs were tucked up in front of her, as she hugged them to her chest. She was so peacefully still, if I hadn't known better I'd have thought she was sleeping. In fact her spirit was just making its journey here. And, when it did, it was our job to get her mind to play catch up.

'Nancy says you can tell a lot about a person's personality by how they roll with this part,' Lorna whispered.

'What do you mean?'

'Well, most dead teens who wind up in the Attesa didn't know they were about to be horribly murdered, so they're kinda blindsided at first. Like, even when you tell them they're as dead as that Elvis guy, they think you're delusional and assume this is all some big old dream they're having instead.'

Been there, got the tombstone. That was totally how I'd reacted.

'And because they don't think we or any of this is real, they don't worry about being parent/teacher conference nice,' Lorna explained. 'Like Nancy always says, "When people are in a dream state, they're the truest version of themselves." She thinks you get to see the real them when they first wake up.' Lorna wrinkled her button nose. 'I guess that's what she means.'

Nancy really needed to pen her guide to the afterlife – *Dealing With Death: A Smart Ghouls' Guide*. Draft one was probably neatly filed in some drawer downstairs in the Agency's office, the Haunting Headquarters. Or HHQ as me and Lorna preferred to call it. Not being into geekspeak as much as Nancy and all.

'She's actually kinda right.' Lorna examined the ends of her hair. 'Like, you got all *it's-my-fault* and were sure you'd fainted down on the subway track in some hella embarrassing way. You were super-worried that, when you woke up, everyone would be laughing or your mom would be going loco because you borrowed her shoes.'

Yeah, that sounded about right.

'And that's totally what you're like in real death,' Lorna said, 'Way lovely, but also angsty and worrying what everyone thinks the whole time. Like, it's your fault if they don't like you or something. But hey, if I'd dated a doofus like David for as long as you did, I'd probably be the same.'

Sorry, had I missed the call for Character Assassination O'clock?

'What about Nancy?' I tried to change the subject. 'How did she react?'

From the couch, Mercy made a small whimper and unclenched her fist.

Lorna dropped her hair, moving closer to our newest recruit to get a better look.

'Oh, Nancy decided it was a dream too, but that the fastest way she'd wake up was by going along with things,' Lorna said. 'Like, if she could solve her murder she'd hear her alarm go off and it would be time for school. She got so frustrated with me trying to explain the Rules, that she took them off me to read by herself. I think by the time she caught on to the fact that this wasn't an Alice in Wonderland deal, she was enjoying all the sleuthing—' Lorna rolled her denim blue eyes '— so much that she'd have been kinda sore to have to go back to her boring old Living life. I swear that girl was born to be dead.'

Mercy's eyelids fluttered open. She looked around the room with a curious stare before focusing on Lorna and me.

'Here we go.' Lorna nudged me in the ribs. She was weirdly strong for someone so slender and small. 'Show time.'

'Oh no! No! Please tell me I didn't faint onstage!' Mercy sat up way quickly, before slumping back down on the couch with a dizzy expression on her face. 'I've got to get back out there – the show must go on and it can't if the audience don't have their Hamlet.'

'See!' Lorna whispered.

Uh huh. Time to take one for the team. I bobbed down to Mercy's level.

'Hey, Mercy. Um, my name's Charlotte. You . . .' Jeez,

how did you phrase this? 'You didn't faint onstage. I'm so, so sorry – I wish you had.' I locked eyes with Lorna, who nodded at me encouragingly. I could do this. Better to be honest with the girl and tell her plaster-whip-off fast.

I cleared my throat. 'Mercy, there's no good way to tell you this so I won't cover it in chocolate: there's no more Hamlet. There's no more anything, really. Something major happened when you were out there onstage. And, well, now you're dead.'

Mercy shook her head in frustration. 'Of course I'm dead – do you have any idea how many scouts from Julliard are out there? Passing out mid-performance is *beyond* amateur. It's not what they expect from Broadway's future players at all. Imagine if I did this when I was opening in *Spring Awakening* at the O'Neill!' She threw an arm in the air and tried to move me out of her way. 'I need to go back out there and give the performance of my life.'

'That ship may already have sailed . . .' I said.

Mercy soaked me in: from Mom's ridiculous heels, to my messy school uniform, up to my unruly brunette waves. I felt like she was studying me in case she could ever channel what she saw in a future role.

Because *Ghost* was such a sold-out success.

'You don't go to PP.' She sat up again, less wobbly this time, taking in the Hotel Attesa's black and white chequerboard tiled floor and luxurious red velvet drapes. 'And this isn't backstage either. It's way too nice. And clean. Where am I?'

Time to shift gear.

50

'Okay, Mercy, you're an actress, right?' I said. 'So I'm going to tell you a story then I'm going to need you to use that amazing imagination of yours to get into, erm, character.' I looked at Lorna helplessly but she was too busy scrutinizing Mercy's fluorescent blue and yellow Nike high-tops to notice. 'Because you're about to take on a major new role.'

Mercy's face lit up like the Rockefeller Christmas tree. 'Oh! I know what's happening – you're an agent, aren't you? You heard how good I was, came to watch the play and now you've whisked me away to your offices to sign me up before someone else does! You even came in disguise as a schoolgirl so you wouldn't be noticed by the other talent scouts!'

Her hand fluttered over the heavy gold metal chain on her chest. 'This is so flattering, but I have to tell you, I'll need to look at what other offers are on the table first. This is my future after all. It's only fair to let the other people have a chance to tell me why I should sign with them before I commit to one agency.'

Man, I sucked at this. Like, majorly. She wasn't getting it at all. If she *was* Alice, Mercy hadn't even realized she was in Wonderland yet – we'd never make it to the Mad Hatter's hood at this rate. There was a very good reason this was Nancy's permanent gig. I wished she hadn't bailed on us to 'observe' Detective Dreamy.

'No, I'm really sorry, but I'm not some big-time agent,' I said. Mercy knitted her fingers together in her lap. 'Or a small-time one either.' Come on Charlotte, be cruel to be kind. 'I'm just your average dead girl. Like you.'

The silence stretched like an elastic hairband.

51

'Here's the deal: this afternoon, while you were onstage playing Hamlet . . .'

'And you were *killing* it, by the way,' Lorna said. 'Whatever Anastasia says about you, I thought you were as perfect for that role as Alexander Wang was for Balenciaga.'

Mercy seemed to notice Lorna for the first time. She let out a small gasp. 'Emma? What are you doing here? Have you been scouted too?' She frowned. 'Oh, you're not . . . Sorry, you just look like—'

'No, she's not Emma – she's *Lorna*,' I interrupted. This was taking as long as a *Bachelor* finale. 'And I'm Charlotte, like I said. And we are all totally, utterly dead.'

Mercy ignored me and scrutinized Lorna, trying to remember where she'd seen her before.

'As I was saying, just as you were getting into the big old solid flesh speech, a terrible thing happened . . .'

'Like, way the terriblest.' I gave Lorna my best *Please shhh!* face.

'There was a terrible incident and, well, a massive lighting rig fell from the rafters and onto your head,' I said. 'Sorry, Mercy, but you're about as dead as Hamlet's dad.'

Mercy blinked again and refolded her fingers.

'Mercy, do you understand what I'm saying?' I asked. She stared at Lorna and shook her head.

I tried to think back to when I'd been here, not so long ago, sat on that very couch. Nancy had explained the whole thing so well to me. Not consolingly, but definitely well. What had finally hit the truth home? Made me accept I'd never wake up? Bingo! I tried again.

'What's the last thing you remember before you opened your eyes and saw us here?' I held Mercy's stare, hoping it would make her concentrate, Nancy-style.

'Being onstage. The lights were so bright. I felt like I always do when I'm out there – as if I truly belong – and—' she turned to Lorna and bestowed her with a winning smile '—I was *so* nailing it because – and you'll know this if you've ever studied the craft – I was basically channelling Hamlet all the way from Denmark to right here on the Upper East Side. It's inexplicably important to try to absorb the feelings of your character in full or the audience won't be with you on the journey, you know?' She took a breath. Old habit. 'And then . . . Oh, and then there was a scream offstage, in the audience, I think. I mean, how rude? Interrupting someone's performance like that. I was just thinking how I was going to tell Miss Ballard that we really needed to vet the people who buy tickets better, when I looked up and . . .' Mercy's eyes widened to the breadth of the Hudson River and she slapped her hand on her forehead. 'The lighting rig had come loose. It was falling at me fast and. Oh. My. God.'

'I think the penny hath dropped, my Lord,' Lorna said.

Mercy let out the world's loudest wail and threw herself off the couch onto the tiled floor.

'I could have guessed she'd be a screamer.' Lorna took a step back like screaming was chicken-pox contagious. 'I hate it when they scream. It prolongs the bad bit and makes me get this fuzzy feeling right down in my ears. Oh *shoot*!'

'What?' I asked.

'She's going to be crying even louder when she realizes she's got to spend eternity dressed as a hipster prince too,' Lorna said. 'If only they'd been staging *Gatsby*.'

Mercy stopped wailing just long enough to lift her head in a *what?* 'But why would it matter what I'm wearing?' she asked through sobs.

'Long story,' I said. 'Which we maybe should cover later.'

Much, much later. Like, when Nancy was good and back.

Mercy kneeled up on the Attesa floor. 'So you're not a theatrical agent then?' I shook my head. 'Or a talent scout?'

'Afraid not.'

'And that heap of metal I saw coming at me when I was onstage didn't land somewhere good?'

'Nuh huh.'

Mercy sighed. '"Thou know'st 'tis common; all that lives must die, passing through nature to eternity",' she said.

'She's quoting *Hamlet* again,' Lorna explained, like I was a total doofus. 'I remember that one. Even I know what it means.'

'Okay, Brainiac, I've got it.'

'It's better to accept my fate than fight the gods.' Mercy pulled herself back onto the sofa. She stared at Lorna again. 'So where do I? Ohh . . .' Mercy thumped the black cushion triumphantly. 'I've got it now!' she exclaimed. 'Lorna! You're Lorna Altman!'

Lorna wasn't sure whether to be freaked or flattered.

'Why of course! That's why I mistook you for *Emma*.'

Mercy slapped the cushion again. Poor cushion. 'You're her big sister after all. I can't believe you're here. Wow, so what's it like? Being a celebrity ghost?'

'Pardon?' Lorna was giving Mercy the kind of attention she only usually reserved for a new season Kate Spade drop.

'Your death – it was *all* over the Upper East Side,' Mercy said. 'It was *quite* the scandal. A beautiful young girl cut down in her prime – in suspicious circumstances *and* at her prom? For God's sake, if it hadn't actually happened some lame-ass writer would have turned it into teen pulp fiction.'

Lorna's death had been a big, scandalous deal? I'd never thought any of ours would be. But when Mercy put it like that . . .

'I was still at junior high, and due to start at PP in the fall—' Mercy expertly intro-ed her story as if we were on *Inside the Actors Studio* '—but even I remember the paparazzi outside the school. The reporters talking to anyone who they thought could give them the inside scoop. You were the splash in the *Post* that week: "Peabody girl killed at prom". Oh and get this!' Mercy grasped Lorna's arm and lowered her voice conspiratorially. 'There were even some TV execs trying to buy the rights to your life story so they could make it into a TV series!'

'There were?' Lorna was starting to sound excited.

Mercy nodded so hard her sleek bob skipped.

Wow.

Lorna beamed. I'd not seen her look this proud since, looking in a Soho boutique window, I'd correctly told

55

the difference between a Victoria Beckham and a Roland Mouret the day before.

'How did I miss all of this?' Lorna asked me. 'Tess told me it was best to keep low in the first days after my death. By the time I felt strong enough to go and spy on my family and friends and decided I wasn't super-sure I wanted my Key anyway, the hoopla must have died down. I can't believe I missed my fifteen minutes.'

'You totally didn't.' Man, Mercy was going to ask for Lorna's autograph in a minute. 'You're still famous within Palmer P. now. Everyone thinks you haunt the Great Hall because that's where you ... you know ... In fact, Lane McAllister saw you there on Halloween night and was so upset she had to take off three days of school! She missed a crucial geography assignment and everything.'

And again, wow.

'I guess I should be thankful that I died doing what I loved most.' It seemed Mercy didn't need a script. The girl could talk forever without any prompting. 'But then I guess most people do, don't they?'

'No, I was pushed under the F Train during rush hour,' I said flatly. 'And I can't say "using public transport" was ever on my bucket list. Look, this whole episode of *E! News* unfolding before my very eyes ... It's been entertaining, but I've got some more bad news.' Time to throw Mercy the next loop. 'You're not just dead. The fact you've shown up here in the Hotel Attesa means you were ... well, murdered too.'

'Murdered? Seriously?! My death really is like something straight out of Shakespeare, isn't it?' Mercy smiled.

Now that was not the reaction I was expecting. I should log it in one of Nancy's files. If she trusted me not to ruin one with my 'scrawly' handwriting, that is.

'But how can you be so sure I was—' Mercy took a second. I was 98 per cent sure purely for dramatic effect '—murdered?' She somehow made the word stretch out to three syllables. 'It could have been an accident. All that metal that crashed onto me – it was the lighting rig, you say? That could easily have just fallen down. Dylan West, that idiot boy from Malton School, was helping out with the production to get some extra credit. He was in charge of the backstage crew. I wouldn't trust him to blow up a kindergartener's birthday balloon, yet alone marshal a set, but Miss Ballard kept insisting that "drama was inclusive" and we had to give him a chance. I bet this is all down to his below par screwing.'

'Sorry, Mercy, but if you're here someone wanted you dead.' I bobbed down to her eye level again and patted her hand. Much as I wasn't sure I liked her any more than Anastasia did, if I was playing What Would Nancy Do? it felt like the natural next move.

'Let me lay this down: when people die, from what we know, they go straight over to the Other Side, but if you're a teen who's murdered in New York City you come here to the Hotel Attesa instead.' I patted her arm some more. Patting seemed to be working. 'When I arrived, Nancy – she's the other dead girl; you'll meet her soon – she told me this hotel was a bit like a waiting room. You stay here, try to solve your murder and when you do you'll get your Key. That's when you can go through the Big Red Door to the Other Side. Whatever's through there.'

I pointed to the corner of the lobby where Big Red sat behind another lavish red velvet curtain. The place where the Tess Incident had happened. There was no point telling Mercy about that now. I'd shattered from the inside out once, there was no need to share my personal trauma with every other murder victim I met. She kinda had stuff on her plate.

'So my Key – you're going to help me find that?' Mercy asked in a strange voice.

I looked down and realized I was squeezing her hand way too hard. Thinking about Tess did that to me. Which was fine when I was holding a book. Less so when it was a fellow ghost – and a new one you didn't want to class you as a total jerk.

'Yes, we're the Dead Girls Detective Agency,' I said.

Nope, didn't get any less tragic, no matter how many times you said it.

'Rather than going through the Door ourselves we've all chosen to stay here and help other dead girls to solve their cases,' Lorna explained.

'Speak for yourself,' I muttered.

Now it was Lorna's turn to pat my arm. 'So this is the part where Nancy usually does the tour,' she told me encouragingly.

I looked over to the wall to the right of the reception desk, where Nancy had helpfully tacked up a list of the most important Rules for new ghosts to get a handle on.

Rule One: The Big Red Door should only be opened by a ghost's personal Key.

Rule Two: In the Attesa, things work in pretty much the same way as they did when you were alive: objects can be picked up and moved without using your ghost powers.

Rule Three: The Attesa is protected – so the Living can't see it or its inhabitants. When ghosts are in the outside world, the Living can't see or hear them unless the ghosts want them to.

Rule Four: Ghosts can't travel over water.

Rule Five: Ghosts should only appear to the Living if it's in the name of solving a case.

Rule Six . . .

Urgh. I could fall asleep just skimming them. If falling asleep was something ghosts were capable of that is.

'Seeing as Teacher's away, shall we skip that?' I asked, palming Mercy the hand-me-down copy of the Rules for her to read in her own sweet time. 'I'm sure Mercy would much rather get back to the school. Her murderer's in a room up there right now and the sooner we put them together, the sooner we can get her out of here.'

'Don't stress it, Mercy,' Lorna said. 'Nancy's an amazing detective. She'll probably have your case wrapped up by the time we port over there.'

'"Port"? What's a port?' Mercy asked, jumping up from the couch.

Lorna put her arms over Mercy's head and beckoned for me to do the same. We created a circle around her so we could transport her spirit at the same time as ours. 'Don't worry about that right now, we'll take you and explain later tonight.'

I took my place opposite Lorna and we locked eyes.

'Like, your murderer is probably someone really obvious – like your understudy,' Lorna joked.

'You better hope not,' Mercy said. 'My understudy was Emma.'

CHAPTER 6

'Wow, I've never seen the gym look like this before.' Mercy's heavily kohled cat eyes did a sweep of Palmer Peabody's sports hall. 'Though cheerleader try-outs probably involve a similar level of interrogation, for sure.'

The place had been turned from an arena usually used to fuel adolescent insecurities into something straight out of *CSI: New York*. Exam tables were dotted around the cavernous room, the police squad manning many of them. As kids – still in *Hipster Hamlet* costume – lined up to give their details to the cops, they blinked under the harsh strip lights which flashed off the gym's immaculately varnished sprung wood floors. All the artificial light was making me feel edgy. Even the cornflower walls and bleachers took on the taste of something from a penitentiary with all the navy NYPD uniforms going on in here. Miss Ballard fluttered about the room like a closet moth checking that no one was as close to a nervous breakdown as she was. Helpful.

'You know she's the school guidance counsellor too,' Lorna whispered, reading my mind. 'Good appointment, huh?'

'About as good as putting Edison in charge of a school spirit club.'

The idea of going to any teacher if I had a problem was a total roadblock, period. But a big bag of neuroses, like Miss Ballard seemed to be? I'd rather get life advice from Lindsay Lohan. I turned my attention to Mercy instead.

'How did you enjoy your first port?' I asked. 'Don't worry if it made you kinda sick. It can do when you're a newbie. You'll nail it in no time. If you're feeling brave, Nancy might even let you port back downtown yourself later on.'

'I didn't feel any sickness at all.' Mercy smiled lazily. It reminded me of the crocodiles in Bronx Zoo. 'In fact if you hadn't spent the last hour convincing me just how dead I am, I'd say I was in sparkling health. I've not felt this good in months.'

Jeez, was this girl making herself hard to like. Not that Anastasia De Witt (and, btw, were there any letters of the alphabet that weren't in her name?) seemed like the sort of person I'd have wanted to go catch a cold with when I was alive much less a band, but I was starting to wonder if she wasn't the Upper East Side's worst character judge after all.

'This is amazing!' Nancy bounded over. She was way too zipadeedoodah for a murder day. 'We've never had an early start on a case like this before. The police still think it's an accident. Still! Can you imagine? And we know different! I can't wait to see how they figure out it *is* a murder. Though I don't blame them – we thought it was nothing sinister too, until Edison arrived. Plus, Detective Lee's methods are incredibly thorough. I've learned heaps just from watching him already.'

She held up her spiral notebook and flipped through five pages full of round, neat handwriting. 'His interview technique is *so* interesting. There are tons of new tactics I want to try the next time we possess one of the Living.' All five foot four of her grinned.

'Erm, Nance, you may want to tone down the "Woo! Murder!" enthusiasm for one second. There's somebody you need to meet,' I said.

Mercy was listening intently as Miss Ballard sobbed about what a 'terrible loss' her death was and how she was devastated to lose such a 'shining talent' from the drama department. As if. She'd have recast the play by Monday for a special memorial performance so that she could raise cash for a new smoke machine or whatever. One of the first things you learn when you die is that most people only appreciate you when you're not around to remind them what a pain in the ass you are.

'Meet Nancy, the final member of the Agency.' I pinched Nancy's overenthusiastic arm in an attempt to bring her earthward.

'Hello, I'm Mercy Grant.' She held her hand out for Nancy to shake. 'I believe you're going to be solving my murder?'

Nancy pumped Mercy's hand up and down like it was a soap dispenser. 'Mercy! I'm stoked to meet you. Though I kind of feel like we met already because I saw you onstage earlier before . . .'

'Before one hundred pounds of metal and low-grade illuminations fell on my head?' Mercy asked coolly.

Even Nancy had the decency to gulp.

'Oh, don't you worry,' Mercy breezed. 'I'm actually surprising myself with how *fine* I am with the dead news already. I'm taking it in my stride. So many truly great actresses died before their time: Judy Garland, Grace Kelly, Vivienne Leigh, Natalie Wood, Marilyn Monroe . . .'

'Amazing Brittany Murphy,' Lorna added.

Mercy ignored her. 'The AV Club were filming tonight's production so – even though we didn't make it past Act One – I'm sure that, in retrospect, I'll be seen as one of the great performers of my time.' She stared off into the distance, no doubt imagining the installation of her star on Hollywood Boulevard. 'Maybe they'll build a Grant Drama Wing in my memory.' She brightened. 'Is there any way to communicate with my parents so I can ask them to fund that?'

Nancy's smile was starting to sag like a tent in a gale. 'Mercy, I know you've had to take in a lot already today, but before we get on to advanced spirit skills like communicating with the Living, I need to ask you some preliminary questions. Then we can get our inquiry moving. It's incredibly important we take advantage of the fact we were actually on the scene when the murder happened.'

'Yeah, usually she makes us recreate it afterwards in HHQ.' Lorna pulled the face of a girl who'd applied out-of-date fake tan. 'And that is fun for nobody.'

'Hey,' I said, swatting her arm. 'I let you be the murderer last time – don't be dissing that.'

'So we know how you died,' Nancy said, 'we just don't know how somebody rigged the, erm, rig to fall down on you like that. It was quite clever really – waiting for the moment when you were the only person on the stage.' Nancy tucked a stray strand of her squirrel-red hair behind her ear. 'Because of that I'm going to hypothesize that anyone who employs that amount of precision didn't just kill you randomly. They weren't going for any old unlucky student who happened to be in fate's path. No, Mercy, it was you they wanted dead and you alone.'

'Er, Nancy,' I cut in. 'You know when I said we should maybe leave off the "Woo! Murder!" vibe for the moment? Mercy's been dead less time than it takes to cook a chicken. Try to take that on.'

'Now, what do you remember about the moments before you went onstage?' Nancy bulldozed on, notepad at the ready. 'Did anything out of the ordinary happen?'

'No. It was the same as always before a performance,' Mercy said. 'First, I led the group in a cast prayer – it was something I saw Madonna do on *In Bed With* . . . and she is one of the greatest performers of our time.'

Oh God, please do not let her break into a rendition of 'Like a Prayer'.

'Then I had some quiet time to get into My Zone.' I could hear her capitalizing the letters with her tongue. 'After that, I did my usual vocal warm-ups . . .'

Which must have been a joy for everyone's ears.

'Then out I went onto the stage.'

'And did you see anyone strange loitering in the wings?' Nancy asked. 'Anybody who shouldn't have been there?'

Mercy puts her fingers to her temples as if she could rub the memory out.

'Think back: were there any weird men you assumed were another kid's dad? Any girls from other schools? A member of staff who was suddenly taking a whole lot of interest in the play? Anyone who didn't have a reason to be hanging around?' Nancy asked.

Mercy dropped her hands with a giant sigh. 'No. No one. I was so focused on the play, I was in my own little bubble. Miss Ballard taught us to cocoon ourselves before a performance so we'd be ready when we took to the stage. The only murderer my mind was on was the one Shakespeare so lyrically invented – that of Denmark's king.'

Nancy had never met someone our age who used words of more syllables than she did. I wasn't sure if she was impressed or feeling a little pushed off her perch.

'Okay, let's try this from another angle,' she said. 'Have you made any enemies recently? Is there anyone at Palmer Peabody who's jealous of you?'

Mercy snorted. 'Sweetie, I was the incredibly talented lead in an innovative production at the best school in the city – most girls are jealous of me.'

Yep, could totally see why someone had brought that rig right down.

'Hey, Mercy,' Lorna interrupted before anyone had time to think of a suitable response. 'How about you and I go round the room together, and see if we can spot anyone new or weird or strange? You can fill me in on all the school gossip as we go. Like, is it true Wilson Burbank's mom had to go into rehab for an addiction to Botox? And what about that affair between Captain Cassidy and his Brazilian driver's son?'

Lorna guided Mercy out into the room, shooting a conspiratorial look back at me.

'Wow. She's . . .' For once Nancy aced-her-SAT-test Radley struggled to find a fitting word.

'Isn't she just?' I said. Something told me it was going to be a major challenge to spend hours and hours with Mercy without blowing a gasket. I didn't want to be snarky with her – it was hard being a newbie. Maybe she was majorly overcompensating and she'd calm it down when she relaxed? I knew how it felt to be the newest ghost in Manhattan, and for someone to go all mean girl on your ass for no good reason. I might be a little bit bitter around the edges right now, but I was not going to turn into Tess. Or . . .

'Where's Edison?' I found myself asking. Uh, could I be any more of a dork?

'Around,' Nancy said. 'I asked him to stay on the stage and see what the cops were uncovering. It's way easier letting them move things around rather than us wasting our powers trying to put our heads into evidence.'

I scanned the room. No sign of tall, dark and . . . bad news.

'I've not seen him for at least three ports and four smokes.' Nancy pushed her notebook back into her pocket. 'I'd love to think that's because he's doing what he was told for a change, but I think we both know that's about as likely as Lorna staying impartial in this investigation.'

Nancy's green eyes softened. 'How's she doing anyway?'

'Honestly? She didn't take the whole walking through her murder sceneiness anywhere near as well as our new friend Mercy. And, even though we know she's been spending time watching Emma for years, she's still way excited to have an excuse to be near her.'

Which I probably hadn't helped before when I suggested we go sit with Emma's crew. I was such an idiot sometimes.

'Hmmm.' Nancy managed to make the noise sound like she was solving Pythagoras's theorem.

'I'll watch her,' I promised, feeling even worse about enabling Lorna before.

'That's great, Charlotte, but who's going to look out for you?'

I let a chubby blonde girl with corkscrew curls and a sword dripping fake-blood walk right through me. I hoped she'd be enough of a distraction to make Nancy stop. She wasn't.

'What you're going through right now – I can't even imagine. If you're feeling a little deadpressed, that's totally to be expected. You know you can talk to me any time. I've actually been doing some research in the case files to see if anyone's ever found a second copy of their Key. Whenever you—'

'Lorna will be fine,' I said firmly, switching the subject. 'As long as too many other people from her old life don't show up on the scene, she'll be as good as gol—'

'Emma!' A willowy woman swept into the gym, her stilettos clattering across the wooden floor. She looked as out of place as a Porsche at a monster truck rally. Her expensive pale-green suit was the colour of glazed pottery and clung to her tennis-toned body beautifully. Her skin was – as Mom would have said – 'glowing', and still lightly tanned from her last winter-sun break. There was something about the way she carried herself that revealed her killer complexion was just as much down to the bank-breaking facials she probably had three times a week as good genes.

'Are you all right, darling?' she asked, scooping Emma into a hug which at once looked totally maternal yet didn't muss up her uber-blonde hair.

'Uh oh,' I said. 'That must be . . .'

'. . . Emma and Lorna's mum,' Nancy finished.

She looked as if she'd accidentally been beamed in from the set of a Hitchcock thriller. Before the gnarly screamy bit of course. Mrs Altman was not a woman who would have screamed. Run the best charity board in the city before hopping off to Monaco to shop, maybe. But a screamer? Never.

'We missed the first act, because we got stuck in traffic. You know us, running late as usual.' Mrs Altman gave the sharp-suited man who'd followed her into the gym a mock scowl. He patted down his salt-and-pepper beard.

Emma pulled herself from her mom's grasp, nodded and smiled. Then turned to Ana and rolled her eyes.

'Who's in charge here?' Mrs Altman swivelled her lovely head, locating the nearest cop. There was a slight trace of a European accent in her voice. 'What right have you got to be detaining my daughter or any of these poor girls after what they've been through today? They should all be at home with their families.'

Nancy gawped at Mrs Altman as if she was the

particularly surprising outcome of a science fair exhibit. I could totally see why. I'd grown up with most of the kids at my school, so I'd known their parents since I was still in a stroller. Ali's mom was practically my mom except she couldn't ground me and always gave me one more cookie instead of taking the box away. But Nancy and Lorna were different. Sure, we'd talked families and I knew enough to be able to ace one of those tragic Mr and Mrs quizzes you get in magazines. But we'd never dwelt on the details. I'd not even been strong enough to port back to my folks' apartment since the F Train hit. Seeing them at my funeral was bad enough, what if I ported in to check they were okay and found out they weren't handling my death? Or, worse, that they were.

No, I didn't need to major in Haunting to know why Nancy and Lorna kept their pasts as pencil sketches. Colouring in between the lines would hurt a hell of a lot more than three Broadways of lights landing on your head.

'Um, Nancy?' She was still staring. 'After everything Lorna's been through today, I'm not sure it's such a good idea that she comes face to face with her mom and dad right now too. It's kinda like topping off getting dumped by finding out your boyfriend's cheating on you already with some girl you hate.'

Wonder why that example popped into my head? Maybe because that's exactly what douchebag David had done to me.

'Mrs Altman's like the Countess from *Upper East Siders*,' Nancy said. She was totally addicted to that stupid TV show.

Nancy snapped back in the room. 'Oh gosh yes, sorry, you're totally right. Where *is* Lorna? How about you take her back to the stage to check how Edison's doing and—'

Pop! Lorna appeared by my side and smoothed down her baby-blue skirt in a casual fashion. Which was anything but. 'Oh, it *is* them. I guess I'd should have realized they'd be here. Figures they'd miss the play and show up for the drama,' Lorna said, lightly.

'If this is too weird for you, Charlotte and I could . . .' Nancy said.

'No, no, it's fine. It's not like I haven't seen them up close before.' Lorna was circling her parents now, taking them in from every angle, making sure nothing had changed in the last few years. 'Maybe I'm meant to be here – it could all be part of some celestial plan, couldn't it, Nancy? Me not feeling like I was ready to go over to the Other Side yet, then another murder taking place so near the scene of mine. It's less than the distance between the Marc Jacobs accessories and mainline shops on Bleecker Street.'

Nancy's expression screeched that she thought it was anything but. Nancy was the kind of girl who colour coded her panties, bra *and* socks. She hated mess. And already this investigation was in danger of getting as tangled up as my old iPod ear buds.

'Lorna, I get that you want to be here with them, but we can't lose sight of what we're here to do – solve Mercy's murder,' Nancy said. 'Not see what your mom's bought from Lululemon.'

'How do you know about that store?' I asked.

71

'They're always talking about it on the TV show,' Nancy whispered. 'I figured if it's good enough for the Countess it's good enough for Lorna's mom.'

Give. Me. Strength.

'Nancy's right,' I told Lorna, even though I knew I'd be acting exactly the same way in her – much more comfortable – shoes. 'Let's go get Mercy, make sure we've not missed any leads here and head back to the hotel. We've not even asked Mercy a ton of the questions we need to yet. How about we do that while Nancy shadows Detective like we planned?'

'Jefferson!' Lorna's mom exclaimed. Her professionally arched brows sprung up into her flaxen bangs as she noticed Detective Lee. 'What are you doing here? Please tell me the press hasn't got wind of this already. We weren't in the audience, but I've talked to other parents who saw the whole event. This is *entirely* different. It doesn't need to be like the last time.'

'Huh?' I said. 'Lorna, how does your mom know Detective Lee?'

She shook her head. 'I have no idea. But my mom knows everyone. Maybe they were on the board for some police charity ball committee together? Organizing events is, like, her hobby. Some people go horse riding or collect expensive plates, she picks out flower displays and place cards.'

'Guys, shhhhh!' Nancy waved her hand in the air. 'What did she mean "the last time"?'

Jefferson stepped forward and held out his hand for the Altmans to take.

'It's Detective Lee now, ma'am,' he said shyly.

'I do love a Southern accent,' Lorna whispered.

'Detective? But how did you . . .' Mrs Altman noticed a clump of slowly melting snow on her tan Dolce boots and stamped them delicately until it fell onto the gym floor.

'Shall we?' he said, gesturing to some plastic chairs. Mr Altman sat down gingerly. They were made to hold an Upper East Side princess, and they weighed way less than six foot three of – what did Lorna say he was? – hedge-funder dad.

'I guess I should have contacted you and told you about this, but I didn't think you'd want to see any more of me. Or get another reminder of Lorna and your loss.'

'Lorna? Did he say *Lorna*? As in me?' she asked.

'While there are probably hundreds of Lornas in this city, I'm going to go out on a limb here and guess you are the Lorna in question,' I said. What the hell was going on? Things were getting messier by the second.

Mrs Altman took a seat and unbuttoned her cashmere coat.

'After covering Lorna's case for the *New York Post*, I felt so helpless I knew I had to do something,' Detective Lee explained.

Nancy and I exchanged looks. 'So he used to be a reporter?' I whispered.

'Seems so,' Nancy said.

His voice had dropped to a gravelly whisper. 'We both know the team who investigated Lorna's murder messed up. Even a rookie outsider like me could see that.' He sighed. 'They didn't secure the scene fast enough – hell, they let the school cleaners come in and destroy any

73

permissible evidence which could have told us who the animal was who kil—who *hurt* Lorna in the way they did.'

Under the table, Mrs Altman quietly took her husband's hand, squeezing it until her knuckles turned white.

'As a crime reporter, I'd been frustrated by cases before, but never that badly. It was the first time in my life I realized maybe I wasn't helping by getting the story out there. Maybe I was just adding to the noise around the tragedy and stopping the truth from coming out.'

Mr Altman gently stroked his wife's hand back.

'Writing about Lorna didn't do jack,' Detective Lee continued, 'so I got to thinking what if I'd been on the scene at the start? What if I'd told those bozos to stop for a second and not just assume this was some dumb high school incident? What if I'd got them to do their damn jobs? Maybe then I could have found your daughter's killer instead of just writing about him or her.'

Detective Lee ran his hands through his thick black hair. 'I decided then and there that if I couldn't change the system from the outside in, I had to get to a place where I could change it from the inside out. So I handed in my notice at the *Post* and signed up as a cop. I told them I wanted to work on the murder squad. I guess my experience in the newsroom fast-tracked things a little, because here I am. I'm only helping out today because my boss knew I was familiar with the school and I wasn't on a murder case.' He hung his head, sadly. 'I cannot believe the irony that I'm back here sitting in front of you.'

'Wow,' Nancy said. 'Imagine being so fired up by the injustice of the death of a kid you've never even met that you'd change your life like that.'

Imagine. I swear Nancy did something close to a swoon. Houston, I think we have a second problem.

'He kind of looks like a hotter, younger version of George Clooney,' Lorna said. 'His eyes would look a lot cuter if he wore a deeper blue suit though. That grey does nothing to make them pop.'

'Honestly, Lorna, this man has given up his entire career so he can avenge your death and all you can do is comment on his wardrobe choices?' Nancy waggled a finger at her.

'I'm just saying that he's got the whole hot detective thing down, but he'd be even hotter with a couple of teeny tweaks,' Lorna said. 'I'm kinda disappointed in my mom for not pointing it out. She's usually so not shy to help people discover their colour types.'

'Oh for f—' Nancy started. 'Oww.'

A weedy girl cop in a one-size-too-big uniform ran straight through Nancy and shivered to a halt.

'Detective Lee, I have news,' she panted. Her face was flushed and kinda sticky. She must be straight out of cop school. I wondered if Mrs Altman could give her colour advice too. 'The girl's death – it was no accident.'

Mrs Altman sharply drew in her breath. The girl held up a Polaroid of the rope. 'Someone cut the end of this to make it fly up into the rafters. See!'

'You're sure?' Detective Lee took the picture from her and stared at it hard, turning it from side to side. Emma grabbed on to Ana's waist. A small group of students began to form around us – Jeez, gossip was about as magnetic as iron filings.

'This is interesting,' Detective Lee said, his upper lip did this cute curling thing when he was concentrating hard, 'but I'm not sure it's proof enough to launch a full-scale murder inquiry, Officer Stigner.' He lowered his voice so only she could hear. 'Wasn't there anything else? We can't leave any stone unturned. Especially not after the last time.'

'This should be enough, sir.' She wiped her cheek and handed a plastic bag to Detective Lee. It was full of small metal screws. 'We found these behind the stage.'

Detective Lee looked like he might barf.

'They're the ones that attach the lights to the rig and keep the whole thing together,' Stigner said. 'Someone must have taken them out before the show.'

'Someone who knew if an object as heavy as a flying rope hit it, the whole rig would come crashing down.' Detective Lee pulled out his cell. 'I'll let the Chief know. And don't let anybody out of this room without getting their name.'

Suddenly, I felt as if I might faint. The gym walls were melting; the bleachers dancing. Someone's arms were around me as the dizziness became overwhelming.

I tried to call out to Nancy, but before I could scream, the entire room spun to black. In darkness's whirl, the last thing I heard was Detective Lee's sad voice. 'I'm so sorry, Mrs Altman. Unfortunately it seems I've just got my first lead case.'

CHAPTER 7

'Original, Edison, super oh-wow original. Like you've never ported me around the city to some weird-ass location against my will before.'

After the black, had come the spinning, then the porting sickness. Eugh. Then I'd opened my eyes to find myself standing not in the gymnasium, but Central Park, the holiday ice-skating rink in front of me and Edison – surprise, surprise – right by my side.

'What's the point in dragging me up here, anyways?' It was early evening now and fairy lights danced on the snow-smattered maple trees. People were buttoned up like Eskimos in thick coats, scarves and gloves. It must be freezing. Not that I could feel it. The all too familiar loss pang kicked me hard. Who knew I'd ever miss runny noses, icy toes and fingers so frozen you could hardly fasten a button on a night this cold?

'In case you hadn't noticed, we're in the middle of a murder investigation. At a *majorly* crucial point. I don't have time to stand here and watch Living kids skating around in circles when I could be helping the new girl out,' I said.

Edison put his hands in his back pockets. 'Look, Ghostgirl, I knew if I asked you politely to spend some time with me, you'd have told me to stick it where the sun don't shine.' He rocked on his heels and looked at me from under his curtain of jet-black hair. 'Don't you think I'd rather get a girl to go on a date with me without having to resort to kidnapping?'

A date? This was his idea of a *date*?

'Come with.'

I was so freaking thrown I let Edison take my hand and lead me to a small flat of human-free grass under a canopy of white leaves. 'You don't have to stay if you don't want to, but just give me a chance first.' He stared at me with those intense green eyes of his. The ones that had got me in trouble before. 'Please.'

Edison moved to one side to show me why we were here, and I let out a little gasp. Somehow he had laid a red and white chequered blanket on the snow-covered grass. Four candles twinkled at the corners of the rug, dripping wax over the lips of green wine bottles. He'd even brought some of the never-wilting pink tulips from the Attesa's lobby and arranged them in an old milk jug.

It was about as out of character as Nancy suggesting we blow off the case and go possess some go-go dancers in a strip club downtown. If I hadn't been so pissed at him or was the kinda girl who was into mushy stuff, I might have thought it was romantic. Awesome as David had been before all the cheerleader-cheating and relationship-disrespecting, he'd not been the Hallmark type. But then Edison wasn't either.

Hmmm ... was it possible to possess the dead?

Because this was not the Edison I knew and definitely did not love.

'The last time I took you some place in the city – how did you put it?—' he was teasing me now '—"against your will", it involved dropping you on a busy subway track, and that went down about as well as mug of orange juice and milk. So I figured I should try a different tack.'

Recreating my death or romantic picnics on the lawn? Was there no middle ground with this guy? Couldn't he just take girls to the movies or out for ice cream like a normal person?

'How did you get all this stuff up here?' I crossed my arms, refusing to sit. I knew I was being snarky, but he totally deserved it. Edison was part of the reason I'd be stuck here forever and that made him a major level jerk. Even if this trick was way nicer than the 'let's put Charlotte in front of the very vehicle that caused her death to teach her to port quickly' one.

'Rule number three hundred and who cares: don't you remember?' he said in his best Nancy voice. Which was actually scary accurate. '"As the Attesa exists in – what we assume to be – a kind of limbo, you interact with everything in here as you did when you were Living." What they don't tell you is that you can bring things out of the hotel too. Like I did with Mercy's "Happy murder!" letter earlier today.'

Trust Edison to have tested how far you could bend a Rule. The very idea of borrowing things that didn't strictly belong to you would have freaked Nancy out about as much as the idea of flunking AP Trig back when she had a pulse.

79

'You never seemed to put two and two together on that one,' he said, 'so I thought it was time to show you – in case you ever wanted to, I don't know, take a good book and go sit down by the Hudson sometime. Helps pass the time.'

Which I had a heap of now there was no freaking chance of me getting off this island. Period.

Edison sat down on the blanket, stretching his long legs in front of him, his tight black T-shirt riding up a little as he leaned back on his hands. Edison Hayes was made for lurking in the back booth of bars not Martha Stewart-ing it up at picnics. He couldn't have looked more out of place at a kids' fifth birthday party in Dylan's Candy Bar. Unless he was in the clown suit.

'Come on, Charlotte, throw me a bone.' He patted the space on the blanket next to him. 'You've been ignoring me for weeks – we've hardly talked since that night. I had to do something. I'm trying my darnedest to make you see that I'm sorry. Would it kill you to take a load off for five minutes and listen to me? It's not like it can make you hate me more.'

I looked up at the skyscrapers towering above the trees, the only reminder that we were still in the city apart from the distant beeping of cab horns. I sat down, making sure there was a person's worth of space between us. A ginormous college quarterback's worth of space.

'So, do you want to start with the elephant in the room or should I make some small talk about how long this festive weather's going to last?' Edison asked, staring out at the rink.

The wind blew the trees above us, throwing a clump

of snow off the branches, down through the air and straight through my right foot. Tickle.

'Elephant,' I said, firmly. 'How about you tell me how we spent all that time alone together – you teaching me all those off-menu ghost skills to help me solve my murder – but didn't think to mention that as soon as I did, she was planning to steal my Key.'

'Hell, that was direct.' Edison tilted his head back and looked up at the sky. It was one of those clear, crisp New York nights where the stars twinkle like they are the set of a pathetic date movie. Bad stars. Didn't they know what I was going through down here?

'Okay, Ghostgirl, if it's the truth you want I'll give it to you, full barrel.'

I wished he wouldn't call me that. It made me feel like we had some special – euggghhh – I don't know, *connection*. Even though his actions had proved we had anything but.

'At first my intentions weren't as white as this snow,' he said. 'I was spending time with you because I was bored, Tess dared me to, and I knew it would piss off Miss Goody Two Shoes if her newest recruit suddenly zombied all over her ass mid-mission.'

I cringed. I'd asked for the zero BS version, but that was no fun to hear.

'You have to make your own amusement round here.' Edison smiled, trying to lighten the moment, but the grin didn't reach his eyes.

'Then . . .' He sat up, picking at the wax on one of the candles. 'Then something about you flicked a switch. I started to not *hate* spending time with you. I started to wish you'd ask me for another off-curriculum lesson. I started to tell you things about my life I'd never felt the need to share with Nancy or Lorna or any other whatever-the-hell-we-are before. And I started to hope you wouldn't find your Key, so we could hang out some more.'

It was one of those moment where, were I still alive, I'd have had to remind myself to breathe.

Ed's expression was serious now. More than I'd ever seen it before. My stomach did its wobble thing. Oh God.

Remember he's a bad man, Charlotte. Remember he's a very bad man.

'And honestly?' he said. 'Even if you hadn't got under my skin with your clumsiness and your come-backs and the cute way you bite your lip when you're scared—' Wait a minute, Edison thought I was *cute*? '—I didn't think in a billion years she'd do it. Tess was all bitter talk and plots and plans, but, deep down, I thought her core was good. There must have been something kind about her for—'

He stopped short and put down the candle. 'After all the years she spent here without any leads to her Key, she'd given up. She knew more than anyone how it felt to have no hope and no way out – it was eating her up inside. That's why I didn't think she'd go *that* far. If she did go Bling Ring on your Key, I was pretty sure that, as soon as she actually had the little sucker in her hand, she'd realize what she was condemning you to and stop.' He sighed heavily. 'But I was wrong.'

We stared at each other. I almost wished he was being all buck-passy and dishonest. At least then I could hate him like he deserved. But instead Edison Hayes was apologizing to me straight out – and that took some guts.

But I'd been here before. And all that had taught me was that trusting him wasn't safe.

A girl my age in a cute red coat and muffs slid onto the rink with all the skill of a baby lamb. She wobbled like a jelly on a plate, until an arty guy whooshed over and skidded to her side, ice flying off his blades. He held her strongly, and she leaned into him. That was the kind of date I should be on aged sixteen. I should be in the back row of the movie theatre, not another dimension. And not with some guy whose heart would never beat faster when he saw me.

'You should have warned me.' I filled the silence. 'If you trusted me enough to tell me about your dad dying, your mom struggling and your brother getting involved with the wrong crowd, why couldn't you tell me what she was thinking?'

'Because you finally seemed to be getting over that class A skater-boy jerk of a boyfriend of yours, and starting to like me back!' Ed knocked the candle clear over. He picked it up and took a second. 'Look, I knew if I told you about her plan, I'd have had to tell you why Tess – who wasn't exactly your favourite person in Limbo back then either – felt she could talk to me about something that dark. And why she expected me to help her out.'

I wasn't sure whether to be devastated or impressed. My mom had never covered this off in our cringe-fest 'girl chats'. Nothing he said changed what he'd done, so his candles and flowers and confessions routine wasn't about to impress this ghost.

'Now you can't go down any further in my estima-
tions, how about you answer that one for me.' Old
Charlotte had never been this hard on a guy in her life.
New Charlotte was majorly harsh. Losing your future
does that to a girl.

'Which one?' he asked.

Nice try, but New Charlotte wasn't biting. 'Do you
need me to communicate at kindergarten level? Why did
she feel she could talk to you – of all people? And why
did she expect you to help her out?'

Edison slapped his hands on his black jeans, wiping
some invisible snow off of them. Blade Boy was still
holding Red Coat Girl up. From the way you couldn't
have got a shard of light between them, I'd say they'd
make it to date two. Unlike us.

'We'd been here the longest – Tess and me,' Edison
said. 'You know this stuff. Before Lorna, Nancy, you –
and any of the others who've come along and gone. Me
and Tess were hardly beer-and-bowling buddies, but
when you've shared a hotel for that long, you get . . .
used to each other, I guess.'

'And did that *used*-ing ever boil over into making
out?' As soon as the words were out of my mouth, I
wished they'd turn to snow so I could make them melt
away.

'No, there was no "making out", okay?' He took the
packet of cigarettes from his back pocket and angrily
popped one out. I wondered if he'd been holding off
until then, trying to impress me without that crutch, but
now he was so mad he'd lost his will. 'Is that what you
need to hear before we can move on?'

'No, I need to hear something else: how did you know her when you were alive?'

Edison was still. 'I didn't.'

'I heard you two talking – that day in the Attesa lobby before she took my Key. She said, "All the people *we* knew – they're still Living. Our lives are frozen."'

'She didn't. She said "all the people I knew". You must have misheard.'

Misheard? Those words had been drumming around my brain since she'd spat them out. Over and over in the moments when I couldn't talk to Lorna or ported to the river to hide from Nancy, I obsessed about those lines and tried to get them to shake into sense. But they were Japanese subtitles in a karaoke bar only Edison could translate.

I tried again. 'She's not even here and you're siding with her? If you really do like me—' just saying those words out loud made my cheeks burn '—like you say you do, then how can you be keeping her secrets when she took everything from me? You know what she did was wrong. You just admitted that. I heard you tell her not to use my Key that day, heard you with my own ears. So why won't you tell me how you knew her instead of giving me this whole Tess Defender act?'

Edison stood up, his black clothes blending into the night sky. 'If my loyalty's misplaced, it's only because it's not placed with the person you think.'

What? Now he wasn't just being the biggest traitor in the tri-state area, he was talking in riddles too. What was so bad? They'd never dated – why wouldn't he tell me?

Edison blew out the candles and began to pack his

Romeo kit up. Looked like our date was as over as Kim and Kris. Bummer. 'It's complicated.' He pulled at the blanket below me waiting for me to get up. 'I promise you, I'm not protecting Tess. She doesn't deserve it. But her secrets aren't my secrets to tell. Can you at least try to understand that?' He looked away at the ice.

'No, Edison, I can't. Why that girl did is something I'll never understand. And—' I scrambled up off his precious rug and closed my eyes preparing to port home '—until you can make me understand, you're going to have to resort to a lot more than kidnap to get me on another date.'

I ported into the night. Leaving Edison with the burnt-down candles he deserved.

CHAPTER 8

'So why are we here again?' I asked.

'Because somedeadbody was stupid enough to ask Mercy where she'd most like to port to in the city,' Lorna said.

'Yeah, epic porting lesson fail, Nance. You totally need to stop that part of the new ghost induction. Never ends well.' I started to count on my fingers. 'There was that stoner boy who went AWOL in the Meadow in Central Park. Korin Johnson apirating in front of her mom before she'd even IDed the body. Me freaking out the ancient security guys up the Empire State . . .'

Nancy ignored us both and strode across the stage to Mercy. 'Why did you bring us here?' Her tiny arm looked lost as she waved it around the cavernous auditorium of the Broadway theatre. 'Is it something to do with a clue to who you think your murderer might be?'

Mercy was hardly listening. She was too intent on looking out into the black hole where an audience should sit. This place was the size of, like, five Bowery Ballrooms. Even though the lights were down and it was

4 a.m., I could make out Mercy taking an imaginary bow to her not-even-there fans.

'I always wanted to know what it looked like from this view.' She sighed. How could someone sound breathless when they had no breath? 'When you said "favourite place", this was what popped into my mind.'

A lone candle flickered towards the back of the stage, dancing in the low draught of the hall. I wondered if Edison had got the ones he'd borrowed from the Attesa back in one piece. Or if he'd moodily left them by a trash can in the park for a celestial janitor to clean up.

'That's not very smart!' Nancy pointed at the candle. 'It's a wonder the whole of Times Square hasn't gone up in flames if that's their idea of health and safety.' She walked towards the candle trying to figure if she had the necessary ghost skills to blow it out – and save the city.

'Leave it,' Mercy said. 'It's an old theatre tradition: actors always let one candle burn in an empty theatre at night. Depending on what story you believe, it's either meant to scare off spirits or give them some light so they can play.'

'Real ghosts need more than one candle,' Nancy said, clicking her fingers so the theatre lights flooded on, bathing the stage and auditorium seats. Still needed somebody to teach me that trick. I'd have to ask them when I wasn't, I dunno, being betrayed, patronized or kidnapped. 'Fancy.'

Nancy was right. Not that I'd ever written a paper on theatre history, but I could see that Mercy had ported us to one of the oldest, grandest ones in New York. Burnished gold pillars embellished with delicate green flowers trailed from the stage to the back of the room. The boxed seats to either side sat suspended like enchanted bumper cars. There was enough red velvet in the place to cover the entire Attesa, not just the lobby. Staring out into the three lavish tiers where the audience sat, with all the lights and staging on display, you felt like you were in the heart of a machine.

'Nancy, I'm not sure that's such a good idea,' Lorna said, shielding her eyes from the lights. 'What if there's, like, a janitor here or we're on CCTV?'

'Then all they'll see is an empty stage with the lights mysteriously flicked on. They'll just think it's a technical hitch.'

'Or a ghost,' Mercy said. 'Did you know most Broadway theatres have one?'

'Why's that impressive? This one's got four right now,' I said. Mercy and her thespy facts were starting to bug me like a stone in my shoe.

Nancy broke the tension and took control. 'You ported here without any help from us.' She beamed at Mercy encouragingly. 'Really good job, by the way. I've not seen someone pick up porting that quickly since Charlotte arrived.' If Nancy could give out little gold stars for ghosting, she so would. 'So let's keep things moving.'

'Where's the Living investigation at?' I hadn't had chance to catch up with the others since my earlier ghostnapping, which was quickly followed by newbie lesson one: how to port.

'Detective Lee is doing such a good job.' Nancy wound a lock of auburn hair around her forefinger. 'He's got the entire situation under tight control. Did you see how quickly he shut down that room and started getting students' statements? It was so *masterful*. He—'

Lorna cut in. 'They're still at the "Isn't that Stigner cop girl awesome for finding the screws and rope?" phase,' she told me. 'Honestly, I've seen trends move faster in Fashion Week.'

Better get this show on the road then, before Mercy tried to form the Dead Girls Drama Club. Whatever was through the Big Red Door – good, bad or hellfire – it couldn't suck as much as an eternity spent running lines and making Mercy props.

'I still can't believe that somebody would make all that effort to murder me,' she said. 'It's kind of like the ultimate fan letter when you think about it. To risk your freedom – if you get caught – just because you feel so strongly about me.' Behind Mercy's back Lorna could not stop staring at the way her blue sports jersey had been paired with those leather-look leggings.

'I bet my murderer has seen all my plays,' Mercy said. 'Oh, maybe they have the programmes at their house in a freakoid Mercy Grant shrine! We've got to find that! What if I'd signed one for them? Ohmigod, it would have been like I was signing my death warrant at the same time!'

'Did you have any mega fans, Mercy?' Lorna asked innocently.

Because if so, we could have this wrapped by 5 a.m. A Dead Girls' PB.

'Not fans as such,' she said, rearranging her beanie hat. 'But my spread in the yearbook was going to look amazing. With all my fund-raising and focus-grouping, I'd single-handedly turned that drama department around. There was no way the Julliard admissions people could ever turn me down.' She stared at me with woeful eyes. 'That course is going to be lot less emotionally rich without me next year.'

I tried real hard not to flip into Tess mean girl mode. Mercy couldn't be all bad if she had two pages in the yearbook, right?

'Were you popular?' I braced myself for the answer.

'Amongst the kids that mattered – Payton and Ryder from PPDC. Lilian and Kate from my English Lit class. Jen was the only Peabody girl who attended my after-school improv group. That is – *was* – enough.' She stopped short. 'My mom always said, if a girl didn't like me she was clearly an idiot, and she didn't want her daughter hanging out with idiots.'

Good philosophy, bad mantra to admit out loud.

'And what about Anastasia De Witt?' Nancy asked. 'There seemed to be some, erm, tension there.'

'As if!' Mercy shook her head in indignation. Her black bob bounced right back into place. 'Anastasia might be clever, but she isn't half as much of a piece of work as she'd like the world to think she is.'

Mercy strode across the stage. Uh oh. Here came the soliloquy.

'Look, even the most beta girls become competitive the second they put on a Palmer Peabody shirt. It goes with the territory, and the blazer.' She looked to Lorna. 'You went there – you'll back me up on this? After all, there aren't many all-girls schools with a reputation for excellence like ours.'

'Or a body count,' I said.

'Hey, only me and Mercy died,' Lorna said. 'You make it sound like my parents paid to put me through the Hunger Games.'

'Ana is your typical type-A overachiever,' Mercy continued. 'She's been racking up activities to boost her Harvard application since she was put in charge of tidying the soft toy corner in kindergarten. I one hundred per cent know her type. I bet you all do. But Ana was nothing I couldn't handle. Even she's not egotistical enough to believe that murder wouldn't hurt her grade point average. That and getting into a good school are all she cares about, not me. You can totally wipe her off the list.'

'And Emma?' I asked. It would be good to wipe her off pronto too. So we could keep moving – and Lorna could keep her sanity.

Mercy smiled slowly. 'Despite the company she keeps, we were good friends.'

Nancy's shoulders slumped. It was super-rare to get a lead on a killer just from quizzing the victim, but that didn't mean she didn't always hope she'd hit a home run.

'Hey, we've got a Chrysler-sized jump on the Living detectives,' I told Nancy. 'We can do this. Plus, we've got something they don't have – Mercy.' Our biggest key to her Key had wandered back to her rightful place – centre stage – and was silently mouthing lines to an empty theatre. Bets on it being that speech the lighting rig had put an end to. 'We just need to tease the truth out of her. Somewhere inside Mercy's brain something useful must be hiding.' Ouch, I really, really did not mean that to sound so harsh. 'Sure, she's a little intense . . .'

'"But, look, the morn, in russet mantle clad, Walks o'er the dew of yon high eastward hill . . ."' Mercy clapped and sprinted back towards us. 'I've got it! If you guys can't get me out of here, I can haunt the Palmer Peabody stage forever and ever! It can't be so bad staying wher-ever-this-is. It's not like you ghosts seem to be in any hurry to move along.'

'A theatre's not a theatre until they've got a ghost. I could haunt some girls in the day, Phantom of the Opera-style. Then—' her feline eyes widened '—I could watch plays every night for the rest of my death from the best seat in the house. Maybe two if I caught the matinee!'

Nancy crouched down on the floor and pulled her lit-tle spiral notebook out of her pocket. This was not going to plan. 'Okay, let's focus: what do we know for sure?' she asked.

Me and Lorna squatted next to her. Even though we were totally lead-less, Nancy's eyes sparkled like a kid deciding what birthday present to open first. This was soo her favourite part. It was cute when she got all detecty.

'Firstly, whoever tampered with the screws and the rope had to have been able to get backstage,' she said.

'And without people thinking it was strange they were there either. Palmer Peabody's the kind of school where everyone notices if you so much as change the way you braid your hair,' Lorna said. 'If a stranger had been hanging around being all menacing someone would have reported it.'

93

'Good insider intel, Lorna.' Nancy scribbled in her pad as fast as her fingers would go. 'You are going to be such an asset on this case.'

As long as we could keep a one-mile exclusion zone between Lorna, her parents and anyone else it would kill her again to see, I thought sadly.

'The fact whoever did this just slipped away afterwards without anyone thinking they were evil murdering scum totally backs that up,' I said.

'Also, the person would have had to have been in the theatre to cut the rope just before Mercy . . .' Lorna stalled.

'*Died*. You can say it. Death holds no fear for me now,' Mercy said.

'Unless "they" was actually two people.' Nancy's eyebrows shot up above her black frames. 'One could have tampered with the screws earlier on, while the other cut the rope!'

'So anyone in the theatre – audience, onstage or off – is a suspect right now?' I asked. 'And we don't know if we're looking for one baddie or two?' That pretty much seemed to sum it up.

'Sounds like I'll get time to finally catch *Death of a Salesman* and *Newsies* then,' Mercy deadpanned. 'Maybe *Jersey Boys* too.'

Nancy finally scowled at her. Just a teensy bit. 'Every investigation has to start somewhere, Mercy.'

'Hey, I get that.' Mercy doffed her beanie hat. It was the least hipster move ever. 'Thanks for helping me out. You've probably got better things to be doing.'

'No, really we don't,' Nancy admitted.

'Great! Then let's get out there and catch my murderer so I can haunt some shows before I head through the Red Door! Oh! What if I actually appirated onstage during *Phantom of the Opera*? Or . . .'

Urgh. This was going to be a *long* case.

CHAPTER 9

Lorna clicked her fingers, and the lights went down with a dull boom that echoed around the room. *Pop!* My friends disappeared.

Standing alone on the stage, I suddenly felt exposed. A hundred eerie eyes could be looking at me right now and I'd have no clue – from the boxes, the director's spot, the orchestra pit, or even hiding in the shadows of the upper tiers. Palmer Peabody's theatre had all these nooks and hideouts too, just on a way less diva scale. Mercy's murderer could have been watching in any of them: waiting until it was the right time to strike. You could see it as stupid that they'd chosen to kill a girl in front of an audience. Or AP-level smart – after all, everyone would be looking at her and no one at you. I shivered. Time to – as my dad used to joke – make like a tree and leave.

I bounced off the stage, making my way to the back of the theatre. As I walked, the shadows changed shape, morphing and sliding every few steps so I couldn't remember if they'd been there a second before or jumped out on me like a cat. In the dark, I couldn't shake the feeling that someone, some*thing*, was watching my every step. Which was totally stupid. I was invisible. And I was a ghost for God's sake. I was the evil in movies so scary they made you throw your popcorn in the air. I was the thought that kept you awake at night when you heard a step on the stairs or a creak in the loft. I shouldn't be scared. It was the Living who were terrified of me.

As I neared the enormous carved oak doors, a gut instinct shot through me and I began to run. Hard. I didn't waste any energy avoiding the ticket stand or the stools in the bar where interval drinks were served. I ploughed through them all, demolition-style – like hurdles at a track event I didn't need to jump. I sprinted through the gloom of the hall, the lobby and out, only stopping when I landed on the sidewalk outside. Instead of being out of breath, my body buzzed from all the objects I'd jumped through. It was like the ghost equivalent of getting a stitch.

The lights on Broadway had been dimmed, the snow freezing to ice on the ground. Instinctively, I pulled my school blazer tighter around my shoulders and began to walk.

At 5 a.m. midtown was as close to a ghost town as it ever got. Above me, the skyscrapers of Times Square were the only ones who hadn't got the memo that they could calm down their act – the only people out were those who couldn't face being at home.

I'd never spent much time in this part of Manhattan when I was alive – hello, tourist trap hell – but since the Tess Incident, I'd found myself porting back more and more. Late at night when the Living were asleep and only people with demons had their eyes open. The regularity of the gaudy fluorescent flashing lights was almost comforting. I had no memories here – unless you counted going to M&M's World for Ali's fifth birthday and eating so many bags of the peanut butter kind, that I was sick on the sidewalk outside – so the ouches were less acute. Two months ago, I'd have said hell was hustly, bustly Times Square. But – as I knew way too well – times change.

A truck pulled up beside me; a few street cleaners got out and began brushing snow from the steps of shops and fast food joints. Steam rose up from the subway grates, as if stretching awake.

I headed down 42nd Street, deliberately kicking through sludge or jumping through ice – tickle. I walked on past the green lampposts of Bryant Park which looked like they'd been Tardised here from one of the prints of Paris Mom hung in our hall, then right down 5th to the New York Library. Someone had made a snowman's head and put it over the face of the giant stone lion on the library steps. A carrot nose was in danger of falling off so I used my kinetic energy to Jab it back on.

The sun was beginning to tease the city now. To mix things up, I half-walked, half-ported the remainder of the way, imagining myself by a particular shop window or green newspaper box, then porting there. I discovered the sickness didn't lessen any even on super-short trips. Instead it was more like a shock of panic, like the moment you're trying on a dress in Urban Outfitters and, as you go to take it off, you realize you're stuck, arms above your head, and wonder if you'll be in that changing room forever. Or worse, have to go out in your panties and ask the too-cool assistant girl for help.

Eventually the neighbourhoods became more leafy and the buildings shorter, until I finally found myself under the arch of Washington Square. Home.

I remembered standing here, on the first night of my death being so scared and confused and not knowing what my future could ever hold now my life had been taken away. Nancy and Lorna were so kind – I'd hardly had time to really think about what it all meant, until I had my Key. And then I didn't.

I walked backwards under the arch, watching the sun reflecting off the Empire State as it rose in the sky. If I let myself, I could see it was beautiful. Being here in the snow and the sun, in my favourite place on Earth. But – what was that saying my gran used to use? – familiarity breeds contempt. How many times would I see those rays before I was as bored of them as I was of my school uniform? Something told me Tess hadn't exactly been a joy in life, but in death she was every bit of the piece of work Mercy said Anastasia was not. Was this how she got so bitter?

I padded down the steps to HHQ, where Nancy was organizing her squad. She'd pulled her chalk-board away from the wall and wiped clean the names of the last set of murder suspects ready for Mercy's to take their place. I wondered how many times she'd done that and if – just once – even Nancy wished her name was scrawled at the top in neat, tight letters

– that it was her murder someone was kindly helping her solve.

'The Living will be awake in—' she checked the clock on the wall '—about a half-hour. The Peabody girls that is. School starts at 9 a.m. right?' she asked Lorna, who nodded, before shooting me a *hello* of a smile. 'Though Detective Lee's probably been awake for hours, writing theories and coming up with leads. He seems like a guy who is very thorough.'

Lorna crossed her eyes at me. I tried not to giggle out loud.

Nancy clapped her hands. She totally thought she could control us like the dogs in the Washington Square run. 'It's a day until winter recess starts, so this is the last one the students will be in class. We need to hit the ground running.'

Whatever *that* meant.

'Charlotte: we'll head to the cops' HQ and shadow the detectives to check they didn't get any leads over night. Lorna: you take Mercy back to Palmer Peabody and recreate her last day from start to . . . *y'know*. It might jog her memory about any weird behaviour or strange people loitering.' Another clap. 'Excellent! So everyone knows what they're doing?'

'Apart from me.' The totally unexpected sound of Edison's voice made all four of us jump.

Lorna coughed.

'That's because you never take part in any of our investigations, Edison.' Nancy so had the you're-cruising-for-a-D-minus homeroom teacher tone down pat. 'I assumed you wouldn't be interested in helping

100

out with this one either. So far all you've done is play messenger boy and take one of my team on a magical mystery tour I'm sure she'd rather forget.'

Jeez, how did she know *everything*? It was bizarre. Maybe mind-reading was in a chapter of the Rules I'd not been bored enough to read yet.

Edison gave her a tight smile. 'I think we all know I've not been the Agency's most *active* member in the past, but right now I've got a lot of bridges to mend.' He looked right at me. I wished he wouldn't. 'I'm more than aware that's not going to happen overnight. I get that you don't trust me one hundred per cent and probably want me around as much as a skunk with a temper, but if you'll just let me, I'd really like to try to make amends. Starting with Mercy's case.'

I stared back at him, trying to figure out what he was thinking behind those green eyes but, as always, I came up short.

'I thought the Agency was for dead *girls*?' Mercy drank Edison in from his vintage Adidas to his skinny jeans and tight T-shirt. His look was as all black as hers was all blue.

'Oh, we're very democratic around here,' Nancy said. 'We let in the occasional man too, but only when they prove their worth. This is Edison, by the way. I'm not sure you've been formally introduced.'

'The more the merrier, isn't that what people say?' Mercy trilled. Man, for someone who claimed she could take an audience on an 'emotional journey', Mercy was crazy-bad at picking up on the mood in a room.

'Okay, Edison, if that's what you want,' Nancy

relented. 'Seeing as you've proved yourself to be such a good teacher in the past, why don't you tag along with Lorna and Mercy – that way you can work on her porting skills on the way up to the school.'

'Which chapter covers that again?' Mercy pulled her Rules book out of her blue sports jersey. A black feather flew out too and gently floated to the floor. It looked almost as if it had an eye in the middle – one with a red iris and blue and purple pupil. Mercy's mouth formed an O.

'What's that?' Lorna asked. 'It's a peacock feather, right? Dolce and Gabbana did an awesome skirt made of them a few seasons back.'

Mercy bent down to pick the feather up. 'It was a prop for a later scene in the play. I was meant to wear it on my head in hipster way or something.'

'Cool!' Lorna said. 'Seeing you in that outfit, I have such warring reactions. Like, it makes me sympathetic you have to spend forever in something so on-trend, but I'm also super-sad I never got to fully explore how I felt about sports-luxe, especially those leggings. I think I could have pulled them off.'

'So!' Nancy tried to bring Lorna back on-message. 'Shall we go?'

She ported out of the room. I focused, closing my eyes to do the same.

'I'm doing this for you, you know that right?' Edison whispered in my ear, so low only I could hear. 'And I'll do it again and again until you believe how sorry I am.'

I screwed my eyes shut even tighter, ignored the buzz humming through the Edison-side of my body, and ported on Nancy's tail.

CHAPTER 10

'I'm not saying a word until Daddy's lawyer gets here.' Payton Cassidy picked an invisible speak of dust off her scrambled egg-coloured Ralph Lauren sleeveless dress and wiggled in her chair. 'I don't see why you called us in and none of the other girls. Can't you see we're not the felon types?'

Dylan sneezed loudly, looking around in vain for a tissue before wiping his nose on his sweater. He was wearing a button that read, 'What would Zuckerberg do?'

Not wear a dirty jumper with Wolverine on the front perhaps?

'Well, *I'm* not a felon anyway.' Payton gave Dylan and his comic book taste in clothes major evils. She shivered. She must be glacial in that flimsy dress. I guess when you're used to being transported from classroom to car, you don't have to think about basic logistics. Like not freezing to death.

'My parents have a summer compound in Connecticut,' she said. 'Did you ever hear of anyone whose parents had a summer compound in Connecticut being stupid enough to murder another girl? Especially this close to college interviews.'

Detective Lee leaned back in his chair and put his hands behind his head. Sergeant Stigner had the face of a woman being forced to watch a particularly disturbing documentary on the Discovery Channel.

'I'm not sure the 19th Precinct has seen anything like this before,' I whispered to Nancy, taking in the scene before us.

Payton, Dylan, Ana, Emma and Marlowe Anderson were sitting in an uncomfortable semicircle in front of Detective Lee's large oak desk. Dylan's scruffy demeanour wasn't entirely out of place – if that boy hadn't been arrested for smoking pot up in the park yet, he would be soon. But the girls looked more like they were attending a meeting of the Junior Board at the Guggenheim than helping the police with their inquiries. There was way too much Barneys-bought loot going on for something as blah as a trip down to East 67th Street. Especially a trip that involved an NYPD station with coffee machines that only served instant and walls the colour of chewed gum.

'You're being questioned, but no one's in trouble here.' Detective Lee leaned forward and folded his hands. 'The reason we've called you guys in is because you were all offstage when the murder happened. I want to get your alibis straight so we can move on with this case. But, hey, if you want to bring along your folks' lawyers that is absolutely your right. It just might mean you're stuck here a little longer. And I thought you were kind of desperate to get to school, so recess can begin?' An officer in a navy uniform brought five polystyrene cups of a greying liquid into the room and carefully put one in front of each kid. Marlowe picked hers up gingerly, before placing it back down like it stung. A poster on the wall showed the old-fashioned green gas lamps in the front of the station. '19th Precinct: in an Upper East Side state of mind,' it read. The look Marlowe gave it suggested this was anything but.

'I don't need a lawyer,' Anastasia said. Unlike Payton, she was wearing her Palmer Peabody uniform, a crisp white shirt tucked into her green and navy plaid kilt. Two bottle-coloured barrettes held back her sunset waves. Even in the slammer, she looked like something from a school prospectus. 'I have nothing to hide. I doubt any of us do, so shall we get on with this so we can get back to school? After everything that happened yesterday, I think Principal Gates would rather we were with our classmates.' She shot Sergeant Stigner a sad smile and squeezed Emma's Wolford tights-covered leg.

'Okay, let's start with you—' Detective Lee ran his finger down the case notes on his desk '—Dylan.' He smiled. 'Gentleman first for a change, hey?'

Dylan shuffled in his chair. Man, that boy needed to brush his hair. It was stuck up in hedgehoggy clumps.

'I was with the props when the . . . the . . .' His hazel eyes filled with tears and his voice wobbled.

'Oh no! Is he going to cry?' Nancy asked. 'Please don't let him cry. These girls will never let him forget it.'

'The props – it was my job to be in charge of the set and the props.' Dylan tried to get a hold of himself as he picked at his dirty sweater sleeve. 'I only left the stage for a few seconds.' He turned to Detective Lee. 'You don't think it's my fault the rigging came down, do you? I tightened those screws so hard. Are you sure it wasn't down to me?'

Detective Lee's expression softened. 'Dylan, I'm sure your DIY skills were diploma-worthy. What happened to Mercy was hideous, but it wasn't an accident. Or your fault. Just for our notes: what prop were you getting?'

Dylan scratched his nest of charcoal hair. 'I was checking everything was ready for the play-within-the-play scene, sir. It's this act where Hamlet gets some players to, um, re-enact the way his dad died. Technically, it's beyond complicated, because you have to move, like, another stage onto the actual stage. That Shakespeare dude liked to mix things up.'

'I can vouch for the fact Dylan was doing just that,' Ana said. Dylan gave a jolt, shocked one of the Peabody girls was actually acknowledging his existence. 'I was with him. Well, I walked off the real stage and tripped over his stupid fake one. I wasn't expecting it to be there. But that's where I and—' she gave Dylan a withering look '—*he* were. Next?'

'Marlowe?' Sergeant Stigner asked a small girl with the thickest brown bangs, which hid half her face.

She crossed her legs, accidentally kicking her cotton navy Amoeba Record bag across the floor. An apple rolled out and clear through my foot. 'I went to the side of the stage to wave at my mom.' She made a face. 'I know how tragic that is, but if you ask her, she'll back me up that I did it.'

'Interesting,' Nancy said. 'What mother wouldn't back up their child? Her alibi's got as many holes in it as a soccer net. We should definitely investigate her further.' She made a note in her spiral pad.

'You can ask Mrs Cassidy, Payton's nanny, my sister, my cousin and Mr and Mrs Grant too if you don't believe me because they all saw me too.' Marlowe turned beet red. 'If the whole Mercy thing hadn't distracted everyone, I'm pretty sure I would have got a major ribbing right now for acting like such a second grader. Like, who waves to their mom from the wings when they've moved out of training bras?'

'Oh.' Nancy let her pad drop to her side.

'So, that's everybody but Payton and Emma covered then,' Detective Lee summed up. 'And you guys were?'

'In the restroom,' they said in unison, then turned to look at each other in confusion.

'Which restroom?' Detective Lee asked.

'The one backstage,' Emma said.

'Same here,' Payton said.

Detective Lee turned to Stigner. 'How many restrooms are there backstage?' he asked.

She consulted her notes. 'Just the one that I could see,' she said.

Detective Lee turned back to the girls. Dylan picked up one of the white polystyrene cups and took a big gulp of the gross drink.

'I was in there,' Payton said.

'No, I was in there.' Emma's denim eyes flashed. 'The second we were sent backstage after Mercy died, I said I was in the restroom, didn't I, Ana? I told you how

I'd gone in there because I was nervous, then the lock jammed and I heard the crash and the screams. That's when I got the lock to move – I guess because I was so super-scared of what was going on outside. I even broke two nails. I came out and the kids were running and Mercy was dead.'

Payton's forehead knotted into two deep lines. 'I didn't hear the crash. I heard it when I got out.'

'So you weren't in the restroom at the same time at all then were you?' Anastasia sighed. 'Payton must have been in first, then she left, but didn't see Emma in the dark. Emma got trapped, then as Payton was making her way back to the stage, someone had already cut that rope and Mercy died.' She ran a manicured finger down the green piping of her blazer and smiled as winningly as she could, considering the subject matter.

'You know I almost wish *she'd* died,' I said. 'Ana could have wrapped her own case up in two seconds flat.'

Nancy scowled at me.

Jefferson scratched his one-day stubble gently. 'Just one last question, while I've got you here, if you don't mind?'

Only Dylan nodded his head.

'You've all been at school with Mercy since – what? – kindergarten? You were at the same one as these girls, right, Dylan?' Detective Lee picked up a cup and swilled the liquid around. 'At least that's what our notes say – correct us if we're wrong.'

This time they all had the decency to bob their heads.

'Can you ever remember anyone taking a dislike to Mercy? Did she make any enemies that you can think of?

It doesn't matter how small or how stupid – any memory you've got which could in some way help us, I'd like to hear it.'

Ana crossed her arms in a very student body president way. 'Detective Lee, if you're seriously going to ask us to draw up a list of everyone Mercy Grant has offended over our short lives, Payton will have roots by the time we get out of here.'

Payton pouted. She looked like a girl who set a BlackBerry reminder for her six-weekly touch-up at Elizabeth Arden's Red Door.

'Much as it pains me to be the one to tell you this, that girl upset a lot of people. Even the teachers.' Ana arched one neat fiery brow. 'For example, have you asked Miss Ballard about the YouTube incident? Now that's a doozy.' Nancy and Sergeant Stigner made identical notes in their spiral books. Boy, death would be so much easier is we could just appirate in front of the damn detectives without scaring them out of their uniforms and work together on this.

Dylan whistled quietly.

Ana pushed back her chair and checked her gold Michael Kors watch. 'Now, if you don't mind, Detective Lee, I have an important job to do. As Student Body President, I have to address three hundred scared and vulnerable young women about what happened yesterday.' She bent down to pick up her aubergine Prada doctor's bag. 'That's if we're finished here?'

Detective Lee stared at her carefully, but nodded.

'Emma, come on, I'll need your support.' Ana pulled Lorna's sister out of her seat and through the door. 'I

109

borrowed Mom's town car – it's waiting outside.' Payton and Marlowe hurried after them. There was definitely no walking ten blocks in that dress.

Dylan stayed in his chair, looking like a little kid whose birthday balloon had just popped.

'You can leave now too, Dylan,' Detective Lee said kindly. 'Unless there's anything else you want to tell us?'

Dylan clumsily stood up, almost knocking over his own chair. 'No, sir, I mean, Detective sir, I mean . . .' He backed away and clattered down the hall. Poor kid. He needed to join a band or start hanging out in Williamsburg and working on his poetry. The girls in this zip code were never going to appreciate Dylan's particular blend of awkward, earnest and unwashed.

'Well, that was illuminating,' said Detective Lee. 'Not.'

'They're just kids, Detective,' Stigner said. 'They could be trying to cover anything up, like smoking backstage or messing about in the wings. I don't trust everything they just said, but that doesn't make them murderers.'

Detective Lee put his head in his large hands and massaged his temples.

Nancy walked around the chairs, as if looking for a clue. 'She didn't question them enough.' She motioned at Stigner. 'If she's going to become a good officer, she needs to play bad cop a bit more to Detective Lee's good one.'

Hmm . . . and something told me Nancy would *love* that job.

'Hey, don't be hard on her,' I said. 'The Upper East Side is one of the most populated places on the planet, but it's hardly an epicentre of crime, is it? It's all dignitaries, diplomats and trust-fund babies as far as the eye can see. I bet the worst crime Stigner's had to deal with lately was someone spilling their non-fat soya latte on the steps of the Met.'

Pop! Lorna ported into the room.

'So I've done my last day on earth orientation thing with Mercy and now people are gathering in the Great Hall for some kinda speech from Ana. Everyone's there. It might be a chance to, like, detect the murderer out,' Lorna told Nancy.

Nancy nodded enthusiastically, closed her eyes and was gone.

'Who were they questioning in here?' Lorna eyed the five chairs.

'It was just a morning briefing with the murder squad,' I lied. I'd bet my dad's baseball card collection that there was the distinct stench of arrogance and Miss Dior in the air. Good thing ghosts could no longer smell or Lorna would spot my fib faster than a Canal Street designer knock-off. 'Let's go.'

'Actually, I'm going to head back to the hotel,' Lorna said, shyly. 'The, um . . . They're holding the address in the Great Hall and I'm not sure it's a super-awesome idea that I set foot in that place twice in two days.' She nibbled her bottom lip.

'I think that's very sensible of you indeed,' I said. Like Nancy said, it was probably better to try to keep Lorna as far away from her past as we could until we knew what direction things were going with the case.

Uptown, the Great Hall was more rammed than a trash

metal mosh pit. Except no girl in the sea of green and blue was fighting to get close to the front. If anything they were pushing to move away from it.

'It's cosy in here.' I found Nancy right by a small group of teachers by the stage. 'They should have held this in the theatre where everyone can fit in.'

'Except it might be a little grim to have Anastasia giving a eulogy about Mercy on a stage where there's still a little bit of Mercy,' Nancy said.

'Ewww. True.'

The chatter dimmed as Ana walked up the steps of the podium. She tapped the mic to check it was on and fixed the crowd with her saddest stare.

'As Palmer Peabody School for Girls Student Body President, I've been asked to represent you all many times.' Her voice was clear and strong. Debating Soc was so a star feature on her résumé. 'But never, when I accepted this honour with an unprecedented ninety-eight per cent of your vote, did I imagine I would have to make a speech like the one I am about to give.'

For a brief moment, Ana looked down at her hands, her thumbs slowly circling each other, as she gave the girls time to reflect.

'Mercy Grant made a colossal contribution to this school.' Ana smiled sadly at the Peabody girls, careful not to miss the teachers out. 'Without her, the drama department would have been a very different place.'

'Yeah, one which some of us stood a chance of being allowed into,' a small, slim brunette to my right muttered under her breath. Her tall pimply friend sniggered.

'Who can forget Mercy's poetry recital-a-thon to raise

funds for the new lead's dressing room? Or her one-woman production of *Seven Brides for Seven Brothers*, which she adapted, directed and starred in alone? Who knows what she would have delighted us with next. Sadly, Mercy takes those ideas with her to the grave.'

I noticed Miss Ballard standing by an older, grey-haired woman who must have been Principal Gates. She was concentrating hard on a spot on the floor, trying not to cry again. Funny, her sob-holding-in face was kinda similar to a smirk.

'Our lives would have been richer had we all had the opportunity to marvel at the wonder of Mercy's unique interpretation of Hamlet. But sadly it's a performance that most of you will never see.' And put a hand to her chest. 'I am just so honoured that I was able to rehearse with her these past few weeks and have a glimpse of how ... *memorable* she would have been,' she told her enraptured audience.

'Y'know, I think it's a good thing Emma has Anastasia De Witt as a best friend,' Nancy said. 'Is it just me, or is that one cyclone you do not want to be on the wrong side of?'

'Mercy's parents haven't yet arranged a funeral. Instead they have told me personally this morning that they'll be following Mercy's wishes and scattering her ashes on Broadway as she always dreamed,' Ana said.

'Because that's classier than a service at St Patrick's Cathedral,' the brunette's friend said.

'What sixteen-year-old thinks about where they want their ashes scattered?' I asked Nancy.

'One who puts on a one-woman show of a play that's meant to have fourteen leads?' Nancy said.

'So if you all keep an eye on the Palmer Peabody Facebook page over the holidays, as soon as there are more details, you'll find them there.' Ana tossed her fiery waves over her left shoulder and paused until she was sure everyone was listening. 'It's Christmas – the season of goodwill. Maybe if there is any lesson we can take from this tragedy, it's that life is short. You have to live every moment as if it's your last, and be thankful for your loved ones always. I know I'll certainly be thinking of that on Christmas Day when I'm on the beach in St Barts and appreciating my family more than ever this year. Thank you and have a good break.'

Ana marched off the podium, the crowd of classmates parting to let her through. She met Emma by the door and they made their way outside.

'Wow, Miss Ballard really is a sucky teacher,' I said, watching Ana's back disappear through the door. 'If that performance was anything to go by, Ana's got more acting talent in her left eyebrow than Mercy had in her entire Mercy.'

'That was hardly a room full of grief and woe.' Nancy frowned, as we made our way outside. 'Yet Mercy says, while she wasn't Miss Popularity, she didn't have any real enemies she can think of. Someone's lying and we're not going to be able to move this investigation forward until we know who it is. We need to find out what Mercy was *really* like before.'

'But how? If she's not been honest with us so far, I don't know what will make her change,' I said.

'Hey Lilian! Kate! We still on for tonight?' Payton shouted across the quad as she ran to catch up with two other girls who were heading our way. She'd still not changed into her uniform. Maybe she was going to use grief as an excuse for wearing designer labels to school.

'That was *not* the epitaph Mercy deserved,' she said. 'If she knew it had been given by Anastasia De Witt—' Payton said her name as if it were a particularly vicious tropical disease '—Mercy would be haunting us right now and giving us hell.'

Be careful what you wish for.

'That's why tonight's so important,' the Lilian girl said. 'It's what Mercy would have wanted.'

'Sure,' Kate added. 'It's just so sad that our start of recess drinks have to be rebranded as Mercy's unofficial wake. I still can't believe the way things have worked out.'

Nancy excitedly elbowed me in the ribs. She was scary strong for someone so small too. Oww.

'Bar above Joe Allen's at eight? I've booked a booth. Ryder and Jen are coming too.' The girls walked away across the quad.

'This is amazing!' Nancy bounced. 'All we need to do is head to this Joe bar place, listen in and we'll get a real insider insight into Mercy. If her friends don't tell the truth about her, no one will.'

I thought back to the white lie I'd told Lorna earlier to stop her worrying some more.

'Because your friends are always honest when you need them to be, right?' I said.

115

CHAPTER 11

'Even if you add up my dead *and* alive years, I'm still not twenty-one.' Nancy frowned. 'Do you think that's a problem?'

We were standing outside Joe Allen's on West 46th. It was only 5 p.m., but winter-night dark. Little fairy lights twinkled in shop windows and you could hear the excited shouts and screams of tourists exploring Times Square. Even for a spook, the orange glow coming from the restaurant looked inviting. Snow clustered on the green canopy above the restaurant door.

'I think you'll be fine,' I said. 'Who's going to ID a teenage girl they can't see? Besides, even if some ghost cop catches you, what they gonna do? Arrest a spirit for drinking spirits?'

Nancy blew out her cheeks. 'Seriously, Charlotte? Like Edison's never made *that* joke before.'

And here I was thinking I was hilarious. I wasn't even as original as him. This day was going from bad to tragic.

'Where is this place anyway?' Nancy asked. 'Payton and Kate said "the bar above Joe Allen's", but all I can see above the restaurant are apartments. It doesn't look very under-age-drinky. There can't be a cocktail joint in there.'

'Sure there can,' I said. 'New Yorkers *love* a speakeasy.'

'A speakwhatsy?' Nancy asked.

'Speakeasy. Fake prohibition bar – goes back to the NYC of the twenties when alcohol was banned. Bars serving hard liquor had to be hidden or pretend they were something else so the cops didn't raid them.' Nancy looked at me open-mouthed. I put a hand on my hip. 'Do not tell me this is the one history lesson I listened to that you skipped?'

'Bartender Studies wasn't on the syllabus at my school,' she put her head clean through the restaurant's large black door. 'No sign of the Peabody girls in there. They must be somewhere else.'

A particularly fat Santa swayed down the street, bashing into the restaurant door, before opening it and heading inside. He was definitely of legal age, but someone should have told him to have a bit less Christmas spirit.

Santa clumsily slammed the door, causing a clump of snow to fall from the canopy onto the street. I looked up at the heavy unmarked oak door in the Victorian brownstone above us. There was no sign, but I'd read *New York Magazine* enough when I was alive to know that was the point . . . And if a bar was hard to find, majorly exclusive and tough to get into, you could bet their last dollop of Crème de la Mer, that it was the kinda place the Peabody girls would want to hang out.

Nancy followed my gaze. 'That sure doesn't look like a bar,' she said.

I stopped myself making a smart remark about how Little Miss in Bed By Ten wouldn't know a bar if it jumped up and did a shot of tequila with her.

'Let's try it anyway.' I gingerly climbed the icy stone steps – no, still not used to the fact I couldn't slip on them any more – and walked through the thick door to the room inside. Tickle.

'Woah,' Nancy said behind me, as our eyes adjusted to the light. 'I thought places like this only existed in Elmore Leonard books.'

Only Nancy could be wowed by a bar and still come up with some literary reference no kid under the age of ancient could understand.

Whoever Elmore Whatevard was, she was right: as soon as you stepped into the room you were in another world. One of low lights, whispered conversations and rich chocolate banquettes. A bartender expertly mixed brightly coloured cocktails at the silver bar, which was surrounded by couples, their heads bent in conversation. This was the kind of place people came to start an affair.

Or teenage girls went to fantasize they were old enough to have one.

'I really hope we see a celebrity tonight,' Lilian said, as she and Kate ploughed right through us. Which, by the way, was becoming my least favourite new thing. 'Like, Katie Holmes has been spotted here a heap of times since she moved to Chelsea. Imagine if she was having a post-Tom meeting At. The. Next. Table. I'd die.'

Kate made a snorting noise.

'Score!' I grabbed Nancy's hand and we followed the girls across the bar to an intimate booth, where Payton and the small girl with caramel hair and pillow lips who'd played Hamlet's dad – Ryder? – were waving just furiously enough to get their friends' attention, but not so furiously that they looked too uncool. Did they practise that in the restroom mirrors of their penthouses when the maid was out?

'This place is *amaze*.' Lilian bounced down on the velvet seat, her apple-green V-neck dress dangerously short for such a manoeuvre.

'Haven't you been here before?' Payton's hand covered her mouth in a delicate yawn. 'We came here all the time – in ninth grade.'

'Oh, us too,' Lilian backtracked. 'That's what I meant: I've not been here in sooo long, I forgot how amaze it was.'

Ouch. And I thought the cheermonsters were rattlesnakes.

'Hey, sorry I'm late.' Another girl with coppery brown curls and a very tight leather pencil skirt tried to shimmy her way into the booth. 'There was some Santa Claus parade going on up on Lex and it took the cab driver an ice age to drive through it.' She plumped her curls with her right hand. 'There should really be a No Seasonal Shit zone in town for those of us who've gone through puberty and are over it.'

Maybe there should be a No Seasonal Grinches zone too?

A tall, broad waiter swept over to the booth, narrowly missing me and walking through Nancy's arm. She gave a little scowl. Hell, if we were gonna keep doing – what did Nance call it? – *surveillance* in such people-heavy

119

areas, we were gonna have to invest in the ghost equivalent of a rear-view mirror.

The waiter barely glanced at the girls before sussing the situation, catwalk-appropriate make-up and designer clothes or not. 'ID,' he said.

Kate looked at him like she wished he'd turn to ash and began rummaging moodily in her blueberry bag. You'd have to have -15 eyesight to miss the enormous intertwining Chanel Cs on its clasp.

'Quick!' Nancy pushed me towards the waiter. 'Possess him before he throws them out!'

'What?' I asked, trying to right myself.

'If the girls are a bit tipsy they're more likely to talk honestly about Mercy. I've never been intoxicated, but that's generally how these things seem to play out on TV.'

Gotcha. I'd bet Kate's entire handbag collection that Nancy had pulled that trick straight out of an episode of *Upper East Siders* too. She was always watching it in HHQ when she thought me and Lorna were out brooding (me) or window-shopping (her).

Right. I took a couple of steps back then ran at the waiter, jumping into him as fast as I could. He shuddered as I took control of his body.

'You in?' Nancy asked.

I turned to her and stuck two thumbs up. It was very weird possessing a fully grown guy. Even his hands were heavy.

The only people I'd ever possessed before were a me-sized girl during my first possession lesson in Times Square just after I died. Oh, and my cheating scumface of an ex-boyfriend when we were trying to cross him off my 'murderer suspects' list. This guy felt different. Like a lot of beautiful waiters in this part of town, he was probably doing the job for tips at night so he could hit up auditions in the day.

I pulled him up to his full six foot plus and looked at our reflection in the mirrored glass above the table. His slicked back dirty blond hair drew attention to how well defined his cheekbones were. I wondered if he was growing it for a part. Or maybe an underwear commercial – he had such big arms. I squeezed one of his muscles with his other hand. They were very . . . firm.

'Ahem?' Kate coughed, looking at me like I was two Pop-Tarts short of a full box. Didn't they teach you better in Manners 101? Actually, all of the drama clique were staring at me very strangely indeed. Kate was holding out the fakest ID I'd seen this side of the one I bought off some guy on the Lower East Side two summers back. Even from my new possessing position of six feet up, I could see the 'Kate' in her supposed ID picture had dark hair, a granny perm and more lines than the entire subway system. Real Kate so had a loyalty card to Liz Earle. Those gentle golden lowlights were not achieved with an at-home kit.

'Fine.' I waved it away with my new big, manly hand. 'What can I get you, *ladies*?' I gave them what I hoped was Hot Waiter Guy's most dazzling smile.

Ryder turned the colour of a can of full-fat Coke and bit on a hangnail. Hmm . . . imagine being able to slay a Park Avenue princess with one look. Must be kinda fun to be him. And hard not to turn into a total A-hole.

'Round of vodkas on the rocks, girls?' Kate asked. 'In memory of Mercy. Ever since she read that article in *Vanity Fair* about how it was Joan Crawford's favourite drink, it was the only one she'd touch too.'

'Joan Crawford? Was she in *Mad Men*?' Lilian asked.

'Five vodkas coming right up,' I said. Big smile. Thank God they'd all ordered the same thing. HWG's black dress pants were too tight to fit a notepad in the pocket. Who knows how he remembered complicated orders. He probably saw it as practice for learning complicated lines.

I tried to edge his body back. He really was very heavy. Plus, it was crazy-hard to see out of HWG's eyes from up here. They were hooded in a brooding Leonardo DiCaprio way. I stood at the table, still giving the girls my megawatt smile. How long could I do that before they realized I/he was a weirdo? Or Ryder exploded.

Nancy Jabbed my right side. 'Charlotte, move. They're not going to start spilling the dirt on Mercy if all you feed them is dreamy looks.' She stared at Ryder. 'Well, it might work on that little one, but the rest seem more impervious to his charms.'

'Fine, fine,' I muttered, edging HWG's body back. I waited for the barman to fix five identical drinks. 'Better make them doubles.' I winked at him. If it was loose-lipped Nancy wanted, it was loose-lipped she was going to get. 'Five vodkas, not too many rocks,' I said as I popped the drinks down.

'To Mercy!' Kate toasted.

'Mercy!' The girls chinked glassed and drank.

A guy with close-shorn blond hair and black Ray-Bans fell into a seat at the table next to us and began reading the *Post*. 'Public school teen murdered!' screamed the headline. Underneath in smaller letters it said: 'Tragedy at play!' In a side panel there was the head of some columnist guy and the words, 'Why nowhere in the city is safe for our kids.'

Ryder sucked in her breath. 'It doesn't feel real, not until you see something like that.'

Jen's copper curls bounced as she shook her head.

'No, but in a really, really weird way, I think Mercy would have loved this,' Kate said, taking a long sip of her drink. 'Her name in the papers. People making a noise over her – finally being famous all over the city.'

'I'll have a Jack and Coke, please,' the blonde boy told me. Uh, what I did not need was another customer. I needed to concentrate on what the Peabody girls were saying. On cue, Nancy leant on the edge of their table, glued to their every word while I ordered the Jack, then pretended to clean. Which, btw, HBG definitely would never do.

'Another round, please,' Ryder asked shyly.

I put five more drinks on their table and slid the Jack and Coke over to Blondie. He'd still got his Ray-Bans on. Urgh. Some people were so try-hard. Did he think he was in a rock band?

'I brought along some pictures of Mercy from kindergarten.' Jen slid an envelope out of her hot pink suede bag. 'Here's our entire class. Look, Payton, Ryder, you're there too! We're sooo small. And here's our first ever school production: the nativity play. Do you remember when I got the part of Mary, then Mercy screamed until I let her do it instead?' Jen giggled fondly. 'Then here's—'

123

'Oh, can we just cut the BS?' Kate said, slamming down her cut-glass tumbler so hard one of the ice cubes jumped onto the table. 'Yes, we were all friends with Mercy, but can't we be truthful for one second in our stupid, fake-smile lives?' She was slurring ever so slightly now. Four shots of vodka in under thirty minutes will do that to a girl. 'Would any of you honest to God say you actually liked Mercy?'

Four pairs of eyes left Kate's and made a dive for the polished chrome table. The hangnail was back in Ryder's mouth.

Kate threw the melting cube back into her glass and lowered her voice. I popped the fresh vodkas on their table, pretending to collect some glasses nearby really slowly. The Miss Dior *parfum* was about to hit the fan.

'C'mon, she's not here to hurt anyone any more. None of you have to be afraid.' Kate smiled, trying to lighten the mood. 'Like, if Mercy is a ghost, do you really think she'd waste her precious wooos haunting us five? She'll be straight on the stage at the AA Theatre possessing Sienna Miller or whoever so she finally knows how it feels to play Miss Julie.'

'Or, if she's made it to heaven,' Payton added, 'she'll be hunting down Sarah Bernhardt and asking to run lines.'

The other girls giggled nervously.

Kate turned to Payton. 'You went for Hamlet too right, but you ended up as grouchy old Gertrude? Why did you pull out before the final audition?'

Payton slouched the ice around her glass, then downed it angrily. 'Because Mercy said if I didn't, she'd tell the whole school I still sleep in my parents' room when there's a thunderstorm.' She slammed the glass on the table.

Lilian hid a snigger.

'And what about you, Lil?' Kate turned to her. 'Would you have been friends with Mercy since kindergarten if your mothers weren't in the same stupid yoga class? And Ryder, if you'd got elected to be president of the Palmer Peabody Drama Group like you should have done, wouldn't you have ditched her from the club on account of the fact that all she ever did was overact and bitch about other people getting roles?'

'Ummm . . .' Ryder managed.

'Wow, good job we didn't bring Mercy along,' Nancy whispered. 'If I'd known this was all you had to do to get girls talking straight, I'd have condoned underage drinking years ago.'

Jeez, this case was like Goldilocks's porridge pot. The list of people who wanted Mercy gone was growing by the second – and we needed it to shrink.

'And, Jen, can you seriously say you, like, *loved* going to that damn improv class with her every Wednesday when you could have been in Barneys with us instead?'

Jen hung her head. 'No, I hated it,' she admitted. 'I sucked at it too. I could never shake the feeling Mercy only guilt-tripped me into going along because she knew I'd make her look good.'

The bartender coughed. He'd mixed up another round of drinks – guess he'd been working long enough to know when people needed them.

'Hey, do any of you know who put that ginormous

"Good luck!" banner up in her dressing room?' Kate asked. 'Mercy went loco when she saw it on opening night.'

'Huh, I don't get it. Wouldn't she be pleased someone was being kind enough to wish her luck?' Lilian asked.

'Nooo, not an actress,' Payton said. 'It's an old theatre tradition: you should never wish anyone good luck before they go onstage, because it's the opposite of that.'

'You can say, "Break a leg" or whatever, but never "Good luck",' Kate explained. 'Personally I think it's a pile of phooey but you know how superstitious Mercy is . . . *was* about that kind of stuff.'

'Turns out she was right to be,' Jen said quietly. 'She wasn't my favourite person, but I didn't want her *dead*. Like, I hoped she'd step on a plug – because *nothing* hurts like that – or even in, like, a dark moment, I wanted her to get a part in some touring show which went waaaay out of town. But I didn't wish for this to happen.'

'None of us did, but it's going to be okay,' Kate said, as much to herself as any of the others. 'Mercy's gone now. The cops seem really on it, especially the cute detective one. I'm sure they'll catch the guy who did this in no time. Then, after the ash-scattering ceremony, we can all move on.'

Out of the corner of my eye, I saw the blond boy straighten up as a small brunette walked towards his booth.

'Hey,' he mumbled. 'Thanks for taking the time to come.' There was something about the way he hunched over the table like that that reminded me of someone.

'Can we change the subject now, please?' Ryder asked.

'I hate talking ill of the dead. Where's everyone spending the Christmas vaycay?'

Wow, nought to vapid in twenty seconds. That had to be a record.

'My family's place in France – the snow's killer at this time of year,' Jen said. 'If my mom and her idiot foetus of a new boyfriend start to drive me cray-cray, can I still come to St Barts with you instead, Ryder?'

'Sure! There's always, like, five spare rooms. Unless my brother brings too many of his stoner lacrosse friends. It's awesome to start the year with a winter tan – you can totally tell the difference between the real thing and bottle-made.'

'Really, you have no idea how much I appreciate you meeting me.' Something in blond boy's tone made my attention flit from the Peabody girls to him. He'd finally taken his damn Ray-Bans off. And that's when I realized why he was so super-familiar.

'Hey, David,' Ali said as she slid into the booth.

'Oh, gawd,' Nancy wailed, taking in my Living best friend sitting opposite my Living ex-boyfriend.

David? Ali? *Here*?

I didn't know what to do. So I did what I guessed Hot Waiter Guy would. I walked over to their table and waited to take their order.

'Another Jack for me, and?' David motioned to Ali who made a 'whatever' motion with her hands. 'Two Jacks and Coke then.' David had shaved his hair short. So short the pink of his scalp shone through. It made his look less like a surfer who'd taken the wrong flight from Cali and more like a member of a punk band. His summer tan had faded. His face was narrower, as if someone had vacuumed away the cushions that used to make up his cheeks. I stood there, staring at him, old David who looked new. I'd not seen his sea-blue eyes since we were up on that roof – where Library Girl confessed the reason she took my life was because she was obsessed with him.

And I was majorly gawking.

'Sorry, dude, do I know you?' David asked. Darn, HWG's legs had totally stopped working. I wasn't sure if that was because they'd gotten too heavy for me to lift after all the possessing, or it was the David effect. Maybe he was the kryptonite to Ghostgirl's powers? Not that I really had any good ones – unless you counted being able to make my right hand glow like the McDonald's sign. I wasn't even sure I could still pull off the zombie trick.

'Oh for Pete's sake,' someone mumbled.

Out of nowhere, the waiter behind me almost fell over, cursing under his breath. The Peabody girls looked from him to me and back again, following a tennis match where they weren't sure which player was acting most weird.

'*This* is what happens when you venture below East 59th.' Jen grabbed her bag closer to her body.

Urgh. Like the Upper East Side had been such a safe place lately.

'Brad, dude!' The other barman slapped me on the arm hard. *Brad*? Was that my name? 'Ross really needs you over at the bar, pronto,' he said, not letting go of my arm and tugging me backwards.

'Brad?' I repeated lamely.

Hey, I know it was only one syllable but right then it was all I could manage.

'Shhhh, it's me! Nancy!' Other Barman whispered in my ear. 'I don't know if your guy's called Brad or not – he just *looked* like a Brad. You know, all chiselled and firm and wow—' he squeezed HBG's arm '—it's like he's actually made of muscle. Sorry to barge in, but you looked like you needed help.' She stared back at Ali and David who were by now having a heated talk.

Nancy lowered Other Barman's head so that his eyes were looking into mine. Or Brad's. Or HBG's. Whatever his name was.

'You've had a shock, Charlotte. Another big one. I mean, what was the probability that *he* would be *here*? And invite *her*? Even I can't do the math.' She stared at David with a level of disgust two below the one she'd been reserving for Edison lately. 'Let's get you out of him.' She motioned to HBG's body. 'Then out of here. I think we've got all the intel we need from those girls.'

I nodded.

'Service!' Ross – if that was his name – the bartender shouted at us in frustration. He looked really mad. Little veins were popping above his brows. His waiters weren't paid to stand around like idiots, acting like they'd smoked a prep-school worth of pot. This was not a 'service!' establishment.

'After three, we step back and wiggle, remember?' Nancy said. 'We need to go. One, two . . .'

Pop!

I threw myself backwards as hard as I could and landed in an ungraceful heap on the bar floor.

'Do I always have to be here to give you a hand, Feldman?' Edison asked, brushing his jeans down from his port.

I was so confused I let him pull me up. 'Wait a second,' I said. 'You weren't here before. What are you . . .?'

Maybe my entire death was an over-eighteens nightmare after all. After the subway, and the murder, the lying and the cheating, this was the part where it got *really* bad – the portion of my dream where my in-no-way-new-boyfriend and my don't-know-what-I-ever-saw-in-him old boyfriend both decided – despite living in different dimensions – to be at the same bar in Manhattan at the exact same moment. While a few murder suspects sat around, drinking overpriced Grey Goose and braying like hyenas.

Yep, that was sooo what was going on. Any second now, I was going to jerk awake, sit up in bed covered in icky, hair-matting sweat and run down the corridor to my parents' room – hugging them and never letting go. I'd even offer to clean my room. Theirs too. Maybe the entire apartment . . . if that just meant this hideous, weakly scripted soap-opera episode went away.

'Edison Hayes! Charlotte asked you a question.' Nancy pulled herself off the floor without the help of a hot bad dead boy, and strode over.

I squeezed my eyes shut, then open again. Bummer. Still here. Still dead. Still in my own personal brand of hell.

'This seemed like the perfect opportunity to wheel out my "A ghost walks through a bar . . ." joke.' Ed smirked. 'When Lorna told me Nancy Radley had gone barfly, I said to myself, Edison this is something you *have* to see.' He took in the room. 'Though this is more civilized and bijou than I was expecting. I was kinda hoping, if you were gonna go off the rails, Nancy, you'd at least have done it in a dive bar where I could put my head in a bottle of Wild Turkey and try to remember how good that tasted.'

When had this got so out of control? Would anyone notice if I ported home and got under the covers?

'How's the detecting been going anyway?' Edison skulked over to the table where the Peabody girls were draining their fourth drinks. This was not going to end well. For anyone. If they all became Betty Ford cases, I was going to feel at least 20 per cent responsible. Okay, maybe thirty.

'Did any of them admit to murdering Mercy Grant yet?' Edison asked, as Lilian pushed her empty glass away. He Jabbed it back at her. She slid it across the table. Ed Jabbed it back. She closed one eye drunkenly, trying to focus and work out exactly what was wrong. 'It looks like the only massacre any of them could commit is one in Bloomingdale's with Daddy's platinum card.' Lilian ignored her haunted glass and slumped onto the table. 'And now even that looks unlikely.'

I focused on Ed, trying to block out the scene enfolding in the booth next to him. The one where Ali was now standing, her shoulders set back indignantly, and picking up her bag ready to stomp out of the bar.

'What?' Edison asked. 'Why are you looking so shifty, Feldman?'

He turned to the one table I was refusing to

acknowledge, a slow wave of recognition spreading across his face.

'What the freak? Did you know he was going to be here?' Edison was pointing at David now. Mad. 'Damn, Charlotte, after everything Blondie did to you – do you never get beat up enough? Is that why you offered to get involved in this mission?'

Awesome. So now David wasn't just messing up my life, he was affecting my death too. For the second time that night, I turned to stone. Only this time I knew it wasn't the David effect that was ruining me, it was the Edison one.

'Of course she didn't know!' Nancy shouted, stepping in between us. 'Firstly, Charlotte has more important things to do than monitor her ex- . . .' She was struggling with her vocab a lot lately. Maybe I should get her a doofus-tionary? 'Ex-*idiot*'s comings and goings. It was my idea we came here, not hers. In fact, it was these five's.' She pointed at the girls' booth, where Kate was trying unsuccessfully to convince Lilian's head that the table was not a bed. 'And, secondly, even if Charlotte did, what would that have to do with you? Nothing, Edison, nothing. Because after everything you've done, that is all she owes you.'

Wow. Could I just give up talking all together and get Nancy to be my personal mouthpiece forever, please? She was way better at this rightly mad stuff than me. Lately, when confrontation hit, my special move seemed to be standing around like a prize numpty.

Edison's shoulders dropped and his fists unclenched. He glanced back at David who was now sitting on his own, watching Ali's back disappear through the door.

Edison popped out a cigarette and sat on the edge of David's table. The sight of the two of them that close and that messed up was something I never needed to see.

'You're right, Nancy, as always.' For Ed, the sarcasm on the last two words dripped lightly. He blew smoke out of his nose and stared directly at me. 'I'm sorry for losing it, Charlotte. Really I am, but he makes me mad. I didn't mean to . . .'

Lilian's head banged back down on the table with an almighty thud. 'Oops!' Kate giggled. 'She's totally going to have a black eye for the Frost Fête now.'

'The Frost Fête? What's that?' Nancy repeated, despite the chaos, still thinking to note an important thing down in her book.

'Can we go somewhere and talk, Charlotte, please?' Edison asked.

I shook my head. My head was moving. This was a breakthrough. Go me.

'You don't have to go anywhere with him you don't want to, Charlotte,' Nancy said. 'Let's head back to the Attesa – add these five to the suspect list. Though I don't actually think they murdered Mercy, do you?'

Ryder and Lilian were slumped in the corner like the raggy dolls department in FAO Schwartz.

'They might not have been Mercy's true friends, but I'm starting to wonder if she had any,' Nancy said. 'If she was too thick-skinned to realize they didn't like her, she could've thought her worst enemies were actually her pals.' She nibbled on her pen. 'It's going to add an extra level of confusion to this investigation.'

'Please, Charlotte.' Edison threw aside his cigarette. 'We need to talk. I oughta explain some things. Everything I meant to say came off wrong last time.'

David threw a twenty on the table and tugged his old army surplus coat on over a vintage AC/DC T-shirt. It bagged in a way it hadn't before. Urgh, why did I care? It wasn't like he'd been worrying about me in the days after my death.

'Charlotte?' Nancy asked.

'Hey Ali! Wait up!' David tore past me.'I've gotta explain.'

'Charlotte?' Edison said.

I looked from one to the other at a total loss. The door slammed hard as David hurtled through it.

'Sorry, guys, but I need to know what's going down in my past before I can face up to my future,' I said.

'I need to make sure there's nothing I can do for Ali.' I ran after David and out onto the street, just in time to see him jump in front of a cab.

The driver yelled, screeching to a snippy stop. David ducked down and climbed into the back seat.

That must be my ride.

CHAPTER 12

The tail lights of the yellow cab were seeping into the night.

Not being a James Bond villain, I'd never jumped into a moving car before. But hey, I'd met my murderer, overseen the possession of a cheerleading squad and developed a thing for a guy who didn't even have a soul any more – there was a first time for everything.

Though hopefully not demons and hellbeasts. Those I was less into.

I ran after the cab as fast as I could, chasing the glowing red lights. On the upside, being dead meant I didn't have any breath to be out of. On the down, losing 125 lbs of body weight hadn't made me any faster either. When it came to running, I still majorly sucked.

As the cab hit the junction with 8th, it braked, the left indicator blinking. I caught up and bobbed down quickly enough to see David's blond head and Ali's silky brunette one inside. I jumped in next to the driver, just as he turned the cab north.

The car was silent, apart from the background crackle

of – I peered at the middle-aged, middle-heavy driver's ID picture: Hal – *Hal*'s radio back to the cab HQ. Was the glass soundproof? I pushed my head through the barrier. From the neck up, I was on the same side as my best friend and my ex. Nope, they were glaring at each other, but saying nothing.

'You know when someone walks out on you, that's not usually an invitation to share a cab home with them,' Ali said finally.

David tugged a black beanie hat out of his messenger bag and pulled it over his scalp.

'I did what you asked,' she said.

The cab pulled another left. Outside the window, Hell's Kitchen was dark compared to the excess of Midtown. Hal swerved to avoid an orange traffic cone where – pre-snowfall – the sidewalk was being fixed up. 'I met with you. I listened to you. I don't have anything else to say. You have to realize, David, that there comes a point where no matter how often you apologize, you can't offload your guilt. This isn't something you can make up for – like you getting so baked, you forget to take Charlotte to the end-of-term dance – this is the loss of someone amazing. And if any of us are ever going to move on, you need to stop this . . . this *fantasy*.'

Hal stopped at a light near 58th Street. Where Reepa Jones – the dead girl right after me – had died after falling under a cab coming out of the Hudson Hotel. We'd solved her murder and discovered her trust-fund-jealous stepsister did it in five days. Simple. I wondered if her ex and BFF were having some tortured conversation about her death across town right now. Double doubted it.

'It's been hard enough for Charlotte's family and *friends*—' Ali clearly counted David as anything but '— trying to get a hold of the fact that that little *thing* from the library could do something like this, without all this BS you're spreading about having seen her ghost.'

My ghost?

Uh oh. So David had been going around telling people what he saw up on the roof? When his only witness to my zombie attack was Library Girl, who was currently in some mental institution upstate? Smart. How had I never realized he was so not smart?

Maybe because I was too distracted by the hot, floppy-haired musician act. Can you spell 'sucker'?

'I know you didn't push Charlotte under the F Train, David, but you do have to take some responsibility in all of this,' Ali was saying. 'Maybe if you hadn't been making eyes at that psycho sophomore . . .'

'Hey, I never made eyes at her!' he protested.

No, you just made *out* with the entire cheersquad before I even had time to decompose.

'All I'm saying is that teenage girls – hormonal as we are – do not go around killing their perfectly lovely classmates without reason. You batting your baby blues at that girl could well have ignited the situation.'

David fell back in the seat in silent frustration.

'Stop with this talk about seeing Charlotte's spirit up on the Sedgewick roof. No one wants to hear it. Not me, not her mom, certainly not her dad.' Ali stared out of the dirty glass as the lights changed. 'I mean, Jeez, who wants to think there could be such a thing as ghosts and that Charlotte's out there, on her own somewhere . . .'

Ali's eyes filled with tears. I wished I could wipe them away.

Hal took the corner at Columbus Circle too hard. David slid towards Ali, as my head almost careered through Hal's lap. Ewwww.

I straightened back up as the cab did. Ali had pulled herself together and hit David with a mom-worthy death stare.

'I get it.' David rearranged his beanie. 'I won't say I'm lying, but I get it. And I won't bother you or the Feldmans any more.'

'Thank you,' Ali said quietly, as we passed the trees and horse-drawn carriages on Central Park West where Emma and Dylan were stood on the corner fighting. In a way – the tiniest, smallest, most microscopic way – I sort of felt sorry for David. Yes, he'd been a total fool, but he'd lost me too. Not that he cared about me as much as I'd cared about him. But I had haunted him quite badly up on the roof. Edison taught me well – Zombie Charlotte was not something you wanted to think about before bed and—

Emma and Dylan! Had I just seen Emma and *Dylan*? Without giving myself time to think of the sickness, I ported out of the cab and onto the pavement by Strawberry Fields.

And there they were: Lorna's sister, wrapped up in a beautiful blood orange mac, and Dylan West, his Wolverine sweater poking out from under an ill-fitting cargo coat. What the . . .?

'Emma, this is serious,' he was saying. 'A girl is dead.'

'Wow, thanks for filling me in on that one, genius. You

really should apply for the next anchor job that comes up at CNN.'

Woah. I didn't get what I was hearing, but I was suddenly very, very glad that Lorna wasn't here. Maybe Nancy too.

'If you don't tell the police, I will,' he said.

Tell the police *what*?

'Dylan, seriously, it will make zero difference to the case.' Emma shrugged him off as if they were discussing the best route uptown in rush hour. 'Talking to them is only going to make them look into my family even more, and I've had about enough of prying cops for a lifetime, haven't you?'

Dylan tried to puff out his chest. I could see Wolverine's clawy fingers. 'Well, I might just go to them anyway.'

'Well, then you might just find yourself on the suspect list and, with your past, I think that's the last thing you want.' Emma's phone beeped. She pulled it out of her matching red tote bag. 'It's my mom. I've gotta . . .' She fixed him with a glacial glare. 'Don't call me out here like this at stupid o'clock for no reason again, okay? It's not worth the risk.'

She disappeared into the night, her long blonde ponytail swinging behind her.

Dylan sniffed, and started to walk in a broken way in the opposite direction.

Um . . .

Sensible Charlotte knew what she had to do: port to the Attesa, tell Nancy and Lorna every second of what I'd just seen and let the investigation go from there.

139

But then I imagined telling Lorna and how her face would fall . . . while Nancy's lit up because I'd just given her another maybe-lead.

It will make zero difference to the case, that's what Emma had said. And Dylan hadn't disputed that, really. She was Lorna's sister. She seemed pretty smart. If she was really some evil murdering girl-witch and Dylan knew that, would a weedy guy like him be meeting her in a dark corner of the park after nightfall? Especially when there was no one but tramps, cab drivers and my fighting Living friends around? Hardly.

No, it was better to keep this one to myself. For the moment at least. If I needed to tell Nancy in the future, I totally could. Lorna too. But there was no point upsetting the apple cart for no reason.

I ported back to the Attesa and made my way down the stairs to HHQ.

'All's not well in Waverly Place,' Edison said. He was standing outside the frosted glass door, lurking and spying. For a change. 'Seems our little corner of Paradise is on course for bumpy times ahead.'

'Oh, will you go get an afterlife, so you can stop ruining mine?' I snapped, as I pushed into our investigation room, ignoring the sort of hurt look which may or may not have been brewing in his eyes.

'Hey,' I said, just in time to see Nancy add Emma to Payton and the other girls on the Mercy's Murder Suspect's List.

And a furious Lorna storm past me, and out into the hall.

CHAPTER 13

Mercy Grant's bedroom was the size of my parents' kitchen, den and hall put together.

'Cosy,' I said.

But no one heard. Nancy was already scoping out the joint for case-breaking clues, while Lorna was admiring the soft furnishings. I'd not heard them say more than a polite 'yes' or 'thank you' to one another since HHQ. Now they were circling each other like wary cats, waiting to see who would deflate the tension first, or restart the fight. Brilliant.

'You know, I would have thought the combo of a four-poster bed, brocade *and* gold satin would be OTT, but it's actually totally Galliano,' Lorna told Mercy as she fell onto the bed. 'And I actually totally love it.'

I rolled my eyes. Saying this room wasn't OTT was like saying Tom Cruise wasn't into Scientology. Two white crushed velvet chairs were very deliberately positioned next to a large gold fireplace. The walls were covered in metallic paint, except for one where some crappy enchanted forest scene had been painted, no doubt at the cost of a year's college fees. There were actually freaking deer. Dancing deer. If you could drag your eyes away from *that* or the poster bed – which FYI would totally sleep four quarterbacks without posing any challenge to their heterosexuality – the opposite corner of the room was taken over by a piece of furniture which normal people would call a dresser. But, Mercy being Mercy, it was surrounded by bright, make-up-perfecting dressing room bulbs and had a large neon flashing sign above it that said 'stage'. You almost had to respect her dedication to the school of more is more.

'Let's get to work,' Detective Lee said, ducking his head to avoid a crystal-look chandelier.

Scratch that, it probably was just crystal.

I thought back to my own Upper West Side shoebox, with its bleached MOMA posters and pinboard heaving with ticket stubs from bands I'd seen, exhibits I'd loved and postcards of places I wanted to visit one day. Who could compete?

And who'd want to?

Stigner double-took the deer. 'There's a lot of, um, stuff in here,' she said. Two more officers were scoping the room, carefully looking under Mercy's bed and through drawers. Signer began to sift through the crap on Mercy's desk instead. Old books, annotated scripts, magazines. 'Any heads up on what we're looking for, Detective?' she asked Lee.

'Yes, what *are* we looking for, Nancy?' Mercy asked from the bed. An ancient copy of *Macbeth* and a sketch of a guy I guessed was Shakespeare was on her side table where most sixteen-year-old girls in their right mind would put a picture of a guy they were into. Or – I dunno – Harry Styles. Even David had that camera phone print of our first date. I wondered if it was still there now he'd seen me as Zombie Girl. That could be as big a turn-off as bad breath or suggesting his 'n' hers Ramones T-shirts.

'This is my room,' Mercy said. 'I lived, breathed and rehearsed here. I get why the detectives want to snoop, but you guys joining in is seven shades of degrading. It's not like you're going to uncover some clue I wasn't already aware of.'

Really? That little confessional we'd overheard above Joe Allen's made me wonder.

Even though she was standing in Mercy's closet, I still heard Nancy sigh. 'There might be something that you think is nothing, but we see in a different light because we've got emotional distance.' She walked back through the closed golden closet doors. 'Let's take an hour to check it out. Now the rest of your cast has alibis, we don't have any other pursuable leads.'

Mercy scowled and flipped over onto her back. 'Didn't the dead boy – what was his name – Harrison? – say he was going to help out with my case? I've not seen him since yesterday.'

A feeling bunny-hopped through me. I refused to let myself identify what it was or where it came from.

'*Edison*,' Lorna said, before I had to, '*is* helping. He's probably off pursuing his own line of inquiry is all.' She gave me a small smile.

'Detective, how far are we going with this search?'

Stigner bent down by a small ivory trash can with tassels. 'There are some mucky papers in here. Do you want them?'

'Bag them up.' Detective Lee handed her a pair of white plastic gloves and some clear bags. 'We'll send them to Forensics this afternoon. They can check for prints. We shouldn't discount anything. A teenage girl's room is like a screen grab of what's going on in her head. We don't know what could become a lead later.'

Nancy shot Mercy a *see! see!* look and put her head into the gilt-edged bedside drawer. What did this 'screen grab' say about Mercy? Either that we had very different taste or she'd accidentally employed Liberace as her interior designer.

Lorna watched with thinly veiled disgust as Stigner pulled three greeting cards and white paper envelopes from the garbage. 'It's way nicer being a dead detective.' She patted down her skirt prissily. 'So much less of the icky stuff. Though at least these guys don't seem to have a stupid, wrong suspect board,' she said pointedly at Nancy.

Miaow! And there was strike one.

'What have you got there?' Lee asked Stigner.

She held up her finds like they were stinky haddock. 'Three cards, I think.' Stigner carefully placed them on the dresser and smoothed them out. 'Yes, good luck ones from . . .' She squinted. 'Aunt Rose, Dylan and "Your biggest fan". With a smiley face and lots of kisses.'

The last card had a large green shamrock on the front. 'Reckon she sent that to herself?' Lorna whispered.

'Why did you put them in the trash?' I asked Mercy.

'Surely they should have pride of place on your mirror or something.'

'Cards are just so pedestrian.' She shrugged. 'I make my own luck. Some over-expensive pieces of paper from a geriatric relative and two of my many admirers aren't going to make me remember my lines any better. It's preparation, skill and raw talent which sees to that.'

I swear – beneath her black-framed glasses – I saw Nancy cross her eyes. Just a little bit.

Mercy had nailed a pinboard to the wall by her mirror. Somehow she'd found one framed with gold leaves. Nice. A sketch of a girl with a severe dark bob, black beanie and black hipster duds was tacked in the middle. It must have been the first draft of Mercy's Hamlet costume. She looked kinda menacing as a cartoon. Like Daria's best friend Jane, but even goth-er.

'Cute,' Lorna said. 'Though they did the right thing making your costume in blue. All that black drains you so much, especially with your hair. This colour totally picks up your green eyes.'

Mercy jumped off the bed and over to her window which overlooked Central Park. The tiny turrets on the roof of the Met Museum framed the green trees like a doily at afternoon tea.

'Bag them and we'll check them for prints later,' Detective Lee said. 'What is this?' He pulled a sheet of paper down from the board where Mercy had written a list of names then messily crossed them out: Payton, Ana, Emma, Marnie, Jen . . . I stared at it quizzically.

'Um, that even I will admit is kinda embarrassing,' Mercy said. 'It's my CL.'

'CL?'

'Competitor List.' She ran a finger over the carved embellishment on her headboard. 'It's this motivational trick Mom taught me back in First Grade when I was auditioning for my first play. The nativity. Whenever you want something, you figure out who your competitors are, then cross them off one by one when they're out of the running. It makes you feel more confident about your chances of hitting your goal. And the more confident you act, the more people will think you deserve it.'

Wow, and there was Alive Me hoping that I could fulfil my dreams of working at a gallery or waiting tables in Paris while I saw the world, without screwing over all my friends. My bad.

At Detective Lee's request, an officer took a shot of Mercy's list, then began flashbulbing all over her room. I was crazy glad the police had initially messed up and thought my death was just an accident. Imagine having these guys in your bedroom before you'd had a chance to tidy or put your three-day-old bras away.

'Was there any luck with the audience attendance list from the school, Detective?' Stigner asked her boss.

'We've got the names of every single parent or relative who bought a ticket to *Hamlet* and used their card, but some people paid in cash.' He picked up a snow globe with a picture of Mercy's mom and dad inside and shook it. 'I checked with Miss Ballard and that always happens – it's usually theatrical agents not wanting anyone to know they're there. I guess they don't wanna get hassled by wannabe Oscar nominees.'

'Hmmm, it's annoying that didn't throw up any leads,' Nancy said.

'Bingo!' the short cop said. 'Detective Lee, I've found Mercy's iPad.' He held it up triumphantly. 'There's got to be some intel in here, surely.'

'Power it up then,' the detective said. 'You know what kids are like, they have their entire lives on those things. Good find.'

Short Cop glowed. 'Oh good, she didn't have a password on it either,' he said, accessing the machine. 'That saves us some time.'

Mercy's tablet sprang to life and a picture of her and – was that Lilian? – playing on some unidentifiable postcard beach appeared. They must have been in kindergarten. Mercy's long black hair was plaited down her back and Lilian was wearing geeky pink-rimmed glasses and train-track braces with bright blue bands.

'Like that's any help to us,' Mercy sighed dramatically.

'It might be.' Nancy moved to the short cop's side. 'Remember: what you don't see as a clue, could be to us.'

'You don't need access to my iPad, silly,' Mercy said. 'You've got actual real dead me right here. There's no need to mess with that. I can tell you anything you want.'

Short Cop scrolled through Mercy's apps.

'Oh! Click the Facebook one.' Stigner leaned over the screen, trying to push her baggy shirtsleeves up. 'We're bound to be able to get a good steer on Mercy's friendships and relationships from there. Kids don't do anything nowadays unless it's online.'

'Eugh.' Mercy threw herself onto her bed like she'd just been told the Afterlife had an 8 p.m. curfew. 'This is the biggest waste of my time. And I say that as somebody who now has eternity to play with.'

'That's weird,' Short Cop said. 'I can't access much on Mercy's page. It seems to have been frozen or something.'

'Let me try,' Stigner said, gently taking the iPad from his hands, little baby-style.

'Erm, Mercy, when was your deathday?' Nancy pushed through Stigner's arm and squinted at the screen.

'Eleventh of December. Oh, wait. Ninth of December? I'm so bad with dates. Mom always said I was the kind of person who'd forget to be at their own funeral.' Mercy sat up and shook out her bob. 'Bet she's regretting joking about that now!'

'Mercy, when did your play open?' I asked.

'The eleventh of December,' she said right off.

Nancy took a millisecond break from the screen to give her an incredulous look.

'The eleventh of December – you're sure about that?' Mercy nodded. 'Well, that's your deathday too then.'

'Oh yes,' Mercy beamed. 'I can definitely remember that then.'

Nancy turned back to the screen. 'That's strange because according to your timeline here, you died on 11 December at 18.09,' she said. 'Which we know is true, but how come the website knew so quickly? Your parents haven't even organized your ash-scattering yet. It's kinda weird they'd have thought to email Facebook to tell them the exact time the rig fell on your head.'

'Maybe they get a letter to their very own silicon valley HHQ?' Lame joke, Charlotte. Remember to engage brain before saying all the lame jokes.

Nancy was staring at the iPad like her eyeballs were UHU'd to it. 'Look, here.' She pointed at Mercy's wall. 'Payton and Ryder posted about how much they'll miss you at 10 p.m. on the night you died. Facebook was pretty new when I died – I didn't even have an account – but surely it takes days and days for the techy people to verify someone's really dead and change their page from a normal one to a memorial? If it was one-click easy, I imagine some sickos would change their friends' pages all the time for a joke?'

What? I stared at the screen too. I wasn't an expert on death on social media, but Nancy was totally right. Mercy's status had switched to dead at 18.09 exactly.

'RIP Mercy. Heaven has a new angel to entertain them xoxoxo Payton Cassidy 22.01'

'I can't believe you were cut off before you finished your big speech! After we ran those lines again and again. WMYED. Ryder xxx 22.04'

'WMYED?' Nancy said. 'What's *that* mean?'

'Will miss you every day.' Mercy gave a little sniff. 'It's what we used to say when we waved goodbye before vacation. She's so cute.'

Yeah, cute as a Care Bear doused in cyanide.

'I'm glad this didn't exist when I died,' Lorna said. 'It's kinda tacky leaving messages like that. What happened to sending flowers? Plus, imagine having no control over your pictures after your death.' She shuddered like a force four had blown through the room. 'Anyone could hate-tag you in a hideous shot and you'd be too dead to change it. Like, I didn't love the picture my parents put out of me after I was killed, but it wasn't so unfortunate

I wanted to appirate and ball them over it. This is too grim.'

'Did she have a diary app?' Stigner asked.

'Yes.' Detective Lee jabbed his big thumb on the icon awkwardly. 'Won't open though.'

'That's because she's got a password on it,' Stigner explained. 'What could it have been? I bet it's the name of a Shakespeare play or something.' Stigner began typing into the password box. The lights in the room surged and the iPad popped off.

Short Cop was so surprised he fell into the wall.

'Hey, don't sweat it. These townhouses are ancient.' Detective Lee pulled him up. 'The electrics in most of them are shot. Nothing to worry about.'

Short Cop tried to regain his composure. 'Sorry, chief, guess I'm just a little on edge. Being in the dead girl's room and all.'

'Happens to the best of us, James.' Detective Lee squeezed his shoulder.

'Stigner, can you take it in to the Tech team and get them working on that passcode? And check in case we've missed anything else?' He started to fold the iPad's baby-blue cover shut. Stigner nodded dutifully.

'You've missed a massive thing!' Nancy shouted at him. 'How can't you see that Mercy's page was turned into a memorial the *second* she died? Look at it again – please, Detective Lee!'

He snapped the cover over the screen.

'Wait!' Stigner said. She couldn't have looked more surprised if Mercy herself had aspirated into the room and gone *boo!*

150

I turned to Nancy who had a look of total concentration on her face. Ah. She was Throwing words into Stigner's mouth.

'How did Mercy's page become a memorial so fast?' Stigner asked in a tight voice.

The creases in Jefferson's rugged forehead deepened. 'What did you say?' He opened up the iPad again and turned it back on. Little Lilian and beach Mercy smiled at him happily.

'See here,' Nancy Threw out of Stigner's mouth as he clicked on the app. 'Facebook knew Mercy was dead before we did.'

'Oh my . . .' Jefferson was gazing at Stigner with a mix of confusion and respect. 'Well spotted, Sergeant,' he said. 'I can't believe I missed that. James!' he called.

Stigner was blowing her lips in and out like she was doing some elaborate vocal warm-up, totally befuddled by what the hell had just happened.

'Get onto our tech support guys and find out what happens to your online imprint when you die, and how someone can change it. You can't have to produce a death certificate – Mercy didn't even have one at 18.09 on the 11th.

'And get someone under the age of seventeen to explain what the hell "WMYED" means.' He passed the iPad to Short Cop again. 'Damned if I know.'

'Well, Mercy—' Nancy tried not to smile too hard as Stigner slumped onto the bed in a bundle of confusion '—it seems your murderer didn't just kill you in real life, but online too. That's got to be a first.'

CHAPTER 14

'Wow. So my party dress shopping pretty much involved Mom palming me two twenties and begging me not to come back with anything that would make Dad pull his Disappointed Face,' I said, studying the room. 'But this is a whole different ball game. Heck, I don't think I was even playing ball. I was stuck on tick, tack, toe.'

Room four in Bergdorf Goodman's personal shopping department was intense. In the perfectly peach dressing room, white orchids sat on a dark wood table; a zebra-print stool and tangerine chaise longue crying out to be reclined on. One whole wall was taken up by hanger after quilted hanger of milk-coloured gowns. Snow White's closet might as well have opened a pop-up shop.

'What you have to understand is that the Frost Fête is a major deal,' Lorna said. 'Like, colossal. The De Witt family have hosted the party every year since my dad's dad's dad's dad was in diapers. It's big-time important you go and look ah-mazing.'

'But it's so nearly Christmas.' I turned away as Emma shrugged off her J Brands and Anastasia helped her shimmy into an elaborate white gown. 'Isn't everyone all tinsel and mistletoed out already?'

'No, it's the last big party of the year,' Lorna explained. 'Lots of families go away for Christmas or New Year so the Frost Fête is basically the last time everyone's together. And people *love* an excuse for competitive fashion. It's, like, practically a registered sport above East 72nd Street.' She stared over my shoulder and smiled. 'Aww, doesn't Emma look like a princess?'

Emma was scrutinizing her reflection in the flatteringly lit carpet-to-ceiling mirror. The floor-length gown she was wearing skimmed her waist and gently hugged her curves as if it had been magically sewn on her by seamstress elves when my back was turned. The ivory embroidered flowers grew larger as they neared the hem.

Yep, that was three kingdoms far, far away from 'princess' than I'd ever look.

'She sure does,' Mercy said, watching Ana adjust the high neckline. 'I adored McQueen when I was alive. That's some dress.'

'Hmm . . .' Jeez, the changing room was bigger than most department stores'. Did people really need this much space just to put on a dress then take it off again?

'Here's the Halston Heritage and the Oscar de la Renta gowns you asked for,' an impeccably dressed sales assistant said as she wheeled another rail into the room. Apparently so.

Lorna sighed like a calorie-counter outside a cupcake shop.

'Can I help with anything else?' the girl asked.

'No, we're good.' Anastasia shooed her out of the room. 'We'll call if we need any other styles or sizes.'

'Come on, Ana, try something on already,' Emma said. 'The Givenchy would look awesome on you.'

'Not that this isn't scintillating, but why are we here again?' Mercy asked. 'I can't see any Keys sewn into the lining of dresses.'

'Because Nancy wanted us to check out what Emma and Ana talked about when they were on their own,' Lorna explained like she was talking to a third-grader. 'In case they said anything that could give us a lead.'

A lead . . . Was now the time to tell Lorna about what I'd heard up by the park? I watched her smiling at her little sister as Emma twisted and turned in front of the mirror. I didn't want to dump a bucket of cold water over Lorna's happy. Maybe it was best to stay all clammed up until I knew if it was important. For now at least.

'What do you think? Can you take a picture of me on my cell so I can see the back?' Anastasia appeared from behind the rail in a silk sheath that I was sure I'd seen some starlet pouting in on a red carpet. Not that I still read Living magazines that featured pouting starlets or red carpets.

Much.

'Mercy! Get out of the way!' Lorna hollered.

'Why?' Mercy asked. 'It's not like they can see me.' She waved her hand in front of Anastasia's freckle-sprinkled face. 'See.'

'No, but sometimes ghosts appear in photographs.' Lorna grabbed Mercy by the shoulder, pulling her out of shot as Emma clicked away. 'What is it Nancy says?

Oh yeah – "cameras detect a broader spectrum of energy than the human eye". If you're going to photobomb anyone's pics, can you not go for my baby sister's? I don't want her upset any more by your death than she is already.'

'Okay, okay.' Mercy threw herself down on the chaise longue and lay back lazily. All she needed was someone to feed her a cluster of grapes. 'I'll do my detecting from over here. Nice and safe and out of the way of scares.'

'Did your mom consider calling the fête off?' Emma asked. 'With, um, everything.'

'When she's got $4,000 of ice sculptures on order at Okamoto? I think not.' Anastasia disappeared behind the rail again, tossing the Givenchy over the top and onto the chaise longue like it was from Forever 21. The dress fell through Mercy. She cat stretched, but didn't move.

'You know my mom, Emm – no dead kid's going to get in the way of her social plans. Unless maybe if it was me.'

In the mirror, Emma's reflection balked. 'Has she been ragging you about Harvard again?' Good subject change.

'Again?' Anastasia swirled out into the room in a minidress, the skirt made entirely of feathers, the unflattering bandeau top a size too tight.

'I'm not so sure that's a look.' Lorna circled her, appraising the outfit. 'Even Cara Delevingne would have trouble making this happen.'

'Mom won't let up until I put my acceptance letter in her hand.' Anastasia grimaced at her reflection. 'If I get one that is. I'm pretty sure Harvard has a closed-door policy on girls who dress like dead ducks.' She pulled at the skirt awkwardly.

'Be serious Ana, you're a cert,' Emma said. 'Your dad went there, your grandmother too. Hell, your parents met there. You're basically a Harvard baby. You wouldn't exist if it weren't for that place.'

'Which is why it's even more important that I get in,' Anastasia said.

'Yes, I get that.' Emma pulled her friend away from the mirror. The dead duck dress was not helping Ana's self-esteem. 'But we're still only Juniors. We don't even need to get our college applications in for another year. You have tons of time to wow the admissions people. There's zero point getting all uptight about this now.'

'Of course there is!' Anastasia yanked at the zipper. 'It used to be enough to have an above average GPA and Latin Soc on your résumé, but now everyone's so joiner-inny. Unless you've got a personal essay that makes Mother Teresa look slack, you cannot afford to relax.'

'She does have a point.' Nancy said as she quietly ported into the room. Pop! 'Good colleges are harder to get into than matrix trigonometry.'

'Gee, could you *be* any more Virgo?' Emma struggled to pull out a ginormous dress with layers and layers of netting for a skirt. 'You're freaking Student Body President, and every teacher's favourite pet. It's not like you've got a rap sheet you need to hide. The naughtiest thing you've ever done is sneak out after curfew and climb down your fire escape so we could go drink bottles of Hard Lemonade by the Alice statue in Central Park.'

Emma gave up on the net number and slid out a light Grecian one instead. 'And if colleges refused to let in students who deceived their parents and had a drink before twenty-one, there wouldn't be one full campus in the country.'

'Ohmigod! The fire escape! Can you believe we used to shimmy down that when you slept over after lights out?' Anastasia giggled. 'My parents must have thought they were so smart putting their teenage daughter in a room on the fifth floor. As if I was closeted away from the dangers of the city like Rapunzel in her tower. They still don't know I used to make a break for it most nights.'

'How'd it go at the high school?' I asked Nancy. 'Did you check out Mercy's dressing room – any clues?'

'Not much to report.' Nancy peered over her black frames at the price tag of a Lanvin dress. 'The murder squad are still down there taking prints now. That's about as exciting as it got.' She counted the zeroes and let out a little squeak. 'Your dressing room was so lovely, Mercy. Does the lead always get that whole room to themselves?'

'It depends how involved the play is,' Mercy said, not bothering to move from her daybed to say hi. 'If it's complex – like *Hamlet* – it's important the star gets some alone time. One doesn't want to be interrupted by adolescent chatter about *America's Next Top Model* when one's trying to immerse in the Bard.'

Imagine.

'Well, that room sure looked like somewhere you'd have the space to do that. Bit like this place really.' Nancy took in the thick carpet and square footage. 'It was incredibly nice of people to send you all those flowers and put up a good luck banner too.' Nancy gave Mercy a long sideways stare. 'Everyone must have really been rooting for you.'

'Well, why wouldn't they?' Mercy dangled her arm off the chair.

'Can you help me with the zipper on this?' Emma had moved on to something more body-con. She slid the material together and waited for Anastasia to pull it up.

The zip zoomed up so easily, Ana grabbed for the tag.

'This is a four and it's loose on you,' she said. 'How come you've dropped weight?'

'I wasn't trying to,' Emma said. 'I guess the last few days have just been kind of . . . stressy. Seeing the detective again and all those cops everywhere . . . It, um, brought some feelings back. About my sister and all . . .'

Ana gave Emma a searching look and squeezed her hand. 'Well, you let me know if you need any help U-turning them. That's what I'm here for. This isn't about Lorna. You've got to remember that.'

Ana walked over to the rack and pulled down a chic, simple Stella McCartney dress. 'Mercy Grant's murder hasn't done squat for my waistline, sadly. Maybe I need someone I *like* to get murdered to hit my goal weight.'

Emma threw a cushion at her, smiling again. 'Ana! You mustn't say such things. Even if it's only to cheer me up. Not everyone knows you're joking.'

'Who said I was joking?' Ana smirked. 'And stop hogging the de la Renta, Altman. Play fair.'

'I can't believe the Frost Fête is real!' Nancy said.

'Um, because a group of socialites getting dressed up and drinking Dom P is way less believable than the abominable snowman or the monster of Loch Ness?' I asked.

'No, because in *Upper East Siders* they have the Blizzard Ball every Christmas and there's always some big scandal,' Nancy said. Uh oh, she was about to bounce. Excited Nancy always bounced. 'For example, last season, the Countess's maid showed up in this gorgeous fancy gown, and everyone was all, "Oh! But why are you here? You're only the maid" and it turned out she was actually the Countess's long lost sister and she'd known that *all* along. That was why she went for the job – to meet her family and see what they were *really* like. And—'

We stared at Nancy like she was speaking Vulcan. Her cheeks turned pink. 'So, um, they have a fictional party every year on the show, and I didn't know it was kind of based on something in real life . . .' Her voice trailed off.

'And I didn't know you could work for *TV Guide*,' I said.

'You'll come to the ash-scattering later with me though, won't you?' Emma asked Anastasia.

'I'd be there like a flash if I didn't have a facial booked.' Ana tried a gold beaded headpiece over her flames of hair.

The spotlight above the mirror snapped off – the bulb quietly blowing. Not that there weren't thirty more in the room.

'*Ana* . . .' Emma warned, staring up at the dead light.

'Okay, okay, I'm joking. I'll put on my game face and go "ohh" at the urn.' Ana bobbed her tongue at Emma.

'If ohhing is required. If it's not, I'll stand there quiet as the proverbial mouse and look like the mourningest mourner Midtown's ever seen.'

'Good girl,' Emma said. 'Now which do I go for: the Jenny Packham or the Halston? Drama or slink?'

'You'll look like an angel in either of them,' Ana said. She retied the sash on her dress innocently. 'You do seem awfully bothered about looking pretty this year though. Someone you want to impress?'

'Bite me,' Emma said.

'I don't think that's appropriate language from a young lady who's applied to be the Frick's junior committee co-chair, do you?' Ana wiggled her finger and pretended to scowl. 'Imagine if your mom heard you talking that way.'

'Can you hold the sarcasm and just help me choose already?' Emma said. 'We can't be late for Mercy's service.'

'And I assume they don't have a matinee and an evening performance we can attend.'

'She's funny,' I said, turning to the others. Lorna was nodding, but Nancy's mouth was in a tight little line. The chaise longue was empty.

'Where's Mercy?' I asked.

'She left a few minutes ago,' Nancy said. 'For all her bluff and bravado, I'm not sure she's at the gallows humour stage of acceptance just yet.'

CHAPTER 15

'I've never been to an ash-scattering before,' Lorna said. 'Do you think there'll be sandwiches? I *hate* it when they serve egg sandwiches. There's always some fossily old uncle who gets a yolky bit stuck in his beard and I think I'm gonna retch.' She pulled her perfect features into an Instagramable barf face. 'Also, like, I'm not sure it's even hygienic to be eating when there are grains of Mercy flying about.'

'Seeing as scattering ashes in a public place is actually illegal under New York health-code law, I don't imagine anyone's going to be hanging around for *hors d'oeuvres*,' Nancy told her, patiently, trying to get things between them back on track. The lights of Broadway's giant *Phantom* billboard made a tiny back-to-front poster reflection in Nancy's glasses. 'Motnahp' sounded like a Turkish ballet. 'You can't just spread ashes willy-nilly. After a cremation, they're meant to be buried or kept in an urn somewhere safe, like on a mantelpiece. Not thrown all over the city.'

Which was, of course, why Mercy wanted hers strewn around willy-nilly. Just to be different. Figured.

It was 2 a.m. and a small group of Peabody girls, Mercy's parents and Miss Ballard were huddled on the corner of Broadway and West 49th, dressed in their darkest clothes, and trying their darndest to look like they weren't about to do anything suspicious. Like, I don't know, throw the remains of a recently deceased, gnarlily murdered teenager onto the streets. A few of the girls were wearing their blue *Hipster Hamlet* T-shirts – a picture of Mercy *en character* across their chests, beanie on, hoodie up.

'Major props on the organizational skills though, Mercy,' I said. 'I didn't even write a will to say who'd get my Converse collection, let alone decide what I wanted to happen to my body when it became worm food.'

My idea of being prepared for the future was reading the vocab list for French class more than ten minutes before homeroom hit. My bad.

'Rehearsing *Hamlet* totally made me think about my own mortality,' Mercy said seriously. '"Thou know'st 'tis common; all that lives must die, Passing through nature to eternity."' Urgh, I wished she'd stop with that already. It was like having a walking Lit revision app around 24/7. 'Concepts like why we're here and what our true purpose in life is. Obviously, my role was to entertain – I wouldn't have been given my gift otherwise.'

I kept my expression as blank as one of the shop mannequins in the window of American Eagle Outfitters across the street. Which was not easy.

'So I thought, rather than being buried in some crappy cemetery uptown, why not scatter me here in Theatre-land instead? That way when my parents came to visit my "grave" they'd remember all the joy I brought them – and everyone who watched me perform – instead of standing at some dreary stone slab, feeling sad.'

Mercy walked into the middle of Broadway and spun around, her arms in the air as if she was about to launch into a big musical number. Chorus line at the ready.

'Because, really, is there a more magical place in the entire world?' she asked.

A tour group of German tourists filed miserably out of one of those chain-fest Italian places which are about as authentic as that time Miley Cyrus went punk.

Totally magical, for sure.

'Where did you guys get buried anyway?' Mercy strutted back onto the sidewalk as the lights changed and a convoy of yellow cabs streamed down Broadway towards Central Park. 'Anywhere I'd know?'

Wow, was where you were buried the new what your parents did? If I said West Side would that make me less of a person than Upper East?

'Okay, let's *focus*.' Sergeant Major Radley tried to pull us back into line. Yes, ma'am! 'Mercy, FYI, funerals – and ash-scatterings too, I guess – are a brilliant time for finding fresh leads. Remember how much we discovered about your classmates at yours, Charlotte?' Her smile morphed into a grimace as she realized what she'd said. Yeah, the whole 'discovery' of David kissing Kristin, my high school's head cheerleader, just as the vicar dude was lowering my coffin into the ground? That was an image which had, sadly, been taken with me to the grave.

'Um, so . . .' Poor Nancy. She was one of my all-time favourite people, but it blew me away how someone could be so book smart, yet so socially dumb at the same time. 'So, let's see who's here, shall we? I'll be quiet now.'

I scanned the assembled shivering gang waiting for urn o'clock, like the world's most depressed flash mob. Mercy's teary folks, daughter-holding vase in hand. A couple of girls I recognized from Ana's Great Hall address – that small, slim actively hostile brunette. The Student Body President herself, Ana, and her BFF Emma. Payton, Lilian, Kate, Ryder and Jen, of course – they might be brave enough to admit they hated Mercy four vodkas and three blocks down, but it wouldn't be the Done Thing to not show at a funeral. Especially a pop-up one (so on trend). And Miss Ballard, floating back and forth at the edge of the group, decked out in a black cape, which looked like something she'd swiped from the costume cupboard for *Macbeth*.

'Where did you get the idea for this anyway?' Lorna asked Mercy. 'Doesn't it freak you out that you'll be spread all over – like, from 12th Avenue all the way to FDR Drive?' She tilted her head to the side, in the direction of the green and black *Wicked* billboard. My favourite. 'What if someone tries to resurrect you one day, and they can't because your left toe was last seen blowing into the park in Union Square?'

'Damon Runyon,' Mercy overenunciated, ignoring the MIA toe portion of Lorna's question.

We gave her looks as blank as a new textbook page.

'The guy who came up with the story for *Guys and Dolls*?' she said. Man, could she talk in a language other than Actrish? Mercy relented. 'I read in this old Hollywood magazine how, in the forties, he was cremated,

164

then his ashes were scattered over Broadway from an airplane up above. Cool, huh?'

Not if you were standing under it, no. Imagine walking along, minding your beeswax, then getting a piece of dusty old playwright guy in your eye. Grim didn't cover it.

'Gypsy! Is that you?' a man called out. All four of us swivelled to see Miss Ballard stopping like she'd been shot with a stun gun. She took in the small old man who was waving at her. We ran over to get a better view. He was a snail of a guy, all wrinkly and a tobacco-aged shade of brown.

'Mr Hill!' she said, quickly flipping her composure button to 'on'. 'I haven't seen you in, what, ten years?' And Miss Ballard was way mortified to see him now if that smile she'd quickly plastered on her face was anything to go by. 'How have you been?'

'Good, my dear, good. Working non-stop, of course,' he said, as if that was akin to a nasty five-year cold. 'I did *The Producers* at the St James, spent two summers in London at the Young Vic . . . I've pretty much been solid at the Amsterdam for the last couple of years. I have been lucky.' His white hair only covered the outer edges of his head, like a tufty picture frame.

'Oh, I'm sure it's not luck.' Miss Ballard was looking at him but all around him at the same time. So if some-Living-one saw them chatting, she'd have time to get away before this became A Thing. 'In this business, it's only the truly brilliant stagehands like you who get such consistent work.' Mr Hill smiled at the compliment – a proper genuine one that made even more wrinkles

165

appear on his crinkly face. He'd definitely smoked for too many years. Is that what Edison would have looked like if he'd been allowed to get old?

'But enough about me, how have *you* been? Everyone in the production was *devastated* that you left in such unfortunate circumstances.' He placed a conciliatory hand on Miss B's cloaked arm. 'We had such high hopes for you, Gypsy. I had you pegged as a great talent. What, with some more guidance and stage miles under your belt, you could have been magnificent!'

Miss Ballard's smile slid a feature down. 'Thank you, but for me that dream just wasn't meant to be.'

He shook his head sadly. 'No, coming back to the stage after what you went through would have taken great courage. But surely enough time has passed now for you to forgive, forget and try again?' His hand was still on her arm. She looked at it like it was a fly she wished she could swat away. 'I know everyone in our little world. I could—'

'That's unspeakably kind, Mr Hill, but really that part of my life is over now.' From the corner of her eye, she caught Mr Grant making his way towards them. She had about fifteen seconds to wrap this up. 'It's lovely to see you and I'm so sorry to be rude, but I have to get back to my students. I'm a drama teacher now, you see. And unfortunately this evening is rather upsetting for them all. They need me.'

'No problem! No problem at all.' He took her hand, lifted it to his puckered mouth and planted a delicate kiss.

'I hope she has some sanitizer in that bag.' Lorna

pointed at the purple velvet tote on Miss Ballard's shoulder.

'I bet she's got half of Duane Reade in that bag,' Nancy said.

'Until next time then.' Mr Hill walked backwards, as if he was carrying out a stage instruction. Exit stage right or whatever.

Miss Ballard spun away from him as fast as was polite. 'Mr Grant! Such a sad, sad day!' she said.

Nancy pulled out her notebook and scribbled quickly.

'What was that about?' Lorna asked. 'Did you know she'd been an actress before, Mercy?'

Mercy shrugged, watching Mr Hill take a right by a tacky gift shop, full of I Heart NY ashtrays and plastic Statue of Liberty teaspoons. Who was actually lame enough to buy that crap? And want it in their house? Maybe it was always an 'ironic' purchase. Or a passive aggressive present for someone back home you *really* hated.

'Yes, of course. Miss Ballard talked about it *all* the time.' She bit on a hangnail. 'But she was only in one Broadway show. I'd almost tread more boards. Hers wasn't a résumé I'd have been shouting about either. But then you know how the saying goes: Those who can, do, and those who can't, teach.'

Ouch! Sorry, did I just cut myself on that comment?

'I think it's time,' Lorna said pointing at Mr Grant, who was giving his wife a hug, while the other girls gathered round. Urn o'clock was chiming.

'Oh, goody!' Mercy bounded over to her family and friends.

Totally the appropriate response when the little that was left of your body was about to become the street sweepers' problem.

Mr Grant gave Mrs Grant a squeeze then turned to the crowd. 'I'll keep this short. As you're all aware, we should not be here. If Detective Lee or one of his colleagues catches us, there'll be hell to pay. But it was Mercy's wish that Broadway be her final resting place, so it wasn't one that we could deny her. It was rather hard to deny Mercy anything – as I'm sure you all know.' He gave the group a sad smile.

There was a polite round of laughter.

'You have to laugh at dad jokes at funerals,' Nancy told me, 'even harder than usual.' Solid tip.

'It's an ineffable understatement to say that the last few days have been beyond horrific,' Mr Grant said. 'But now, in this moment, let's take a few seconds to remember Mercy. Her life, her talent, her smile, her strength. When I look around at all of you, in this electric place, I truly feel that, in some way, Mercy's here in spirit.'

'You better believe it,' Lorna said. I tried not to spoil the mood with a giggle.

'Shall we?' he asked, holding his hand out to Mrs Grant.

'Have I missed it? I have, haven't I? I'm so sorry – I was rebuilding the motherboard on my Mac and I totally lost track of the time!' Dylan raced past the orange lights of Tad's Steaks, skidding to a halt and showering Payton's J Crew black tailored pants with a thick film of city grime-stained, sludgy snow.

She glared at him like she wished he was in the urn

too. 'Sorry,' he repeated, smoothing out his T-shirt. Sweet – he'd put on the *Hipster Hamlet* one too.

'Geek,' Ryder said under her breath. The word turned into a little ball of white steam in the freezing night air. Dylan watched it cool and fall to the sidewalk floor.

'No, thank *you* for taking the time to be here.' Mr Grant smiled at Dylan, welcoming him into the circle. 'This is the kind of turnout Mercy deserved.'

'And wanted,' Kate said quietly.

'So – what is it you say on the stage?' he asked Miss Ballard. 'Take two?'

'That's the movies,' she said kindly. 'How about "Let's take it from the top"?'

'Let's do that then.' Mr Grant stood away from the crowd, waiting for a suitable gap in the traffic – of cars and humans – before he unscrewed the urn's metal lid. 'Goodbye, my darling, may you play on these stages forever.'

'This is beautiful.' Mercy's voice wobbled. 'I couldn't have scripted it better myself.'

Mr Grant gently turned the small silver container over and watched as the dust flew out of it, catching on the breeze and travelling through the night air until it mingled with the steam rising from the subway grates.

'Goodnight.' He took Mrs Grant by the shoulder and they silently walked away.

'That was actually pretty moving,' Nancy said, dabbing her nose. Not that it had run since her townhouse blew up – with Nancy inside. 'Good scattering, Mercy.'

'Yes, I think they pulled that off,' she said proudly. 'I'd have liked a little more build-up to the actual opening of my urn, but hey, you can't be the director of every production, can you?'

'You know the Hindus scatter their loved ones' ashes when they die?' Miss Ballard was still staring at the subway steam as it escaped into the cold air. 'They believe that our bodies are given to us as a gift from the gods, so when a person dies, their ashes should be thrown into the sacred waters of the Ganges river, as an offering to higher powers.'

The Ganges and the subway grates of Midtown. Totally the same thing.

'That was an entrance Mercy would totally have approved of, Dylan,' Payton said, her leg still damp. The annoyance on her face hadn't dried off any either. 'Interesting, because I didn't have you pegged as a founding member of the Mercy Grant fan club. Why are you here?'

Dylan shuffled awkwardly, kicking a clump of green snow. I didn't want to think what could possibly have turned it that colour. 'The girl died,' he said. 'Right in front of us. I wanted to show my respect.'

Anastasia coughed deliberately. 'Oh, did you now?'

'Yes, we worked together for four weeks – Mercy was very particular about the props she wanted Hamlet to have. I spent hours programming the control desk so that the spotlight was just strong enough when she made her first big speech. I got to know her enough to want to come down here and say goodbye.' He patted down his thick black hair, but it only stuck up higher.

'But not enough to drag yourself away from your motherboard fifteen minutes earlier?' Emma asked, right eyebrow raised. The others giggled.

'You know, I'm curious too,' Ana said. 'Seeing as you're here in person, Dylan, maybe you can clear something up?'

He nodded helpfully. Uh oh. Big mistake. Huge.

'Why were you so keen to get involved in the play? You don't even go to our school. Don't Malton put on their own productions?' She was like a python plumping its prey before she went in for the kill. 'Was it that you didn't think your technical prowess would make the grade over there? Or was there something else drawing you to us like – and let me think of a simile you can relate to here – Captain Kirk's tractor beam?'

'Ana!' Emma swatted her friend's arm. 'Lay off him, already. He was just being nice.'

Lorna beamed proudly at her sister. 'That's my girl,' she said.

'Yes, Miss De Witt, Miss Cassidy, I suggest you both retire your sarcastic streaks until we're in an environment where it's more fitting,' Miss Ballard said. 'In case it is a genuine "curiosity", Dylan was helping out because his father and I are old college friends. He wanted to get some extra-curricular experience for his Cal Tech application. An example many of you could learn from.'

Miss Ballard eyeballed the group, daring anyone to take her on. 'Now, it's late. You should all be making your way home.'

The girls began to trickle away.

'Should we go back to the Attesa too?' Lorna asked. 'There's not much more to see here. Unless you want to play watch the drunken tourist spew outside McDonald's.'

171

'Just one second.' Nancy was staring at a student I'd hardly noticed before, three lanes of furrows between her eyes. Her target was a tall Asian girl, her hair tied back in a rough bun. 'There's one more thing I want to check.'

Nancy clicked her fingers to get Lorna's attention, then motioned with her hands towards Mercy, who was busy staring with real reverence at the seven-storey pulsing orange and yellow *Hair* billboard opposite the Crown Plaza.

Now there was a production I was glad we'd never have to see her in.

What? Lorna mouthed. 'Oh,' she said, catching on to the fact that Nancy was trying to get her to occupy Mercy and keep her away. But from what?

Nancy beckoned me over. 'Something's been bothering me.' The red artificial lights were turning her hair a crazy colour. 'That girl over there—' she pointed to Bun Girl '—she was in charge of costumes, right?'

Was this the time to admit I had about as much of a clue as I did of the atomic number of carbon? I nodded. Safer to just go along than admit to bad detectressing.

'I need to ask her something. If I was going to possess one of the other girls fast, who's the most likely to talk to her do you think? To ask her about why she made certain decisions about what she dressed the girls in.'

I surveyed Mercy's inner circle who were standing on the corner of 49th, no doubt waiting for someone's daddy's town car to take them home. 'Not Payton. Too feisty. Or Lilian. If you ask anything too clever, people will know something is up.' I bit my lower lip. 'Jen

172

doesn't seem like a total bear-trap.' I pointed at the girl stood next to Payton. 'I'd go for her.'

'I will then.' Nancy looked over her shoulder to check Lorna had Mercy covered. Our newbie was giving Lorna a detailed rundown on how famous you had to be for the lights on Broadway to be dimmed when you died. Lorna couldn't have looked more bored if she was sitting through a fashion show of four season's old clothes. She gave me a small thumbs-up and stifled a yawn.

'We're good to go,' I confirmed, but Nancy was already running at Jen. She jumped into her body, causing her to shiver, her copper curls bouncing.

'What's up, Jennifer?' Payton asked. 'Someone walk over your grave?'

Jen wobbled a little, then ran a hand through her hair. 'Ha ha, very funny.' Which it totally wasn't to anyone but us. 'Can you give me two secs? I just need to talk to . . .' She pointed at Costume Girl. I smiled. Like Nancy knew her name either. She and the hostile brunette were about to cross the road and hail a cab. Nancy jerked Jen's legs into a semi-run and tore after them.

'Hey,' she said, catching up. 'That was *so* moving.'

Costume Girl looked at her like she was a straight A on a test she'd done no study for. Those were clearly the only five words Jen had ever said to her. Or the only civil five. She raised her eyebrows waiting for an explanation.

'I wanted to talk to you before everyone went away for the break,' Jen said. 'I thought you did such an amazing job with the costumes, and I'm not sure, in all the drama over everything that's happened since, anyone's taken the time to tell you that. Everyone looked so authentic.

173

Like they'd stepped straight out of . . . of . . .' Nancy struggled to think of a suitably hipster locale.

'Pete's Candy Store,' I whispered fast.

'. . . Pete's Candy Store!' Nancy said. Who said all those years spent reading the listings in *New York Magazine* were a waste of my time, Mom? Costume Girl's expression did a 360. She lit up like *Hair*. I guess backstage wasn't where there was a lot of the praise was to be found.

'Like, changing Hamlet's costume from the trad black to that cool blue was way inspired,' Nancy said. 'It totally stood out against everyone else's fluoro outfits, and made the whole point about him being the, like, depressed outsider and . . .'

Costume Girl balked at Jen like she'd just claimed the alphabet was her own invention. 'You're joking, right?' Nancy shook Jen's head. 'Man, how did you miss that explosion?'

Costume Girl looked to the hostile brunette for backup. 'So Mercy totally wanted her costume to be all black. Like, reinventing Hamlet as some beanie-hatted, flat white-drinking, Animal Collective-obsessive wasn't stretching the Bard's text? But not having Hamlet in black like Shakespeare suggested was wrong? Actresses . . .' she muttered.

'I sooo missed all this,' Nancy said, trying to encourage CG to spill more.

'So yeah, I went with the all-black Hamlet outfit. Creatively, I thought it was a mistake – like, she was going to disappear into the whole black backdrop Miss Ballard and that freaky-haired Dylan kid had planned out. But, you know, it was basically worth it to shut Mercy the hell up. But then, when we get to the costume rehearsal hours before curtain-up and the outfits arrive, someone's sent us blue leggings, a blue crop-top and a blue hoodie instead.'

'Noooo,' Jen said. 'And Mercy went off?'

'Like a pistol. She was spitting. And shouting.'

'Not the nicest combo,' the hostile brunette added. I was starting to wonder if she wasn't so hostile after all. Maybe just approaching her idiot limit for the year.

'I tried to tell Mercy I'd not done it, but honestly? Like she believed me. Even when I called the costume shop and put them on speakerphone and she heard the sales girl say that they'd received an order for all blue stuff. She was ranting on about how she couldn't go onstage in blue, how it was bad luck.'

It was bad luck to wear blue onstage? Seriously? I was with hostile girl. Actresses . . .

'That's when my knight in shining kaftans came to the rescue,' CG said. 'Miss B told Mercy she was being lame, and that no one believed that stuff since, like, the days when there were actually witches in *Macbeth* or whatever. She totally talked her down.'

'Wow,' Jen said. 'I had no idea. I just thought it looked good.'

'Yeah, except now I do feel freaking awful,' Costume Girl admitted. 'If Mercy *had* had awesome luck onstage, we wouldn't be stood here freezing our butts off on some street corner in a part of town I've not been to since I got too old for Ripley's Believe It Or Not! museum.'

'I'm with you.' Her friend finally flagged down a cab. 'Speaking of which we need to . . .'

'Yeah, we do. But thank you. Thank you for taking the time to come on over,' Costume Girl said. 'The next time I hear someone in the halls say you're just a jumped-up trustie with more Clinique loyalty points than brain cells, I'm gonna put them straight.' Hostile nodded. 'See you around.'

Jen shuddered and took a sudden step forward into the traffic, as Nancy fell out of her body. A cab swerved and honked. 'Hey! You on a suicide mission or what?' the driver asked in a thick Jersey accent. Jen jolted to attention with a small yelp and leap back onto the sidewalk.

It wasn't like Nancy to be so careless. Leaving a body somewhere it needed havoc lights. But then Nancy didn't look like Nancy at that moment. She looked majorly pissed.

'Right,' she spat, trying to pull herself up off the sludgy sidewalk where she landed as she left Jen. 'RIGHT.'

I'd seen Nancy mad before. Mad at Tess. Mad at Edison. Mad at Lorna for having time-management issues whenever she was in a three-block vicinity of any store stocking Burberry goods. But I'd not seen her properly, scary fired-up mad before. Not like this.

She jumped to her feet.

'Nancy?' I asked helplessly. 'Can I . . .?'

'No!' She strode over to where Lorna and Mercy were discussing whether Matthew Broderick's latest billing was big enough at twelve feet high. Lorna turned, pleased to see us, so she could escape the clutches of Thespzilla. Then she got a load of Nancy's face and took a step back.

'Mercy Grant!' Nancy was right up close to her now,

so furious her glasses were slipping down her button nose. She rammed them back onto her face like it was them she wanted to bench for four games. 'Do you want to explain why you've been holding out on us for the last three days?'

Mercy casually examined her hangnail. Woah, ignoring Nancy? That was fighting talk. 'I haven't been holding out on you, Nancy,' she said calmly. 'What on earth do you mean?'

'The peacock feather, your blue costume, the T-shirts everyone was wearing tonight . . .'

Mercy's eyes widened as she suddenly began to get Nancy's drift.

'Someone's been holding up our investigation by not telling the truth,' Nancy said, 'and I'm desperate to know why that person is *you*.'

CHAPTER 16

'Right.' Nancy flipped over HHQ's blackboard from the side where – two days ago – she'd written 'Mercy's murder: suspects' to the clean one. 'Right.'

'*Right*? Is that her new word of the week?' Lorna swivelled her chair towards mine so we could talk without being heard. 'At least she's picked one I can understand for a change. Do you remember when she made me port to Harlem every time I used "literally" wrong and I got all dizzy and confusedy?'

Nancy carefully wiped the board with a yellow cloth. It was spotless already, but she was in one of those Nancy moods where everything had to be done right. And that meant by Nancy and Nancy alone.

'Also, can I just say how happy I am that porting takes no time at all?' Lorna looked over at Mercy who was sitting in HHQ's back corner, biting on her hangnail like she still got hungry. 'Tense journeys where people are mad at each other are the *worst*. It's like, when your mom and dad have a big old shouting match in the car about map reading, or restaurants, or your grandma's cooking, and you're, like, sat in the back, hoping it doesn't go silent. Because that's totally the worst part of any fight. The silent bit.'

Just like now, then? Nancy kept cleaning. Mercy kept biting.

'Right.' Nancy grabbed a piece of green chalk as if it was a cat trying to make a break for its flap.

'Do you think she's stuck in a loop like an old video?' Lorna asked. 'Maybe we need to get Dylan to show us how to unbuffer her or something? He looks smart enough to help with that.'

'Peacock feather.' 'Blue costume.' 'Good luck banner.' 'Good luck cards.'

Nancy scratched words onto the board. I was sooo glad I wasn't that piece of green chalk. It was not long for this world. I wondered if it got to go through a Big Red Door after Nancy murdered it too?

'Hamlet T-shirts.' 'Dressing room flowers.' 'Copy of Macbeth.'

She spun on her heels to face Mercy. 'Anything I've missed?' she asked, tucking her hair behind her ear, not noticing she'd gotten green chalk dust on her cheek.

Mercy shifted uncomfortably in her chair. 'No. Yes. Um, there was the iPod thing – the playlist with all the songs with the whistling. I guess that could fit in too.' She stared helplessly up at the three oblong windows that covered the top of the opposite wall – the ones at street level with Waverly Place outside. The snow was falling again now, thicker than before, sticking to the Village's leafy streets and covering the bottom of the glass pane like dainty cotton wool.

'*Playlist,*' Nancy scrawled on the board.

'What whistling songs?' I asked. Banners and blue I couldn't help with. But songs? Totally. Well, maybe.

'"Tighten Up" by the Black Keys, "My Number" by the Foals, Tame Impala's "Elephant", that one about the "Young Folks" . . .' Mercy recited the list in an exhausted voice.

'Good memory,' I said. 'And good playlist too. Totally in keeping with the *Hipster Hamlet* vibe.' Well, take me down and file me in 'impressed'. Who knew Mercy was a secret muso?

'When something's been haunting you for weeks, Charlotte, it's very hard to get it out of your head,' she said solemnly.

I knew Peter, Bjorn and John were hardly everyone's bag, but I'd never heard them discussed like that before.

'Um, guys.' Lorna spun her chair back to centre. 'I'm sorry to sound snail-mail slow, but it's like you've all switched to another language and forgot to put the subtitles on. What do feathers and flowers and whistling songs that no one – apart from Charlotte and probably Ed – have heard of have to do with Mercy's case?'

The girl had a point. Very nice hair and a very good point.

'Fine. Want to explain, Mercy? Because you know full well, don't you?' Nancy followed her gaze up to the window. The winter sun was beginning to rise now, turning the air outside dove grey.

'I . . . Um . . .' For once Mercy seemed unable to remember her next line.

'Fine,' Nancy said. 'Fine' seemed to be the new 'right'.

She picked an old leather-bound book off HHQ's table and slid it over to Lorna. The title *A History of the Theatre* was written on the cover in swirly golden type.

'Page sixty,' Nancy instructed. 'Take a look.'

'Books? Can't you just tell me?' Lorna wailed. 'Seriously, Nancy, you know I hate books. I've been here for four years and I've still not been able to finish *The Rules*.'

'I'm not plot-spoiling, but no one dies at the end – totally safe to finish it,' I said. The joke fell flatter than three-day-old lemonade. Okay . . .

Lorna stared at Nancy impetuously. '*Fine*,' she said. 'Page sixty.' She thumbed through the thick book until she found it. 'It's a chapter called "Theatre Superstitions". Is that right?' She looked to Nancy, none the wiser. Which I really wasn't either.

'Theatre superstitions? Is that, like, things actors worry will screw up a play if they happen?' I asked.

'Disco. Why don't you read the opening section out loud?' Nancy asked Lorna. 'I think you'll find it sheds a soccer stadium of light. If you don't mind, that is,' she added, trying to show it wasn't Lorna she was sore with. Right now.

Lorna pulled the book closer and cleared her throat. '"Theatre folk are a superstitious breed. Performances being live, many things can, and do, go wrong – from a vital prop not working to cues being missed or actors accidentally injuring themselves on a faulty piece of the set . . . Unsurprisingly in such a creative environment, over hundreds of years, folklore has arisen which explains away – and helps guards players from – these misfortunes. Many actors and actresses genuinely believe that if they adhere to certain rules, they will get through a play unscathed and leave the stage to rapturous applause.

'"Whether turning your back on these superstitions genuinely puts a production and its actors at risk, is the stuff of legend – and interpretation."'

'Sooooo?' Lorna asked.

'So?' Nancy batted her question over to Mercy.

'So . . . you know the way my dream was to be a great actress?' Mercy said in an unsure voice I'd never heard before.

'That was about as obvious as Edison trying to win Charlotte back.' Lorna ran one perfectly manicured finger down the book's ancient spine.

'Go on,' Nancy said.

Wait, *obvious*? Edison was being obvious? And trying to *what*?

'Someone was messing with me because of my dream,' Mercy admitted.

'Elaborate, please.' The chalk was still in Nancy's right hand, waiting for its chance to write.

'It's just as Lorna read,' Mercy said. 'The theatre has all these old traditions – don't do a play on a Monday, don't wish people good luck before you go onstage, players should never wear blue . . . If you go against any of them it's seen as really, really bad luck. As in, something bad could happen to the production or the actors in it.'

Mercy gulped hard, even though she had nothing to swallow. 'I think somebody had researched all of the superstitions. Someone who knew I totally believed them. In the run up to *Hipster Hamlet* I think they were making them happen to me to freak me out.'

What the . . . Somebody had been messing with Mercy for weeks and she'd waited until . . . oh, four days into our investigation to mention that? Now I got why even Nancy had lost her cool.

'How did it start?' Nancy asked, quietly. 'Take us back.'

'A few weeks back, with the good luck cards, I guess,' Mercy said in a quiet voice. 'My eighty-eight-year-old auntie and dumb-as Dylan, they sent them to my house. I figured they were both too clueless to realize what sending a card like that meant in theatreland – bad luck instead of good – so I binned them and didn't say a word. But then I got another anonymous one, signed from my "biggest fan". At first I brushed it off. Then the other stuff started happening.'

The room was silent apart from the gentle tap of the snow on the windowpane. Now she had our full and undivided attention.

'Like?' Nancy asked.

'Like a copy of—' she paused '—*the Scottish play* arrived at my house – addressed to Mom.'

'The Scottish play?' Lorna asked.

'*Macbeth*,' Nancy explained. Mercy bristled. 'What? I don't believe those silly superstitions, Mercy. I'm a ghost – the Living think you can get rid of me by burning some sage or reciting some Latin over my grave, and we all know that's ridiculous.'

Nancy turned to Lorna. 'Actors have this thing about saying the word "Macbeth" out loud. They think it's the worst jinx ever. Something to do with witches in olden times, right?' Mercy nodded. 'So they always just say "the Scottish play" instead.'

'So when some idiot posts a copy to your mom, who opens it in front of you at the breakfast table, she's gonna say the name of the play out loud and wonder why she's been sent a copy,' Mercy said.

Was it just me or was this 'idiot' valedictorian smart?

'Then there was the enormous "Good Luck!" banner that appeared overnight in my dressing room. I thought even people with a basic knowledge of the theatre knew you shouldn't say that to an actor. It's the worst. You're meant to say "Break a leg!" instead.'

Which was ironic, seeing as Mercy hadn't just broken that, but every bone in her body.

'Then I get to the theatre for the dress rehearsal and my room's decked out with flowers which are also bad luck,' Mercy continued.

'How can flowers be bad luck?' Lorna asked. 'I loved getting flowers when I was alive.'

'Because it's like putting a hex on a performer,' Mercy explained. 'You're congratulating an actress on being brilliant before she's had a chance to be. Ditto with any kind of merchandise linked to the play. You don't want to see people wearing a *Hipster Hamlet* T-shirt before there's been one performance of *Hipster Hamlet* – what if it never goes ahead? What if it blows so badly the reviewers can't even be bothered to write one line about it?'

Or your leading lady dies horribly in the first act? That could damage ticket sales.

'That's why you went psycho when someone ordered you a blue costume?' Nancy said. 'Wearing blue is bad luck too?'

Mercy nodded.

'Boy, being an actress is haaard,' Lorna said. 'I thought it was just a lot of standing on a red carpet and hoping you could adopt a child with Brad Pitt, but it turns out you don't just have to learn scripts, you have to memorize all this loco stuff too? Maybe our Rules aren't so bad after all.'

Nancy swallowed a smile.

'So it's the opening night of the show,' I said, 'your dressing room is covered in evil performance-killing flowers, there are nasty good luck signs everywhere, you have to wear your least happy colour, and your mom's said the Bad Word at least twice in your presence. Then—' I was getting it now '—you put on your iPod to try to chill the hell out and some bogus punk has set it to play songs that feature a whole lot of whistling. Which – and I'm no Drama Major – but I guess is meant to put a jinx on you too?'

'Exactly.' Mercy looked broken. 'No one should *ever* whistle in a theatre.'

Boy, someone went to a lot of trouble to mess with her head. It was messing with mine and I didn't even go in for any of this creepy deeky stuff. I mean, I'd walked under a ladder on my way to the F train platform and that had turned out—

Oh . . .

'Then just as I went onstage, I put my hand in my pocket to check for my lucky coin – I'd had it since I played Matilda in second grade – and somebody had switched it for a peacock's feather which is—'

'Bad luck,' all three of us said in union. Bummer.

We silently listened to the snow falling outside. I wondered if Ali would be rushing to the park straight after breakfast like we used to do as soon as school was out. We'd make a snow Simpson – usually Bart because he has the best hair – then, when we were so cold we thought our fingers would never work again, we'd run to Serendipity for a frozen hot chocolate to make us feel even worse.

'You know, in a sick way, I almost admire whoever did this,' Nancy said, shaking her head. 'They went to an awful lot of trouble to unsettle you. Or more – if we look into the hypothesis that whoever was doing all this could have killed you too.'

Nancy pushed her glasses up onto her head like an Alice band and rubbed her eyes. 'Mercy, why weren't you just straight with us from the beginning? Knowing all this could have saved us so much time.'

Mercy sniffed. 'Because I know I come across as a tad overconfident sometimes . . .'

Sometimes? That was like saying the beardy guy from Man Vs Food occasionally enjoyed a sandwich.

'. . . but the truth is that deep down I get insecure too.' She looked up from under her bobbed bangs. 'I know it's impossible to imagine, especially when you've seen me killing it onstage . . .'

Being killed more like.

'. . . but under this actress's brave shell beats the heart of a vulnerable young woman. On a bad day, I'm almost as needy as Charlotte.'

Hey!

'And as you might have noticed, I wasn't *quite* as popular at high school as I originally made out. I'd got on the wrong side of a couple of girls. I know what I want and I go out to get it. I'm not going to apologize for that. When Anastaia acts that way she's "driven" and "cool". When I do it, it only serves to give those higher up the food chain something else to laugh about.'

Mercy hung her head. 'When I came here, I thought maybe I could change that. That death was my clean slate. That I could show my new friends the Mercy I wanted people to see. Not some drama geek whose classmates joke about her behind her back. Or the one who they think it's funny to mess with by going all *Punk'd* on her ass.' Mercy looked at us so very sadly. 'You still like me now, don't you? Even though I sort of maybe lied?'

'Oh, Mercy of course we do!' Lorna bundled her into a hug, nodding up at me to get involved.

'We don't hate you,' I said, gingerly patting Mercy's back. 'You can be kinda pedal to the metal, but that's what makes the world a varied and exciting place.'

Could I sound more Oprah?

'Charlotte's right.' Nancy gave her a squeeze too. 'We're not judgemental here. Everyone who passes through these doors has died in horrible circumstances – no matter how you treated people in life, you didn't deserve to be murdered for it.' She pulled away and looked Mercy straight on. 'Now can we agree on an honesty amnesty, please – no more lies or leaving things out, okay?'

Mercy nodded so hard her beanie nearly fell off.

Nancy motioned to the blackboard. 'We've got plenty

of leads to get going with now.' She fixed Mercy with a stern stare. 'Is that definitely it? You're not hiding anything more?'

'There is one last *little* thing.' Mercy nibbled her nail.

'How little?' Lorna asked.

'So little it might be nothing,' Mercy breezed, 'but I'm going to mention it anyway. Honesty amnesty and all.' She held up her little finger in a Girl Scout promise. Nancy expectantly pushed her glasses back down onto her nose. 'So a couple of weeks back – after the pranks had started already – I got this friend request on Facebook from someone I didn't know called Thespis.'

'Thespis? What kind of name is that?' I asked. He or she sounded like Def Jam's latest signing.

'Exactly!' Mercy said. 'So I Googled him, clearly. I couldn't find an actual Thespis-named guy, but according to Wikipedia, Thespis was the first person to ever go on a stage as an actor in a play – like, in Greek times or whatever.'

I could totally pass Drama class after today. If only I'd been show pony enough to take it.

'I thought it was a really cool username. Anyone who was into the theatre so much they'd have that as their Facebook handle had to be someone I'd want to be friends with. I mean, I'd accepted Marlowe Anderson and I'd never said more than six words to her in real life since she stole my panties during swim class in third grade. I was totally going to friend accept some young, potentially hot guy who was into drama too.'

'How did you know he was a he? And young and potentially hot?' Nancy asked.

'Because people don't just go around friending people they're not into, silly.' Mercy sighed. 'And in his profile picture he had this cool grey mask on, which you could totally tell he was hot behind. Plus he was sent me all these love lyrics – quotes from Shakespeare's sonnets. You've probably never read any but they are *so* romantic. I figured he was totally some guy who'd admired me from afar and was too shy to make his move.'

'So this Thesbos dude – he wasn't part of the superstition pranks?' Lorna asked. 'I'm confused again.'

'I didn't think so. Not at all,' Mercy said. 'But then in the days before I died his messages started to change.'

'In what way?' Nancy was pretty much going to be qualified as a dentist after all the teeth pulling she'd done today.

'The sonnets went and he sent me different Shakespeare quotes instead. One's about—' she paused '—um, death.'

Nancy threw the green chalk on the floor and it smashed into thirty teeny pieces. 'Mercy Grant!' she shouted. 'Honestly, you waited until now to tell us this? When we were on that Broadway stage on your first day here and I said, "Can you think of anyone who might have wanted to kill you?" and you said no. Did you not think right there, right then, that maybe – aside from all the weird pranks and hoopla that had been going on – maybe, just maybe you should have mentioned that some potential psycho on the Internet was sending you daily messages about death?'

Lorna wheeled her chair back a couple of inches. I so didn't blame her.

189

There was a moment-breaking creak as HHQ's door opened and Edison put his head around the half-frosted, half-wood door.

'Guys, you better come quick,' he said, looking straight at Lorna. 'I've been shadowing the cops overnight and they've found something. They're . . . well, they're taking Emma in for questioning again. Lorna, I'm sorry.'

Nancy slowly bent down to dust the ruined chalk off the floor.

I heard Lorna's chair slide across the floor as he hurried to get to her sister.

CHAPTER 17

We ported onto grime-stained steps of Precinct 19, just as the Altmans' town car pulled up. I'd never noticed black could be so clean before, but their limo changed my mind.

The driver opened her door and Mrs Altman slid out as if she was stepping onto a paparazzi-packed red carpet, not some dingy cross street the wrong side of Lex. The roads had been salted that morning to melt any ice. Her tan heel landed centimetres from a deep puddle of sludge.

'Mom?' Lorna said, as Mrs Altman unknowingly strode past the ghost of her firstborn and up the steps into the station. Lorna sadly followed her inside. This was why I never visited my folks – what if I ported into the den and they didn't feel my presence at all? Would that mean they hadn't truly loved me when I'd been around? Or just that they'd learnt to block the pain out?

'Jefferson, it's terribly early in the morning to be summoning us here.' Mrs Altman shed her grape twill trench in a way that would have made a snake jealous, simultaneously brushing off an officer's offer of a coffee with a day-making smile. If I'd lived to 100, I could not imagine her lips coming into contact with one of those white polystyrene cups. 'Payard is not even open for breakfast yet.'

'Wow, that's Oscar de la Renta!' Lorna pointed at her mom's coat. 'Mom has the *best* taste in clothes. She always looks so appropriate,' she said, like 'police station dressing' was a fashion dilemma they covered in *Vogue*.

'I realize that.' The detective rubbed his stubble with his forefinger. 'Actually I have no idea what a "Payard" is, Mrs Altman. What I meant is that I know it's early. I apologize for bringing you folks in like this, but we received some new information last night regarding the case and I wanted to talk to Emma about it, first chance I got.'

Emma had quietly entered the station with her dad. His suit suggested he had a major meeting to attend any second. Surely, even hedge-funders took holiday this close to Christmas?

'Is it anything we should be concerned about, Jefferson?' Mr Altman asked. He had one of those boomy voices that made you trust every word he said. Like he could be saying, 'French fries – they're so awesome for your diet' or 'Teenage boys – never led by what's in their pants instead of their head', and you'd take the fifth on it. Some skanky investment firm should totally hire him to do the voiceovers on their commercials.

'I hope not.' He shifted his focus to Emma who was deeply engrossed in her cell. 'I hope it's going to be a simple case of clearing something up. You're welcome to sit in of course, Mr Altman – Emma being a minor.'

Emma slid her finger over her iPhone screen and dropped it into the black and emerald doctor's bag which she was balancing in the crook of her arm. 'Don't worry, Daddy, that won't be necessary – like you always say, better to try to solve a problem yourself before getting the help of others.' She stood on her tiptoes and planted a light peck on her father's cheek, just above the spot his salt-and-pepper beard neatly ended. 'I've got this covered.'

'Good girl.' Mr Altman lowered himself down onto one of the grey bucket seats and motioned for his wife to follow. Beside me, I felt Lorna stiffen. It was like watching an episode of *The Waltons: the Penitentiary Years*.

'Now, where do you want me?' Emma brushed past Detective Lee, her knee-high black boots clopping across the floor. Black python-look skinny jeans poked out of the top. If Lorna wasn't so thrown she'd totally be telling me where those were from too. 'Or is me finding the interview room the first part of the test?' Emma giggled.

Detective Lee led her down a dingy corridor to another grey room where Officer Stigner was already sitting. 'You two met already.' It was less of a question, more of a statement. He shut the door just as Mercy, Lorna, Nancy and I jumped through.

'So what's this about?' Emma removed her black leather gloves and dropped them into her bag.

'I was hoping you could help us with something.' Detective Lee waited for her to take a seat. 'Before *Hamlet* started, what were you doing?'

'Talking to Anastasia in the dressing room, going over

my lines, booking a table at Plunge for after curtain call –
not that that was on Miss Ballard's list of pre-play warm
up moves.' She flashed him a disarming smile.

'So you didn't talk to anyone before you went onstage?'
He pulled out his small notepad from his pocket and
turned to a half scrawled on page.

'No,' she said. 'Well, yes, it depends where you draw
that line of "before" at, doesn't it?'

'Had there been any tension between the cast lately?'
Detective Lee didn't look up from his pad.

'Not that I was aware of,' Emma leant her elbows on
the table. Her blonde hair was neatly pulled back in
her signature ponytail. 'But teenage girls will be girls.
Especially at somewhere as competitive at Palmer P. I've
heard people fighting over who would be first to get in
the lunch queue before.'

'Was that what you and Mercy Grant were arguing
about?' He finally looked up and locked her eyes. 'Who
would get to the salad bar first?'

Emma slid back in her seat. 'I'm sorry, Detective Lee,
but I don't know what you're talking about. Why would
Mercy and I be "arguing" over salad?'

'I didn't say it was salad, I was just wondering what
the topic was.' He let the statement hang in the air like a
kestrel and went back to his notes.

Emma's phone beeped in her bag. She ignored it.
Whose move was it next?

Stigner balled up her hands. 'It's been brought to our
attention that Mercy had an argument with somebody
just before she went onstage,' she said. Emma stared
at her, her expression as unchanging as the Statue of

Liberty's. 'And the person who brought it to our attention, well, they say Mercy's fight was with you.'

'Do they now?' Emma asked sweetly. 'And what do you think?'

'Mercy? Were you two fighting?' Nancy turned to face her so fast, her hip slipped through the table.

Mercy threw a palm to her head. 'Yes, but it was only a little disagreement, nothing to run to Mommy about. I can hardly even remember what started it now – something about my entrance? Or the music? Or . . .?'

'Mercy! We discussed this!' Nancy said. 'Honesty amnesty, remember? No more lies!'

'I wasn't lying,' Mercy wailed. 'It just didn't even cross my mind that it mattered. Like I said, I was always having a difference of opinion with someone. Emma and I were almost friends.' She looked nervously at Lorna. 'She's not the one. I'm sure of it.'

'Me too.' Lorna walked through the table and to get closer to her sister. 'Look at her – Emma's so vulnerable. She's not capable of something like that.'

Nancy coughed.

'I think you wouldn't tell us even if you were.' Detective Lee pushed back his chair.

Emma laughed again. 'You don't seriously have any reason to think I was capable of killing Mercy, do you?'

Detective Lee picked up a large file from on top of the cabinet behind him, put it on the table and slid it towards Emma. 'What's this?' she asked. 'A transcript of our "argument"?'

'No, it's your school file, Emma,' he said. 'We took everyone's out – it's a matter of course in a wide open

195

case like this – but I have to say yours made for particularly interesting reading.'

Lorna and Emma stared at the crumpled blue folder as if it could give them both cooties. It was three thumbnails thick. Even David's hadn't been three thumbnails thick. What the . . .?

'I guess you don't need to open it. You already know exactly what's inside, don't you?' He pulled the file back across the table and flipped it open. Someone had put Post-its on pages they wanted to flag up.

Lorna didn't move.

'Tenth of September – around three months after your sister died,' Detective Lee read. 'It says here that you were taken to the principal's office for speaking out in class. Thirtieth September, same year – called in again, this time for shouting at a teacher and throwing a chair.'

Emma stared him down, her navy polished mani poking over the edges of her tan crossed arms, daring him to go on.

'Some of the same. October wasn't brilliant either. Quiet November. And then we get to December,' he said. 'Now, correct me if I'm wrong, but December that year was not a good month for you, was it, Miss Altman?'

Emma refused to reply.

'What did she do, Lorna?' Nancy asked.

'I don't know exactly,' Lorna said. 'It was just before I got brave enough to go visit my family. I hadn't come to terms with being dead yet. Everything was so new. If I'd gone to see them, I wasn't sure what I'd—'

'To refresh your memory, in December, you very nearly got expelled,' Detective Lee said. 'In fact, it says here that you did. Then—' he pulled out a lemon piece of paper '—according to this, your parents made a *very* generous donation to the Great Hall restoration fund, you left for the holidays early and come January . . .' He looked back at the first report. 'Yep, seems you're back at school again.

'Now, Emma, can you tell me why you were – sorry – *nearly* were expelled?' He shut the file.

'Of course, but I don't see that it's worth my time, seeing as you clearly already know the answer, Jefferson.'

'It's Detective Lee,' Stigner said.

'It's okay,' he whispered. 'All right, Emma, if that's how you want it.' He opened the file again and found his place. 'In December there was an "argument" – there we go, that word again – with another pupil . . . Marlowe Anderson, it seems. And you, you were so incensed during this, you pushed her at the top of the school steps – she ended up in hospital with a broken leg.' He looked at the report. 'Seeing as you pushed her down two flights of marble, I'd say she was pretty lucky to be alive.'

'I didn't mean to do it.' Emma knotted her fingers together. 'I've been through this a gazillion times with a gazillion people – teachers, therapists, my parents . . . She was teasing me about having to get extra help in math. She said I was just as dumb as my sist— As my . . .' She took a deep yoga breath. 'She said I was dumb. I am not dumb. I saw red and I pushed her. I apologized. I've apologized about sixty-eight times in the last three years. Why are you bringing this up now? What's it got to do with Mercy's case?'

'What it's got to do is this,' Detective Lee said.

'Someone saw you fighting with Mercy before she died. You may have been the last person to talk to her – in a language other than Shakespeare. When someone taunts you, you've been known to – how did you put it? – "see red". Lorna, I wouldn't be doing my job if I didn't bring you in here and ask you about it.'

Emma stopped breathing. The colour faded from her lovely face.

'Lorna?' Mercy asked. 'Did he call her Lorna?'

'Shoot!' Detective Lee realized his mistake. 'I'm sorry, I'm sorry, I didn't mean to . . .' He took a second. 'It's just that you look so much like her, Emma – people must have told you that before.' He looked at her sadly. 'Your eyes are the exact same shade of blue – almost navy. And your colouring, it's . . .'

'It's what? The same as Lorna's too?' Emma's voice was rising. Pink spreading angrily across her cheeks. 'Give me a break, *Jefferson*. Like you ever met her in real life. You only saw her in those stupid school photographs all the papers ran. Like that rag you worked for. How the hell would you know what my big sister looked like?' she shouted, hitting the table. 'Who the hell would know but me?'

Stigner's pen rolled off the table and onto the floor, bouncing twice. The only sound in the room was Emma's ragged breath.

She got a hold of herself. Fast. 'I'm sorry, I . . . It just hurts.' She looked up at Detective Lee with her enormous blue eyes. He was right, they were a perfect colour match. The photographs the Altmans gave the press might not have done Lorna's cover-girl pretty justice, but there was no denying how alike they were – the uber-blondeness, the long limbs, the way they moved like seahorses on the ocean bed. Was it more pronounced now they were both sixteen? Lorna would be frozen this way forever while Emma's features grew and aged.

Detective Lee's face softened and he opened his mouth to speak. Then a switch flicked and his cop gene kicked in.

'That kind of outburst isn't going to convince anyone that you had nothing to do with this.' He slammed the file shut. 'You've got a history of violence, your alibi doesn't stack up, and we know you weren't on good terms with the victim – as her understudy you were one of the few people who had something to gain from her death.' He stood up to walk out of the room.

At the door, he paused. 'We may not have the evidence we need to prosecute the murderer yet, but sooner or later we always get our man – or woman. If you're holding back any information that is stopping us doing that, I suggest you reconsider.'

His footsteps echoed down the corridor.

Emma crossed her arms and stared down Stigner. 'Seeing as he doesn't have anything other than some failed theories and a Jesus complex, I take it I'm free to go?' she asked.

Stigner nodded. Emma pushed back her chair slowly. Was it just me or did she deliberately make it scrape loudly across the tiled floor? Stigner followed her through the door, showing her out of the station.

We stood in silence for a second. Two. Mercy

uncharacteristically quiet. Nancy and I eyeing Lorna, totally unsure what to say. Finally, Lorna turned to us, indignantly flicking her hair over her shoulder, so it landed in a golden wave.

'So, it looks like we have two crimes to solve,' she said. 'Who killed Mercy Grant, and who's framing my sister.'

CHAPTER 18

'Festive.' I took in Washington Square, the park right by the Attesa. Snow was still falling in thick lazy waves, cloaking the concrete with an eye-blinding layer of white. The annual Christmas tree was rocking so many baubles and lights you could hardly tell that, underneath, it was actually green. It almost filled the entire marble arch that marked the spot where the square ended and Fifth Avenue began – which, considering you could probably fit every hot-dog seller in the city in that hole, was not a seasonal miracle to be sniffed at.

'Usually at this time of year, my biggest drama is whether to watch *It's a Wonderful Life* for the sixty-eighth time, eat some Hershey's or actually start present shopping.' I dropped onto an empty bench. Urgh, I could totally feel a wave of woe-is-me threatening to wash. I had to get a life. Which was basically the problem.

'I *love It's a Wonderful Life*.' Mercy sat on the arm of my bench, swinging her legs onto the seat. The girl had less concept of personal space than my fourth grade boyfriend. 'So life-affirming. I totally have a new slant on what George Bailey was going through after the whole dead experience.'

When I wasn't revisiting the urge to push her head through the nearest Living wall so I'd have some quiet for five minutes, I loved how upbeat Mercy was. Somehow she still saw her heinous, bloody death as fuel for inspiration, instead of sobbing/smoking/ stealing Keys like the rest of us. Maybe Miss Ballard wasn't such a sucky guidance counsellor after all. All things considered, Mercy was crazy well adjusted.

She jumped up on the bench and held out one arm with a flourish. '"Each man's life touches so many other lives,"' she quoted the old movie. '"When he isn't around he leaves an awful hole."'

Live from Washington Square: it's Mercy Grant, in the greatest performance of her death! Who needed Netflix when you had your own spooktacular every night?

'What I don't get is, are we the equivalent of George – spying on his old life to see what it's like without him in it? Or Clarence, the guardian angel – someone on a mission from above?' Mercy sat back down, letting the question hang.

Lorna groaned. 'I don't know about anybody else, but this is way too deep for this time on a Monday morning. Especially when a dry double-shot soya latte's out of the question. For, like, ever.'

'It's a made-up story anyway,' Nancy said. 'I've been here for two years and I've not seen so much as a flap of a white feathered wing. Unless you count the glittery ones on the girl students during the orientation parties at NYU, and they don't look so angelic.'

After the greyness and the bombshelling of Precinct 19, Nancy had suggested we head here, rather than to HHQ in case a different backdrop helped us 'think straight'. We were already wiggling all over.

'Debates on the devil-and-the-deep-blue wardrobe options for women when it comes to fancy dress aside, should we not work out our next move?' I asked Nancy. 'Mercy's not getting any younger, you know. Not that she's gonna.'

'Sarcasm really is your favourite form of wit, isn't it?' Mercy studied me carefully. 'Why is that?'

'Look, I know this case has got a little weird.' Nancy threw a worried glance at Lorna who was thankfully too busy staring at three model-tall label-heads walking through the square with Barneys CO-OP bags. 'But if you compare where we are now with a day ago, we're positively overflowing with leads!' Nancy was using her excited voice. Ever since we possessed those cheerleaders, I'd been worried she had the inclination and know-how to break into a 'Go team!' chant at any moment. I was just waiting for her to actually grow the balls to do it.

'Investigating who pulled all the pranks on Mercy would be the logical place to start.' Out came Nancy's trusty notebook. 'The feathers, the script, the playlist, the good luck stuff, reordering her outfit in blue, setting up Thespis's Facebook page.'

Was it just me or did that sound like a summer school of work? Anyway, how did you interrogate an iPod into telling you who programmed it? Maybe we'd need to stop it working, wait for Detective Lee to get so mad he threw it at a wall, then it would rock up at the Attesa and the questioning could begin. Or . . .

'How can you be sure that whoever set up the pranks was the murderer?' Lorna watched the model girls walk under the arch, easily hailing a cab on Fifth. Oh, to be young, hot and visible. 'No offence, Mercy, but we know you upset half the island at some point over the last sixteen years; what if the theatre superstition stuff had nothing to do with your actual murder?'

'That's a really good point, and one that we need to keep in mind the whole way through this investigation,' Nancy replied, a little – it has to be said – dismissively, 'but we've got to start somewhere. Checking out the pranks is our best lead right now. Unless anyone's got any other ideas?'

'Do we know any more about where the cops are with the case?' I asked. 'Apart from where they, um, were earlier?'

Lorna's shoulders sagged. Brilliant, why didn't I just bound over and ask if she thought Emma had the colouring to pull off an orange boiler suit.

'Not really,' Nancy said. 'I gave Edison cop-watching duty and apart from his cliffhanger of an appearance this morning, he's not exactly been feeding back.'

I felt my shoulders sag too. I tried my best to pull them back on up. I thought he said he was going to help out 'again and again until you believe how sorry I am'? As if.

'Detective Lee might just have taken Emma in to psyche her out,' Nancy told Lorna kindly. 'The murder squad will have a list of suspects in exactly the same way we do. Sometimes it's just as much about discovering someone's innocent, as it is about nailing the killer.'

'Except it isn't really, is it?' Mercy said, idly swiping her hand back and forth through the bench. 'One million innocent people aren't going to get me through that Door. One guilty person will.'

It was getting harder to see through the thick snowy air. Uptown, the Empire State loomed like a giant's shadow.

'Okay.' Time to change the subject. 'Pranksville it is. We can't do anything about the good luck cards – the cops took those. I saw Stigner with the baggie.'

'If Detective Lee's as hot as Nancy thinks he is, he'll be getting them fingerprinted right now.' Lorna smiled into her cuticles, pretending to check them.

Nancy didn't know where to look. Aww, cute.

'The iPod playlist puzzle sounds like a task for people with bodies, tech departments and NYPD badges they can flash to jump the line at the Apple store,' I said. Nancy nodded. 'That leaves us with the *Macbeth* script, the peacock feathers, the magical colour-changing costume and the origin of the *Hipster Hamlet* T-shirts.'

Pretty much everything then?

'Um, everyone, not wanting to rain on your parade, but there's one teeny problem,' Lorna said. 'You're kinda relying on the police to be looking into this too. But while *we* know someone was scaring Mercy with all this stuff, the cops don't, do they? Nancy figured it out because she's super-smart. I don't think they have anyone that clever on their team.'

Nancy did an internal cheer-jump. Really, I was going

to have to watch her on that. She'd be making pompoms from the placemats before you could say 'touchdown'.

'They have my iPad though,' Mercy said. 'Much as I'd rather they didn't, if they manage to unlock my journal app, they'll know everything you guys do – I wrote about all the superstitions and the pranks as they happened.' She shrugged. 'I was a really enthusiastic writer actually. I figured that if I got it all down now, writing my memoirs later would be as easy as speaking in iambic pentameter.'

Even Nancy looked confused.

'Ow!' she said angrily as a snowball crashed through her head. 'That tickled!' You did not want to be the small boy who threw that.

Or the very tall boy. 'Sorry, I meant for that to hit the fountain, not you.' Edison emerged from the tunnel of trees to our left. 'Gee, you girls are hard to track down. The next time you leave the house without Mom's permission, could you at least leave a trail of breadcrumbs for me to follow?'

'Edison, nice of you to make the time in your hectic schedule,' Nancy said. 'Tough morning smoking, smoking and . . . sorry, what else is it you do?'

If I thought I was having trouble letting go of the Tess Incident, turns out I had competition.

'Have you been tailing the police all morning like you said you would?' she asked. 'Or helping someone else steal Keys?'

Ouch. Ed kicked a lump of snow across the floor in frustration. Mercy enviously watched as it shattered into delicate flakes. That wasn't even one of his good ghost tricks. Wait 'til she got a load of the zombie-transformation

206

one. Not that I wanted him to be showing other girls how to be a zombie.

'Not exactly,' he said. 'I had this other lead on a case. I hoped it was a promising one, but unfortunately it didn't pan out.'

'Wow, Ed, can you ditch the mysterious loner boy act for ten seconds?' Lorna said. 'It's getting increasingly tired and, FYI, that Cullen kid had it down *years* before you stopped breathing. We're trying to prove my little sister isn't guilty of murder here. You could at least pretend to give a damn.'

'Funny, I thought we were trying to discover who killed *me*,' Mercy said.

'We are, we are.' Poor Nancy. This was basically like herding cats. 'And at the same time getting Emma an out-of-jail card too. Not that she's in jail. Yet. Officially.'

Lorna glared at her with a fever usually reserved for people who tried to hoard at a sample sale. Was it time to mention what I'd heard Emma and Dylan say up by the park? Probably not. That time was going to be round around five minutes past never.

'Can we talk?' Edison asked me. 'It's kind of important.' He brushed his black bangs across his face.

'Like, solving a girl's murder important or more of the standard "Boo hoo, Charlotte, I'm really sorry I helped some girl take your Key" fare?'

This new sensitive Edison was freaking me out. Of course, I totally wanted him to apologize (some more), and tell me the truth about him and Tess (as long as it wasn't bad bad). But I'd rather he did it without getting all *Notebook* on my ass.

Nancy waded in. She liked her soaps on the TV, not playing out in front of her eyes. 'How about you tell me your iDiary password, Mercy, I go to Precinct 19, Throw it into Stigner's mouth and then we'll all be on the same page?'

'Genius. And we'll go to Mercy's and take a closer look at that *Macbeth* book,' I said.

Mercy shuddered at the word, then coughed deliberately. 'Can I get a say in my own murder investigation?'

'Of course you can but—'

Mercy cut Nancy off. 'Now we've got some solid investigating to do, I want to learn some more ghost moves.' Mercy pulled out her copy of the Rules and thumbed the pages. 'Porting: I could totally get a straight A in. We've been up and down the city more often than a mayoral candidate in election week. Possession: you guys have only done that while I've not been around, so it's a grey area, *but* I think that seeing as I have a talent for taking over a character onstage, doing the same to a body will be a piece of pie. Appirating: you've not shown me that one yet either.' She looked at Nancy. 'That only takes us up to Chapter Five – I've been here as many days and I could hardly scare a pre-schooler. What if you guys suddenly got pulled into another dimension and I was left here to fight evil on my own? I'd be ruined.'

'C'mon, is the invisibility thing not enough? Harry, Ron and that Hermione kid were knocked out by invisibility,' Ed said.

'Mercy, we're at a critical point in your case,' Nancy said. 'If we lose an afternoon to apparition lessons now, we could miss something big. And, as teaching Charlotte that skill illustrated, it's not always as easy to control as you might imagine.'

Honestly, you accidentally appear up the world's most visited tourist attraction, when two security guards and a whole lot of CCTV is watching, and you never hear the end of it . . .

Mercy hung her head. 'It's like you guys are all off doing your superhero thing, while I'm left here benched like Lois Lane. Share the special powers already.'

'Fine,' Nancy relented, 'you guys go uptown, look for your mom's copy of *Mac— that* book, and maybe Charlotte and Lorna can teach you something along the way.'

'Nancy, I'm not sure that's such a . . .' Lorna said as Mercy big-time beamed.

'Charlotte, please, can we talk?' Edison tried to touch my hand. 'There's something I have to tell you.'

I actually preferred it when he was porting me onto live subway tracks. At least I knew where I was then. Even if it was getting run down.

'Up, up and away!' Mercy shouted. 'What? It's what Superman says, isn't it? I'm just getting in character. Let's port!'

And we did. Leaving Edison and his 'something important' being pelted with snow.

CHAPTER 19

'It was by your bedside table,' I said. 'I saw it.'

'I just want to make sure it's not in the breakfast room first,' Mercy shouted through the wall. 'That was where we were when Mom opened the parcel.'

'Yes, but that's not where it was last. You just want to sneak all over your parents' apartment and check out if the *Wicked*-sized Mercy Grant memorial painting's been commissioned and hung yet.'

'Do not! Besides, ample as our living room is, there is no way you could fit the *Wicked* billboard in there. That would just be tacky.'

I pushed past Mercy into her bedroom, accidentally passing my arm through one of the gold poles of her four-poster bed. 'The *Macbeth* script is in here!' I shouted, staring at the copy which hadn't moved since we were in the Grants' apartment yesterday. It was still right next to the freaky framed Shakespeare print. Mercy walked through the hall wall to stand by me.

'Don't call it that!' Mercy pulled the bobble on her beanie in horror. 'It's *the Scottish play*. I know you're not superstitious, Charlotte, but I am and we so do not need any more bad luck.'

Bad luck? Seriously, you did not have to explain that concept of bad luck to two girls who'd both had the extreme misfortune of running into teenocidal lunatics, while the rest of their class were busy deciding which top looked cutest for their yearbook picture. A little credit, please.

'Eugh. That copy is older than Edison Hayes' icky sneakers.' Lorna refused to touch the aged leather cover. 'Whoever this Thespis guy is, he must have got it from a rare book shop. I bet it cost more than a pair of Jimmy Choo pumps.' The concept was clearly blowing her mind. 'What kind of person spends all that money on a dirty old book when all they're gonna use it for is a prank?'

'Someone who had a lot of it,' I said, 'or access to Daddy's platinum card.'

'Where *is* Harrison, anyhow?' Mercy asked, peering at the book. 'He's such a broody loner boy cliché. Here, there, off who knows where. What's his deal?'

Edison was not a topic I needed to be getting into with Mercy Grant. She'd have me role-playing my feelings before you could say 'damaged teenage boy with abandonment issues'.

'Okay, Lois Lane, you're up,' I said, trying to distract her. 'You wanted to learn more ghost skills? Let's start with the Jab.'

Mercy lit up like the Chrysler Building. 'Will a Jab mean I can appear onstage during a performance and get to scare people?' she asked, her black bob bouncing.

'Easy, tiger, let's not run before we can possess someone well enough to walk,' I said. 'Lorna, you wanna take this one?'

'Sure, that would be fun.' She'd sat through enough of Nancy's newbie inductions to be able to explain this stuff in her sleep. Not that ghosts *did* sleep. No wonder the Living were so petrified of what we got up to at night when we were bored. When it came to David, chain clanking and sheet pulling had totally crossed my mind.

'Here's how our powers work: ghosts have all this ... kinetic energy. It's, like, what Nancy thinks we're made of now, instead of skin and bone and all those other grisly bits.' She wrinkled her button nose. 'To pull most ghost tricks, all you need is to find the place where your energy, like, goes when it's having a little sit down.'

She closed her long dark lashes and focused. 'Then you kind of wake up the energy, and push it to where you want it. For instance, if you wanted to pull off a Jab, that would be into your fingers.' Lorna wiggled hers. 'Wait until they feel good and buzzy, then bam!' Her eyes flew open and she pushed over the first page of the book. 'You Jab!'

'Cool!' Mercy said. 'That's the kind of thing I was talking about. What's the point in being dead if you can't do all the stuff spirits do in the movies? Or at least spy on hot guys when they're in the shower.' Whoa, why had I never thought of that? 'That looked easy. Plus, I'm so used to taking emotion from deep within me, moving my energy's got to be kinda the same, for sure.'

Haunting and acting: basically the same thing. The

Royal Spookspeare Company was just crying out to be founded.

Without waiting a second, Mercy closed her eyes, pulled her shoulders back hard, and did some funny breathing thing. It must be her pre-show warm-up. She sounded like a rhinoceros drowning in a puddle of mud.

'Hey, Lois, you know those exercises won't work now you're dead? The whole not breathing any more thing – we discussed that *days* ago.'

Mercy's eyes snapped open and she Jabbed the book so hard it flipped over, back cover up. 'You think?' she said.

I had to admit the girl had skills.

'A Jab is basically telekinesis then, just with a really literal name?' she asked.

'Don't be blaming us—' had everyone been raised on *Most Haunted* apart from me? '—we didn't name nothing. We're just here to help you out. Now this book . . .'

We leaned over it, hoping a clue would jump out and say hi!, but it just looked like an old, craggy script. I kinda didn't blame Lorna for not wanting to touch it. I bet it had been touched by a lot of people. Some of them not BFFs with sanitation or soap.

'This is one of those times when we really need Nancy,' I said. She was taking a very long time to Throw that password into Stigner's mouth. I bet I *so* knew why. 'She'd be able to take one look at that thing and analyse the hell out of it.'

Mercy threw her hands in the air. 'Hello? Am I here?' she whined. 'Have you learned nothing about me since I slipped off my mortal coil? What was my passion in Living life?'

'Acting,' Lorna and I sounded like kindergarten kids learning the letter A.

'So what am I an expert in, even in death?'

'Doing lots of those big gesturey things with your arms?' Lorna asked.

'No, *scripts*, silly,' Mercy said.

Uh oh. Lorna might not always seem like an Ivy League cert, but she was crazy-smart in lots of ways. It was really not wise to call her 'silly'.

'Step aside,' Mercy said grandly. If only she had a cape to swoosh. No matter what she did with it, her beanie hat did not scream drama.

Lorna moved away from the fussy gold bedside table like the moody teen I was. 'After I was nice enough to teach her Jabbing too,' she muttered.

Mercy inspected the book, concentrating hard on pushing her energy down her fingers. She Jabbed back to the title page first time. Impressive. 'It was published in 1903, see it says so here. And by the Oxford University Press. Which makes it old and – you're right, Lorna – very expensive.'

'Wait, what's that?' Lorna pointed to some a piece of paper poking out, a couple of pages in. Mercy flipped the script open there.

'It's a price tag for $249,' she said.

'Seriously, you could get some killer heels for that. Some people have more money than sense.' Lorna sniffed.

I peered at the tag. In red ink was a logo and two words: Strand Kiosk. Touchdown.

'What's that? A rope shop?' Mercy asked.

'No, *silly*,' I said, 'it's the most famous bookshop in the city, Strand Books. And it's just off your favourite place – Broadway. The ashes of your little finger might be floating round there this very second.'

'What's their slogan?' Lorna glared at me. If we were telepathic, right now she would so be telling me to lay off the cremation jokes. Honestly, some people were so prissy. 'I've seen it on their canvas totes. So cute.'

'Erm . . . Oh.' My face fell as the memory hit. 'Their slogan is: *18 Miles of Books*,' I said. 'Brilliant. Out of all the shops in all of Manhattan, this Thespis dude had to go to the biggest, hardest to find a clue in one.' Figured.

'It doesn't sound like you could fit eighteen miles into a *kiosk* though,' Mercy said. 'Isn't that where tourists buy those horrible, swirly white ice creams?'

Kiosk, kiosk . . . Oh! I remembered it now.

'That's because you can't!' I said triumphantly. 'Sure, there's the mother ship in Midtown, but there's another, smaller branch of Strand Books uptown – a green hut right on the edge of Central Park. Right where the Upper East Side begins.'

Opposite Bergdorf's. Real near my rock. Which, FYI, I hadn't been brave enough to visit since the day of my funeral. Why did it *still* feel like someone had ripped out my insides, put them in a waste disposal unit and used them as fertilizer when I thought about that?

'Not that I've hung out there heaps,' I said, 'but when I've walked by, there only ever seem to be a couple of guys working the place. And they look like total librarian-level experts. If only there was a way to show them this copy of *Macbeth* . . .' Mercy sucked in her breath as I said the jinxy word. 'I figure they'd totally remember selling something as old and collectory as this.'

'But there is!' Lorna said. 'We just *apport* it. Easy as picking up a Mulberry Lana of questionable provenance on the Internet.' As if Lorna had ever bought a fake.

'Sorry, we could app*what* it?' Mercy said. 'That sounds like something you download in the Apple store.'

'*Apport*.' Lorna gave Mercy her best *who's-silly-now?* look. 'It's another ghost power for you to learn. Apporting is, like, the paranormal transference of an article from one place to another. Or in Mercy-terms, when a ghost moves an object from here to there. Happens a lot in séances, apaz.'

I grabbed Lorna's shoulders. 'Excuse me, but who are you and what have you done with my friend?' I asked.

'Funny, Charlotte, way funny,' Lorna said.

'How does it work? This transference trick,' Mercy asked.

'Kinda like porting, except you imagine the *object* moving instead of you. If you focus on something hard enough, it should go where you want it to.' Lorna stared at the worn teddy bear on Mercy's bed then snapped her eyes shut. It disappeared into thin air. 'Done!'

'Ohmigod! What did you do with him?' Mercy wailed. 'Laurence Olivibear is precious! He's not a piece of apparatus for spectral science experiments!'

'Relax. Turn round,' Lorna said. And there, behind Mercy was her precious bear. Not a clump of fur out of place. Pretty awesome.

'Uh, I've been dead for two months – how have you never shown me this?' I asked. Zombieing, yes. The simple moving of objects around a room, no. Where were these people's priorities?

'In case you hadn't noticed, I don't exactly get to lead the orientation part of the newbie process,' Lorna said. 'Not unless you're around and being nice about it.' She smiled.

'So how come you're such an apporting genius?' I asked.

Lorna flopped down on the bed. 'Well, a few months after I died, I was pretty bummed I hadn't made a will,' she explained. 'All my stuff was just sitting in my closet waiting to go out of fashion. Then Nancy told me about the apporting power one afternoon when we were bored, and I thought, *Hello, I can totally use it to bequeath my favourite bags to my friends!* Like, how I would have done if I'd known I was going to be too dead to accessorize anytime soon.'

Yes. Actually, no.

'So I apported the handbags I loved-loved to my main girls, but the weird thing was instead of being super-happy, they were all *really* freaked out.' She cocked her head to the side. 'Like, Lina actually screamed when she found hers. I do not know why. How can you be scared of gifted Gucci?'

The mind boggled. If only I'd known about this when we were investigating my murder. Maybe I could've apported a credible playlist into my parents' hands, and I wouldn't have been the only kid in the city to have Evan-freaking-escense played at their funeral.

'Who wants to do the honours then?' I nodded towards the book. I really hoped one of the Strand guys remembered it, and that they didn't have an entire stall of $249 *Macbeth* scripts on special that week.

'Me! I want to try!' Mercy's blue hood bobbed up and down as she bounced. 'It's apporting to the Strand Kiosk at the Bergdorf corner of the park?' I nodded. She shut her eyes and did her funny breathing thing. The book slowly lifted in the air. It wiggled for a moment, unsure whether to drop back down on the table or not. Then poof! It was gone.

'Did it work?' Mercy opened one cautious lid and looked around. Her bedside table was empty.

'You're the naturalest natural.' Lorna smiled. 'Must be my expert teaching skills. I'm soo telling Nancy she's no longer queen teacher bee.'

'Shall we join the book?' I asked.

We ported to the edge of the park and found the little green Strand hut where I remembered it – right by a hot-dog seller's cart, billowing steam into the freezing air.

The kiosk was open and jammed with shelf after shelf of awesome books. The snow had stopped falling now and a table of novels had been laid out front of the mini-store. *A Clockwork Orange*, *The Great Gatsby*, *Wuthering Heights* and hey! right on top – there it was. Mercy's *Macbeth*.

'Guys! It worked!' I waved them over. 'Check it out! The *Mac*—Scottish play, it's here.'

'Not bad for my first try.' Mercy was the poster girl for delighted. 'Imagine what I'll be able to move when I get some proper practice.'

'Now what?' Lorna asked. 'Please tell me we don't have to possess someone *again*.' She balked at the only

218

Living person around: a hassled, greying dad in a Yankees cap. He was simultaneously trying to talk to the book guy and stop his two little boys from using a stack of precious Fitzgeralds as snowball target practice.

Even though it was freezing, he looked sticky as hell under his sweater and puffa coat. Not prime possession real estate.

'Agreed.' I preferred to savour the memory of Hot Waiter Guy instead of jumping into Sticky Dad. If that didn't make me a total freak.

'Why don't we Throw the questions into his mouth instead?' Mercy suggested. 'That way none of us have to possess anyone, but we can still talk to the stall guy.'

'Plan.' Lorna raised her arm.

'Do you have an old copy of *Macbeth*?' Hassled Dad asked as she Threw the words into his mouth. 'It doesn't have to be clean.'

As soon as the last syllable was out, he turned to his kids to see if they were somehow behind the trick, but they were too busy making a snow dog on the sidewalk. He looked back at the storekeeper, trying to work out what had just happened. This was very weird.

'You know I did have a gorgeous script a couple of weeks back,' Strand Guy said. 'It was turn of the century, if you can believe those things are still intact. Oxford Press.' He sighed wistfully up at the canopy of white trees above his head. 'Beautiful piece.'

'Isn't that a *Macbeth* on the table?' Hassled Dad clapped his hands over his mouth, his brows linking into one hairy caterpillar line. 'What the . . .?'

Maybe he could put the weirdness down to sleep

deprivation. One of the terror twins was now making the snow dog do a snow doggy do – they definitely looked like they'd stop 99 per cent of parents catching any zeds.

'Oh my!' Strand Guy said, reaching for the *Macbeth* on the pile. 'This is it! Maybe she brought it back? She seemed so desperate to buy it too. Why didn't Daniel restack it on the correct shelf?'

'*She*?' Mercy said. 'Did he say *she*? Is my murderer a *she*? I'm not sure how I feel about that. It's not very feminist, is it? Going around killing other girls instead of helping each other to get ahead.'

'Who?' I Threw to Hassled Dad.

He crouched down and put his throbbing head between his legs and groaned. Aww, I felt kinda bad for using him like this. He looked like a nice guy. I wished we had a memory-eraser trick – a dead girl equivalent of those sticks the agents use in *Men in Black*. Sadly, that was just a movie.

Mr Kiosk snapped his fingers. 'She was so specific that it was *Macbeth* she wanted, even though I had a more reasonably priced *Much Ado* on sale. I assumed it was for a present – she was in such a hurry to buy it, she accidentally left her blazer by the register and I had to run after her to give it back.'

'Um, good memory,' Hassled Dad said quietly.

'OMG, we *so* detected things! Without Nancy too!' Lorna said. 'We know Mercy's prankster could be female and that she has a blazer. Nancy's going to be stoked when we report back. We've found out heaps without her.'

'Yeah, we have my case cracked.' Mercy sarcastically

narrowed her feline eyes. 'We're looking for a woman with a blazer. In Manhattan. That narrows it down *plenty*.'

'I'm sorry,' I whispered to Hassled Dad as I Threw one last question into his mouth.

'What did she look like?' He was so distracted, his kids mashed a snowball into his leg and he didn't even holler. We were Bad People. Very Bad Dead People. 'The woman sounds just like my . . . sister.'

'Well, it was the end of the day and dark, so I'm not sure I could pick her out of a line-up.' Even Strand Guy was looking at the dad weirdly now. 'Long hair, tied back. Could have been anything from sixteen to twenty-six – you know the way young women are these days. It's impossible to age them. Maybe you should ask your *sister* yourself?'

'Ummm,' Hassled Dad managed.

'Guys, the only solid proof we've got out of this little interrogation is that we need to step things up a notch,' Mercy said. 'If we keep floundering around cluelessly chasing books or checking out the alibi of every woman in the city, I'm going to be here until every lead on Broadway's played by a woman.'

She kicked the boys' snow dog to dust. Where'd she learn that trick? One of the boys started to cry, then the other . . . Ohhh, poor Hassled Dad.

'We need to be aggressive – to start actively taking suspects off the table – or we're never going to narrow the list down and find my murderer,' Mercy said. 'We all know Emma didn't kill me, so how about we start by crossing her off Nancy's list? We could possess Anastasia and get Emma to admit she's innocent?'

Lorna's blue eyes flashed. 'Why don't we take one of the others "off the table" first?' she said. 'Payton wanted to be Hamlet, didn't she? Her family live up on Fifth. She must have walked past this kiosk every day. She wears a blazer to school. Or Ryder – didn't she go for Drama Club President, but you talked her down? She's been acting since she was a little kid. She must know all the theatre superstitions too.'

Mercy's eyes shrunk to slits, an idea forming. 'Or we could possess Emma, walk her up to the kiosk and see if the stall guy remembers her? If they don't know her, then we could try Payton next? Then Ryder? Then Kate? We could get through most of Peabody by five.'

'No, no, no! Are you clinically insane?' Lorna asked. 'I didn't lend out my vintage *Vogue* collection when I was alive, so I'm totally not lending out my little sister now I'm dead!'

'Dad!' one of the boys screeched. It was impossible to think with all this noise. Small children were as annoying as a ladder in new tights.

'Beside, you don't even know that would work, Mercy. Maybe the script isn't related to your murder after all?' Lorna said. 'Like, maybe some girl bought the *Macbeth*—' she made a point of enunciating every syllable '—and sent it to your mom just to be nice?'

'Sorry, but teenage girls being nice for no reason is up there with unicorns and mermaids on the list of things I don't believe in,' Mercy said. The boy was still screaming. If only I could apport him five blocks away without upsetting his nice dad.

'Actually, Nancy's always talking about this research

paper she read that proves unicorns could exist,' Lorna said. 'They're basically just horses with a horn on their foreheads – what's so magical about that?'

'Can we go to the zoo?' the kid said. It was more of a demand than an ask. 'I want to see the pandas and the penguins and the peacocks. Pleassseeeeeeeee.'

We all swivelled to look at him. 'Peacocks – there are peacocks at Central Park Zoo?' I asked. I'd not been since I was in diapers – how would I remember?

'Yes, if Scream-a-lot here's to be believed,' Mercy said. 'And if there are, that means the Scottish play script is totally linked to the other pranks. Like, my murderer must have come up here, bought the book, then gone to the zoo to pull out a peacock's plume – two scares for the price of one.'

'No, *silly*,' Lorna said. 'They wouldn't have to. There's a souvenir shop in there that sells that kinda stuff. It's called the Zootique.' Of course she knew about that. Put Lorna near any form of culture and she'd be able to tell you the location of the nearest shop.

Across the street, the red and white flags of the Pierre Hotel jack-rabbited in the wind. Its white entrance was meant to look like a Greek amphitheatre from before-time-began or something. The effect was slightly ruined by the doormen in their pristine black suits and shiny hats. Right now, they were helping two girls hail a cab. Two girls who looked just like . . .

'Hey! Across the street – there's Ryder and Kate right now.' Lorna waved, like they could see her.

'Brilliant!' Mercy said. 'See, this is a Sign. You guys possess them and bring them over here for the book man to see. We can find out whether they killed me or not right now!'

'What are they doing here?' I asked.

'This whole area is Peabody central,' Lorna said. 'We all grew up in a ten-block radius. Ryder and Kate being here doesn't suddenly mean we've caught them red-handed. Sorry.' She lowered her voice, turning away from Mercy. 'Um, Charlotte, I don't feel very comfortable going forward with the whole possession plan until we've run it by Nancy. Like, I know some of her ideas have been *way* off the mark lately, but I do think she should lead the show.'

She was right. I knew that.

'Mercy,' I said, watching Hassled Dad take his he-beasts in the direction of the zoo, 'let's go get Nancy. If she thinks this is a good idea, we can bring their bodies back here later. The kiosk won't close for hours yet.'

'I do love Ryder's coat though.' Lorna squinted across the road, where Ryder was striding purposely to the kerb. 'That has to be Elizabeth and James. You can tell from the detailing. If we do possess them, can I have Ryder so I can feel what it's like to wear tha—'

Lorna never finished her sentence. Because at that exact moment, Ryder's heel gave way, and she fell head first into the traffic speeding downtown.

Above the blaring cab horns, I heard Kate scream.

CHAPTER 20

'Thanks to Sergeant Stigner's inspired suggestion on Mercy's password—' Detective Lee smiled down at Stigner from the podium. Stigner glowed like a sixty-watt light bulb '—we've really moved the case forward in the last twelve hours.'

In between Mercy and me, Nancy made a muffled noise. If I didn't know better, I'd say someone had just stepped on a very small, cute kitten's tail.

'This morning we were finally able to gain access to Mercy Grant's journal app via her iPad,' Detective Lee told the assembled cops of Precinct 19. 'Let's just say, it couldn't have been more illuminating.' He picked up the pile of white papers on the lectern and rammed them untidily into a standard-issue beige folder.

'Stigner: do you want to catch everybody up, seeing as this breakthrough was down to you?' he asked, stepping aside to let Stigner take his spot.

Detective Lee had changed into a clean navy suit, but it was just as crumpled as the last one. Black stubble was threatening to conquer his entire chin and put up a victory flag. Somehow the look totally bypassed down-and-out and screamed screen-god-in-the-making.

'Good job on the theatrical research by the way,' Jefferson whispered as they switched places. 'You're doing an amazing job on this case, Sergeant. It's like you've actually got inside Mercy Grant's head.'

'Or got a ghost who knows her telling you what she thinks!' Nancy mumbled.

'Sssh!' Mercy mouthed at her. Boy, she loved nothing more than people talking about her. Even if it was people talking about her in a 'who hated Mercy enough to kill her?' way. There really was no such thing as bad publicity to some people.

Stigner turned to face the room and grimaced as the harsh lights of the desk projector hit her eyes. She took an unsteady step to the right so she could see the crowd.

'Don't stress it, Nancy,' Mercy said. 'That woman can't even position herself on a podium correctly. Detective Lee won't honestly think she's the brains behind this case.'

Nancy watched Detective Lee take his seat in the front row, her eyes Krazy Glued to his back as he unsuccessfully tried to fold his long legs under the plastic chair.

'Now, now, guys, play nice,' I said. 'It's not Stigner's fault she's got a crime-fighting guardian angel helping her out. We're all here to solve Mercy's murder – it's not an extra credit deal.'

Gee, was it just me or did that sound like a classic Nancy speech? Since when did we play teen movie body swap?

'From reading Mercy's private iPad journal, we've learned that someone was taking advantage of the fact she believed in old theatre superstitions,' Stigner explained. 'Someone who was – we assume – trying to scare Mercy Grant. It goes without saying that our priority now is to discover who this person is, so we can ascertain if they are the murderer or not. Now firstly, I'll give you some necessary background.'

She pointed a remote down at the projector. A picture from *A History of the Theatre*, the book Nancy had been reading, flipped up. 'Sorry if this gets a little like Lit class, guys.'

'Eugh.' Nancy clicked her fingers, instantly turning the sound off in the room and motioned for me to port outside with her. We left Mercy hanging on every word of her homicide on the back bench.

'Sorry for that,' Nancy said. 'I know Mercy loves it, but I didn't think either of us needed to sit through the whole feather/ *Macbeth*/ scary blue list again. We've been "caught up" on it for days.'

A cop sprinted down the corridor as if someone's life depended on him. Nancy's expression turned serious. 'Shoot! I don't know what's wrong with me. I've been so focused on Mercy's case, I completely forgot to ask: how's Ryder doing?'

'Lorna spent most of the night in the hospital, keeping watch,' I said. 'We think she's going to be okay. The doctors kept saying how lucky it was she fell at the split second she did. If she'd tripped in *between* two cars, rather than sort of sliding over one of them, she wouldn't be here now. No way.'

Nancy shuddered. 'What a freaky accident. Her heel snapping like that in the busiest street in the city.'

'You know, I think for one self-obsessed moment Mercy was kinda hoping Ryder wouldn't pull through. Then she'd have one of her old friends here to talk school and drama club with and stuff.'

'*One* self-obsessed moment?' Nancy raised her eyebrow with a smile.

Yep, there'd definitely been a body swap.

'Except Mercy wouldn't have had Ryder here,' I said, 'because kids who've died in accidents go straight over to the Other Side. You taught me that even before Rule One.'

Nancy nodded, looking up at the clock on the hallway wall. 'I guess we should go back inside. Stigner should almost be done with the hocus pocus portion of the talk by now. Thank God we haven't taught Mercy to apparite yet – now seems like the exact sort of moment she'd love to get her glow on and make an entrance.' We strode through the thick grey station wall. Triple tickle.

'. . . no leads there,' Stigner was saying. Nope, not missed a thing. Wouldn't it have been awesome to be able to do this in school? 'Three good luck cards were mailed to Mercy in the week before her death. One from her aunt who lives upstate and has confirmed she sent it. One from Dylan West, a boy from a nearby private school who was working as a stagehand on the production for extra credit.' She flipped through her notes carefully. 'He's admitted he sent the card too and didn't see why it would have offended her.'

'And the third?' Mercy asked out loud.

'The third is from Mercy's "Greatest fan, T xoxoxo" – who we couldn't initially identify,' Stigner said. 'We've run it for prints, but there are none. It was posted from a box on West 4th which doesn't tell us much either – it's not like we bother training CCTV on those things any more.'

The cops laughed. Was that a police force in-joke? Did mailboxes and CCTV suddenly become funny when you got a badge?

'But "T" becomes even more important when you cross-reference the T on the superstition-baiting card with the name of Mercy's newest Facebook friend – a guy called "Thespis".'

'They're *so* two days behind.' Nancy gave a smug sigh.

The cops had stopped joking around now. Stigner clicked the projector and a black and white picture of a guy's face appeared – he was wearing a grey stone mask like a statue from ancient Greece. Yeah, that was creepy.

'Which just happens to be the name of this guy who's a legendary theatre mischief maker or spirit – if you believe in that stuff.'

A low murmur rattled around the room.

'Ugh, she's got that wrong! He was the first *actor*, then he turned into a ghost,' Mercy said.

Even Nancy Fact-Stickler Radley ignored her, looking forward at Stinger instead.

'Here are some examples of the messages Thespis sent Mercy Grant over the last few weeks.' Stigner clicked to the next slide – two old quotes:

Nothing in his life Became him like the leaving it.

Ah, what a sign it is of evil life,

Where death's approach is seen so terrible!

'And here are some more,' she said flipping to the next page of her presentation. 'They're all from Shakespeare. Mercy's favourite playwright.'

Tis a vile thing to die, my gracious lord, When men are unprepared and look not for it.

He that dies pays all debts.

'I don't think any of you need another Lit refresher from me to understand the meaning,' Stigner said seriously. 'Based on this, we're going to assume that Thespis and the person pulling the pranks are one and the same. Whoever sent those messages, the card, the flowers . . . they wanted to hurt Mercy Grant. Certainly psychologically. Whether they hurt her physically as well or not, that's what we need to work on now.'

She nodded thanks to the room and returned to her seat.

'Am I allowed to say I think she handled that quite well?' Mercy asked Nancy.

She shrugged. 'She got her murder mojo going at the end, for sure.'

'The Tech team have been working on this for the last few hours.' Detective Lee returned to the podium. 'Here's what we know: the Facebook account was set up from an email – Thespis.one@pmail.com. About as generic as you get.'

A few cops shuffled in their chairs.

'They're currently trying to track the IP address where Thespis accessed his email and Facebook account to send Mercy those menacing messages.'

'That's such a smart move,' Nancy said. 'I wish we had a Tech team. Right now, I'd trade in Edison for half a geek. HHQ and all the old case files are brilliant, but some computer help would really speed things up.'

'Hey, don't knock the old files,' I said. 'They've been very useful.' Edison? Currently ice cube-sunhat status.

'In the next few hours we should have a list of addresses in Manhattan, right guys?' The Tech guys nodded at Detective Lee. 'Then we'll have a much clearer line of inquiry to move down.'

'So that's where we're at. We've got a team tracking the origin of the *Hipster Hamlet* T-shirts – clearly, we're hoping they were paid for on a credit card, but I'm going to assume Thespis is too clever for that. The *Macbeth* script from Mercy's bedroom has gone missing, weirdly. We're sending a squad up there now to turn the place over until we find it. It might be the key.'

Detective Lee took a step back from the podium and pushed his hands into his pockets. His dark hair fell over his face, as he focused on the room.

'Before you leave today, I want to remind you of one very important thing,' he said seriously. 'Somewhere out there is the person who stole Mercy Grant's life.'

He clicked the remote and a picture of a smiling Mercy filled the screen. Her bob was fresh, her eyes made up and shining. She looked relaxed, happy – like she was ready to take on the world.

'Mercy was sixteen years old. *Sixteen*. Think back to when you were her age. Think about everything you had yet to achieve.'

Detective Lee clicked the button again. A shot of a cute teenage guy appeared – one that had been put through a retro camera app. He was wearing a rolled-up check green plaid shirt, which matched his enormous, dark-lashed eyes. His black wavy hair was almost cheek length and he smiled crookedly at the camera, every bit as happily as Mercy had seconds before.

'Ohmigod—' I turned to Nancy— 'is that . . .?'

Now it was her turn to *sssh*.

'Sixteen-year-old Jefferson Lee had a *lot* yet to achieve,' he said. 'Sure, he'd been on a first date, but it was too disastrous to end in a kiss. He loved plenty of things – writing, grunge, the fact high school was nearly over – but he'd never met a girl he could fall for. He'd not yet been thrown out of his college dorm for playing music too loud, not landed the front-page story of his student paper, nor got his dream job at the *Post* . . . or left it to get his *real* dream job with you guys. It would be years before he could look in the mirror and be happy with the guy staring back at him. And when this was taken, sixteen-year-old me had *no* idea that in about twenty years' time, that cheerleader who'd just turned down his kind invite to prom was totally gonna encounter serious mid-thirties spread.'

Jefferson pushed his hands into his back pockets. 'Remember how it felt to be sixteen. Please. Then think about how the Grant family must be feeling right now – knowing that Mercy will never have the chance to mess up, pick herself up and learn from all her wonderful mistakes.'

He flipped the shot back to Mercy's smiling face and stared at the back of the room, where Nancy, me and ghost Mercy were sitting.

'Four years ago, we – all of us – let Lorna Altman's killer go. For Lorna and every other sixteen-year-old in Manhattan who has everything still to achieve, we need to catch this son of a—' he screwed up his eyes '—this *person* so he or she can't hurt another Mercy Grant. Let's go get 'em. Thank you.'

Wow.

'Okay, I get it,' Mercy said, slowly shaking her head at Nancy. 'The whole tortured soul thing does not do it for me at all. But even I am currently thinking he's *hot*.'

'What?' Nancy innocently tucked her notepad into the pocket of her denim skirt with the smallest of smiles. 'I have no idea what you're talking about. No idea at all.'

'I'm gonna go talk to the drama teacher,' Detective Lee told the burly sprinting cop, as he walked past us and towards the door.

'Want me to come with?' Stigner shouted across at him.

'"Want me to come with?"' Mercy mimicked back. It had to be said, pretty crazy accurately.

'No, I'm good. You focus on the IP addresses, then get me some real bricks and mortar addresses of Internet cafés or whatever. I'll head down to the Village and speak to Miss Ballard. See if she can fill in any information-shaped holes.'

Nancy jumped off the table, dragging me and Mercy with her and followed Detective Lee through the door.

The Village? That was where the Attesa was. 'Miss Ballard must live near us then,' I said. Who knew? Not that we were the *Hey, can I borrow a cup of sugar?* types. 'Should we port there or—'

Nancy walked through Precinct 19's blue wooden doors. 'Or we could we go in the cop car? I've always my entire life and death wanted to go in a cop car.' She tucked her hair behind her ear. 'Now I'm not in the same dimension as my mom, she can't bawl me out for ending up in one. Plus, it kinda makes sense to travel with Detective Lee. That way, we'll make sure we don't lose him on the way.'

Because she was likely to let *that* happen.

'He might get an, um, lead from base camp on the radio while we're in the car.' Nancy walked towards the black Chevy as Detective Lee swung into the front seat. 'We wouldn't want to miss that, would we?'

'We would not,' I said. 'Let's go.'

We jumped through the metal door and onto the black leather back seat. I tried to ignore the fact I was sitting in a Dunkin' Donuts cup that looked like it had been here since teen Jefferson graduated high school. Nancy Jabbed it onto the floor like it was nothing. Awww, Her Geekiness had a crush on a messy Living cop. Three days ago, I would have been bummed if I'd drawn that in a 'most likely to happen before you build a snowman in Hell' sweepstake. But now . . .

'Let's go.' Detective Lee slammed the door, glancing at the back seat in his mirror as he pulled out onto the cross street. He stared right through us.

'Considering he's so thoughtful, he's not as spirit sensitive as I expected.' I leaned forward in my seat as we whizzed down Fifth. 'Look!' I waved my hand in front of his face. 'He's got no idea we're here at all.'

'No, he doesn't, does he?' Nancy turned away to look out the window, as the shopping district blended into Midtown before we finally hit Washington Square, where Detective Lee pulled a left. He stopped by a brownstone, got out and made his way down the basement steps.

'I was hoping he'd put his siren on and floor it.' I ignored the shut door and climbed out through the windscreen. Just because, y'know, I could. Mercy looked at me with a cocktail of pity and respect.

'Oh, Charlotte, do stop dithering.' Nancy beckoned us over to a lower floor flat where Detective Lee was jamming the buzzer. I jumped on the sidewalk just in time to see a purple kaftan-clad figure shutting the door behind them. Miss Ballard.

Inside Miss B's apartment was exactly how I'd imagined. Not that I spent a lot of time dreaming in *Elle Deco*. She'd painted the place the colour of clay pots. A black and white old movie poster of Woody Allen's *Manhattan* took up most of one wall. Turkish lamps hung from every inch of the ceiling. No wonder her clothes mostly seemed to be thrift or borrowed from the Peabody costume department – her electricity bill must be through the roof. It felt as if you were in a Bedouin tent, not just off West 4th.

'I was wondering how long it would take you to come find me.' She moved a blazer off a velvet-covered chair so Detective Lee could sit down.

235

'Tea?' She switched the kettle on without waiting for his answer and threw two green tea bags into a cracked pot. It took her less than two seconds to cross her entire apartment again.

'Miss Ballard, I'm sorry to crash in on you like this, but it would be amazing to get your take on some things if you have the time?' Detective Lee pulled out his note-book not waiting for her answer either.

'Gypsy, please. Call me Gypsy,' she said. Detective Lee tried his darnedest to look like he met girls called 'Gypsy' every day. 'I know, I know, it's an unusual name. Mom loved the theatre just as much as I do. *Gypsy* was her favourite musical when she was expecting me. The fact it's essentially about a stripper . . .' Miss Ballard turned beet red. '*That* she was never able to explain in a way which made me feel like she'd properly thought it through. But I guess that was my mom. Or pregnancy hormones. Go figure.'

'I quite like it.' Nancy took in ceiling lamps. 'I actually can't think of a name that would suit her more.'

The kettle whistled and Miss Ballard passed Detective Lee a mug of something hot and murky. He tried to sit up to take it, but slumped back into the beat-up velvet chair.

'Thanks. Obviously we're looking into a few lines of inquiry at the moment, but I'd like to exhaust all the ones at the school first.' He took a sip of tea and hid a gag. 'Which is why I wanted to talk to you. I guess I might as well come straight out with it: were there any girls who had a particular grudge against Mercy?'

Miss Ballard took too big a sip of her tea and choked a little. For totally different reasons.

'Oh come on!' Mercy said. 'I spent every waking moment down at your drama studio practising my thees and thous. Some loyalty please.'

'To say she was headstrong is something of an under-statement from what we've discovered so far,' Detective Lee said. 'That must have rubbed a couple of people up the wrong way? You – way more than me – know what teenage girls are like. Did you ever catch any of them playing tricks on Mercy?'

Miss Ballard thought for the longest time, as if she was trying to interpret an expecially tough scene. 'No, I can't say I caught anyone doing anything specifically like that. But, like you say, Mercy was headstrong and teenage girls can be . . .' She took another sip of tea.

'Mercy was a star of the drama club – there's no doubt about that,' Miss B said.

'Erm, *the* star!' Mercy corrected.

'And yes, Mercy's ambition didn't always endear her to the entire class. But then we have a lot of ambitious young women at Palmer Peabody, Detective Lee, as I'm sure you're already aware.' She stirred her drink. 'Especially with your history with the school.'

Detective Lee ignored the inference and walked over to the movie poster. The word 'Manhattan' was made from navy skyscrapers, above it a sad-looking couple were silhouetted on a bench below the Brooklyn Bridge.

'This I love, but I've never caught this show.' Detective Lee pointed from *Manhattan* to a framed smaller poster below it. 'Was it any good?'

Miss Ballard laughed hollowly. 'It could have been.'

'Why's that funny?' Nancy asked. 'Is—' she peered at the poster '—*High Society* a comedy?'

'Wait, she's about to explain.' Mercy gently took a seat on the arm of the chair where Detective Lee had been sitting.

'I was an actress once,' Miss Ballard said. 'Have you detected that yet?'

Detective Lee shook his head. Negative.

'I was on Broadway, believe it or not, in that very production.' She looked out of her window, as if she could imagine her faded floral curtains were some distant relation of the ones that hung either side of a Broadway stage.

'Opening night was electric. I said all the right lines, cried when I should, laughed when I shouldn't, didn't trip over the hem of my dress. And the reviews! Detective Lee, the reviews were amazing. I was a "rising star". "Preternaturally talented". And one critic even named me a "Tony cert of the future".'

I could picture her excitedly cutting the reviews out of newspapers now and mailing them to her mom.

'But you know the one thing they never teach you in drama school? Being good can make you bad.' Her smile melted away like snowflakes on your tongue. 'As soon as I had a reputation to lose – even the very beginnings of one – I panicked. I began to doubt every instinct that had gotten me to where I was. Before I knew it, every entrance felt like climbing the Himalayas. Every word like reading the entire works of Chaucer out loud.'

'I have no idea who that dude is,' I whispered to

Nancy, 'but I do know I never want to read him. Out loud or otherwise.'

'Then finally one night I got onstage and I couldn't remember one line. Not one!' Miss Ballard bowed her head in shame. 'If you look me up on YouTube, sadly the whole thing's there. Some idiot with a camera caught it. Me dying. The audience laughing. Me crying as I run from the stage.'

Her hands fluttered to her chest. 'It was the worst moment of my life. And that was when I had to face up to the truth: I did not have it in me to act. I wasn't courageous enough.' She rested her chin on her fingers. 'So I figured, how could I take something good from this? Maybe, if I could help another Gypsy learn from my mistakes, maybe everything hadn't been in vain.' Her eyes clouded over.

'That's *so* sad,' Nancy said. 'Imagine. Achieving your dream then watching it disappear.'

'Pathetic more like.' Mercy slowly got up from the arm and pulled her track top around her. 'Having what you want and letting it go.'

'Anyway, my story's not helping you to catch Mercy's murderer, is it?' Miss B snapped back to the present. 'The true tragedy is that because of her personality, I have no doubt Mercy Grant would have been the success I never was. She had that killer streak. Mercy wouldn't have let anyone tell her she was anything other than a rock star, because that's what she believed she was. And that's what you need to succeed. More than connections or bone structure or talent.'

Gypsy's brick of a phone beeped.

'Who's that?' Detective Lee grimaced at his words. 'Sorry, that was so rude.' He gave her a lopsided grin. 'It's a side effect of the job. You spend 24/7 asking people to explain themselves and sometimes you forget where the job ends and other people's private lives begin.'

'It's okay.' Gypsy stared at her cell screen. 'Teaching is like that too in a way. You spend all your time and emotional energy doing everything for these girls, trying to help them get a start in life . . . Then school ends and they disappear without so much as a "thank you".' She scrolled down her messages. 'Though the one thing seven years' teaching has taught *me* is that they mostly get what they deserve.' She looked up at Detective Lee shyly.

'What I meant was, I didn't think you were being rude.' Her phone beeped again. 'And in answer to your question it's only a message from Dylan – did I mention that his dad's an old college tutor friend of mine? – letting me know he's going back to Peabody to pick up his kit. He was worried in case anyone saw the lights on and thought he was a burglar.' She smiled. 'He's such a good kid. I'm about as technical as my great-grandma. But every time my laptop conjures up some screen in a language I don't understand, Dylan helps me out. He even set up my email account. Can you believe I'm twenty-eight and I was so feeble I didn't know how to do that?'

Mercy muttered a not-so-quiet, 'Yes.'

'While we're on the subject of Dylan,' Detective Lee said, 'didn't you at any point think it was strange that a boy like him would volunteer to work on something like the Peabody Christmas play? I don't mean to judge him by my low standards, but when I was Dylan's age, I was out chasing girls or getting myself in trouble trying to underage DJ in bars on the Lower East Side.'

Of course he was.

'You're right,' Miss B admitted. 'He certainly didn't need to get involved with a production like ours, especially with all the egos involved. But he did it to help me out as a favour to his dad. And for the résumé points. To be candid, I was having trouble finding any of the girls who wanted to work behind the scenes. There are a lot of ugly sisters at Palmer Peabody, Detective Lee, and not many Cinderellas.' She drained her tea. 'So is that all you needed?'

'Oh for God's sake.' Mercy stretched her left hand in the air in frustration. 'I've been a ghost detective for – what? – less than a week and even I can tell when someone's just given us a major suspect. What's with you people?'

'Mercy, don't get ahead of yourself,' Nancy said. 'We don't have any proof Dylan was involved. That man up at Strand, he said the person who bought your *Macbeth* was a girl.'

'And Dylan could have got any woman to buy that for him, even his mom,' Mercy hissed.

She did have a point. A very shaky one, but it wasn't like any of ours were any better.

'Of course we have proof!' Mercy said. 'The cops think my murderer is this Thespis guy, right? Miss Dullard just admitted she thinks Dylan is the biggest Internet geek this side of that guy out of *The Social Network*.'

'Mark Zuckerberg, his name is Mark Zuckerberg,' Nancy said.

'Hey, I thought Facebook was hardly invented when you popped your clogs?' I said.

'That's as may be, but it doesn't mean I don't keep up on current affairs,' Nancy sniffed.

'Whatever.' Mercy rolled her eyes. 'One: Dylan is a web wonder who was freaky and friendless enough to be majorly jealous of someone like me who had a personality they hadn't downloaded from *Computer Dweebs Today*. Two: he was poking around a set he had no right to be on, as chief douche-hand for weeks. Three: it was his job, for God's sake, to make sure the stage set worked, and didn't, y'know, fall down on cast members' heads.' She took a breath. Then remembered she didn't need to now. Which only seemed to fire her up even more. 'Which means, four: if anyone killed me it was Dylan Weirdo West. I just know it!'

She screwed up her eyes, and did her rhino-breathing thing, preparing to port.

'Where are you going?' I asked, like I didn't know. I tried to grab her arm, but she shrugged me off as if I was no more than an annoying fan.

'To do what one of you should have done days ago – find my murderer.' *Pop!* Mercy disappeared from the room.

'Shall we—' Nancy started.

'Don't worry, I've got this one.' I screwed up my eyes.

Someone needed to stop Mercy Grant and her ego before it was too late.

CHAPTER 21

'Mercy?' I called into the darkness. Palmer Peabody's theatre was deserted. Where was she? I couldn't see her. Or Dylan for that matter. Maybe Miss Ballard was wrong. Maybe Dylan had got his kitbag already and left.

There was a shuffling noise to the side of the stage – in the right wing where Dylan had been standing just before the rig crashed down. The shuffling got aggressive. Oh. Either there was a large clumsy raccoon going Tyson on a garbage can back there, or that was Dylan searching for his bag.

'Mercy!' I shouted louder this time. Maybe she'd decided the whole 'confront Dylan' plan was a lame idea and headed back to the Attesa instead? That was what a sensible ghost would do. Except everything about Mercy told me she wasn't currently in Sensible Ghost mode.

An ominous boom reverberated around me as every light in the auditorium flipped on. The sound of the bulbs firing up echoed off the stage and back over the seats in a dull wave. The stage was still set for Act One of *Hipster Hamlet*, the graffitied battlements up, the grey backdrop of a faux-Williamsburg street painted on the wooden slats. The only thing that told you something terrible had happened here was a small area at the front of the stage cordoned off with blue and white police tape – over the spot where Mercy had breathed her last.

Time to get outty. 'Mercy!' I shouted again. Still nothing. 'Mercy?'

A small dark-haired boy emerged from the wings, blinking in the harsh fluorescent light. That KOed the raccoon theory then. Though Dylan's hair did look like he'd spent the last two hours looking for bugs in the undergrowth.

'Hello?' he asked. 'Anybody here?' Dylan's voice ricocheted through the stalls like the bulbs before it. He walked to the front of the stage and gently jumped down to where the lighting desk lived, trying to work out if some weird electrical fault had caused the place to light up like Disneyland. He rubbed between his eyebrows, then flipped a couple of switches. With a more gentle boom, the lights went back down. The stage was dark again.

Maybe it had simply been an electrical fault? Dylan vaulted back up on the stage, careful to avoid the place where Mercy fell.

I should head back to the Attesa. See where Nancy and Lorna were at. If Mercy wasn't here—

Boom. As Dylan reached centre, a lone spotlight hit him, bathing him in severe green light. 'What *the* . . .?' he said.

'Mercy?' I asked impatiently. What was going on? Sure she'd said she was 'coming after' Dylan, but she

244

couldn't be behind this – Mercy was a newbie. Staging this kinda light show wasn't a week-one trick. She didn't have the ghost skills.

There was a click as the smoke machine beside me whirled on and swiftly started spilling white mist across the stage. Dylan jumped, staring at it like it was a wild animal. Even though he was wearing an oversized beat-up black pea coat, he began to shiver hard, hugging his arms around his body.

Uh oh. As a ghost, I might not be able to feel heat or cold any more, but I knew what was going down. The room was getting arctic. Someone was changing the temperature. That was no freak electrical fault or stage trick. That had to be a ghost. And one who'd been *majorly* practising their powers.

'Mercy, if this is you, I'm crazy-impressed, but stop already,' I said. 'You don't know Dylan killed you – this is achieving nothing. Let's go back to the hotel. We'll talk to Nancy. This isn't the way to get your Key.'

As if in answer, the ice machine beside me cranked up a notch. The smoke rising faster than out of an over-heated engine.

Move, Dylan, get out of here now, I pleaded. But he just stood there, as if someone had sneaked up and cemented his navy sneakers to the spot.

'*Wooooo, woooooo!*' A ghostly wail came from the back of the stage. Dylan looked out over the seats as the the-atre's projector flipped on too, dust dancing in its harsh beam of light.

I'd heard that sound before – on the night of Mercy's murder. I knew what it meant. But how was she . . .? The projector swivelled to point upwards, above Dylan's head. Ohmigod, here he came . . .

'*Wooooo, woooooo!*' The projection of Hamlet's dad walked across the top of the battlements. A transparent Ryder, all dressed in white. Now *that* was eerie.

'*Revenge his foul and unnatural murder!*' Ryder's vocoded voice boomed across the stage. '*Revenge his foul and unnatural murder!*' The volume rose and rose until Dylan threw his palms over his ears.

Okay, so I was dead and this was majorly starting to freak *me* out.

'*Murder most foul, strange and unnatural! Murder most foul, strange and unnatural!*' Hamlet's dad chanted.

'Whoever's doing this, it's not funny,' Dylan managed. Someone was spanking him across the face by his own personal version of *Paranormal Activity* and I really wanted them to stop.

'*Revenge his foul and unnatural murder! Revenge his foul and unnatural murder!*' The recording of Ryder's voice looped. It was campfire-story unsettling when you considered the real Ryder was lying in a hospital bed a few blocks away, having just cheated death herself.

Finally, Dylan got his legs to do what his brain was telling them. He grabbed his rucksack and jumped off the stage, making for the nearest door as fast as a guy being haunted could go. There was a firm click as someone locked it. Dylan wrestled with the handle, twisting and pulling it, but the door wouldn't budge.

He ran to the next door, but there was another loud click as that locked too.

'Mercy Grant if this is you, get out here now!' I

shouted. 'You're going to put him in the hospital with Ryder. And believe me, you do not want that – I know from experience that it's way harder to get the clinically insane ones to confess.'

'Dylaaaannnn,' a girl's voice echoed around the room.

'Murder most foul, strange and unnatural! Murder most foul, strange and unnatural!' The projection of Ryder walking back and forth across the battlements moved in small jerky movements.

'Dylaaaannnn,' the voice teased.

Broken, Dylan gave up on the doors. Slowly, so slowly, he turned back to face the stage, and the source of the new voice.

'Wh-who are you?' He tried his best to stand up tall. His pea coat was crumpled, his shoelace untied. 'What do you want from me?'

A low wind began to blow across the auditorium, making the *Hipster Hamlet* posters on the wall flutter. Programmes discarded by parents in their rush to get the hell out of the room skipped over seats. Seriously, *wind*? If I wasn't so mad right now, I'd be asking Nancy for make-up lessons stat.

Mercy calmly walked onto the battlements and stood next to Hamlet's dad.

'MERCY!' I shouted up at her. She looked down at me and shook her head, as she closed her eyes and started to do her weird actress breathing thing. That meant she was concentrating again. Which meant she was about to? Oh, *God*. Had she somehow taught herself to appirate too?

I considered porting back to the Attesa to get some Nancy-shaped backup, but there wasn't time. Who knew what she could do to Dylan if I left them alone for one second?

Mercy opened her eyes as she focused on the farthest corner of the room. From the feet up, her body began to take on a rosy pink glow, like an empty glass being filled with cherry soda – first her fluoro Nikes, then her leggings, then her cropped T-shirt and finally her face, surrounded by that severe bob.

Mercy's ghost appeared on the battlement, next to Ryder's – as transparent as one another. There was a dull thud as Dylan tripped over his laces and hit the deck.

'I am here to revenge my foullll and unnatural murderrr.' Mercy's voice had that spooky echo every ghost's did when we appeared to the Living. 'You . . . youuu killed meeeee.'

'Revenge his foul and unnatural murder! Revenge his foul and unnatural murder!' the recording parroted mechanically.

'Urgh,' Mercy sighed in frustration. She turned to the film of Ryder, clicking her fingers. The projector shut down, the recording stopped and Hamlet's dad faded away.

Clearly this was not a moment where Mercy was willing to share the stage.

'You killed meeee.' She fixed Dylan with an imperious stare. Was it just me or was she enjoying this improv way too much? 'You unscrewed the rig-ig-ig.'

Dylan scrambled back up on his feet. 'No! No, I didn't! Mercy, I'm so sorry. I . . . The rig. I should have been able to stop the rig falling,' he said. 'But someone had tampered with it when I wasn't looking. I didn't notice. I *should* have noticed. It was my job to notice. I'm sorry. I'm so sorry.'

He felt behind him for the door handle. Still locked. Mercy raised her arms and the wind cranked up a knot, blowing Dylan's hair back from his face. He shielded his eyes.

Enough.

I ported up to the fake battlement and slapped Mercy on the arm.

'There! Did you hear that? The poor boy is TERRIFED,' I shouted. 'Look at him.'

Dylan had fallen to the floor and was hugging his knees to his scrawny chest.

'He did *not* do it,' I said. 'He said so himself. He's not capable of handling his own laundry – how would he commit a murder? Stop this now. Let him leave and we'll go solve your murder instead of terrorizing innocent guys, on nothing more than a whim.'

Mercy nodded quietly, the wind slowing. She clicked her fingers and the theatre doors unlocked. The temperature in the room began to warm up again – when Dylan breathed out in ragged breaths, it no longer made small balls of steam in the air. The sound of doors unlocking, one by one, echoed through the room.

Mercy's rosy glow began to drain away, until she was no longer visible. Just a pale spirit standing sadly above the stage. One who looked seriously beat.

Dylan heard the locks and bolted through the nearest door, his kitbag in his hand, the wood slamming hard behind him.

Mercy slumped to the battlement floor.

'Look, Mercy, I get it, really I do.' I bobbed down beside her. 'I know how you feel. But it's no excuse to scare someone like Dylan that badly, especially when you didn't have any solid evidence against him.' Based on the way he'd just acted, I was petitioning to put a big red cross through his name on Nancy's chalkboard list.

'You don't know how I feel!' Mercy hit a frustrated hand on the set – it went clear through the battlement wall. 'You're happy here, with all your friends and your detecting and your living in that weird-ass hotel. I'm not. What if I never find my Key? What if I'm stuck here forever?'

Mercy stood up and pushed her hands into her pockets like she wished the fabric would tear. 'I know I've been making out like being dead is one big breeze, but it's actually pretty scary, Charlotte. Can you remember back to when you were as newly dead as me?'

I nodded quietly. Of course I could. It wasn't so long ago. I'd never forget.

'Why didn't you say anything?' I asked. 'You should have admitted you were finding it hard. There's no shame in that.'

Mercy scuffed her Nikes on the stage awkwardly. 'My mom always told me, "If you're scared, act the opposite." Like, if you pretend everything is okay, eventually you'll believe it so much, it just will be. "Fake it till you make it" – that's pretty much been my mantra my entire life. When I got here and learned that I'd been murdered, well, I figured that if I acted like I wasn't totally terrified by *this*'— she threw her arms around helplessly; it was the least stagey gesture I'd ever seen her make '—maybe

I could get through it. Guess that plan big-time sucked.'
She shook her head. 'Wow. You don't need to be a Psych
major to figure me out, do you? I'm as transparent as,
well, you and me.'

Where had the real Mercy been hanging out since the
lighting rig went down? I didn't get why she'd been hiding her. Real Mercy was way cooler than the other girl
she'd been playing for the last five days.

'Since the rig came down and Nancy gave me the
Rules, I've been practising in my room every night. I'm
sorry for not waiting to be taught all the lessons – it
just seemed like Nancy wasn't crazy keen to show me
anything other than porting. And I wanted to be able to
move my case along if I had to.'

Totally something I could identify with. Props to
Mercy for doing it on her own without having to ask for
the help of the dead boy next door, like me.

'I found my Key.' The truth tumbled out before I could
stop it. 'It took a week, but we found it.'

I had Mercy's full attention now. 'But you're still . . .'

'Here. I know.' My voice sounded strange. Scratchy.
'I don't have my Key any more. I decided not to go
through the Door straight away. You're right – I was
liking it here too much. But then another girl stole it.
Another girl who couldn't solve her case. Tess. She was
called Tess.'

I hadn't said her name out loud since that day. It stuck
on my tongue.

'Ohmigod, Charlotte! *Really*? That's beyond terrible.
Why didn't you say so? No wonder you've been pulling
the sulky teenager act since I got here.'

And there was me thinking I'd been doing such an awesome job of pretending there was nothing wrong.

'And this was recently?' Mercy asked.

'A week after I died. On Halloween.'

For once, Mercy was lost for words. Well, for two seconds.

'And Keys – what happens if someone steals yours? I'm guessing there's not some spectral maintenance guy you took yours to for a spare before this Tess witch took it?'

I shook my head. 'No, unlike your SATs, Keys are pretty much a one-time deal.'

'Do you feel as if you'd lived the life you wanted?' she asked quietly.

Um, direct, much?

I thought for a moment before replying. I'd spent so long on this one, yet now I had to finally verbalize it, I had no idea how to put my feelings into words.

'Does anyone? It wasn't like "write your bucket list" was a school assignment we'd ever been set,' I said. 'I wanted to go to college, watch the sun set over Paris, properly fall in love. Hell, even figure out if I preferred Peeta to Gale. At least in life you get to choose. Brown over Stanford. High-tops over low ones. Sprinkles over plain. Here, that's taken from you. What choices do we have?

'But you know what? It's okay,' I said. 'I'm slowly coming it terms with it. I mean, sure, the afterlife isn't advanced enough to offer a counselling service yet. Especially not one for Post-traumatic Tess Disorder.' Mercy smiled weakly at my joke. 'But when they do I'll

252

be first in the queue,' I said. 'I guess this isn't exactly a common problem. The whole scenario is meant to play out with more harps, endless sunshine and good hair eternities, right?'

I stood back up too. 'I'm not telling you this so you give me Poor You face,' I said. 'I'm just saying that it's still real early in your case. You've spent enough time around Nancy to know that she doesn't leave off until she's solved a murder. I'm her only failure, and I wasn't exactly her fault. Most of the time she's like a big enthusiastic stripy dog with a murderer's bone.'

Boy did that sound wrong. Very, very wrong.

'My point is, I do know how you feel,' I said. 'Really I do. But please don't panic yet. You've got all of us working on your case. And the Living team too – no one's ever had so much help as far as I know. We *will* get your Key.'

'Thanks, Charlotte. You're right. Maybe I am being overdramatic. Which – as you know – is *so* unlike me.' She gave me an evil smile. Ohhh, Real Mercy was way better than Stage Mercy.

'And even if it takes a little while, there are worse people to be stuck here with than me and Nancy and Lorna and . . .'

And him.

'. . . and Edison?' Mercy finished my sentence. 'Look, I'm not prying, but seeing as you've just seen me apparite, scare an innocent boy out of his grubby skin and try to upstage Hamlet's dad, this does seem to be lay-it-on-the-line time. What is it with Edison anyway? Or should I say, with you guys. I've seen the way he looks at you, Charlotte. It's like you're a new Gibson.'

Was it wrong that I instantly liked her 50 per cent more because she could name a cool guitar brand?

'Were you ever . . .?'

'No! Well, yes, almost, but . . .' Man, this was *way* harder to explain than the Tess stuff. I guess because I had at least a snowball's chance of changing the way things were going with Edison – if I even knew which way I wanted them to go. Oh what the hell . . .

'He was friends with her *before*. Edison knew Tess was plotting to steal my Key.'

Mercy's mouth goldfished.

'It wasn't like he helped her or anything—' why was I apologizing for that plankton-feeding pond-life? '—but he could have warned me that some bitch was about to Hamburglar her way out of here. It wasn't like she was trying to steal my lunch money or my third-grade boy-friend. This was kinda major stuff.'

'Um, understatement city. This happened two months ago, right? Have you talked to him about it yet?' Mercy asked.

'Yes, but he won't be straight with me – he won't say why she confided in him. He says it's not "his secret to tell".'

'Wow.' Mercy adjusted her beanie hat. 'Seems Mr Hayes really does have a collection of bones in his closet then. And here was me assuming it was all an act fuelled by his raging Bryon complex. I guess anyone whose jeans are that tight can't be all good.'

I held out my hand. 'Hi, I'm Charlotte Feldman,' I

254

said. 'I don't think we were introduced properly when you died. Good to meet you.'

'Mercy Grant.' She shook it and smiled. 'Nice to finally meet you too.'

CHAPTER 22

'When I said it would be good to get some time on our own to talk, this wasn't *exactly* what I had in mind.' Edison held out his hand to help me out of the garbage bag I'd accidentally ported straight into. Even in Mom's killer DvF heels, I was standing in it up to my knees.

'We're not here for a session with Ricki Lake.' I refused his help, shuffling through the trash and onto the sidewalk, while simultaneously trying to ignore the rat that scurried out with me. Were they spirit sensitive like cats? If so, that was *so* not a piece of information I was sharing with Lorna anytime soon. 'We're here to work, not "talk", Edison. Please remember that.'

'Yes, ma'am.' Edison doffed an imaginary hat in my direction as the rat ran through Mom's boots. His eyes were laughing at me. No matter what his mouth was doing, I could tell.

'Can we just find the place already?' I clumsily moved my feet out of the way of the rat. 'We don't have time to chit-chat.'

After Mercy and I had ported back to the Attesa from

Palmer P, we'd found Nancy bouncing around HHQ like a yo-yo on a string. Precinct 19's Tech team had got their geek on and somehow tracked the addresses of three computers in Manhattan where Thespis had accessed his email or Facebook accounts. Right now, the cops – and, not that they knew it, but Mercy and Lorna too – were looking over the CCTV from a Starbucks near Grand Central to see if they recognized anyone on the footage. While Nancy was tailing Detective Lee to an Internet cafe in Koreatown. Which meant I'd got the fuzzy end of the lollipop: heading to the Lower East Side with Edison to find In the Net, another Internet place we knew Thespis had hung out.

'It's Edison's Living neighbourhood,' Nancy had patiently explained, when I'd said I'd rather sit in a bath of cold porridge than spend an evening with him. 'And you know that area a lot better than Lorna or me.'

Translation: *You'll freak out less in that area than Lorna or me.*

'It'll only take a couple of hours, Charlotte. Max.' Nancy lowered her voice, just enough to sound like she was being polite, but totally still loud enough for Edison to hear. 'Plus, based on his current track record, I can't trust Edison to check out such an important lead on his own.'

She pretended to be all confused when he gave her a death stare. I loved Nancy.

Standing in the Lower East Side now, I took in Stanton Street. In the Net (hello, lame much?) was meant to be somewhere before you hit Chrystie and the park at the end.

257

'So I guess you've been here before?' Edison asked, as we set off down the slightly grubby street.

Been here? When I was alive I'd loved this place. Sure, it didn't have the shine of the Upper East Side, you never saw families here (unless they were very lost tourist ones) like you did in my neighbourhood on the Upper West, and it wasn't as leafy as the Village where the Attesa stood, but the Lower East totally had its charms.

It was full of awesome record shops, hip bars and places for new bands to play – ones who were so just-formed they didn't even have a name yet. Everyone here was in on the secret – yeah, the shop windows might be covered in New York City grime, but it was actually the coolest area in town. And behind every in-need-of-a-paint-job door was someone creating something cool and different.

'Of course I've been here,' I snapped. 'Camels On the Freeway, the band David managed, played at Arlene's Grocery all the time.' I pointed at the artfully scruffy red and yellow venue as we walked past. 'Well, before the headliners sound-checked and the paying customers came in.'

'Oh yes, I forgot about Blondie's "music" career.' Edison smirked, lazily kicking a lump of ice with his black Adidas. 'Camels must be shooting their *Rolling Stone* cover round about now, right?'

Funny. Excuse me, but where did Edison Hayes get off acting like he was so much better than David anyway? Okay, he hadn't said he loved me then put his tongue down the nearest *90210* extra's throat, but it wasn't like he'd been super-keen to fulfil his promises either. I felt my toes tingle. Mr I'm Gonna Hang Around Until You Know I've Changed had been about as AWOL as 100 per cent polyester during Fashion Week lately. And Nancy wasn't the only person who wasn't impressed with his behaviour.

He was such a douche-canoe. The warm, wiggly feeling rose up my calves.

We walked past an arty boutique. Small trees filled the window, handmade jewellery hanging prettily off the branches and leaves. I stopped, trying to take a moment to calm down. There was no point getting into this with Edison now. Not when we had more important things to do – like find Mercy's killer.

'I didn't have you pegged as the window-worshipping type.' Edison stood behind me. 'I thought staring at the pretties was more Lorna's bag.'

A display of gold rings was at my eye level. The metal band on each one had been bent so it spelt out words – 'fate', 'life', 'kiss'.

I tried not to notice that Edison was standing so close that if he stretched out his arms, he could easily loop them around my waist. My legs were warm. Right now the ring I needed would read 'help'.

'The last time you were feeling blue, didn't Nancy and Lorna port you all over for a tour of the city?' he asked.

Blue? What was this, 1958?

'After Nancy and Lorna ported me all over to make me feel less *blue*,' I mimicked, 'you thought it would be fun to drop me in front of a speeding vehicle and onto the track.'

'I ran you over with a subway train and it only made

me like you more,' Edison said. 'Isn't that the biggest compliment ever?'

As soon as he saw my face, he had the decency to cringe. 'You know, I've been thinking a lot since the other night in the park. I'll admit that moment down on the platform wasn't my *finest* hour, but I think I went a bit too far in the opposite direction with the picnic and the flowers.'

Ohmigod, were we seriously having this conversation? He'd basically aided and abetted the girl who'd stolen my future and Edison thought I was mad about getting run down by a second subway train or flowers? What was it with me and idiot men? Even when I was dead, I couldn't avoid them. I spun around to face him.

'A bit too far?' I shouted. 'Exactly what do you think was "a bit too far" about kidnapping somebody, taking them on what you say is a date, refusing to tell them anything they want to know, then getting all bad moody when you are totally the one in the wrong?' I was definitely feeling warmer now.

'Then the next time I see you, you're all, "Ohhh I'm soooo sorry, Charlotte. I promise I'll make it up." Then you disappear when – forget me – *we* need your help with the investigation.' I was ranting now. I knew I was, but I couldn't find my internal brake to stop. 'What is your PROBLEM?'

Edison stared down at my legs. The dimple in his chin deepened as he took a step backwards. 'Er, Ghostgirl, you might wanna—'

'You're like a traffic light boy – you can't decide if you want to stop or go.' I put a hand on my hip. It was classic

Lorna, but who cared? 'You need to work out what you want from death. You can't be all—'

A loud scream pierced the night air. I stared over Edison's shoulder to the other side of the sidewalk and the source of the sound: a blonde girl with thick bangs was pointing right at me, her red lipsticked mouth gearing up for another scream. What was she . . .? I looked down. Oh. Edison had made me so mad, I'd appirated my legs and feet. The poor girl had left Arlene's after a few cans of Pabst to find half a transparent body standing on the street. Awesome.

'Blow,' Edison instructed. Reluctantly, I did as I was told. The energy drained out of me and I became invisible again.

'What?' the girl's boyfriend asked, as he turned to stare at the air where my legs had been.

'I thought I saw a . . . a . . .' she stuttered. 'It might be time to . . .' She held out her arm to hail a yellow taxi as it turned into Stanton. Grey sludge flew up on the sidewalk as it slowed to let them in.

Edison eyed my legs suspiciously, checking they were all appirated out. 'Well if I'd known I had *that* effect on women . . .' He pointed at the bonnet of a burgundy Ford parked right by us. 'Sit?' he asked. I sat.

Edison stretched his arms up into the air, taking a moment too. I just really wished his didn't involve his tight black T-shirt riding up and revealing a couple of inches of Edison flesh.

'I didn't know you were *that* mad at me,' he said finally.

I stared back at the jewellery shop and nodded, nibbling

my bottom lip. Right now my word ring wouldn't be spelling out anything. I suddenly felt end-of-semester tired.

'Why didn't you come talk to me about it, if me not being all over Mercy's case was upsetting you so much?' Edison rested his hands on the bonnet to the left of my legs. His eyes were on a level with mine. I unsuccessfully tried to drag my gaze away.

'Because you're the one who set the Not Talking agenda, not me.' Inside, my chest felt like a block of Swiss cheese, all hard and holey. 'You didn't tell me you knew Tess before. And you wouldn't tell me how. Then you said you'd be around to make it up to me, and you disappeared faster than my feet in front of that girl.'

Edison reached into his pocket to pull out his packet of cigarettes. 'No.' I pushed his hand down. 'You can talk without that.'

He clapped his hands on his jeans instead, looking crazy-annoyed. I wondered if I'd gone too far. If he would port out of here taking all the answers I needed with him. Then I realized, if he did, I didn't care. Edison made me feel like a kid on the first day of kindergarten, for sure – excited, scared, like this was the start of something big – but that wasn't enough. If anything was going to happen to make us, whatever *we* were, us again, he was going to have to give a little. Or I couldn't give anything else.

'Why did you say you'd help with Mercy's case then do the opposite?' I asked. 'Was it because you couldn't be bothered with all the detecting? Or because you weren't really as sorry as you said?'

262

Wow, that was the most honest I'd ever been with a guy. If it wasn't for the decomposition, I'd say death was starting to have a genius effect on my self-esteem.

'No,' he said. 'It was because I was helping out with a more important case.' His hand almost found mine, then pulled away. 'Yours.'

'Excuse me?'

Ed went to reach for that cigarette, stopping himself with a small sour smile. 'Your case, Charlotte; I was trying to help you get out of here. Seeing as you arrived in the Attesa months before Mercyl Streep, I think you top the Other Side waiting list above her.'

Oh. Oh?

'But we know who killed me,' I said. 'We found that out already. Library Girl pushed me onto the subway track because she was obsessed with David. She confessed. You were there. I got my Key.'

'And I was trying to get you another one.' Edison jumped off the car and paced the pavement. 'Look, I know Nancy's case files and books and the Rules don't say anything about ghosts getting a second Key, but I figured that could simply be because no one's ever needed one before.'

He had me now. 'Go on,' I said.

'So I thought, if we don't have previous, maybe some other ghost does. I called in the big guns – I went to the adult hotel,' he said.

'You did what? But . . .' I thought back. On my first dead day, Nancy and Lorna had told me about it. How murdered teenagers came to the Attesa and adults went to another hotel uptown. But I'd never actually *seen* one of them, or it. Nancy had said some kid before me – Jimmy, was that his name? – had badly haunted a guy he thought was his murderer. Like, haunted him in a gnarly, psycho zombie way. Because Jimmy was making a show of himself, he'd been taken from the Attesa by two adult ghosts . . . and never come back.

The crazy thing was, I'd pretty much assumed that was just a story invented to keep us in line. I hadn't let my mind process the idea that there could be a grown-up detective agency working uptown. That was too much, too weird.

But there was. And Edison had potentially risked everything by going up there to talk to them. What if the adults had decided, like Jimmy, he was a loose cannon of a threat? What if they'd done with Edison what they'd done with him? What if he'd lost his freedom on some half-baked mission to help me?

'How did you find it?'

He shrugged. 'Nancy had said it was up near the park. I guessed it was next to a Living hotel the way the Attesa is, so I ported around them one by one until bingo! It took a while. Ages in fact. That's why I've not been around.' He threw me a look which was the closest someone as barricades-up as Edison Hayes would ever get to upset. 'Not because I wasn't keeping my promise to you. Because I was trying to go one better.'

A cab hurtled down Orchard Street. I looked help-lessly up at the old brown tenement buildings with their tangle of zigzagging fire escapes and tried to imagine how someone could have done all that for me.

'And my Key?' I already knew the answer. If there

was good news – if Edison had miraculously been given another copy – he wouldn't have waited until we were stood on a street full of dive bars to tell me about it. This was the closest I'd been to hope in months. But already I could see it disappearing into the distance like the cab's red tail lights.

Edison stopped pacing. 'The adults had never had a case where a ghost had their Key stolen before, either.' He stood right in front of me. 'They said you don't get a go-over. It's one Key per ghost and if you lose it, well . . .' He touched my hand, finding the courage to pick it up this time. 'I'm so sorry, Charlotte. I tried to make everything better, but all I did was make you think I didn't care. I screwed everything up for both of us. Again.'

Before I had a chance to think about what I was about to do – whether it was a smart, sane, Nancy-approved or if there'd be no going back – I put my hands on his shoulders and pulled him towards me. Because right then I didn't care what happened next. Just that I was sitting on a dirty car bonnet, in the snow, kissing a hot dead guy who'd just done the nicest thing anyone had ever done for me. In life or death. This time the tingle didn't stop in my legs. And I knew no amount of blowing out would make it subside fast either.

'So this is where you lived when you was still breathing, then?' I came to my senses and pulled back. Crap, had I actually just done that? I was so not the grab-a-guy type. It'd taken weeks for David to kiss me. Not that *that* relationship was a case study to build on.

Ed's confused frown slid into a smile. His black bangs

fell across his face. It took Olympian levels of restraint to stop myself from brushing them back.

'This—' he stretched his arms wide taking in the whole street '—the bad end of the Lower East Side, is where I grew up. You, rightly, must have a ton of questions. If I can't answer them, how about I show you instead?'

'But what about Mercy's mu—'

'Honestly, that girl can wait.' He grabbed my hand and I jumped off the bonnet. 'If Nancy Drew, the NYPD's sharpest brains and Lorna can't solve her murder, I don't think us goofing off for fifteen minutes is really going to impact on the case, do you?'

Ed pulled me back down Ludlow and onto Delancey – the artery that pushed traffic from Brooklyn into the city. He pointed up at a beige five-storey apartment block above a twenty-four-hour convenience store.

'That's where we lived. The family Hayes.' The way he said it was like he was talking in Technicolor. One layer proud, another sad, two reminiscent for something he maybe never had. I tried to untangle them one by one and figure which mattered the most.

'Neat,' I said. What was the correct response to some-one who was being brave enough to show you where their entire life began to unravel – from their father's death to the discovery that their younger brother had been into some heavy stuff that led to their own death? This was so not a second date conversation.

Not that we were on one.

'I think we both know it's incredibly unlikely to make it as the location for the CW's next big teen show, but thanks anyway,' Edison said.

At the end of the road, the lights on the Williamsburg Bridge twinkled in the icy air. The real hipsters – not the ones from the Peabody girls' play – had taken their guitars, organic coffee and directional hair across it years back, around the same time kids like me felt safe enough to hang out here and the fancy hotel chains set up shop.

I remembered the first time mom and dad let me go across it to Brooklyn on my own. They'd made this big song and dance about how, even though I was a born and bred city kid, but I was way too young to leave the island without them. Then the second I turned sixteen they instantly gave in.

The weird thing about parents is that they don't give you more responsibility when you do something good, or are super well behaved. With them, it's a numbers game. They actually seem to think that something clicks inside you overnight on the eve of your sixteenth birthday. Like, you go to bed a kid and wake up as someone who can be trusted to get the L train from Union Square without getting mugged.

'Of course, back then this was all fields,' Edison joked. I kinda doubted there'd been fields here even when Christopher Columbus showed up.

'So, Ghostgirl, seeing as you've cruelly been ignoring my existence for the last few days, we have some catching up to do.' He steered me back up Ludlow. Clearly this section of Ancient Edison History was drawing to a close. 'Anyone taught you any good tricks lately?'

'Weirdly it's been crazy hard to top "Becoming a Zombie 101",' I said. He had one hand on my shoulder. It was real hard to focus on anything but my one shoulder. Come on, Charlotte, you can do this. Engage brain. Engage just an M&M-sized part of your brain.

'Actually that's not true,' I said, as we walked past a cool barber's off the corner of Rivington. Outside was another garbage bag mountain. This time I was fast enough to sidestep it. 'Yesterday Lorna – of all people – showed me and Mercy how to do this trick called "apporting". You know, when you move an object from one place to another. We moved Mercy's copy of *Macbeth* from her penthouse to the Strand Books kiosk. That was pretty fancy.'

Ed squeezed my shoulder sharply. 'Don't mess with that stuff.' He stopped, his voice suddenly serious. 'I'm surprised Nancy let you do it.'

Hello, this coming from my zombie teacher? It was like a daredevil base jumper telling me to be careful crossing the road. His hand dropped back down by his side as he walked on.

'She wasn't around at the time—' why was he acting so weird? '—plus "How to Apport an Object" is a chapter in the Rules, so it's a totally Radley-approved ghost trick. Unlike with all that ectoplasm-producing jazz you're into, you don't get any spooking points on your licence for using it.'

My joke didn't even raise the smallest of smiles.

'I know I sound like your dad, but you need to be careful with that one.'

We rounded the corner back onto Stanton where more drunk kids were pouring out of Arlene's and trying to find their way home. A guy even taller than Ed fell into a stack of Citi Bikes as he tried to pull his cell out of his Brooklyn Industries duffle.

'It's one thing moving a book across the city, but if you try anything more, it can have . . . consequences,' he said.

'Don't tell me in your darker days, you got so bored you tried to move the Statue of Liberty from the Battery up to Central Park. I know she'd look good up in Sheep's Meadow, but I don't think—'

'Don't joke, Charlotte.' Boy, he was actually bent out of shape about this. 'I've had bad experiences with apporting before, is all.'

And? He was not getting away with it that easily. Not after the entire conversation we'd just had.

I stopped just after the bike rack and faced Ed. 'Hey, you went to the adult hotel for me – isn't that enough to call a sort of honesty amnesty now, Mr Mystery?' I said, stealing Nancy's phrase. 'No more daggers and cloaks and skeletons in your man cave. You've got to tell me what's going on in that head of yours.'

That high-cheekboned, two-day stubbled, cute chin-dimpled head. Man, was I in trouble. I needed to stop with this. And *fast*.

'Okay, okay,' Ed relented. 'There was this one time when I tried to apport a Living person.'

He *what*?

'My brother to be exact. I tried to apport my own brother.' Ed carried on down the street like he hadn't just dropped a bomb. 'He needed to be somewhere – fast. There was a problem with his . . . She—' He picked up the pace. 'It doesn't matter why, but I had to get Matt from one side of Manhattan to the other in the blink of an eye. I thought about possessing him, but he already knew where he had to go and that he had to be there yesterday. I tried apporting him the usual way, by concentrating all I could. But it was no good. He wasn't moving. So I tried something else.'

'Which was . . .'

'Which was that I possessed him, then ported myself to where he needed to be. I took his body with my spirit. Some kind of porting/apporting mash-up trick, I guess.' He stopped and looked at the shop signs around us. 'I helped him, but I was, well, it wiped me out for days. Crucial days as it turned out.'

'I don't understand, why would you need to—'

'We've found it.' Edison pointed across the street at In the Net. A dirty white shack done up to look like a boat. Little plastic seagulls hung inside the windows, which were framed by curtains made out of sails. The owner had painted messy blue waves where the sidewalk ended and the brick of the storefront began.

A large 'CLOSED FOR BUSINESS' sign was out front, alongside one advertising the space to rent. Oh.

'After you,' Edison said. 'Now we're here we better check for clues or Nancy will define ballistic.'

I walked through the window glass. Inside In the Net was deserted. Anchor-decorated wooden tables where computers must have once sat were now dusty and empty. A large sea scene had been painted on one wall, an actual nautical net hung across the ceiling. Behind the disused cash register desk was a large boat's wheel, the kind Jack Sparrow used to steer the Black Pearl.

'So they were playing on "net" as in fishing net, and

"net" as in Internet?' I rolled my eyes. From the looks of things, it was a concept too far, even on the Lower East Side. Edison didn't even try to follow up my joke.

'Whatever sunk the business, this place is no help to us now,' Edison said. 'We better report back.' He walked through the door and out onto the street without looking back. 'You coming?'

Somewhere between the drunk guy, the apporting conversation and this stupid excuse for a café something in Edison had reset. The boy who'd risked everything to get me a new Key had gone into hiding again. I had no idea how to bring him back.

I followed Edison outside.

'You know what, I might hang around here a while.' He pointed a thumb back in the direction of his mom's apartment and began walking backwards. 'You're okay to port yourself home, right? It's not far.' He didn't even wait for my answer before he turned away, hands in his pockets, shoulders hunched.

'Sure. I . . .' As the night air stole my words, I realized he hadn't said if she still lived there. Or if Matt did too. In fact, he hadn't answered the one question I needed unfurled more than anything – about his friendship with Tess.

As I watched Edison's tall black figure join the long shadows of Stanton Street, I realized he might have tried to save me, but he hadn't really told me anything at all.

CHAPTER 23

'I know this is may not be the smartest thing to admit to my boss, but the Upper East Side creeps me out,' Stigner whispered as she walked into the elevator with Detective Lee.

And Lorna, Mercy, Nancy and me. Cosy.

'It's all the not having to think about money,' she said. 'It takes a really strong person not to be an asshole when they don't have to think about money.'

'What floor?' The elevator operator was dressed in a bottle-green suit, patent black hat and white gloves. That uniform must suck in summer.

'The Altman's penthouse, please,' Stigner replied. 'They're expecting us.' She pulled down on her navy regulation sweater uncomfortably and checked her cell.

'Are you sure you want to be here for this?' Nancy asked Lorna, as the operator put his arm through Nancy's belly to press the button marked 'PH'.

'These idiot cops are coming to question my sister for the one millionth time – and in our own *home*? Of course I want to be here for this.' Lorna stared down Stigner.

'This girl *so* has it in for my sister,' Lorna said. 'All she seems to talk about is where Emma was, what Emma did, why Emma could have hurt Mercy. We know she's wasting everyone's time, right? She's a terrible detective.'

'No, she isn't.' Nancy watched the numbers above the doors rise as we sped from floor to floor. 'She's just trying to do her job. Like us.'

'All I'm saying is that I may be dead, but I'm still a fair person who doesn't victimize innocent people and knows how to dress. Which is more than I can say for *her*.' Lorna crossed her arms defiantly over her chest. Meow.

Seven people – three Living, four not – collectively sighed in relief as the bell pinged for the penthouse. As the polished silver elevator doors slid open, Mr Altman's handsome face appeared. He was wearing a fancy pistachio blazer, crisp white shirt and navy tailored pants. Did the man ever just loaf around in sweats? Lorna gripped herself a little more tightly.

'Jefferson, hello.' He firmly shook Detective Lee's hand. 'Sergeant Stigner.' He paused, unsure whether to kiss her cheek, before deciding it wasn't that kind of social situation. 'Emma is in the living room with her mother. Come through.'

An Altman full house. Exactly what Lorna needed when she was feeling this defensive.

'I trust this isn't going to take long?' he asked.

Detective Lee shook his head. 'Thank you so much for seeing us today, Mr Altman. It's really kind of you. We had a couple more questions for Emma, so I thought it might be easier to talk here, rather than dragging her down the station and scaring her unnecessari—'

273

A black-framed photograph filling the hallway wall made him stop short. The girl in it had long silky blonde hair, twinkling blue eyes and the kind of smile which somehow simultaneously floored parents, teachers *and* guys. It looked like a shot from a professional glossy modelling campaign.

My eyes found Lorna nervously, but she seemed to be taking a whole heap more interest in the state of her cuticles than in the ginormous picture of her hanging in her family home.

'Oh, I *love* this shot of you,' Mercy said. 'Lorna, you look gorgeous. If you were trying out for a role, you could totally send this with your résumé. Why didn't your parents release this to the media when you were killed? The one of you in your Peabody uniform was cute, but this is so much more sophisticated.'

'Sophistication being the criteria for families when they're picking out police shots of the recently deceased,' Nancy said.

'I just . . . Sorry, I wasn't expecting to see her picture. It wasn't here when I came to the house before and . . .' Detective Lee shuffled awkwardly. It didn't suit him. 'I can't get over how much Emma's grown to look like her.'

'My wife and I think that every day.' Mr Altman smiled sadly at the shot. 'We had this blown up and framed last year. I know it's ridiculous, but it took that long to feel ready to see her every day. It will be five years since it happened in May. Five, Jefferson. Can you believe that?'

Detective Lee stroked his stubble like it had only just occurred to him that maybe he should have shaved.

'It seems like a second ago she was heading to the prom. If only I'd been one of those overprotective fathers who doesn't let their children go to that sort of thing, maybe she'd still be . . .' Mr Altman adjusted his cufflinks. 'Well, it's too late to think like that now. I've thought about it enough.' He motioned to a door down the white carpeted hallway. 'Shall we?'

'You had a lovely home,' Nancy said taking in the vanilla-white hallway walls peppered with photographs of the Altman family, all in the same stylish black frames. Two little blonde angels opening their mountain of presents one Christmas morning. Emma – or was it Lorna? – learning to ride a pony. Mr and Mrs Altman's *Brides*-worthy wedding day shot, taken on some far away beach. Emma's first day at school. 'It's so beautifully decorated. Your mom has great taste.'

'Uh huh.' Lorna swept past us and followed her dad and the cops into the family room. Emma and Mrs Altman were poised on a caramel couch as if they were waiting for their slot with the Dean of Admissions at Princeton, not to be grilled about a murder inquiry.

'No, don't get up.' Detective Lee shooed them to stay put and took a seat opposite on a darker leather ottoman. He misjudged how low it was and just saved himself from wobbling off the stool and onto the floor. Easy.

'I wanted to ask you something about the play, Emma.' Detective Lee straightened himself up. 'You guys had special *Hipster Hamlet* T-shirts made, didn't you? I've seen some of the girls wearing them since.'

Stigner hovered next to him. I figured scared if she sat down someone would realize she didn't have the salary to afford a ninth of that sofa and throw her out. It was weird the way money said just as much about the people who didn't have it as the ones who did.

'Yes, someone suggested it'd be a cool idea to get our own merchandise made.' Emma smoothed down the pussy bow of her sleeveless white silk blouse. Little red hearts were dotted all over it. It was so not a top many girls could pull off. 'Marlowe designed them. Her sister wants to major in Photography at NYU, so she took the shot of Mercy as Hamlet, the logo from the programme and designed the whole thing.' Emma smiled politely.

'So you didn't have anything to do with the T-shirts?' Stigner asked.

Emma craned up at her. 'Not really. To be perfectly honest, I thought they were a bit of a waste of time. I mean, who really wants a shirt from their junior-year high school play?'

'Er, hello, *everyone*,' Mercy said.

'So why did you pay for them on your credit card?' Stigner asked.

Mrs Altman looked at her daughter in surprise.

Emma crossed her legs delicately. Her navy shorts were totally wrong for winter, but even I had to admit they looked fierce.

'Because Marlowe asked me to,' she said smoothly. 'She'd gone Imelda Marcos with hers in APC the week before, and her mom wasn't pleased. Marlowe said she'd frozen it.' Sargent Stigner scribbled a note in her book. 'She asked me to help out and pay.'

She turned to Mrs Altman. 'Sorry, Mom, but it was only $200. I hoped you wouldn't mind.'

'And Marlowe – a girl from a family like that – didn't have a second card she could lose $200 on?' Stigner focused on the page.

'No, Sergeant, she didn't.' Emma paused until Stigner was forced to look up. 'Despite what you've seen on *Upper East Siders*, not all of us have instant access to the kind of trust funds that allow you to lose $200. Some parents in *families like that* like their kids' feet to stay on the ground.'

A mottled red rash was growing on Stigner's chest.

'Your sister's a lot more, erm, spirited than you, isn't she?' Nancy said.

That was one way of putting it.

'Look, Emma's been through a *lot*.' Lorna walked to her sister's side. 'You guys don't have siblings. You don't know what it's like to die and leave a sister behind. Especially one as young and sensitive as Emma. She's inherited the worst case of only-child syndrome there could be.'

'Can I take a look at your credit card receipt, Emma?' Detective Lee butted in. 'It would be great to cross-check it with what we got from the T-shirt printing store.' He looked at Mr Altman for permission. 'If you don't mind, that is?'

Mr Altman pushed his hands into the pleated pockets of his pants.

'Jefferson, I'm sorry, but I don't understand what Emma helping a classmate out has to do with the inquiry into Mercy Grant's murder. Do I need to be worried here?'

'Go get it, Emma,' Mrs Altman said. This was the wrong time to be crushing on her accent, wasn't it? It was just that she sounded like some kind of Scandi snow princess. 'You have nothing to hide. Let's clear this up so we can move on with the holidays.'

'Um, there's just one problem with that.' Emma recrossed her legs. 'I don't have it, Mom.' She pulled her best *sorry* face. 'It was in my blue Miu Miu purse last week with the card itself and I left it in the back of a cab. I think.'

'Emma Altman! Why didn't you tell me this before? Anyone could have been racking up who knows what on that card all over the city.' Mr Altman reached into his jacket and pulled out his cell. 'I can't remember what limit I set on it.'

'There we go, Nancy. That's exactly the kind of dappy behaviour we'd expect from someone related to Lorna,' I said.

'It's *kinda* different,' Mercy said. 'Lorna lost her life. Emma can't keep track of where her credit card is.'

'Dad, don't panic, I cancelled it already,' Emma said. 'Another one will be through soon. No one put anything on it. I checked.'

He flashed Emma a *good girl* smile.

'And when was this?' Stigner asked.

'When was what?' Emma's eyes really were enormous. Like a Disney baby rabbit's.

'When did you lose your Me Me wallet with the card and receipt in it?'

Emma resisted the urge to correct her. 'I don't know. Last Tuesday. No, it was Monday. I was running late for dinner, so I took a cab on my way back from ballet class.'

Detective Lee got up off the ottoman – not entirely

ungracefully – and walked over to the sash windows in the centre of the family room. From up here Central Park looked like a scene in a snow dome. You almost felt big enough to pick it up and shake it. Detective Lee stepped away from the ledge quickly, grabbing onto the wall.

'Are you all right, Jefferson?' Mr Altman asked.

'Yes, fine.' He leant on the plaster for the briefest of seconds then took a seat on the edge of the couch. 'Vertigo. It comes up at the strangest times. The guys at the *Post* used to rag me about it all the time. Us working on one of the top floors in that skyscraper over on Avenue of the Americas and everything. Man, those jokes never got old.'

'A crime-fighting detective who's scared of heights in a city full of scrapers?' Mercy giggled. 'That's got to be a buzzkill. "Oh no sorry, Commissioner, I can't go solve that mass homicide at Top of the Rock. My head gets kinda blurry when I leave the fourth floor."'

'Mercy Grant, don't you mock him,' Nancy said. 'Vertigo is a proper medical disorder. It's incredibly hard to treat. Considering he suffers from that, I think it's even braver of him to have become a cop.'

'Tell me, Nancy, have you registered at Bloomingdale's yet?' Mercy asked. 'I hear they have some *great* wedding gift lists. I'm sure you and Jefferson will have an awesome future together. The fact you're a high school junior and he's pushing thirty should be fine. The only teeny problem might be that one of you is *dead*.'

If breathing fire out of your nose was a power in the Rules, that was the moment Nancy would have slam-dunked it.

Detective Lee turned back to Emma. 'One last thing, and excuse me for sounding dumb, but it's years since I graduated high school and even then I wasn't into the arts.' He smiled crookedly at Mrs Altman. 'To be honest, I was more about goofing off. The amount of time I spent on detention, I was on first name terms with the night janitor.'

Emma raised one arched eyebrow. If he was a Malton boy, not a senior detective, she'd majorly tell him to get to the point already.

'The one thing I wanted you to help me with was this: if I'd said "good luck" to you before you went onstage, what would you have thought?'

'What's he doing?' Lorna asked. 'He totally knows the answer to this.'

'I think someone's been watching too many episodes of *Columbo*,' I said. 'It's the classic act dumb, trap the perp trick.'

'Except my sister isn't the perp,' Lorna said.

'If you wished me good luck, I'd say that you were either being very stupid or very mean,' Emma said.

'Why?' Detective Lee asked.

'Because everyone who's cracked a book knows you should never wish an actor good luck before a play. It's an old theatre superstition. If you say "good luck" it's meant to bring anything but.'

'That's very interesting, isn't it?' Detective Lee turned to a nodding Stigner. 'Especially seeing as someone with access to the backstage area had put a large "Good Luck!" banner up in Mercy's dressing room. Any idea who would have been very stupid or

– sorry what did you say? – very mean enough to do that?'

Emma's eyes narrowed until they look liked two pieces of chalk. 'No, I try not to hang out with mean or stupid people. It's just a rule I have.' She recrossed her long legs again.

'Okay, I think we've got everything we need here.' Detective Lee clapped his hands. 'Stigner, let's not take up any more of these kind people's time.'

'Hmmm . . . Maybe we should check on what Emma said – you know, about Marlowe's mom taking away her credit card?' Nancy asked, as the cops headed for the elevator. 'If Emma did pay for the T-shirts which freaked out Mercy then . . .'

'Then what, Nancy?' Lorna drew herself up as tall as she could in her ballet flats.

'Then we'll know that Emma ordered them and—'

'*And*? We'll know she was being a good friend? We'll know she helped someone out of a jam? I don't see what that's going to prove either way. Paying for some crummy drama squad T-shirts doesn't mean my sister murdered Mercy. Does it, Mercy?'

'No, it doesn't,' Mercy said slowly, unsure who's side to take. 'I honestly don't think Emma would have hurt me. The detectives are looking for someone who's a tech whizz too, remember? I sat next to Emma in seventh grade Computer class. Believe me, she is not good with things that go beep. Unless it's an emergency BBM to her nail artist for an appointment.'

Lorna put both hands on her hips in a *see!* way.

'You know what, Nancy, I'm getting kinda sick of

281

having to live with your superiority complex,' Lorna said. 'Who died and made you head detectress anyhow?'

'No one, seeing as we were *all* dead in the first place.' Nancy threw her hands in the air in frustration.

Uh oh. The ectoplasm was totally about to hit the fan.

Pop!

'Oooh, is some ace detecting going on in here?' Edison ported into the room, stopping Lorna before she could speak. I'd never been more glad to see him in my entire death.

'I thought you might need some male perspective on the case, but I guess I—' He stopped talking and stared from Lorna to Nancy and Nancy to Lorna. Their faces both dead ringers for the sky over the Hudson before a July storm broke. 'Charlotte, I need to talk to you about . . . that *thing.*'

He pulled me away from the others. 'Look, I don't know what I walked into here, but coming from a guy who lost his life in a failed drugs bust, I think you should listen to me when I say I do not think this is going to stay PG-rated for long.'

Over Edison's shoulder, I saw Mercy taking a step back as Lorna prepared to blow.

'I'm guessing this is about Mini-Me being our main suspect again?' he asked. I nodded. 'How about you take Lorna somewhere sparkly, get her to cool off and I'll escort the other girls back to the Attesa?' Ed said. 'Maybe if they have a break from each other they'll get the perspective they need?'

'Because if you and your *fake* Living boyfriend over there were the super-awesome detectives you think you are, you wouldn't be focusing on an innocent girl like my sister!' Lorna shouted. Her hair was out of place. Yep, this was bad.

'Oh, will you just port off and mourn the fact you no longer have a reflection?' Nancy said.

The second the words hit Lorna's ears, Nancy grimaced. 'Lorna, I'm so sorry,' she said, trying to touch her friend's arm. 'I really, really didn't mean that. It's just this case. It's been so stressful. And we've all been working such long hours. And I really, really didn't—'

'Um, Lorna, how about we go someplace?' I stepped between them.

Lorna linked my arm. 'That's the only sensible thing anyone's said all day, Charlotte. I guess it takes something like this for you to realize who your true friends are, doesn't it?'

Sorry, I mouthed at Nancy. *Thank you*, I mouthed at Edison.

As Lorna and I ported out of the room, the last thing I saw was Nancy starting to cry.

CHAPTER 24

I opened my eyes to find myself face to face with a lifeless porcelain mannequin. She had huge black sunglasses for eyes and was reaching an eerie arm up towards a white paper fir tree. Behind her was an entire wall of shiny cans. Her bustled dress had been created from thousands of fanned silver paper plates; her headdress a circle of forks.

Sweet Jesus. I appeared to have ported us into the Tin Woman's evil lair.

'How did you know this was my happy place?' Lorna squeezed my arm in delight.

Happy place? Right now the Christmas window of Barney's department store was scaring the bejeezus out of me, but each to her own.

'Lorna, anywhere with a surfeit of shoes that cost the same as the lease to a small island will always be your happy place.' I took a step away from the glass. Nope, tin woman was still staring. And still borderline terrifying. 'It wasn't like I was betting on the Sox to win the next series.'

'You'd bet on socks?' she asked, wrinkling up her nose. 'But they're so *Clueless* circa 1995. I know grunge had that comeback, but patterned tights are way more A/W '14.'

Sometimes Lorna's mouth opened and English words seemed to come out, yet I could not understand one of them.

'I *love* this place.' Lorna whirled to the next humungous window where a headless snow queen covered in white netting was standing in front of the words like 'glad tidings' and 'cheer'. Candles shivered in the background. Um, what was wrong with Rudolph and some elves?

'Thank you for bringing me here,' Lorna said. 'That whole scene was getting soo big sceney. I'm feeling more Lorna again already.'

'Good,' I said. 'Always glad to help via the restorative powers of festivity and fashion.'

Above us, the entire building had been tied up with a colossal red velvet ribbon, as if Jack's giant had wrapped it as a present for Goliath. Okay, that was kinda cool.

'New York is Christmas on a stick.' Lorna pushed her head through the window to get a better look at the queen's ghostly gown. 'The lights, the singing, the skating, the shops . . .'

Could I ban her from mentioning the skating without telling her why I suddenly had an allergy to the skating? Probably not.

'Phew. I'm glad you're feeling a bit less—' Lorna pulled her head out and shot me a look which left me under no illusion I better be *very* careful which word I chose next '—*stressed*. I was gonna port us to Tiffany's first, but I wasn't sure there were enough clothes in there to make you this smiley.'

'Tiffany's? Uh, it's, like, an inner ring of engagement hell. All those guys slopping round, clutching their wallets, looking scared.'

'Hey, Miss Picky,' I joked. Was it safe to make a joke yet? 'I'm doing my best here. Can you at least try not to sound so bummed?'

'I am not.' Lorna looked wistfully from Queenie's designer dress to her own. 'I majorly appreciate it, Charlotte. Really I do. If I'd been in that room with those people a moment longer, why I . . .' She pulled her hair into a ponytail then let it fall back onto her shoulders in waves. 'Now, can we go look at some more windows already?'

Like she hadn't judged every single one in the city by now.

'Henri Bendel's are always crazy-stylish. One year, instead of baubles, they had Chanel lipsticks hanging from their trees. It was immense.' Lorna's baby blues widened like that was akin to discovering a way to stop yawning being contagious. Which in her eyes, it probably was.

'Okay, okay,' I said. 'But if this whole thing gets too like a shopping montage from an eighties movie, I will be forced to leave.'

We ported five blocks down and two across to where Bendel's sat on Fifth Avenue. There were a lot more high fashion green dresses and red sparkly backdrops down here. The mannequins still didn't have eyes, but they didn't look like they wanted to eat mine either, which was a definite move in the right direction.

'The problem is, Nancy just doesn't get it.' Lorna twisted a lock of blonde around her fingers as the mannequins spun to 'White Christmas'. 'She's so sure what the police are doing is right, she's stopped using her Nancy Intuition. She's forgotten how important that is.'

So we were talking about this now? Okay . . .

'She's just—' I didn't want to shut Lorna down, but I was in what my mom called a rock-and-a-hard-place situation '—doing what she thinks is best. You know Nancy, she'd never deliberately hurt anyone. She's one of the most genuinely good people I know.'

'Uh huh.' Lorna made a clicking noise that sounded like it came from my fourth-grade homeroom teacher.

In the fight-stopping stakes, there wasn't about to be a miracle on 34th Street tonight. Where Emma was concerned, Lorna was as sure of her sister as Nancy was of Detective Lee. Bummer.

I thought back to the night after Mercy died. To when I ported out of that taxi and heard Emma and Dylan arguing by the park. Maybe this was the moment to tell Lorna what they said? I hated having secrets from her as much as I hated manufactured boy bands, but would the information really help? Right now, Lorna was already convinced one of her best friends was working against her. I didn't want to double that number by suggesting Emma really *did* have something to hide.

Besides, the whole thing might have been totally innocent. Maybe Dylan wanted Emma to tell Detective Lee that she charged the T-shirts to her card? Or that he felt bad for sending Mercy that good luck card because he'd realized what it meant? Maybe they weren't talking about the cops at all. *Maybe* they were talking about another kind of police. Like that geriatric band my dad loved? Or the sunglasses brand?

Urgh, who was I trying to kid? It looked as bad as Queenie's artfully severed head. But I totally got why Lorna wasn't ready to deal with that. Period.

A gold boy mannequin jerked its arm up and down, scattering silver snow around the scene. The music switched to 'All I Want For Christmas Is You'. I hummed along, hating myself with every bar. Maybe I could bring up the Dylan and Emma thing without actually mentioning Dylan and Emma? That was possible. Wasn't it?

'It's got to be hard, being this close to your sister again,' I said carefully. 'Like, I know you've kept an eye on her since you died, but not like this. Emma must have changed heaps in the last four years. I mean, when I was twelve, I thought I was going to marry Joel Madden. But by sixteen, I was in a box in the ground.'

Some may say that was a lucky escape.

'I know that's not your average teenage journey,' I said. 'All this violence, adult content and strong language wasn't what any of us signed up for. I'm just saying that everyone grows up a hell of a lot during those years. Emma must have changed too?'

From your cute pre-teen, clothes-stealing little sister into a drop-dead, school-ruling junior with a murderous streak? I seriously hoped not.

'Emma's not so different,' Lorna said. 'She might be a

little tougher on the outside than she would have been, but underneath she's still my kid sister.'

'But all that stuff the cops pulled out of her school file . . .'

Lorna blinked as the mannequins slowly whirled. 'I knew about it. Of course I did. I'm not stupid.' Her voice caught. 'I know more than anyone how much my death affected her. Why do you think I've been hanging around here all these years? I know you all assume it's so I don't miss McQueen's next season or whatever, but I'm not quite that shallow. Well, not all the time.'

She gave me a sad smile. I let her speak.

'When I arrived, the Attesa was a majorly different place. Like, imagine Celine before Phoebe Philo took over and you're not even close.'

That I could definitely not imagine – or understand – but I stayed sshhh.

'There was no Nancy, so no Agency really. At least not one that works like hers—' she caught herself '—ours does now. Sure, Edison and Tess were there, but like I told you before, there was no orientation tour to show me where they kept the kegs.'

The thought of Edison or Tess at college? Yep, that was about as alien as Nancy skipping out on it.

'Tess taught me to port, but apart from that all I got was a copy of the Rules. I was confused and sad and lonely. I know you didn't have the easiest time when you showed up, but at least you had us to talk to.'

Lorna put a hand on the glass, tracing the word 'Noel' with her fingers. 'When it came to solving my case, I didn't know where to start. I followed the cops around for a while, but that was a major buzzkill. All that hanging about in grey police stations listening to them talk about how they didn't know who my killer was . . . Pretty soon I figured, if they couldn't solve my case, what hope did a girl like me who couldn't even pass History have?'

'So that's when you decided to stay around?' I asked.

Lorna made two little circles around the 'e'. 'One day, I was brave enough to go visit my folks,' she explained. 'They were holding up okay. My mom *never* holds up anything but okay. But Emma . . . Emma was a mess. She'd started getting upset. Acting out, they called it – I heard them talking about all that stuff with Marlowe and the stairs and that's when I made my decision: to stay here and make sure she *was* okay. At least until Emma didn't need me any more.'

She fanned her fingers through the glass. 'After all these years of wishing I had a reason to be close to her, now I have one, I just want it to go away.' She threw me a sad sideways glance. 'I never thought she'd need me like *this*.

'So yes, of course I know all that stuff in her file,' she said. 'It's the reason I'm here. I know my baby sister, so I know Nancy's wrong to think for a half a second she had anything to do with Mercy's death.' She sighed. 'In a way, instead of losing my Key to Tess, I gave it to Emma, but unlike you I did it willingly.'

Oh boy. Was now *not* the time to bring up what I'd heard by the park.

'Jeez, we're poor excuses for ghosts.' I bounced through the window and Jabbed the green top hats off three of the boy mannequins' heads. The tourist girls window-shopping next to us ohhh-ed like it was part of the show.

'I was meant to be making you smile,' I said. 'Most dead kids would be having a ball right now. Getting their *Christmas Carol* on, playing Ghost of Christmas Past and haunting people who really deserve it.'

I lifted one of the hats back in the air theatrically. This was the best show the out-of-towners had ever seen. 'Do you think now I've lost my Key forever, there'd be trouble if I ported over to Kristin the head cheermonster's townhouse and booed and wooed right in her pretty face?'

Instead of giggling, Lorna's features turned oh-so-serious. Not that was not the effect I'd been going for.

'What's up?' I said. 'Someone die?'

The serious face refused to shift. 'You don't have to be Team Upbeat the entire time, you know?' she said quietly. 'You are allowed to be sad that you lost your Key.'

Erm, hello, I thought this was meant to be her counselling session not mine? I didn't agree to lie on any couches.

'You know, much as I love you, the whole "fashion does festive" vibe isn't doing it for me. We need some proper cheer-you-up New York seasonal pizzazz,' I said. 'Race you to the angels in Rockefeller Plaza? Last one there's a mouldy sprig of mistletoe.'

I ported away before she could stop me, landing right in front of the city's most epic Christmas tree. It was as tall as four regular houses stacked on top of each other and heaving with dancing red lights. A tunnel of golden angels trumpeted its tree-lined entrance. A choir was singing old-fashioned carols, and little kids with red noses and matching bobble hats were squealing in delight. Now *this* was Christmas.

As she ported in, even Lorna took a second to be impressed. 'Woah, I've not been here at this time of year in forever.'

'Did you know the tallest tree ever was 100 feet tall?' I told her.

'How big's that?' she asked.

'About eighteen Charlottes high,' I said. 'Don't look at me like I'm crazy. My dad *loves* facts. Did I ever tell you that? Sports facts mostly, but Christmas ones are his all-time favourites. He brought me here every year since I was a little kid to watch the lights switch on.'

I pointed up at the tree. 'There's more than thirty thousand of them on there. Did you know that? It takes, like, five miles of wiring to power up that thing. Awesome, huh? Five miles: that's almost half the length of Manhattan. The first tree came from Jersey. And it—'

'Charlotte, STOP!' Lorna's words slapped me like a January wind. 'Will you stop avoiding the subject and just tell me what happened that day – before me and Nancy showed up?'

'You know this,' I said quietly. 'There's no need. I walked into the lobby and I could hear Edison and Tess arguing. She wanted to take my Key.'

'And Edison?'

'Edi-who?' I said.

'Edison.' Lorna said. 'Handsome, dead, hot for you . . . There ain't many of them around, Charlotte.'

She wasn't going to let up, was she?

'Edison was trying to make her stop.' I sidestepped a sledging pre-schooler. 'He said what Tess was trying to do was a big bag of wrong and that she shouldn't do it because I'd be stuck here forever.'

I'd replayed the words over and over on my internal iPod. They were pretty impossible to forget. If only they were available to download, I'd have a million-seller on my hands.

'But it was the way they were talking that was weird,' I admitted. 'It was almost as if she blamed him for not finding her Key.'

'I know she's been gone a whole month, but you remember Tess, right?' Lorna said. 'Brunette, bitter, about yey high? Being all blamey was pretty much her USP. It doesn't mean Edison actually had anything to do with her Key not turning up.'

'Maybe, but one thing's for sure: your theory about them knowing each other before *here* – that has to be right. She talked about the people *they* knew. She kept saying Edison owed her.'

'So is that why you're making things so bad with Edison now? Because you think he helped her in some way?'

Duh.

'What's worse is he won't tell me how he knew Tess, so that's pretty much put the road closed sign up on anything ever happening between us.' I watched as a dad pulled his daughter along on a sleigh. Cute. Christmas made me such a schmuck. 'Not that there was an "anything".'

'Oh, but there so was,' Lorna said. 'I've been here with Edison for four years and I've never seen him go wiggy over a girl before.'

Wiggy? 'I make him wiggy?'

'Charlotte, the guy's been a) helping with the world's toughest investigation, just to impress you, b) looking even more sullen than usual, which I think we can both agree is quite some feat and c) moping in his room all day and night. He's one step away from killing Taylor Swift so she can sing him some of the more poignant ballads in her back catalogue. If you went back to HHQ, dusted off Nancy's nasty old dictionary and looked up "wiggy", you'd totally find Ed there.'

'Okay, okay, but it doesn't change the fact he lied to me.'

'He didn't really, though,' she said. 'He just didn't tell you what Tess was up to because he was probably scared if he admitted they had some kinda history you'd go off him. Plus, honestly, who would have thought she'd actually do something like she did?'

Erm, had Edison been feeding her lines?

'But he won't tell me what's in their past. He says it's not his story to tell.'

'Then maybe you need to trust him on that?' she said. 'The kinda guy who promises to keep a secret, then still won't spill it no matter how dark times get – he sounds trustworthy to me. No matter how many schoolmarm faces Nancy pulls.'

'Yes, but he . . .'

Lorna stood next to the angel. In the hazy evening air, the lights it threw off beamed through her. She was like the good version of Hamlet's dad.

'I just figure, like it or hate it you're going to be here a while longer,' she said. 'No, Edison hasn't behaved like a prince. But murdered teen princes are kinda thin on the ground in this city. He likes you. You like him. Somewhere under all those bad gothy clothing choices is a good person. Maybe you should stop punishing yourself.'

'Maybe, but I . . .'

'Plus he can be super-sensitive too,' she said. 'I might have been as mad as a slingback-wearer in a thunderstorm, but even I noticed the way Ed asked you to get me out of my parent's penthouse before me or Nancy said something we really regretted. The way he's acted lately – I don't think he's all bad.'

Since when did Lorna become the wise one?

'You know what, Lorna Altman, I can't think of anyone I'd rather be stuck here for eternity with but you and Nancy.' I gave her a mammoth bear hug. She pretended to be upset it was mussing up her hair. 'I know Nancy's acting a little loony tunes right now, but we've also got to remember she's basically in the throes of her first crush. Hopefully she'll get over it soon.'

Lorna pulled away from me sharply – an idea stubbing. 'Ohmigod, what if Detective Lee gets murdered on the case, goes to the adult hotel and she ends up meeting him for *real*.'

'Lor, I really don't think that's very like—'

'Then you would have Edison, and Nancy'd be all stalky over Detective Crumpled Shirt.'

'Lorna, that's not going to hap—'

'And I'd have no one to talk to but Mercy Grant.'

295

She sat on the angel's slightly soily leg. She must be distraught. 'When I was alive, I never had a problem getting a date. I could find them as easy as cute clutch bags.' She itched her button nose. 'Now I have no idea where all the cute guys have gone.'

'Hey, I'm sure your Mr Right's out there,' I said. 'He's just not died yet.' I had a thunderbolt. 'Actually that is a genius strapline for a dead girls' dating agency.'

'Oh! It *so* is.' Lorna let me pull her back up on her feet again. 'Ohhh, you could call it Soul Mates! Or . . . should it be No Soul Mates?'

'Forget Match.com, welcome to Despatch.com – your leading source for other singles who've left this world,' I boomed à *la* Mercy's best stage voice.

Lorna giggled so hard she had to lean on the angel again. It was good to see.

'Come on, let's go back to HHQ,' she said when she'd managed to compose herself. 'There's a dead boy you need to see.'

There was. But only when *I* was ready.

CHAPTER 25

We ported back to HHQ, to find the place empty.

'I would make some joke about it being like a ghost town in here, but I think I blew my punchline already.' Lorna checked the lobby. Nope, no dead people. Neither of us had to admit how relieved we were.

'Do you think Nancy and Mercy went to the Frost Fête already?' The Attesa clock read 7.05 p.m. 'The party started five minutes ago,' I said. 'Guess we better port over to Chateau De Witt.'

Lorna stared at me as if I'd just washed my best whites with a red sock. 'Have you *never* been to a party on the Upper East Side?'

Because my inbox was busting with society invites along with all that life insurance spam before I died.

Which, actually, maybe I should have taken up.

'The invitation might say 7 p.m., but what that means is "Turn up at seven and you're the biggest loser in town". If it says seven, you can't show up at seven. Right about now, everyone who's anyone will be instructing the maid, fixing their hair and choosing between the Dior and the Wu.'

The who?

'Which also means my parents and Emma will still be at our house. Can we go see? I want to check she's okay after everything that went down today.' Lorna shot me a shy smile. 'And see how heartbreak pretty she looks in her dress too.'

'Sure.' It wouldn't hurt for Nancy and Lorna to have a little more time apart. I wasn't crazy-keen to hang around here and wait for Mr Issues to put in an appearance either.

We ported into the Altmans' townhouse, landing by the private elevator we'd ridden with the cops. Lorna beckoned for me to follow her up the marble stairs. A Kandinsky was casually hanging on the wall. I'd had the same abstract print taped to the front of my Math file. Except the Altmans had the real thing. Holy smoke.

'Emma! Are you ready?' Mr Altman's voice boomed behind us.

'Almost,' she shouted down. I was in an Altman sound sandwich. Excellent. 'I'll be ready in fifteen. You and Mom take the town car, then send it back for me. You know she hates being too late.'

I climbed past another awesome piece of modern art. Blue triangles intersected with purple squares and silver paint splashed over the top. This was less like a murder investigation and more like a class trip to MOMA.

'Okay, honey, I'll tell Richard to be out front at 7.45. See you there.' His shoes tap-tapped down the hall, then squeaked to a stop. 'You look beautiful, by the way. I *love* what you've done with your hair! And that dress.'

Lorna giggled.

'Your dad's very, um, metro,' I said. She was climbing

so fast, her Pretty Ballerinas were on a level with my chin. 'When I dyed my hair pink in sixth grade, mine didn't notice for two days. Whereas Mom made the Incredible Hulk look calm when she got home.'

'He can't see what she looks like. That's just Dad trying to be funny.' I could practically hear Lorna roll her eyes. 'Being the only guy in the house, he says it's impossible to keep up with who's been to the salon or is wearing a new dress. So he always says he *loves* our look, even when he can't see us. It cracks him up most when he does it down the phone.'

I felt the familiar pang of loss. If you'd told me six months ago that I'd give up my fake ID just to hear one of Dad's lame dad-jokes, I'd have laughed till the sun hit the Hudson.

Lorna reached the landing above and stopped at a firmly shut light-blue door. 'That was my room,' she said quietly. Her fingers twitched for the handle, then drew them back.

I wondered how it looked inside. If her parents had left the overflowing closets and the make-up palettes as I imagined Lorna had left them. She'd been murdered at prom. Was the room still a total mess of discarded Dior and – what was the other one? – *Wu* from Lorna trying on a hundred dresses before she left that night? Or had her parents paid the maid to neatly pack up her belongings and send them to the Goodwill? Had I been dead so long for my mom and dad to have emptied my room? Maybe they'd sent my clothes away because it was all too painful for them. Maybe some girl in Alabama was wearing my favourite vintage Hole T-shirt now.

'This way.' Lorna led me down the porcelain hall towards the boom boom of music. Emma was sitting at a large white dressing table. For once, she hadn't scooped her long blonde hair up in a tight ponytail. Instead, it fell in gentle waves over her tan shoulders – just as Lorna's did. A mascara wand was in her hand, but it hovered inches from her face as she studied her reflection as if seeing it for the first time. She looked so, so sad.

There was a shout downstairs and she snapped out of her trance, throwing the wand carelessly onto the dresser. As she swept past us, I noticed for the first time that she was a couple of inches taller than Lorna now. More so when she pushed her painted toes into her heels. Emma's white dress plunged at the front into a deep V, one shoulder covered with delicate fabric daisies, which travelled down the cinched bodice. The voluminous, netted skirts billowing behind her only made Emma look more like an escapee from the nearest fairy tale.

'She went with the Jenny Packham.' Lorna beamed approvingly. 'That's sooo perfect for the Frost Fête. I can't get over how beautiful she looks. She's grown up so. How did it happen that fast?'

'Dad?' Emma shouted down the stairs, as she held up the hem of her gown and hurried down in her silver Louboutins.

'Did you guys forget something?' she asked. 'You should have just called me, I could have brought it along if—Oh!' Emma stopped suddenly three steps from the hall.

She wasn't expecting the scene that met her in the lobby. None of us were.

'I'm so sorry, Miss Altman,' the elevator guy was saying. His black patent hat was all askew. He was what my grandma would call 'distressed'. 'I tried to stop them coming up, but they had police badges and they wouldn't take no for an answer, no matter how hard I tried.'

'It's okay, Barney. You don't like to be told "no", do you, Detective Lee?' She eyeballed Jefferson who was standing behind him. Stigner and another cop I'd never seen before made their way out of the elevator too.

Followed by Nancy and Mercy. Of course.

'What the hell?' Lorna hissed. 'It's the Frost Fête! Couldn't he leave her alone for one lousy night?'

'Lorna, I think we should—' Nancy tried to guide Lorna away from her sister with her eyes '—there's something you need to know and it might be better if you hear it from me.'

'No!' Lorna moved down a step to be by Emma's side. 'I'm not leaving Emma to deal with these people all alone.'

'Miss Altman, do you want me to call Mr Altman's cell?' Barney was freaking out his pink slip was in the mail. 'They only left five minutes ago. I could contact the driver and ask him to turn their car around?'

Emma swooped down the stairs. 'No, Barney, thank you for all of your help, but I'm fine. The detective and I go back a long way. As I'm sure he's aware, I've got the Fête to attend tonight. You won't keep me long will you, Jefferson?'

Detective Lee turned strawberry pink when she used his first name. I couldn't tell if he was embarrassed, uncomfortable or plain mad.

'Honestly, Barney, you can go,' she said. He gave the cops a Medusa-worthy stare, and retreated into the elevator.

Emma calmly turned to Detective Lee. Thanks to her heels, they were almost eye to eye. 'Thank you for taking the time to check in on me, but as you can see I do need to be some place.' She motioned down at her dress, before eyeing Detective Lee's black suit. There was an unidentifiable grease stain on the lapel. Nancy had to have caught that.

'Seeing as you clearly didn't get the memo about the dress code, I'll take it you weren't invited to the De Witts party and—'

'Why did you kill Mercy Grant?' Detective Lee asked.

Lorna gasped.

Woah, how out of the blue? And that from the girl who was run down by a subway train.

'Seriously?' Emma laughed, the tinkling sound dancing down the hall. 'You bug me all week, turn up here on the biggest night of the year and you come out with *that*?'

'Emma, I need you to stop lying now,' Detective Lee said firmly. His face was back to being the kind of white you got from spending your life behind a desk. 'You're only going to make it worse.'

'Please.' She rolled her enormous eyes. 'Can't you do better than that? It's like you learned that interview technique watching *The Wire*.'

'We have reason to believe you were the one pulling pranks on Mercy Grant. I'm going to need to take you down to Precinct 19 and question you formally.'

Emma's expression was as unreadable as *Ulysses*. 'If someone was pulling pranks on Mercy Grant, it wasn't me. I do have a life you know.'

'Which is more than I can say,' Mercy muttered.

'There are two ways we can do this: easy or hard,' the detective said. 'Take your pick.'

'Actually I think you stole your approach from *NYPD Blue*,' Emma said. 'It's not *dynamic* enough for HBO.'

'If that's the way you want to play it, fine.' Detective Lee took off his jacket and threw it on the violet hallway couch. 'Let's break this down. Firstly, you charged the *Hipster Hamlet* T-shirts to your card.'

'I told you, I was helping Marlowe out. And how is that a "prank"?'

'It is a prank because we also know that when you made that order, you asked the clerk to send one special delivery T-shirt to Mercy Grant – two nights before the rest. Two nights before the first show.'

'I was being nice. I wanted her to have something to spur her on.'

'Why are they doing this?' Lorna sat down on the step, a crumpled paper doll. 'She didn't do anything wrong.'

'That's interesting,' Detective Lee continued. 'Especially seeing as we got access to the costume shop's phone records too. Do you want to know the cell number of the person who called up to change the colour of Mercy's outfit from black to blue?'

'No, not particularly.' Emma examined her silver nails. They were the exact same shade as her heels.

'Well, I'll tell you – it's yours.'

'Someone could have borrowed my phone. I was always lending it to people back stage. I don't see the—'

'The good luck flowers and banner, they were a little tougher to track down,' Detective Lee said. Behind him, Nancy grimaced. 'But you know what they say about policing? If you put in the legwork, the rewards will come.'

He pointed to the new cop. 'Thomas here has been to most of the florists on the island in the last few days. Five sold banners exactly like the one someone put in Mercy's dressing room. But only one sold a banner along with three bouquets of lilies the night before Mercy was murdered. The person who bought them paid in cash.'

Emma rearranged her clouds of skirts. 'What does that prove? You can't trace dollars.'

'No, you can't, but what you can do is show the florist a picture like this—' Detective Lee held up a shot of Emma in her uniform, her hair high in a head girl pony, her blazer brand new '—and then you can take a statement from the florist when he confirms that *this* was the girl who bought the banner and asked for the flowers to be delivered to her high school. A girl who stood out from your average teen on account of the fact she didn't blink as she paid with a $100 bill.'

Emma slowly dragged her eyes from her dress up to Detective Lee's face.

I wanted to look at Lorna – really I did – but I didn't dare.

'So you see, Emma, we have concrete proof that you ordered Mercy's T-shirt, you sent her the flowers, you most probably put a good luck banner up in her dressing room, and you most definitely changed the colour of her costume. You did all these things to scare her. I can't pin the peacock feathers or the *Macbeth* script on you, but I do think that when we take your laptop in as evidence in this case, we'll see you've been downloading a whole lot of the Black Keys.'

He waited for the longest time. 'Am I wrong?'

Emma slumped onto the couch, crumpling his jacket further. Suddenly she looked so small.

'Okay.' She hugged her long arms around her body. 'Fine, I was messing with Mercy Grant. Is that what you want to hear?'

Lorna sucked in a balloon of air. I bobbed down beside her and squeezed her hand. Oh boy.

'You've interviewed enough Peabody girls over the past six days to know Mercy Grant wasn't all sugar and spice.' Emma's voice was quieter now. I had to strain to hear her. 'Mercy had a hurricane of a personality. Sometimes she made people feel the size of subway mouse. I don't think she did it deliberately, but she did.'

'Hey! That's not fair! I never—' Nancy slapped her hand right over Mercy's mouth. I was glad she'd been the one near enough to do that.

'Lately, I was one of them,' Emma said.

'Go on.'

Stigner silently took a seat on the edge of the couch.

Emma took a breath as big as her sister's. 'Mercy knew something about me and she was threatening to tell everyone. She thought it was funny. I didn't want it getting out.'

Mercy pulled back from Nancy, tripping over her own trainers. 'Oh. Oh noo.'

'Was this secret why Ryder heard you two fighting, just before you went onstage on opening night?' Stigner asked.

'Jeez! I should have guessed she was the one who went to you with that,' Emma spat, all fire again. 'Ryder's worse than Mercy at times. At least when Mercy was mean she was straight about it. Every time you talk to Ryder you have to check there's not a sharp piece of metal in your back. You should really enrol her on your recruitment drive now, Detective Lee. Before the FBI sign her up.'

'Mercy, what were you teasing Emma about?' Nancy asked.

'Honestly, Nance, I didn't know I was upsetting her.' Mercy's pupils were the size of a kid's before they go over a roller-coaster loop. 'Really I didn't. I thought we were joking about. We were friends – I thought I could do that.'

'Did you have stand-up rows with a lot of your "friends" before going onstage?' Lorna asked.

Mercy looked at me helplessly.

Detective Lee communicated something to Stigner with his eyes. She sat up straighter.

'We're capable of recruiting our own talent,' Detective Lee told Emma. 'Seeing as I have four pieces of solid evidence showing you were harassing our murder victim in the weeks preceding her death, why don't you finish the story with a bit less of the attitude?'

'What secret did Mercy know?' Stigner asked, softly

pulling out her notebook. What was this – the good cop, bad cop routine?

'Is it really that important?' Emma uncrossed her arms.

'Most judges would say I've got grounds to charge you this second,' Detective Lee said. 'Does that make it important enough?'

'Fine. I was dating someone.'

Detective Lee waited for Emma to fill the silence.

'It was Dylan, okay?' Emma said. 'Dylan was – Dylan *is* – my boyfriend.'

Colour me shocked, I was not expecting that.

'*She's* seeing *him*?' Nancy pushed her glasses on top of her head. 'But he's so . . . and she's so . . .'

Yes, she was and yes, he was, but it didn't stop me shooting Nancy a *leave it* look.

'Go on, Emma,' Stigner said kindly.

Her eyes rested on the photograph of Lorna, staring at it for the longest time, before she began to speak.

'To say that school was harsh after Lorna died, is like saying Genghis Khan wasn't a very nice man.' Emma pulled her hair up into a high ponytail and let it fall over her shoulders. 'I wasn't Emma Altman any more. I was the Girl Whose Sister Died. My picture was in the newspapers and all over TV. Kids who'd never said three words to me suddenly wanted to be my best friend. Except they didn't want to get to know me – they wanted to know *her*. What she wore, who she hung out with, what she was like, the last thing she'd said. They wanted information so they could solve Manhattan's big whodunnit. I'd lost my sister and, to some idiots, it was just a game.'

Stigner stopped scribbling in her notebook. The pen wavered in her hand.

'The staring and the whispering and the sudden quietness whenever I walked into a room – that I learned to deal with. Fast. What I couldn't handle was the way every person in this stupid city thought they knew my big sister better than I did. Everyone had a theory. Everyone thought they knew why she died.'

Emma looked up at Detective Lee. 'You included, Jefferson. You spent enough time befriending my family, getting the background, the colour, profiling the victim. You tell me: who murdered Lorna Altman? You must think you know.'

'Emma, I—' His eyes grew glassy. 'I don't. No one knows. If we did, the person wouldn't be out there. They'd be in a cell paying for what they did. I promise you that.'

'Emma,' Stigner said. Why had I never noticed how young the sergeant was? Sitting beside Emma, she could have passed for a new college grad. 'We were talking about Dylan. You need to tell us about Mercy in relation to you and him.'

'I was.' Emma swallowed hard. 'With every new friend who let me down, and every old one who let me shatter apart, I started to realize: the world is full of phonies.'

Lorna squeezed my hand hard. How was she sitting through this? At least no one – at first – knew I'd been murdered. At least my family hadn't been put through a show like this.

'After Lorna ... There weren't that many people I could talk to,' Emma said. 'Not my parents. They were

308

making out like they'd only ever had one daughter any-way. He wasn't like that. He understood.'

'He? Dylan?' Stigner asked.

'Dylan.' Emma nodded. 'She used to babysit him. He didn't have a big sister, so he loved mine. He was the only one who talked about Lorna like she was a person, not a story. He put me back together. We became best friends. Then one day, more.'

Wow.

'I don't get it.' Stigner had abandoned her notes completely. 'He sounds amazing. Why would you want to hide your relationship? Why would Mercy telling people you were together be so bad?'

'Because no one knew we were dating. That was the way we wanted it.' Emma was getting exasperated. Why didn't Stigner understand? 'Oh, I know you're looking at me and thinking, *Shallow little rich girl*. Like I'm the type who doesn't want her cool, debutante friends to know she's dating a geek. You think I was worried I'd be shipped to Social Siberia for the rest of my high school days if it got out. Well, it wasn't like that.'

'Of course it wasn't,' Detective Lee said. 'You two have too much in common for you to see Dylan in that way, don't you?'

Emma stared at him, tilting her head to the side as if she was an auctioneer appraising the worth of an antique vase.

'It was because of what happened to his mom, right?' Detective Lee continued. 'Oh, don't look at me like I'm some nosey curtain-twitcher, Emma. I read about her in his police file when we were doing background checks on all you kids. Dylan was the only one apart from you who had one, because you both had a relative who'd died.'

'His mom?' Mercy asked. 'I didn't know anything about his mom.'

'*Murdered*, Detective, not "died". Why don't you just call a spade a spade?' Emma asked.

'Dylan's mother was killed when he was one.' Detective Lee told Stigner, ignoring Emma's tone. 'She was shot out in Brooklyn waiting for a cab.'

'Oh wait. West! Dylan's mom is Holly West?' Stigner asked. Jefferson nodded sadly. 'Wow, I remember the case now. I was at college – a young mother, out alone with her baby son for the first time. Shot by some drunk. She was from some perfect society family. It was so tragic. It devastated the whole of Manhattan. No one could believe it. It was in the news for weeks and weeks.'

'Mr West told me his wife had died in an accident,' Lorna said. 'I never knew he was dealing with all of this.'

'Dylan was too young to remember,' Emma said. 'But reporters never forget. Every couple of years, one would knock on the Wests' apartment door, asking to run a "positive uplifting piece" on the anniversary – about the little boy who'd survived. His dad always told them to take a long walk off a short cliff. But that didn't stop them. The next year there'd be more.'

'Oh.' For Stigner the penny was finally dropping. 'So when you two started dating . . .'

'When we started dating, we didn't want to tell a soul,' Emma said. 'It's the five-year anniversary of

310

Lorna's death in May, do you know that, Jefferson? It's still a *Vanity Fair* article of a scandal that her murderer's never been found. Reporters are sniffing around already, looking for an angle to fill a page. Imagine it: the boy who never knew his mom and the sister of the murdered Upper East Side princess? Two sob stories with one happy ending, yours for the price of one.'

'And the fact you look more and more like Lorna every day would make it even more compelling,' Detective Lee shook his head.

'Fancy pitching us to your old editor? Once a journalist, always a journalist, after all.' Emma's smile was lemon-bitter. 'I'm sick of my life being a slow news day solution. Dylan's too. After everything he's supported me through, I didn't want him being dragged into my dramas too. So we hid our relationship. We saw each other in secret. Dylan even volunteered for that crummy stage manger job to get to see me more. Then Mercy caught us kissing. And I didn't think her "jokes" about telling everyone were so funny any more.'

'Erm.' It felt like the first time Nancy had said anything in days. 'Is it just me or does anyone else feel like they need a few hours to take all this in?'

Or weeks?

'Hey, sorry to sound all me-me-me, but I'm confused. Does this mean Emma's *actually* my murderer?' Mercy asked. 'Because I don't think she confessed yet. I haven't got my Key.'

'So you started pranking Mercy to give her a taste of her own medicine for a change,' Stigner said.

Emma nodded some more. 'It was just a silly game

at first. Dylan wasn't involved – he's too packed full of integrity for it to be his style. I thought I'd do a couple of gags, scare her off the play and maybe she'd – I don't know – actually learn something about herself from it. Like, think about why someone was doing it to her, and be nicer in future.'

'But that didn't work?' Stigner asked.

'No,' Emma said. 'After I reprogrammed her dressing-room iPod and sent the *Macbeth* script to her house, she went into diva *overload*. She wasn't getting the message. If anything she was being harsher to people than ever. That's when I switched her costume so it was blue. Oh, and ordered the T-shirts and put the feather in her pocket. When she saw the good luck banner and the flowers before opening night, I knew she'd flip. I hoped that would do it.'

'And when it didn't, you set up Thespis's Facebook page,' Stigner said.

Emma looked confused. 'Pardon?'

'The Facebook page. Come on, Emma, there's no point starting to lie again now. Tell us why you set up the account,' Detective Lee said.

'I'm sorry, Detective, but I genuinely do not know what you're talking about.'

Detective Lee pushed his hair back off his face. 'Emma, please. You were annoyed at Mercy. We know you set up the Facebook page to send her threatening messages. And when none of that put Mercy off her path, you realized you had to take serious action – you had to get her out of you and Dylan's lives for good.'

'No!' Emma shouted.

'The last four years have been horrendous for you,' he said. 'I can see how things have spiralled so out of control. I'm sure a judge will too.'

Emma's mouth set in a hard line. 'I'm a screwed-up part-time bitch, that I'll admit, Detective Lee, but I'm no murderer. Mercy was a pain in most of Palmer Peabody's ass at one point or another, but I didn't kill her for it. Don't try to make out that I did.'

Stigner stood up. 'Emma, after everything you've told us tonight, we've got no choice. We have to take you in.'

'No!' Lorna shouted. 'They can't do this. She's been honest about the pranks, why would she lie more? Nancy, you've gotta do something. She didn't hurt Mercy – you heard her!'

'I don't know what to do – we can't interfere with the Living investigation now or they'll know we're here and the adults could take us all away,' Nancy said. 'We can hardly get Mercy to appirate and say she doesn't think Emma's her murderer, can we?'

The cops helped Emma through the elevator doors.

'We have to stop them!' Lorna shouted.

Or maybe we had to admit that Emma could have killed Mercy Grant.

CHAPTER 26

'I've been in this place more than my body over the last week.' Mercy looked around Precinct 19's interview room. Still here. Still grey. 'If someone had told me my afterlife was going to involve quite this many municipal buildings, I would have demanded a do-over on Day One.'

'Okay, Emma, you sit here.' Detective Lee showed her in. The hem of her white lace gown was grey with dirt. 'I'm going to need you to tell me everything you just did about Mercy and the pranks in an official statement, then we'll—'

'Why?' Emma interrupted. 'I tried to clear things up, but you didn't listen. You're too intent on wrapping up this case before someone calls you out on how long it's taking you to solve the damn thing. You think I'm the one who made the rig come down on Mercy's head? I'm not saying another word until my parents and a lawyer are present.'

'Good girl,' Lorna said. 'They can't just bring a minor down here and intimidate her!'

Down the hall, someone was shouting. I couldn't make out whole words through the thick wall, but they sounded way mad.

'Fine, your parents are at the De Witts' party? I'll get them over. In the meantime . . .'

The shouting out front went from loud to noise complaint.

Nancy raised her eyebrows. 'Just after I've . . .' Detective Lee pushed open the door. Woah. Shout o'clock. 'Excuse me for one moment.' He headed commotion-ward down the hall, four dead girls trailing behind him.

'But I need to see Detective Lee NOW!' Dylan was shouting at the ancient front desk clerk. 'I have some information about Mercy Grant's murder that he needs to hear.'

'And, as I said, if you'll just take a seat, young man, I'll get someone to come and take a statement from you in a second,' the officer said not looking the least bit intimidated by Dylan. He probably had to deal with drunks, dealers and annoyed parents who'd come to bail out their pot-smoking Ivy League-applying offspring on a daily basis. A messy kid in a Captain America sweater, packing nothing more than an iPod Mini, was no threat round here.

'But it's important. He needs to hear it right now!' Even Dylan looked shocked by the decibel he was hitting.

'It's okay, Western.' Detective Lee took in the scene with a sigh. 'I'll talk to him. Dylan? This better be good.'

'Oh it is, sir.' He nodded furiously.

'And it better be *fast*,' Detective Lee said.

'Understood. So it's about the case,' Dylan said.

'Mercy's murder case.' Detective Lee fixed him with his harshest *come on already* stare. 'I have new information. Emma Altman has not been telling you the truth.'

Ohmigod, he was going to talk about the park argument, wasn't he? Man, I should have just told them about the park argument as soon as I'd seen it. Secrets always explode in the end. Lorna didn't look like she could take many more cliffhangers this evening.

'You know Emma said she was in the restroom when Mercy died?' Dylan said. 'Well, she wasn't – she was, um, backstage with me. So you see, you don't need to question her again like you did this afternoon. She couldn't have hurt Mercy. You can take her off your suspect list. Really you can.'

'Seriously, Dylan? Don't you think it's rather convenient you're suddenly coming in here now with this piece of information? Why would we believe anything Emma's boyfriend tells us? Especially when he knows she's in big trouble?' Detective Lee asked.

Dylan's eyes bulged. 'You know me and Emma are . . .? But—'

'Emma told us herself,' Detective Lee said.

'Oh, I . . .'

'So thank you for the new information, but I need to get back in the interview room now,' Detective Lee said.

'But I just told you something important.' Dylan grabbed the arm of the detective's coat. 'Emma didn't kill Mercy. I promise you. I was with her in the wings when the rig went down. We were together when I heard it crash. I wanted her to tell you days ago, but I figure she was too embarrassed. We were having some, um, alone time. And—'

'Eugh!' Lorna put her hands over her ears. 'I am going to pretend I never ever heard that.'

'And I will bear your information in mind, Dylan, but I have a more urgent line of inquiry I need to follow up on right now.' Detective Lee turned on his heel.

Dylan was owl-eyed. 'Do you need me to stick around and sign something that says I testify to that?'

Detective Lee had already moved on.

'The understudy did it? That's one cliché away from the butler in the drawing room with a lead piping,' Stigner said as he reached her down the corridor. 'I wouldn't want to be a character witness for Emma Altman right now, sir, but do you really think Mercy threatening to unveil who her boyfriend was would be enough to make a girl like Emma commit murder?'

Detective Lee massaged his temples. 'I hoped not. Really I did. After what happened to Lorna, more than any other kid, I didn't want Emma to be involved. That family have been through too much. But you have to look at the hard facts, Kat.'

'*Kat*? Did he just call her by her first name?' Nancy threw her hand clear through the grey wall.

'To say Emma's had a rough few years is the understatement of the century. She lost the person closest to her when she was twelve years old. That's a vital stage in child development,' Detective Lee said. 'When you were at Brown, how many studies did you read in psych class that showed what you go through at that age affects you into adulthood and beyond?'

'Too many to remember four years after graduation.' Stigner shook her head.

'Exactly. Emma didn't just lose a sister, she lost a sense of boundaries that day too. She probably has no idea what's acceptable in society,' Detective Lee said. 'If someone could get away with killing Lorna, then why couldn't Emma push it on the small stuff? Tests, friendships, fights. We know from her school file that Emma became physically aggressive in the months after Lorna's death. She's been a cocktail of anger, frustration and bitterness for more than four years. Mercy Grant, she wasn't the easiest person to get on with. Maybe she was the final blow that upset Emma's delicate balance?'

'I guess she doesn't have a solid alibi either – we can't trust what Dylan says about her being nowhere near that rig. Not now we know how he feels about her,' Stigner said. 'And we do know for a fact that Emma and Mercy were fighting before they went onstage. We have a witness who'll testify to that.' She kicked her heel against the grey skirting board. 'It's just . . .'

'Just what?'

'Just that my instinct says she didn't do it,' Stigner blurted. 'I know all the evidence points towards Emma, but I can't shake the feeling we're wrong.'

'Finally,' Lorna said, 'someone other than me is standing up for my sister! I've got to say, I'm kinda amazed it's Little Miss Ill-Fitting Pants over here.'

'Look, instinct's one of the most important cop skills,' Detective Lee said. 'But we have to go with fact. You've done brilliant work on this case, Stigner. You're going to be a great asset to the squad.'

318

'Eugh,' Nancy said.

'Oh stop being a meanie,' Lorna said. 'She's not so bad.'

'But yesterday you were saying how much you hate—'

'Let's go do this.' Detective Lee walked back to the room where Emma was sitting defiantly on her blue plastic chair. We followed numbly through the wall after him.

'Emma,' Detective Lee said, 'more than anyone I didn't want things to end this way, but I don't have any choice. You don't have a good alibi, you've admitted you were trying to scare Mercy and we know you were fighting with her before she went onstage. I wish you'd just admit that you're Thespis too – if you cooperate with us, things won't be as bad.'

Detective Lee opened Mercy's iPad and scrolled to Thespis's profile page. The creepy mask face stared out at the room. How had Mercy thought he was a hot guy? Emma ignored it, instead examining the yellowing plasterboard tiles on the ceiling.

Detective Lee took a deep breath. 'Fine,' he said. 'Emma Olivia Altman, I'm charging you with the murder of Mercy Grant. I'll notify your parents now. I'm sure they'll have a lawyer with you within the hour. Until then . . .'

'No, they can't do this!' Lorna moved to Emma's side. 'It's wrong! He's wrong! Even the Stigner girl thinks so! Nancy, do something – *anything*. Make them realize it wasn't my little sister.'

Nancy looked at her miserably, not sure what to do or say.

'Mercy?' Lorna said. '*Please*. Think of a reason it couldn't be Emma and I'll Throw it into Stigner's mouth.'

'Um, I . . .' Mercy was looking at Emma strangely.

Dah dah dah! On the table, Mercy's iPad chimed a three-note scale, lighting up. A small box popped up to say she'd got a new Facebook message.

'That was nothing to do with me,' Nancy said.

'Me neither,' said Mercy.

Stigner grabbed the tablet. 'Sorry, Detective, it's probably just another message on Mercy's memorial page. It makes that noise when one gets posted. I'll switch it off.'

'That's okay, let's . . .' He turned back to Emma. Even after everything she'd been through and everything she was facing now, she refused to cry. 'Actually, Stigner, can you pass me that thing?' Detective Lee said.

He flipped off the baby-blue cover. The little blue globe at the top of the screen had turned white, a red number '1' over it. One new notification. Lee clicked it and the list of Mercy's friends' activity flopped down, filling the screen. The top box was new, unread, the background lemon. 'Thespis mentioned you in a comment,' it said.

'But how could . . .?' Lee touched the screen again, his large thumbs nearly missing the right place. The screen flipped and this time a new message appeared, next to the profile picture of the dead-eyed grey stone mask.

'Sure you've cracked it?' the message from Thespis read.

'So if he's sending a message right now, then Emma can't be Thespis! Right?' For the first time in hours, Lorna dared a small smile.

'I guess but . . .' Mercy said.

'When was this posted?' Stigner's voice broke on the last syllable.

Detective Lee looked from the screen to monochrome clock on the wall. 'Twenty thirteen – one minute ago.'

Emma sat up in her chair. 'See! Jefferson, how could I have done that when I've been sat here? You took my phone on the way in. It's not like I've got another one I've been updating on under the table.' She put her hands in the air to show they were empty and mobileless.

'May I?' Stigner took the tablet and hit the back button. Unlike Detective Lee, she didn't handle the computer like it was from the future. She scrolled down, then her eyes widened. 'Detective, according to this, Thespis is online. Right now. Look.'

We all leaned over the screen, Lorna putting her head through Stigner's shoulder to get the best view.

There was a small green circle next to Thespis's name showing that he or she was accessing the site – from a mobile phone.

'James!' Detective Lee hollered, going for the door. 'Get in here now!'

Short Cop bolted into the room, his face flushed. 'Sir?'

'Thespis is apparently online right now – get Tech to find out the location of the cell where he or she is posting from.' James didn't move. 'NOW!' Detective Lee shouted. 'This is the best lead we've had all case.' James rushed out of the room.

Emma sat back and crossed her arms. 'So can I go now? You're going to un-charge me, right?'

'No, you're going to stay right here, where we can keep an eye on you,' Detective Lee said. 'There are still a lot of question marks over you. If Mercy's killer is out there, I don't want you running around and ruining the chance of the alibi you've just been given. Stigner: can you take Miss Altman back to my office and get another officer to keep her there?'

'On what charge?' Emma asked.

'On the one where you'll do what I say if you know what's good for you,' Detective Lee snapped back. 'I might book you for harassment for the tricks you pulled on Mercy Grant yet.'

Emma flipped her hair angrily, her eyes on fire.

'Emma, please,' he added more gently. 'It's for you and your family's good.'

'Please do as he says, Emma,' Lorna pleaded, even though her sister would never hear.

'Fine,' she said.

James skidded back into the room, nearly taking the spare chair by Stigner with him in his haste. 'Detective, we've got it!' He held up a small piece of white paper. 'The address, I mean. Because Thespis was online, the guys were able to track it in majorly fast time.'

'Good work.' Detective Lee took the paper from him. 'One one three eight Fifth Avenue,' he read. 'That's . . .'

'The De Witts' townhouse,' Emma said. 'Anyone who's anyone in Manhattan is there right now for the Frost Fête party.'

'Then we've got no time to lose.' Detective Lee pulled his charcoal jacket off the back of his chair and nodded for Stigner to follow him. 'James, get a team to follow us over – we might not know who we're looking for, but we can't let anyone leave that party.'

'Us too,' Nancy said. 'Lorna: port back to the Attesa, get Edison – we need all the help we can get. Charlotte: we'll get a head start on these guys.' She ported away.

Stigner led Emma out of the room. I grabbed Lorna's hand. 'It's going to be okay, you'll see,' I said. 'Ready?'

A young officer poked his head around the door. 'Thespis is offline already, sir,' he said. 'If the pattern of log-ins is anything to go by, we don't think he'll be back for a while.'

'Then we're just going to have to find him or her in the real world,' Detective Lee said. 'Let's nail this guy.'

CHAPTER 27

'It's way, like, more restrained than last year.' Kate adjusted her white butterfly mask so she could get a better look around the room. 'Do you think the De Witts decided going all out was inappropriate under the gnarly circumstances?'

'Totally.' Lilian shrugged off her cherry cashmere coat and handed it to the door dude without even looking at him. She, Kate and Jen were top to toe in lustrous white – like every guest in the room. 'Mercy was hardly Anastasia's BFF, but what with her murder being a week ago, Mr and Mrs DW probably thought it would be crass to be too jingle all the way.'

'*This* is restrained?' Nancy blew out her cheeks. 'Boy, they sure do things differently on this side of the Reservoir.'

Didn't they hell. Overnight, the De Witts' five-floor townhouse had been turned into the chicest of winter wonderlands. The antique furniture had been removed by some very careful elves and replaced by tulip armchairs, a dance floor and bar. Pristine white satin sheets covered the walnut panelled walls, up-lit by delicate green bulbs expertly placed along the white carpet – which Ana's mom had had laid especially for the event. It was like Mrs Claus had won big on the lottery and taken *Real Housewives* as an interiors reference point.

Every surface was the kind of perfect white my mom never let me wear because she knew it would end up latte-coloured with dirt within seconds. The polished tables, linebacker-sized standing lamps, cocktail trays, candles – everything was alabaster. The only object in the room that wasn't was the De Witts' two-storey high Norwegian Christmas tree. Its branches were unadorned – as if to say, decorations are sooo 2012. Just looking at the damn place made me worry I'd smudge the perfection.

This was most definitely a drunken-Santa-free zone.

'Is Payton here yet?' Kate asked. 'I thought she was getting a ride in your car, Lil.'

'She texted about an hour ago and said she was running late. Something about visiting Ryder and final adjustments to her dress.' Lilian unnecessarily straightened the spaghetti strap on hers. 'You know what she's like – probably just wanted to make an entrance.'

'They look like they've fallen straight off the top of the tree,' Nancy whispered, pointing at the Peabody girls in their designer maxis.

Like they were angelic enough to have scored a job up there.

'Jesus, can you get snow blindness when there isn't actually any snow?' Edison ported into the room and pretended to shield his eyes. Mercy and Lorna arrived a beat after him. In this weird-as setting, Edison looked like something off a Greek vase I'd seen at the Met – the only dark figure in a sea of frost. The bulbs made his eyes an even more intense emerald. I gave myself an internal slap for noticing.

'Seeing as this is the first big social event since my death, you'd have thought they'd have some sort of memorial to me here.' Mercy scanned the room. 'Like a photo on a table or an option to make a donation to a suitable charity in my memory.'

'Because the Whoops! I Angered A Pyscho Foundation is crying out for cash.' Ed shot me a smile.

I tried not to return it. This was not the time for guy drama. Much as I was enjoying this insight into the lives of the rich and ridiculous, we did have a murder to solve. And a Dead Girl to offload to the Other Side. 'Nancy, what's the plan?'

Nancy flipped to business mode. 'Okay, here's what we know for sure: Thespis sent a Facebook message from inside this house about ten minutes ago.'

I took in the room. Even though I'd only been scraping a B-minus in Math before my painful, messy and untimely death, even I could see there had to be over two hundred people here. How did you find a psycho in a haystack?

'And he did it from a mobile.' Nancy held up a second finger, counting her two pieces of evidence on her left hand. 'He's not used a computer for weeks. The cops' Tech guys detected that. Why change his habits now?'

'Maybe we just need to wait for Detective Lee to get here then?' Mercy stepped aside to make way for a waiter with a tray of smoking glasses with green-frosted rims. 'The cops could have traced his actual cell number by now. Maybe all they need to do is bound in here, surprise the guests, shut off the music and call Thespis's cell? When it rings, they'll have him!'

'Except Thespis is as clever as the guy who invented the boyfriend jean,' Lorna said. 'What? I know they're not super-flattering on everyone, but they hide a multitude of sins if you're having a fat day, let me tell you.'

Like she ever had those.

'Thespis isn't gonna send some cop-baiting nuh-nuh-nuh-nuh-nuh! message then just leave his mobile switched on to be found,' Lorna said. 'He's totally not the rookie mistake type.'

'No, I agree, his cell will be off already.' I tucked a stray wave behind my ear, trying not to be so aware of how close Edison was standing. 'And stowed in his pocket? Or if he's a she, her purse?'

'Yeah, come on, a bit of gender equality for the murderer,' Edison said. 'Stop with the "he's" already.'

'Everyone in here's probably got two cells, an iPad and a BlackBerry at least.'

So all we needed to do was find a person with one of those on them in a room full of millionaire workaholics, Internet obsessives and gossip queens? Easy days.

Lorna looked like a girl who'd just run round the sports track three times and her gym teacher had told her to do another two laps.

Nancy pulled out her trusty notebook and began flipping the pages, hoping for a lightning bolt of inspiration. We had less leads than a retired pet walker.

But I didn't want to verbalize that, because while we were freaking out, somewhere nearby, Mercy's own personal Norman Bates was enjoying a chilled crystal-cut flute of ten-year-old Moët and debating whether to enter the charity draw to win a weekend in Maine or Mauritius. Awesome.

'But Thespis is also getting cocky.' Nancy tapped her pen on the crowded page of notes. 'Think about it: why else would he send that message to the police, taunting them like that? He's stopped being so careful all of a sudden. He's enjoying playing the game now and that means he might get sloppy.'

'He or *she* better get sloppy fast,' Edison said. 'Because we still have an Emma in jail, a murderer on the loose and a dead drama queen *sans* Key.'

'How did Thespis know the cops had Mercy's iPad?' Lorna's brow wrinkled. 'Don't you think that was kinda odd?'

Nancy shrugged. 'Could be a heap of ways – let's not worry about that right now. Lorna, Mercy, you've been to these things a million times: how do they usually play out?'

Lorna looked enviously at a woman in an expertly cut cream dress. It was a bit Pippa-at-the-wedding for me, but Lorna could totally have worked it. 'People mill, discuss the scandal *du jour*, which right now is still you, Mercy – and probably the NYPD's intense interest in my little sister – then try to figure how early they can leave without being talked about too.'

'How about we divide up the room then?' I asked. 'Check out if anyone's missing?' It wasn't really a plan-plan, but no one seemed to have anything better.

Nancy mentally carved up the place into three large murderer-holding slabs. 'Lorna, you and I will take to the right of the tree . . .'

Lorna gave her a small smile. Now that Emma was – hopefully – off the suspect list, I really hoped they could make this up.

'. . . Charlotte, you and Edison to the left. Mercy, I want you to cover the area beyond the grand piano – you know everyone. Monitor who's coming through the door. If they're just arriving now, they can't have sent the message earlier – we can strike them off the list.'

'Yes, ma'am.' Mercy bobbed a little bow and headed to her station.

Edison touched my shoulder, making the whole room slide like your grip on a melting frappucino cup. Seriously, we were going to have to talk about him just doing that. 'Shall we?'

'Let's do this!' Nancy clapped her hands. 'He or she's in here. We can crack this tonight. Maybe even without Detective Lee's help. I can feel it.' She and Lorna disappeared into the crowd.

'So this is what a Frost Fête looks like.' Edison pointed at my school uniform. 'You really haven't observed the dress code, Ghostgirl.' We were alone now. Well, as alone as you can get in a Living room. 'Ever attend something this fancy when you were alive?'

I snorted. Which was *so* attractive. 'Hardly. This is about as unreal to me as the *Hamlet* set. You?'

'Sure, I escorted the odd debutante to her cotillion, but

329

I can't say it ever flew my kite as much as an evening spent porting around Internet joints on the Lower East Side.'

I tried to focus on the group of tuxed-up guys beside us and not think about the last time I'd seen him – and my boy-grabby behaviour. 'Do you ever not turn a perfectly sensible question into a joke?' I asked.

'Um, coming from the most sarcastic girl this city's seen since Mae West bit the dust, I think that's a little fresh.'

'I have no idea who you're talking about. I'm just trying to help Mercy get her Key.' It came out snarkier than it had sounded in my head.

'Jeez, what's a guy got to do to get a break around here?' Edison asked. 'I thought we talked and cleared the air the other night? Now you seem to be mad at me again. Your brain must be getting whiplash from all the changing of direction it's doing this week.'

'My brain? What about yours?' I asked. 'Am I a nice guy or a bad guy? Nice guy or a moron? Nice guy or a—'

Out of nowhere, Edison bent down and pressed his lips to mine. I remembered Miss Jackson, my Lit teacher, once telling us how there weren't certain words in the English language to express how some things felt. Like, we had one word for 'ice' and Inuits had fifty. I didn't know which word I was looking for to describe how I felt, but I knew I didn't dare open my eyes until I was sure I could without toppling over.

'Sorry, what incredibly important thing you were saying?' Ed grinned down at me, his hand still burning on the small of my back. Brilliant. My brain and feet seemed to have severed communications completely.

'I was *saying* . . . Er . . . I . . .' Way to go, Charlotte. Way to impress.

Two waitresses carrying an ice sculpture of an eagle brushed past and Edison moved a step closer again to stop a full on walk-through.

'I was . . . saying that we better . . .'

'Anastasia!' an elderly woman with black, pokey-uppy hair shouted past us, totally breaking the moment. Without wanting to sound like a panellist from *Fashion Police*, she looked like a big white igloo. I wondered how many words the Inuits had for that.

'Oh hey, Mrs West.' Anastasia delicately popped a polenta, fig and goat's cheese canapé into her mouth. Boy, I wished I still needed to eat. Ana's fiery waves looked even more dramatic against her white Grecian dress. I couldn't believe we hadn't noticed her as soon as we ported in. 'Where's your grandson?'

'So that's Dylan's grandmother?' Edison asked taking in her sour expression.

'I guess.'

Mrs West senior scanned the room as if Ana had just asked her to Hoover the place.

'I've not seen him since the maid took our coats at the door twenty minutes ago,' she said. 'His father refuses to attend events like this and I got horribly sidetracked talking to Captain Cassidy about those terrible lies about him and the chauffeur.' She refocused on Ana. 'Dylan will be skulking around somewhere and avoiding conversation, no doubt. I was hoping Emma Altman was going to be a positive influence on him – they seem to have been together quite a lot of late – but now that seems to be *far* from the mark.'

Ana balled up her napkin and tossed it on the floor. 'And why is that, Mrs West?' I'd heard that temperature in Ana's voice before. This could turn bad.

'Because since poor Mercy passed, Emma Altman has been in and out of Precinct 19 more often than a pair of handcuffs. I feel for her parents. They gave those girls everything. First Lorna, now this.' Mrs West senior inspected her string of heirloom pearls.

'*This* is not a *this*.' Ana shooed another waitress away before Mrs West had a chance to take a Brie and cranberry pastry bite from the tray. 'Emma's not been charged with anything. She was *friends* with Mercy. We all were. I don't think it's your place to go around defaming people because you don't know the entire story, do you?' Her cheeks were so pink, her freckles almost disappeared.

'Anything of any note?' Nancy asked porting over with Lorna. 'All anyone's discussing over that side of the room is share prices and the cost of a compound with a pool upstate.'

'I'd forgotten just how dull these evenings can be,' Lorna said, before noticing Ana's face of thunder. 'Or is it about to get interesting?'

'Ana! Please! You have no right to talk to a lady of Mrs West's standing that way.' A beautiful older redhead rushed over. 'Jane, I'm sorry.' She touched Mrs West's arm. 'Ana's been under a lot of strain this week. All the girls have. Dylan too I imagine – he was there too after all.'

'Mom, that's as may be, but Mrs West is a guest in *our*

house and I won't have anybody bad-mouthing Emma.' Ana ran a hand through her hair in frustration, her gold ring glinting under the lights.

'*She* was being mean about my sister?' Lorna asked. 'You know she spends hundreds in Orlo, this super-duper swanky salon that, like, Gwynnie and SJP and Beyoncé go to. And she's still got the family scarecrow hair. Like my mom says, some people get the follicles they deserve.'

'Lorna, wait.' I was staring at Anastasia's hand. The ring. I'd seen one like it somewhere. Small and gold, a thin rope band of swirling letters, that spelt out . . . Oh.

I spun to face Ed. 'Her hand – where have we seen a ring like that before?'

Ed bent down by Ana's side to see, then stood up fast. 'It's one of those gold slogan rings, from that place on Delancey – the one right opposite—'

'In the Net, the Internet café where Thespis accessed his Facebook page,' I finished.

'Don't be silly.' Lorna's voice broke. 'Thespis can't be Ana, she's Emma's best friend. She'd never let her take the fall, let her be questioned while she was out here at some ball.'

'Unless she knew that Emma was being questioned and decided to log on one last time, send a message and get her best friend off the hook?' Nancy said.

'But she . . . why would she . . .'

'I want you all to know right now that I am taking this one for the team.' Edison grimaced and jumped straight into old Mrs West. 'Urgh,' she shivered.

'Pardon, Jane, did you say something?' Mrs De Witt

asked. 'Can I get you some more champagne? You look a little low.'

'I was just admiring Anastasia's lovely ring. Where did you get it from, dear?' Possessed Granny Dylan asked.

Ana looked at her like she was certifiably insane – suddenly changing from being Dylan's tiger gran to a jewellery fanatic.

'Oh, some place downtown. You wouldn't know it.' She shrugged.

'Try me,' Mrs West said. 'I might want to get one for my niece.'

'Fine,' she sighed. 'It was a place down on the Lower East Side.'

'Oh, I think I know the one you mean, opposite that Internet coffee shop. The one with the funny name? In the something.'

'Net. It's called In the Net.' Anastasia cocked her head staring at Mrs West very strangely. 'Though I can't ever imagine *you* down there.'

Mrs West's body shivered as Edison fell out.

'So Ana's been to the Lower East Side, plenty of girls like to slum it once in a while,' Lorna said. 'Where's Payton? She's got psycho written through her like a stick of rock. She could be squirrelled away, in some room upstairs, updating Thespis's account again as we—'

Pop! As usual Mercy arrived as if she'd been given a cue. 'Sorry, but nothing exciting was going on over there. I checked out the doorman's list and most people are here now. I'm leadless once more. I'm guessing you guys are too?'

We stared at her, no one quite sure what to say.

The head catering dude rushed over, his face as pink as a sausage. 'Mrs De Witt, sorry to interrupt but my security team say the police have just pulled up.' He touched his earpiece with his finger. 'And there's a lot of them. What do you want us to do?'

If I didn't know better, I'd have assumed the crescendo of sirens building under the DJ's music were just part of the track.

Mrs De Witt paled. 'I'll assume your team won't be letting them up without very good reason.' She turned to her daughter. 'Anastasia, can you go and find your father for me please? Ana?'

But Ana had gone. Her fiery head was nowhere to be seen.

CHAPTER 28

'Quick! We can't let her go!' Nancy ported to the other side of the room, ready to run through the grand wooden door. 'Guys, come on! Anastasia can't have gone far. Living girls don't move that fast, remember?'

Edison grabbed my hand. We bailed through the party guests, landing seconds after Mercy and Lorna.

'What kept you?' Nancy shouted. 'Let's go!'

Lorna waited for a guest to open the door, then strolled through, Mercy numbly trailing after her.

'Nancy,' she said. 'I'm not sure about this. Yes, Anastasia's been to that café where Thespis went on his Facebook page, but that doesn't mean she *is* him, or that she killed Mercy.' Lorna stood in the hallway, refusing to move while the De Witts' security team buzzed around her. 'I know you want to wrap up this case, but let's not do anything mulehardy.'

'Foolhardy, it's *fool*hardy.' Nancy took off her glasses and rubbed her eyes. 'The word refers to idiots, not stupid donkeys.'

She pushed her glasses back on and faced her friend.

'Lorna, with the greatest, greatest respect, you have been too close to this case to see the wood for the green stuff from the beginning,' Nancy said. 'You said Emma was nothing but sweetness and light, then we discovered she'd been pranking Mercy to shake her up. Now you don't think Ana – her best friend – could have done something bad either? I don't want to sound harsh, but if we were talking about any group of people apart from your family and friends here, you would be coming to the same conclusions as me. Please say you can see that.'

Lorna eyed her coolly. 'No, Nancy, I can't. All I can see is a tangled case where we don't have all the answers, and you're jumping from suspect to suspect like a monkey in a tree.' Lorna's eyes darted up the stairs as the banister made a low creak. 'Take a second to think this through.'

Nancy's gaze followed the noise. Ten guesses who'd just bolted up there.

'I can't,' Nancy said. 'We have to check out Anastasia before we lose our chance. She's been to In the Net. She disappeared the second she heard the cops were on their way. She could have sent that Facebook message from here. If Dylan really was with Emma when the rig came down, then her alibi's vanished too.' Nancy's expression softened. 'If I'm wrong, I promise I'll say I'm wrong, but right now we don't have time to debate this. Someone's up there and I'd bet every case file in the Attesa that it's Ana. Let's finish this one way or another.'

'They've got a warrant,' the doorman mountain told the head security guy. 'We've got to let them in, no matter what the De Witts say.'

'Fine.' He pressed his earpiece lightly again. 'But can you stall them for five minutes so I can prepare the family before all hell breaks loose?' The doorman nodded, as the head of security strode back into the party room.

'See!' Nancy said. 'The murder squad won't be here for another five minutes; we owe it to Mercy not to waste one second of them.'

Mercy. In all the drama, I'd almost forgotten about her.

She was standing silently at the bottom of the staircase, her hand hovering just above the banister, her face as much of a mask as the ones Lilian and Kate wore earlier. I tried to remember how it felt to be in this moment – the one where, for you, it could finally be over. The rush that you'd nearly, maybe, solved the case you were left on earth to crack. The sickening dullness that everything that you'd clung to since the worst happened – no matter how heartbreaking or confusing or downright lame – was about to be taken away. And wondering – what would be left?

The DJ's music shut off exposing a low hum of confused chatter.

'Where's Ana's room?' Nancy held out her hand to Lorna to lead the way.

'Up four flights, to the right. Unless she's moved wings since I last babysat.' Lorna left Nancy's palm floating sadly in the air.

As we climbed up the marble stairs, the lights from the party dimmed to dusk. The De Witts hadn't been expecting guests to venture up here tonight. Only the buzz of Ed's hand holding mine anchored me to the fact that this wasn't a dream.

Soon the stairs ran out and we saw a horizontal sliver of yellow light, peeking out from under a door. 'This is Ana's room?' Nancy asked.

I could just make out the motion of Lorna's blonde head nodding in the gloom.

'Let's do this.' Nancy stepped through the closed door. One by one we followed. Tickle. Tickle. Tickle.

It took my eyes a second to adjust. From the length of the shadows, I could tell Ana's room was even bigger than Mercy's, and with less clutter and chintz. It was charcoal dark apart from the far left corner, where someone had thrown on a lamp. A silhouette darted across it.

And that's when I saw it. The proof. Ana determinedly trying to push open her heavy bedroom window, a lifeless cell phone beside her on the ledge.

Lorna let out a little moan.

'She's got a phone. Do you think that means . . .?' Mercy pushed her palms together.

'It means we need to get Detective Lee, and fast,' Nancy strode towards Ana. 'There's no point in us getting a confession out of her if Jefferson's not here to hear it. He needs enough ammo to arrest her. We can't let her dump the cell – it's the final piece of evidence that Anastasia is Thespis. We mustn't scare her dumb like you did with Library Girl, Charlotte.' She looked at me with a worried face, like I was about to zombie uncontrollably all over the place.

'I can't see too well.' Mercy tripped through a footstool.

Nancy impatiently clicked her fingers and the room was bathed in light. Ana looked up in shock and pushed the window harder. We didn't have long.

'Should I go possess Detective Lee and walk him up here?' I pointed a thumb towards the door. 'It might take a while – he's going to be heavy. Plus, we don't even know if he's been let in the building yet by Dumb and Dumber.'

The window gave a little squeak.

'Quick, someone do something!' Mercy wailed. 'If Ana goes through that window, she's taking my Key with her.' Now she was awake.

Ana was unscrewing the ancient locks in the window frame now. Any second she'd have it open.

'No time.' Ed's voice was low. 'I've got it covered.'

Ana threw the lock on the floor and impatiently began to push up the window. Nancy bolted to her side, Jabbing it shut and using her energy to hold it there.

I knew in a second of looking into his eyes what he was about to do. 'Edison, are you sure about this? Like Mercy said, he's a big guy. You know what it did to you the last time.'

'The last time? What last time?' Lorna asked.

Nancy was losing hold of the window. 'Edison, if you've got some secret magic trick up your sleeve which is going to stop Anastasia getting away with murder, get down with your dark arts *now*.' She was strong, but couldn't win against Ana for much longer.

I looked down and realized I was still holding Ed's hand. I squeezed it. Even from across the room, I could feel Nancy's eyes on me, but at that moment I really didn't care. 'Be careful, okay?' I said.

Edison face broke into crooked smile. 'Don't worry your pretty head about me, Ghostgirl. What's the worst that could happen? I'm already dead.'

Then he was gone.

'What the freak is wrong with this thing?' Ana cursed as she tried to lift the window. She slammed it upwards with her shoulder. Nancy fell backwards in a bundle of stripes and skirt – energy gone. The window shot up with such unexpected force, Ana fell onto the carpet beside her.

'Fine!' Lorna stepped up to where Nancy's hands had been. 'I'm still not one gazillion per cent behind this, Nancy, but I am behind you.' I watched as she pushed her power up her body, focusing it into her hands. She slammed the window shut once more.

'What the hell?' Ana jumped up, but once more it was held fast, some invisible force working against her.

'Oh for God's sake,' she muttered, taking a paper-weight from her desk and throwing it through the glass.

Didn't see that one coming. Shoot.

The pane shattered outward. Ana took a pillow from her bed and pushed it into the gap, taking the last few deadly pieces of glass with it.

'Anyone would think she'd done that before,' Mercy said.

Ana pulled the upholstered footstool over to the window and climbed on it, shimmying up her long white skirt, ready to climb through the glassless gap.

'Charlotte, quick, she's going to get away!' Nancy was right. We couldn't wait for Edison. His plan was a major gamble. Maybe the trick only worked on Matt because he was Ed's brother? Edison didn't have the same emotional link to Detective Lee. Maybe that meant he couldn't port his body in the same way?

I ran to the window and tried to Jab the stool away. If I couldn't stop Ana, at least I could slow her down. The footstool was as heavy as ten Christmas cakes. Damn the Upper East Siders and their stupid antiques. What was wrong with furnishing your kids' rooms with IKEA like the rest of the planet? I Jabbed it again. The stool barely wobbled. Ana lifted her foot, ready to climb through the window.

Lorna rushed to my side. 'On one, two . . .' she counted, as we prepped to use our joint strength to push the stool away.

There was a loud crash from the other side of the room. Ana and Nancy squealed in unison.

The crash-maker stood up with a jolt. All six foot three of him. Ana froze like her mom's ice sculpture.

He brushed down his charcoal suit, looking even more confused than her. Then shivered and took a step forwards, as Edison fell out of him and onto the bedroom floor in a defeated heap.

'Detective Lee? But, Edison, how did you . . .?' It was a trick to blow even Nancy's galaxy-sized mind.

'I'll explain later,' I whispered, trying to get a clear view round Detective Lee's bulk at an unmoving Ed.

Jefferson sprang to his senses like a TV coming off standby. He took in the scene: an empty room, shattered glass, Anastasia De Witt by a broken window, a cell in one hand, the window frame in the other. A suspect trying to escape.

'Stop!' he said, somehow simultaneously radioing down to Stigner that he was in what he assumed to be Ana's room.

'Wow, he's good,' Nancy said from the floor.

'With *our* help,' Lorna added.

Jefferson ran to the window, but Ana was fast. In the time it took him to cross the room, she'd ducked through the frame and onto the fire escape outside.

'Guys, come on!' Nancy used all her remaining energy to pull herself up and out after her. Lorna and Mercy pushed the window up for Detective Lee to climb through. He barely blinked as it magically rose like an automatic shop door.

I threw a helpless look at Edison who was lying on his back on the floor, barely moving.

'Go.' His voice sounded like someone else's. 'Nancy needs you.'

I didn't want to leave him – really I didn't – but I didn't want what he'd just done to be in vain. Reluctantly, I followed the others outside. Ana was standing on the black bars of the fire escape grate away from the window.

'Anastasia, why don't you come back inside already?' Unlike Ana, Detective Lee's back was firmly against the townhouse's red-brick exterior. 'Whatever you've done, there's no need for you to be out here.' He moved a hand off the wall and held it out towards her.

'Really? Then why are you chasing me through my own home and out onto the fifth floor?' She wobbled on her gold heels. They were designed for strutting, not balancing on icy metal grates. Ana gripped the rail harder to steady herself.

'I really don't like this,' Lorna said. 'Can't we do anything to get her back inside? Jab her in?'

Detective Lee changed tack. 'Look, we know all about

the pranks Emma was pulling on Mercy and why. But she didn't kill her, did she?'

'As the old saying goes, "No shit, Sherlock."' Ana's left heel slipped through the grate and she stumbled forward. *If I still had a heart, it would have been in my mouth.*

'He needs to get her away from there *now*,' Lorna said. 'It's not safe.'

'Like it wasn't safe when I went out onstage that night?' Mercy's eyes had turned to glass.

Ana gracefully leaned down and took off one stiletto, then the other. She casually tossed them into the backstreet below. *It took a full four beats before I heard them hit the bed of snow.*

'We know that Thespis sent a message from a cell somewhere inside this house tonight.' Detective Lee watched as she curled her red-polished toes over the bars beneath her feet. 'And do you know what's been bothering me ever since we received it? Why he – or she – would do a thing like that.'

Ana stretched her arms across on the rail and leaned back, her volcanic hair falling down her back.

'I mean, it's kind of stupid,' Detective Lee continued. 'Between you and me, our leads were drying up. Thespis knew we had a scapegoat in custody and were ready to arrest her. He was getting away with murder. Why risk being caught by turning a disposable cell on again and sending a message to let us know we had the wrong person all along?'

Despite herself, Ana shivered. *It must be five below.*

'Then it struck me – you'd only do that for one of two

344

reasons.' Detective Lee and Ana were only five feet apart but it felt like an ocean.

'Why's he not moving towards her?' Lorna asked. 'He's strong. He could grab her and take her inside.'

'The vertigo,' Nancy said. 'Detective Lee is scared of heights, remember? He must be terrified.'

'The first reason would be that Thespis was wholly psychotic.' Detective Lee's tone was level and calm. 'So psychotic, he got a kick out of messing with us. But I don't think that fits in with Thespis's profile. He's smart – look at the way he used computers in cafés that were about to close or didn't have CCTV.'

'Where's he going with this?' Mercy asked.

'The second reason would be that Thespis cared for the scapegoat. A great deal. If he'd, say, been through pure hell with her – like, watching her lose her big sister – and loved her like a best friend. Maybe then he'd be brave enough to risk his own freedom – even in the smallest way – to ensure Emma had hers?' Detective Lee let the question hang in the freezing night air.

'Oh, will you just get to the point, Detective,' Ana said. 'We've been through this. I didn't like Mercy Grant – I've told you that – but I sure as hell didn't kill her. What reason would I possibly have to do that?' Ana's breath turned to white steam.

'Now, you see, that was bothering me too.' He tried to take a step away from the wall, balked and failed. 'Then Stigner made something of what we call a *breakthrough*.'

'Without me?' Nancy asked.

'I don't know why we didn't see it before.' Detective Lee's shoe squeaked on the painted metal. 'It was in a folder marked "For Harvard". We were stupid, really, not to spot it, but we just saw Mercy's admission essays in there and didn't think to check through the rest of the documents.'

Detective Lee pulled Mercy's iPad from behind his back. He must have been holding it when Ed brought him here. He'd been too crushed against the wall for me to notice it until now.

'What is that?' Ana blinked at the screen as Detective Lee clicked open a file.

'Don't play dumb, Anastasia,' he said. 'You're more than aware of what this is.'

'I'm not playing anything.' Her eyes flashed defiantly. 'You tell me what that is and then tell me what it's got to do with me.'

Detective Lee zoomed in on a shot. 'It's a picture of you: dancing on a table, looking pretty wasted, smoking something that is clearly not a normal cigarette.'

'Oh come on!' Her hair spun around her face like a halo of fire. 'My three-year-old nephew could have created that on Photoshop. You've found out enough about Mercy Grant by now to know that she wasn't about to win Humanitarian of the Year any time soon. She probably doctored that herself. Like that would have bothered me.'

'Mercy!' Nancy said. 'What is that picture? Is it real?'

'That was *months* ago, I don't know why he's . . .' Mercy stuttered.

'Anastasia, we found the email – the one where Mercy told you if you went for the part of Hamlet, she'd make sure the dean of admissions at Harvard saw that picture.'

Ana looked down to the backstreet below. The snow was so thick there.

'We know she was threatening you, threatening your future. We know she was upsetting your best friend. You are currently standing on a fire escape in arctic temperatures holding a cell which I guarantee if I turn on will be the one Thespis sent that Facebook message from.' He sighed. 'Come clean and admit you *are* him and things will be a lot easier.'

Ana closed her eyes. She took a long breath.

'I could take Mercy threatening to send that picture of me to Harvard,' she said finally. 'Hell knows what she would have held over me next, but I could deal with someone like *her*. A bit of snooping. A few rumours. If she'd really tried to mess with me, I could have shattered Mercy Grant's reputation more easily than that window frame. But when she tried to break Emma – I had enough.'

'Uh oh,' I heard myself say.

'You know what Emma's been through.' She opened her amber eyes and stared at the detective. 'You saw her after Lorna's murder. Something died in her along with her sister. She was a mess for so long. Nothing I could do would pick her back up. Nothing.'

She traced a finger across the rail. 'Then Dylan came along, with his stories about Lorna and his puppy dog adoration and he started to change that,' Ana said. 'I get why she didn't want their relationship getting out. After what Emma's been through, she has a right to be bruised and brittle and paranoid.'

'Jeez, do I have to say I'm sorry about this again?'

347

Mercy asked. 'I really, really didn't know all the circumstances. I'm not *that* much of a biyatch.'

'If you want your Key, shhhh.' I put a finger to my lips, as Lorna scowled at her.

'That's why I put the idea in Emma's mind,' Ana said, 'why not give Mercy some of her own medicine. We'd set up some harmless, schoolgirl pranks to make her stop and think about her actions. Best case scenario: she'd be so scared she'd pull out of the play and someone like Payton could have a starring role for a change. Worst case: she learnt nothing. Of course the problem was that my plan failed. Nothing we did stopped Mercy Grant being her horrendous self.'

'Hey!' Mercy said.

'So I decided to take things a step further. To deal with her in a language that she could really understand. I did some more research and I made Thespis – the theatre's greatest prankster – come to life online. God, even then Mercy didn't seem that bothered. So that's when I decided I was really going to scare her, and I sent the email turning her page into a memorial.' Ana shook her head. 'A little too dark all things now considered, that even I'll admit.'

'Ana, I need you to come with me now.' Detective Lee held out a hand. 'I need you to say all of that at the station.'

'Why? So you can hold me the way you're holding Emma?' She made her way towards the escape's ladder, pushing it down. 'Who's going to send the message that gets me off the hook, Detective Lee?'

'If you just admit it, I can get you help,' he said, edging forward. 'You owe it to Emma. Mercy too.'

Her eyes darkened. 'I don't. I don't owe Mercy Grant anything.' She hitched up her gown and swung a leg onto the metal steps. The ladder noisily creaked.

'You killed Mercy Grant,' Detective Lee said. 'I will prove that.'

'What?' Ana stopped mid-swing and put her other leg back on the grate. 'You think *I* killed Mercy?' She laughed.

'Gee, has she finally lost it?' Nancy asked, looking back into Ana's room where we could see Stigner and the cops appearing as if on cue. 'She just confessed. Why's she still running? There are police guys everywhere. She won't make it one block.'

Ana hauled herself over onto the ladder. 'Fine.' She smiled. 'I killed Mercy Grant. Is that what you want to hear? Will that wrap up your case in some neat little bow so you can file it with all the others?' Ana pushed her full weight backwards onto the ladder. 'Bite me, Detective Lee.'

There was a scream of metal as the ladder ripped away from the rail. Ana's eyes widened in horror.

Detective Lee ran across the grate. 'Quick! Give me your hand,' he shouted. 'I can . . .' But he was too late.

The ladder pulled away from the wall with a nauseating wail. Behind us, Stigner reached the window and screamed.

The ladder broke away, falling onto the street below.

This time I didn't count the beats before it hit the snow.

CHAPTER 29

'So how does this work?' Mercy scuffed her blue and yellow Adidas. They squeaked on the Attesa's tiled lobby floor. 'Does some spectral mail dude turn up with my Key in special delivery?'

'Depends,' Nancy said, helping me to lower Edison onto the black leather couch. Man, he was wiped out. And heavy. Without leaning on me, Ed could barely stand. I wasn't sure if this new vulnerable, reliance thing was hot. But the gallantly stepping-in-to-save-the-day thing? Definitely.

'As soon as your murderer confesses, a ghost usually gets pulled back to the hotel by a some sort of force, then when they arrive they have their Key,' Nancy explained. 'For instance, Charlotte's was in her hand when she got back.'

Sure he was down safely, Nancy let go of Edison and straightened her Breton top. 'It makes sense really – whatever controls this world wants us to go through the Big Red Door and to the Other Side as soon as possible, as we should have done if we hadn't been murdered. Plus ...' She looked at me uncomfortably.

'It's okay, Nance, you can say it. *Plus* if you don't get your ghostly ass through the Door asap, some evil, stuck-here, bitter nut-job could go cuckoo on your Key. I mean, why waste valuable time finding your own Key when there's a perfectly good one just sitting on a table waiting to be stolen?' I took a seat on the edge of the couch. No, I wasn't ever going to be able to talk about that without sounding like vinegar.

Edison moaned, and his eyes blinked open, locking on mine.

I was suddenly very glad I was sitting down. The new reliance thing was totally hot.

'So I just wait then?' Mercy really needed to stop with the nervous shoe-scuffing. Couldn't she go run through some walls to ease the frustration like a normal dead person?

Pop! Lorna ported into the lobby. Her eyes were shining and there was a small smile back on her lips. It was as if between the De Witts' townhouse and here somebody had charged her battery back up to 100 per cent. 'I went to the police station – Emma's been let out! You should have seen my mom and dad. They were so happy. Dylan too. Emma even hugged him in front of them!'

'Did they tell her about Ana yet?' I asked.

The light in Lorna's eyes dimmed and I immediately regretted asking the question.

Now that was a conversation-stopper.

She nodded slowly. 'She was super, super-upset. No, she was devastated. She totally couldn't believe it. She kept saying over and over that Ana would never do anything like that, how the detectives must have it wrong. But I guess that's the grief talking, right? She's been through an unbelievable amount in the last twenty-four hours – losing her closest friend on top *and* finding out Emma wasn't who she thought she was. Even Nancy couldn't process that amount of drama easily.'

Mercy looped an arm around Lorna's waist. 'I was majorly shocked when we found out that Anastasia had killed me, too. Hands up, we were never within three blocks of being friends. And I *had* been messing with her just to make the mighty Ana sweat, but I thought the worst she'd do was start a rumour about me or go to my mom. I didn't think she'd cyber-stalk me, then send a lighting rig crashing down on my head. It's kind of an overreaction.' Mercy forced a smile. 'Emma's a good person. It's so, so much to take in. But she'll be okay.'

Lorna gave Mercy a quick *thanks* squeeze.

'Should I start packing then?' Mercy asked, breaking away. 'Not that I've got a lot of stuff. Or, actually, *any* stuff. When I get out of here, can I change out of this ridiculous get-up?' She pointed down at her leggings, crop top, chunky necklace and beanie hat. It was the necklace that did it. It was the Worst.

'It was bad enough meeting you guys in this outfit, but at least you had context,' Mercy said. 'The next ghosts I meet might just think I'm a total fool. Like I wore these kind of clothes every day.'

The next ghosts? I'd never really wondered about the next ghosts. I'd not let myself – not now I'd lost my key and knew I'd never meet them.

'Oh, I don't know!' Lorna said. 'How did I never think about that before? Maybe you finally get to choose what you want to wear? Like, if you're going to be on the Other Side forever, there must be some fashion plan. Even people who work for those drab city banks might get a wardrobe allowance. Nancy, do you think there's—'

Wah! Wah! Wah!

We looked at each other in confusion. The new ghost alarm. Talk about bad timing.

Wah! Wah! Wah!

Edison squeezed my hand and tried unsuccessfully to get up. Dizzy Boy was going to have to sit this one out.

Nancy rushed over to the old-fashioned mail chute at the front desk. The light above it was flashing madly. I squeezed Ed's hand back.

Same as always, a letter sealed with red wax appeared. Even though we'd only just solved the last murder and not even seen Mercy get her Key yet, Nancy couldn't hide her excitement as she tore it open.

She scanned the words, then took a step back, clumsily bumping into the desk. That was a Charlotte move, not a Nancy one. Something was wrong. Something big.

'Um, I . . .' she managed.

'What's up?' Lorna asked. 'Tell us already. Oh no, did someone you knew and hated in Living life die? I always worry about that. Because you'd have to, like, help them solve their case. But you'd have to be nice to them when you were doing it and . . .'

'The new arrival . . .' Nancy was unable to finish the sentence. Her eyes welled.

Woah, how had the new boy or girl been killed? It

must be in seriously gnarly circumstances for Nancy to be balking. Thank God we turned up here looking as we had before we died. Or I'd be rocking subway track chic.

I jumped up from the couch and walked to the desk to help. I tried to ease the letter out of Nancy's hand, but she was holding it way too tight.

'Oh, Charlotte,' she said, finding my eyes. 'We've done something wrong. So very, very wrong.'

'What?' Lorna rushed over. 'Tell us. We can work it out together – whatever it is we can make it right.'

'And I'll help all I can,' Mercy said. 'Well, until my Key arrives. Do you think that letter slowed it down?' She looked up the mail chute for signs of her Key. 'Maybe it can only deliver one thing at a time. Ohmigod, can Keys get lost in the mail?' She pulled a panicked face. 'Could it have gone to the wrong hotel?'

Nancy's bottom lip fluttered, her eyes sad. 'Mercy, we might need to wait a little while for it to appear.'

'Why? Has it got lost? There must be someone we can complain to.' Mercy pulled herself up to her full height. 'I bet there's someone from USPS in the adult hotel – you can't tell me no one's been driven to murder by their service before. And—'

Pop! 'Where the *hell* am I?' an angry voice shouted from the other side of the lobby. 'Did I pass out? If this is another idiotic, ineffectual police station, I'm telling you right now, I am not saying another word until my lawyer gets here. I'm sick to death of being persecuted like this. Why can't you people get on with your proper jobs – you know, like, actually catching criminals – instead of wasting your time on me?'

Oh. My. God.

I turned. We all did. And there she was. In her gorgeous floor-length white designer dress, her red hair spilling over her shoulders like a still from a Rita Hayworth film, looking more like you imagine a ghost would than anyone who'd ever ported through the Attesa's door.

'Anastasia?' Mercy was the first to find her voice. 'But . . . what are you doing here? *You* killed *me*. You just admitted it to the cops. I heard you. Why would you be here?'

Ana took in Mercy and recoiled. 'Brilliant. Now I'm in a cop-induced faint and dreaming about Mercy *freaking* Grant. The girl is even gatecrashing my subconscious! There must be some very expensive effective therapy I can get for this.'

I turned to Nancy – what was going on? Ana fell from the fire escape, we'd all seen her. It just gave way when she put her weight on it. How could she have been murdered? Oh. Unless . . .

'Anastasia, hey, it's me.' Lorna snapped to her senses and walked towards Ana slowly, like she was approaching one of the tamer squirrels in the park. 'You're not dreaming. You, um, fell off the fire escape, do you remember? Just after you confessed to killing Mercy. Think back. I know this is hard but try.'

At the sight of her, Ana let out a little gasp. '*Lorna*? What are you . . .?' She shook her head. 'Jeez, this is some messed-up crap. Like, why would I be dream-imagining *you* in the same room as *her*? This is the last time I allow my mother to serve Époisses at a social function. It might be haute as hell, but it makes your dreams crazy trippy.'

'Nancy,' I said. 'Can I see that letter, please?'

She stared numbly at Ana, weakly letting me prise the old piece of paper out of her hand. How could Ana be here?

'"Anastasia de Witt, sixteen, was murdered at 21.08, at 1138 Fifth Avenue, on the Upper East Side, this evening",' I read quietly. '"She was killed when the fire escape she was walking down gave way and she fell to her death – someone had tampered with it deliberately to make it unsafe. Please expect her arrival soon. As usual, until Anastasia's Key is found, she must stay in the Hotel Attesa.'

'So if she's here,' I said, trying to make my mind shift into gear, 'and Mercy's Key is not . . .'

This was like the dead girl equivalent of ice-cream brain freeze. Without the mint choc chip and sprinkles first.

'Then Ana wasn't the one who killed Mercy,' Nancy said dully. 'We were wrong. She's not the murderer. We didn't solve the case. We wasted time on a bad lead. Then we pushed the cops in a direction that wasn't right either. And we stood by and watched an innocent girl die – right before our eyes – for the second time this week.'

'Ana didn't kill me?' Mercy spun on her aggressively fluoro sneakers. No getting rid of those babies just yet. 'But she just confessed.'

Ana sighed. 'Wow, even Pass Out Mercy is as annoying as an overly chatty cab driver. You must really have bugged me when you were alive for me to be conjuring you up *this* accurately.'

Lorna took two more small steps towards Ana. 'Hey,' she said softly. 'I was confused when I got here too. I'll help you, I promise. I know it's not quite the right emotion now, but I'm so, so relieved you didn't hurt Mercy. Emma was right – you could never have done something as bad as that.'

'*Lorna*?' Ana was looking at her like she was a mismatched pair of shoes. 'I suppose it makes sense that I'm dreaming you the way you were the night you died – in that cute blue dress and your Pretty Ballerina flats. I'm your age now. If you'd lived, you'd be at college. Emma misses you so much. She's so sad right now. Maybe that's why I thought you here.'

Lorna double-blinked. 'Ana, I know it's going to take a while for you to take all of this in, but why did you tell the cops you'd killed Mercy? Weren't you Thespis?'

Ana frowned. 'Wow, this is some specific dream shit,' she said, looking down at her white Grecian dress and killer gold heels in confusion. 'Okay, I'll play along until I wake up. That's how these dreams work, right? Behave yourself and you'll hear your mom calling for you to get out of bed, or you'll miss the bus to school?'

She pointed at Mercy. 'Emma and I were pranking you,' she said. 'You were a Flatiron Building-sized pain in my ass and you deserved to get yours. Emma ran with the theatre wind-ups – the *Macbeth* book, the feathers, the flowers, the good luck cards, your blue costume. Which BTW, you look ravishing in in dreamland tonight. But you didn't seem too fazed by that. You've got a skin as thick as city smog in July.'

Mercy shrugged. 'In my business you have to learn to ignore the haters or you'd never go on.'

'This is what I mean – even when I'm not conscious, you are *so* annoying!' Ana pinched her arm, trying to wake herself up. I'd done that too. I clearly remembered. I wished I could tell her that it didn't help. 'Jeez, the sooner I get away from Pass Out Mercy, the better.'

The Big Red Door began to gently shake, a low rumble filling the room. Erm, hello? What was going on today? Things sure were rotten in the state of Limbo.

Mercy ignored it. 'And what about Thespis?'

Ana sighed, putting a hand on her chest to swear the truth. 'Yeah, yeah, that was me. Like I said, the theatre tricks weren't freaking you out enough, so I decided to take things to the next level.' She smiled at Lorna. 'A level I knew your sister wouldn't be comfortable with – even after everything that's happened, she's not as bad-ass as she pretends. So I set up the Thespis account and started sending you messages. Not the finest use of an Ivy League brain, but you were threatening me. I needed to fight fire with fire.'

A slow, steady swirl of white smoke danced underneath the Door and onto the Attesa's chequerboard floor.

Mercy frowned. 'Then you took it even further and tampered with the lighting rig – you killed me!'

'No! No! No!' Ana shouted. 'I'm not brainless – why would I do that, Pass Out Mercy? I've been itching to get out of my Peabody uniform for years, why would I want to replace that with a New York Penitentiary one? Plus an orange boiler suit with *this* hair? Prison is so not my colour.'

'Then why did you tell the cops you killed me?' Mercy asked.

'I didn't. I owned up to the other stuff, but I didn't say that.'

'You did too.'

'I did not.' Ana rolled her eyes. 'I was mad. It was cold. That wannabe cop, Detective Lee, was harassing me. I said, "Fine, I did it – prove it". I was being sarcastic. Or is that an emotion that you can't act?'

'So if you didn't kill me, who did?' Mercy asked.

'Um, and who killed Ana?' Lorna said. 'Because for her to be here, someone must have tampered with the fire escape. The cops think Ana's death was some big karmic accident. They're not looking for Ana's murderer because they don't know she has one. And they've stopped looking for Mercy's because they think Ana was it. Nancy, what are we going to do?'

But Nancy wasn't listening. She was watching the smoke. It slowly covered the floor until you couldn't see where one black tile ended and a white one begun. I heard myself gasp.

'If we didn't put a Key in the Big Red Door, why is it doing *that*?' Lorna asked. 'Did you touch it? Did someone find their Key and not say?' She turned to Nancy, her brow furrowed into neat little lines, sure she'd have the answer.

But Lorna's shock and confusion was mirrored on Nancy's face. For once, Her Geekiness didn't have the answers either.

'So, I may have only been passed out here for, like, ten minutes max,' Ana said, 'and I'm hoping I won't remember any of "here" tomorrow morning when the maid comes in—' she gave Mercy a special glare '—but I'm guessing this Cirque du Soleil smoky shit is not a good thing?'

I felt Edison's hand squeeze my shoulder. He'd pulled himself off the couch, but was standing like he's just climbed Mount Royal. His jaw was clenched, his eyes fixed on the humming vibrations of the red wood.

His posture told me everything I needed to know: this wasn't one of those things he'd been holding back about. Like Lorna and Nancy, he'd never seen the Door do this before: activate without a Key. Maybe no dead kid had.

'Edison.' Nancy cleared her throat, trying to cough back the fear. 'Do you, er, think we should . . .?'

'Get the hell out of here before some wanton, hungry hell-beast devil breaks through that door and eats us all?' Lorna wailed. 'HELL YES.'

A squeak. Then another. Ohmigod, the door handle was turning. The smoke was hitting the sides of the lobby now, bouncing up the walls in delicate waves, before losing its momentum and falling back into the misty smoky sea.

'No,' Nancy said, her voice firm now. 'No one's going anywhere. Maybe this is a reaction to what's happening with Mercy and Ana, some penance for us not solving the case. We need to deal with whatever is about to happen head-on.'

Despite myself, I leaned into Edison. I part hated, part loved the way my body fitted so neatly into his side.

The door swung open with a low creak.

A creature skidded into the lobby, with such force it

had either been pushing the Door hard, or it had been forcibly shoved through it. It landed in a crumpled heap on the Attesa floor with a sickening thud, its limbs appearing and disappearing into the smoky fog.

As always, Nancy was the first of us to come round. She cleared her throat again.

'H-hello?' she said.

The creature's head was down, its back hunched. It wasn't that big, not much larger than me. Maybe if things did get nasty, we could fight it and win? There were six of us now after all. The biggest Agency ever. Sure, Ana was too new to have any proper skills, but Mercy, well, she'd been picking everything up like a pro. And Lorna and Nancy – I'd been here long enough to know they were way more powerful than they liked to admit. And Ed, he wasn't on form at this exact moment but—

The thing gave a jolt, as if suddenly remembering it had the spirit of a body. Slowly – so slowly – it unfurled its limbs. Muscle by muscle, vertebra by vertebra it seemed to gain strength, uncurling until it was standing tall. Its face covered by a mass of dark hair.

It shook its head, the tangled locks falling away from its eyes and looked around with an unfocused stare. It rolled its shoulders and stretched.

Nancy let out a small yelp.

'Is . . . is it a demon?' Mercy asked, grabbing my other arm tight.

'You could call it that,' Lorna said.

Suddenly aware it wasn't the only being in the room, the creature turned to us. Then I realized the truth: it wasn't a creature after all. Or a hellbeast. Or a devil. Oh no. It was a dead girl. Just like me.

And as soon as she turned her cold, green eyes to me, I knew.

'Tess?' I said.